Matthew's Meadow

By Corinne Demas Bliss
Pictures by Ted Lewin

Voyager Books

Harcourt Brace & Company

San Diego   New York   London

Requests for permission to make copies of any part of the work
should be mailed to: Permissions Department,
Harcourt Brace & Company, 6277 Sea Harbor Drive,
Orlando, Florida 32887-6777.

First Voyager Books edition 1997
Voyager Books is a registered trademark of
Harcourt Brace & Company.

Library of Congress Cataloging-in-Publication Data
Bliss, Corinne Demas.
Matthew's meadow/by Corinne Demas Bliss; pictures by
Ted Lewin.
p. cm.
Summary: Every year at blackberry time Matthew visits the
red-tailed hawk in the black walnut tree in the meadow,
and she teaches him how to use his senses to fully
appreciate the natural world.
ISBN 0-15-200759-8
ISBN 0-15-201500-0 (pbk.)
[1. Hawks—Fiction. 2. Senses and sensation—Fiction.
3. Nature—Fiction.] I. Lewin, Ted, ill. II. Title.
PZ7.B61917Mat   1992
[E]—dc20   91–10840

A C E F D B

Printed in Singapore

FOR *Austin* AND *Artemis*
— C. D. B.

For Louis Agassiz Fuertes,

who made birds speak to me
— T. L.

The illustrations in this book were done in watercolors on
D'Arches 300-lb. cold press watercolor paper.
The display and text type were set in ITC Garamond Book by
Thompson Type, San Diego, California.
Color separations were made by Bright Arts, Ltd., Singapore.
Printed and bound by Tien Wah Press, Singapore
This book was printed on Leykam recycled paper, which
contains more than 20 percent postconsumer waste and has a total
recycled content of at least 50 percent.
Production supervision by Stan Redfern and Ginger Boyer
Designed by Camilla Filancia

Fₐᵣ ᵤₚ ₒₙ ₜₕₑ ₕᵢₗₗ, far beyond where the eyes of the house could see, was a meadow of long, soft grass. A forest circled this meadow, and once this meadow had been forest, too. Someone had cleared the trees, leaving only one tree to grow tall in the center, a black walnut tree, taller than any tree around. The red-tailed hawk perched in this tree and looked out over the meadow and the whole hillside below.

This was Matthew's meadow, and he shared it with no one except the red-tailed hawk, and the deer who came there to sleep at night and at daybreak disappeared back into the woods. Matthew had never seen the deer because he had never been there at night. The meadow was far up the hillside, far from the house, far from his own room and his own bed. But he could see where the deer had flattened the grass when they slept and he could lie in the shallow hollows where they had lain.

This was Matthew's meadow because he thought of it as his, though he never told anyone about it. When his mother or father asked where he was off to, when his chores were done, he would say he was just going up the hill for a while. He went to his meadow when he wanted a place to think and when he wanted a place not to think at all. He would lie in the long, soft grass and watch the sky and watch the wind stirring the leaves of the black walnut tree. He would watch the red-tailed hawk survey the mountains and then fly off, to be lost, finally, in the sky.

One afternoon Matthew brought field glasses up to his meadow and focused on the red-tailed hawk who perched on a branch above him. The hawk looked right back at him and Matthew realized the hawk could see him just as well with her plain eyes. They stared at each other for a while and when Matthew put the field glasses down by his side the hawk spoke up.

"I surprise you," said the hawk, "but that's to be expected. Soon you will get used to my voice and you won't find it strange that I speak to you, that we speak with each other."

Matthew knew, just as you do, that birds and animals speak in stories but that real life is a different thing. Matthew is part of this story now, but, when the story took place, he was as real as you are. So of course he was amazed to hear the hawk speak.

But very quickly, and without knowing why, he

forgot his amazement. And soon the hawk's voice seemed as
natural to him as his own.

"Do you know how this meadow came to be here?" asked
the hawk.

"No," said Matthew. The meadow had been there for as
long as he could remember. He thought it had always been
there.

"Your grandmother made this meadow for you. The black walnut tree has kept the forest back, as black walnut trees do, but it was she who cleared out the brambles and the bushes, and she who planted the grass. She wanted you to have a place in the forest where you could see the sky."

"Is she there?" asked Matthew. "Is she there in the sky?" As he said this he felt it was a silly question, a question he would have asked when he was a little child. Matthew's grandmother had died when he was just old enough to remember her. She had been buried, he knew, in the cemetery in town. But when he thought of her, and he thought of her often when he came up to his meadow, he liked to think of her somewhere up in the sky, watching him from a cloud.

"If that's where you like to think of her," said the red-tailed hawk, "then that's where she is."

"Do you know?" asked Matthew. "How do you know?"

The hawk flew down and perched on the lowest branch of the black walnut tree. She was the closest she had ever been.

"There are things that I can tell you," said the hawk, "and there are things that I can't. There are things I will tell you that you won't understand until you are older, and there are some things you may never understand. And if you don't understand something you must try to think about it for a year before you ask me to explain."

Matthew said he would. He stood up very quietly. The red-tailed hawk was preening her feathers. She looked just like a bird, a bird who could not speak, and for a moment

Matthew thought that the voice must have been in a dream, in his mind. As if she had heard Matthew's doubts, the hawk looked down at him and asked loudly, "How old are you?"

"Nine," said Matthew. "I just turned nine."

"Can you remember today?" asked the hawk. "Can you remember to be here this day next year?"

"I think so," said Matthew. "I'll try."

"Go to the edge of the meadow," said the hawk, "where the blackberry bushes grow. See if they can help you."

Matthew ran through the grass to the edge of the meadow where the wild blackberries grew. They had just turned from deep red to the color of crows, and they came off easily in his hand. A few days before, they had held on to the stem.

"Next year," said the hawk, "blackberry time."

"Next year," repeated Matthew, "blackberry time."

"Come back here next year and I'll have something to teach you. Come back here every year at blackberry time and you will learn something new. And when you are old enough to understand things for yourself you will find a way to let your grandmother know what you learned. For the things that I will tell you all come from her."

"From her?" asked Matthew. "Did you speak with her, too?"

"Many years ago," said the red-tailed hawk, "when you were just a baby, your grandmother carried you up here to show you to me. She was not an ordinary woman, your grandmother; she knew many special things, and she wanted you to know them, too. She asked me to teach you these things as you grew older, because she knew she would not be alive to teach them to you herself."

"How did she know I would talk to you?" asked Matthew.

"How did she know you would make this your meadow?" asked the hawk, and she flew off, leaving her question as the answer.

And now, you must wonder: what did Matthew say when he came down from his meadow and went back to his house? Although birds can talk to children in the real world, that's not something grown-ups would ever believe. Matthew walked down the hillside, eating blackberries, and by the time he got home he did not remember that the hawk had spoken. He remembered what the hawk had said, but he thought they were his own words, inside his head. He thought he had come to know all this while he was in his meadow watching the sky by himself.

Exactly a year later, when Matthew was ten, he went up the hill to his meadow. He brought his scythe with him, as he sometimes did, to keep the meadow clear, and he brought a basket, too. Three days before, the blackberries had not been quite ripe enough to pick, but this day they came off easily in his hand. As he was picking he began to think that there was something he should remember.

"Blackberry time," he said to himself, "blackberry time."

He took his half-filled basket and went to lie in the long, soft grass at the foot of the black walnut tree. He lay back in the grass and looked up at the sky and watched the fat, white clouds move past like floats in a parade. Then he noticed a familiar shape against the sun. When he shaded his eyes he saw the red-tailed hawk watching him from a branch above and he felt a burst of excitement. Now, a red-tailed hawk is a magnificent sight to see, just on its own, but Matthew knew, though he was not sure why, there was more to it than that. When the hawk spoke he was not surprised.

"Hello," said the hawk, as if she had expected Matthew to turn up. "I have a job for you to do."

Matthew stood up.

"Go find a milkweed pod that survived the winter," said the hawk, "and bring it back here."

Matthew knew that the milkweed grew at one side of the meadow. The monarch larvae lived on milkweed, and at the end of summer the plump yellow-striped caterpillars turned into pupae there, and then into butterflies that flew off for the winter. The milkweed was green again, the monarchs were back, but Matthew was able to find an old pod that was still sealed.

"Open it very carefully," said the hawk, "and let out just a few seeds, one at a time."

Matthew cracked open the pod of the milkweed along its seam. The seeds, with their silky white threads, were packed tight, and Matthew knew they would billow out like feathers from a ripped pillow. He plucked out a few strands, and as soon as he

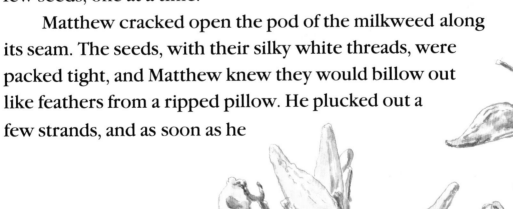

opened his palm the wind lifted them into the air and carried
them off toward the sky.

"A few more," said the hawk, "and listen to them this
time."

Matthew bent toward the milkweed pod and nudged
a few more seeds away from the pack. They took off quickly
into space.

"I don't hear anything," he said to the hawk.

"Try again," said the hawk. "Close off all your other
senses, if you have to, but open yourself to listening. Become
your ears."

Matthew tried again. He put his ear close to the milkweed

and he thought about listening. He closed himself off from
the sight of the blue sky and the fat, white clouds. He closed
himself off from the taste of blackberries in his mouth and the
feel of the sun on his arms. And he listened as hard as he could.

And then, slowly, as each seed lifted into space, he
began to hear them. At first what he heard was the sound
of the wind. But the hawk told him to listen better. Matthew
listened so hard he became his ears, and soon he could hear
the sound of each milkweed seed as it lost its grip on the
cluster and flew off, perhaps to become a milkweed plant of
its own. And each milkweed seed made a beautiful sweet
sound, like a note from a harp.

"Now you know how to really listen," said the hawk. "There are things to hear that you've never thought to listen to before. Everything in nature has its own sound. Listen to things move, listen to things grow, listen to things change. Listen to stillness. In the winter, when it snows, you will discover that even each snowflake has its own sound."

"Will I remember all this when winter comes?" asked Matthew.

"Did you remember to come here at blackberry time?" asked the hawk, and she flew off. Matthew was not surprised. He had learned that questions can be answers, too.

When he came down from the mountain, carrying his half-filled basket, Matthew remembered what the hawk had taught him, but he did not remember that it was the hawk who had been his teacher. He thought he had come to know these things by himself.

And during the year, he found that he could hear things he had never heard before. When he listened he was able

to hear the sound of the smallest insect making its way
along the stem of a plant. He could hear the sound of toads
moving through the grass, and the sound of water moving
underground, and the sound of leaves dying as winter
came, and the sound of the earth beginning to freeze.
In the winter, when it snowed, he listened to the snow and
he discovered the secret of snowflakes. He had known
that every snowflake has a different shape, but now
he found that each snowflake falling made a
different sound, like the chime of a miniature bell,
and that together the snowflakes
sounded like a carillon.

At the same time the next year, when Matthew was eleven, he went up to his meadow. He knew there was a special reason for him to be there, but he was not sure what it was.

He lay in the long, soft grass, eating blackberries, and listening to the clouds move in the sky. When he looked up into the black walnut tree and saw the red-tailed hawk, he remembered instantly why he was there.

"Can you listen now?" asked the hawk. "Can you hear the smallest things?"

"Yes," said Matthew. "I can hear the water lilies on the pond close up when evening comes. I can hear the dew dry from the grass."

"And the snowflakes," asked the hawk, "can you hear them?"

"Every one," said Matthew.

"Good," said the hawk. "You have learned how to listen. This time, I'd like to teach you something new. Stand up and tell me, can you feel the wind?"

Matthew stood up in the grass and faced into the light wind. His hair blew back from his face and his shirt moved against his skin.

"Yes," he said, "I feel the wind."

"Now," said the hawk, "I want you to feel the wind on your forehead alone. And then I want you to feel the wind on your cheeks. And then I want you to tilt up your chin and feel the wind on your neck."

Matthew held his face into the wind and felt it touch his forehead, then his cheeks, then his neck.

"Now," said the hawk, "hold out your hand and turn it slowly. I want you to feel the wind on your palm, and then I want you to feel each finger in the wind, one at a time. The wind on your forehead is different from the wind on your cheeks. Even each finger feels different in the wind."

Matthew held out his hand and felt the wind brush across the top, then the palm. The hawk counted off his fingers as he held them out into the wind, one by one.

"Now," said the hawk, "I want you to forget about the wind. I want you to think about the sun. Hold your face to the sun, and then hold out your hand."

Matthew thought about the sun on his forehead and his cheeks. He tilted his chin and felt the sun on his neck. Then he turned his hand in the sun and felt it on his fingers one by one.

"Your skin is not a shell to hold all of you inside," said the hawk. "Your skin is like a million windows, open to touch. This year you'll learn about how much there is to feel, just as last year you learned how much there was to listen to."

"Will you be here next year? Again?" asked Matthew.

"Will you come to your meadow at blackberry time?" asked the hawk, and she left her question behind her as she flew off.

When Matthew came down from the meadow, he remembered what the hawk had taught him, but he did not remember that it was the hawk who had been his teacher. He thought he had come to know these things by himself. All year long he felt things he had never felt before; the world had a new texture for him. When he swam in the pond he found that the water on his shoulder felt different from the water on his belly and the water on his toes. In winter he felt the differences between snowflakes as each one landed on his face. At night he could feel the moonlight as it touched him and the starlight that tingled on his skin. He could feel the blood chugging through his body and he could feel the thoughts churning in his mind.

For the next four years, just at blackberry time, Matthew came up to the meadow and found the red-tailed hawk waiting for him in the black walnut tree. And each year the hawk taught him something new.

When Matthew was twelve he learned how to smell where the deer had lain. He could smell a rainstorm far away and he could smell the coming of night.

When Matthew was thirteen he learned to taste all the intricacies of an apple. He could taste one blackberry from another.

When Matthew was fourteen the hawk taught him to notice things that were too small for him to have noticed before, and to take in things that had been too big. He could observe the habits of mites and comprehend the curvature of the earth. The hawk taught him how to watch for changes

that had been too slow for him to see before, like the erosion of the mountains, and to watch movements that passed too quickly for him, like the beating of a hummingbird's wings. His eyes could follow the progress of the stone that he sent skipping across the surface of the pond as if it were in slow motion.

When Matthew was fifteen, the hawk showed him that the eyes inside his mind — his memory and his imagination — saw more than the eyes of his face, and the hawk taught him how to use those eyes together. So when Matthew looked at a leaf he could see its underside as well. And he could see, with

his memory, how the leaf had looked before it had unfolded into green, when it was first formed, tightly wrapped. And with the help of his imagination he could see it as it would become, turning to a hot orange in the fall, exhausting itself in color, and then falling brown and brittle to the ground. The hawk taught him that his memory could store all his senses as well, so that in addition to seeing, he could feel and smell and taste and hear what he wanted to, right in his mind.

All of these things he learned from the hawk, but he did not remember that it was the hawk who had taught him. He thought that he had come to learn these things, in his meadow, on his own.

When Matthew was sixteen he went up to his meadow at blackberry time, just as he had the seven years before. As

Matthew had gotten older, the hawk had gotten older, too. She seemed smaller to Matthew, just as the meadow seemed smaller and the black walnut tree seemed smaller. Only the sky hadn't changed. It was just as immense, just as far away, just as elusive as the life before he had been born.

Matthew lay on his back in the long, soft grass and looked up at the red-tailed hawk. And although he did not remember to expect it, when the hawk began to speak, he was not surprised. The hawk's voice was weaker than it had ever been, and Matthew stood up to hear her better.

"Now," said the hawk, "your five senses are fully awake. You know all the secrets that your grandmother asked me to reveal to you. You are sixteen. You're on the brink of becoming a man. Today I want to tell you about one last thing, something that comes from me, something that will help you in the years ahead."

Matthew suddenly felt sadness move through him. He heard, in his mind, a coming farewell.

"I wish you could speak to my grandmother now," said Matthew. "I wish you could tell her that I learned what she wanted me to learn. I wish you could thank her for me."

"That," said the hawk, "is something you'll have to do yourself."

"How can I?" asked Matthew.

"When you were a little child," said the hawk, "all kinds of things seemed possible. As you got older and wiser you

learned more and more about the boundaries of your world, and you got more and more used to thinking within those boundaries. The unknown is simply the not-yet-known.

Most people look for solutions within the known. If this is something you want to do, and you think it is impossible, I want you to look outside the known, not within it. I want you to learn to think beyond your thoughts."

Matthew had always listened unquestioningly to the red-tailed hawk. But he was older now. Although it was not the first time that the hawk's ideas had puzzled him, it was the first time he spoke up.

"You've always talked in riddles," said Matthew. "Although I never remembered you were my teacher, in time what you said made sense. Now I don't understand you at all."

"How long did I ask you to think about the things I said?"

"A year," said Matthew. "And in a year I learned."

"What I told you today is much harder to understand," said the hawk. "Ten times harder. So it will take you ten times as long. Put it away in a back pocket of your mind and take it out now and then and turn it over when you have a chance. And in ten years come back up to your meadow —"

"In ten years —" began Matthew.

"You'll be grown up completely by then," said the hawk, "you'll be a man."

But that wasn't what Matthew wanted to ask.

"Will you —?" he began.

"Can you watch me?" asked the hawk. "Can you watch me even when you can't see me anymore?" She pushed off from her branch and sailed up into the sky, circling and soaring higher and farther away. Matthew watched as her shape grew indistinct, and watched as she became just a tiny,

dark spot, and watched her in his mind when she was too far away for him to see her with his eyes.

Matthew came sadly down from his meadow and walked across the fields to his house. In his mind he listened to the words "think beyond your thoughts," but he did not know where they had come from and he did not know what they meant. He put them in a back pocket of his mind, and now and then he would take them out and turn them over and over again.

The next year, when blackberry time came, Matthew was seventeen. He was too old to be interested in picking berries.

He was busy working in the fields. He did not go up to his meadow at blackberry time in the coming years, but he went there at other times to watch the sky and to think his thoughts and to not think at all.

He knew that it was in the meadow, when he was a boy, that his senses had awakened, one by one. He remembered the red-tailed hawk who used to perch above him in the black walnut tree, but he did not remember that the hawk had spoken with him, that it was the hawk who had taught him how to really listen, feel, smell, taste, and see.

As Matthew grew up he started taking over more and more of the work on his parents' farm, and when they got older they turned the farm over to him. He was a good farmer, because they had taught him all about the land. But he felt it was from his grandmother, though he didn't understand how, that he had learned about himself. He felt that somehow, in the meadow she had cleared for him, he had discovered all the things she had wanted him to learn, and he wished he could find a way to let her know, and to thank her for these gifts. For his life, although much of it was spent alone, was a very rich one. He could listen to his hay growing. He could feel the pattern of sun on his hands. He could smell evening move across his fields. He could remember the tastes of the cornbread he had eaten at breakfast. He could see the face of the girl whom he was beginning to care for. And more and more often he took out the words "think beyond your thoughts," from the back pocket of his mind and turned them over and over again.

When Matthew was twenty-six years old, he went up
again to his meadow at blackberry time, carrying his baby
daughter. The meadow seemed small to him, just a grassy
plot, and the black walnut tree seemed no taller than the trees
in the forest around it. But when he looked up at the sky it
seemed as immense as it had when he was a little boy. And
as he watched the fat, white clouds move across the sky
he remembered how, as a child, he used to think that his
grandmother was somewhere in the sky, watching him from
a cloud. More than ever before, he wanted to reach out to

her, through time, through space, and tell her what he had learned. As he thought of her, he thought about the red-tailed hawk and for the first time he remembered that the red-tailed hawk had actually spoken to him.

There was no red-tailed hawk perched in the black walnut tree this blackberry time; there was no red-tailed hawk circling high overhead. But Matthew could see her clearly with the eyes inside his mind. He could see her circling in the sky and at the same time he could see her on a branch overhead, and in his mind he could hear the hawk's voice, which was as clear as the first time she had spoken.

"The unknown," said the hawk, "is simply the not-yet-known. Think beyond your thoughts so that you can find a way to do what you once thought impossible."

Matthew lay in the long, soft grass, his baby asleep in his arms. In his mind he watched the red-tailed hawk coast across the sky, and he began, slowly, to think beyond his thoughts.

He began to wander in a region where his mind had never wandered before, and there he discovered something he hadn't known. He hadn't known it because he had been thinking in words, and this was an idea that came to him not in words but some other way.

There was, he realized, a language of the land. It was there in nature, in the way the mountains grew and eroded, in the way the stream meandered. The earth was — when you looked at it and touched it and listened to it — its own design. The meadow his grandmother had cleared for him gave him the forest and the sky. Gave him the black walnut tree and the red-tailed hawk. His grandmother had spoken to him through the land. He, too, could speak to her through the land itself.

And so, when Matthew came down from his meadow, he began his message. The trees that he planted, the pond that he banked, the fields that he tilled, were the way he spoke. From the sky above the message was clear; but the message went underground, into the earth, as well. As he worked through the language of the land, he told his grandmother the story of his life. He told her how he had learned from her. He thanked her and told her of his love.

And when Matthew smelled the coming of spring and listened to the blackberries grow, and saw in his mind the red-tailed hawk perched in the black walnut tree, which towered over his meadow as it had when he was a boy, he knew that she had heard.

The Idea Magazine For Teachers®

PRESCHOOL

1998–1999

YEARBOOK

Jayne M. Gammons, Senior Editor

The Education Center, Inc.
Greensboro, North Carolina

The Mailbox® 1998–1999 Yearbook

Editor In Chief: Margaret Michel
Magazine Director: Karen P. Shelton
Editorial Administrative Director: Stephen Levy
Senior Editor: Jayne M. Gammons
Editorial Traffic Manager: Lisa K. Pitts
Contributing Editors: Michele M. Dare, Ada Goren, Lori Kent, Allison E. Ward
Copy Editors: Karen Brewer Grossman, Karen L. Huffman, Tracy Johnson, Scott Lyons, Debbie Shoffner, Gina Sutphin
Staff Artists: Cathy Spangler Bruce, Pam Crane, Nick Greenwood, Clevell Harris, Susan Hodnett, Sheila Krill, Rob Mayworth, Kimberly Richard, Rebecca Saunders, Barry Slate, Donna K. Teal, Jennifer L. Tipton
Cover Artist: Lois Axeman
Editorial Assistants: Terrie Head, Laura Slaughter, Wendy Svartz, Karen White
Librarian: Elizabeth A. Findley

ISBN 1–56234–293–2
ISSN 1088–5536

The Education Center, Inc.
P.O. Box 9753
Greensboro, NC 27429-0753

Look for *The Mailbox®* 1999–2000 Preschool Yearbook in the summer of 2000. The Education Center, Inc., is the publisher of *The Mailbox®, Teacher's Helper®, The Mailbox® BOOKBAG®* , *Learning®,* and *The Mailbox® Teacher* magazines, as well as other fine products. Look for these wherever quality teacher materials are sold, or call 1-800-714-7991 to request a free catalog.

Contents

Thematic And Contributor Units

Cock-a-doodle-doo!

Howdy! Welcome

Welcome "baa-ck!" This farm-themed, welcome-to-preschool unit is sure to get you in the "moo-ed" and ready to raise a new crop of preschoolers.

ideas contributed by farmhand Susan Bunyan

Who's In The Barnyard? Who's In The Barn?

On the first day of school, youngsters and their parents will know they've arrived at the right place when they see this farmyard scene and barn-door entrance to your room. Using bulletin-board paper, create a scene with a blue sky, rolling green pastures, and a fence. For each child, duplicate onto construction paper a pair of the animal patterns on pages 9 and 10. Color the patterns; then laminate them for durability. Cut out the patterns. Label the baby animal with a child's name. To prepare the baby animal for use as a nametag, punch a hole where indicated on the pattern. Permanently mount the parent animal to the display; then use self-adhesive Velcro® to attach the baby animal to the display beside the parent animal.

Mount red bulletin-board paper on your door and the wall around your door to create a barn and barn-door entrance. Label the door with the name of your classroom farm.

As a parent and child arrive at your door, have them remove the child's animal from the display. Explain that even though the baby animal is leaving his parent to go in the barn, he will rejoin his parent on the display later in the day. Safety-pin the nametag to the child's clothing; then welcome him to the farm. A quick glance at the display will show who's in the barnyard and who's in the barn.

What's Your Name, Barnyard Buddy?

This activity may be corny, but it's sure to help your barnyard buddies learn one another's names. Seat youngsters in a circle. Give one child a plastic or real ear of corn. Instruct the children to pass the ear of corn around the circle as you play a lively musical selection. Stop the music and ask the children to join you in asking the child holding the corn, "What's your name, barnyard buddy?" After the child says her name, the group responds by shouting, "Howdy, [child's name]!" Continue until the group has greeted every child with a fine "How-do-ye-do"!

To The Farm!

Moo, moo, moo!

Barnyard Scramble

This game will help youngsters learn to follow directions, as well as improve their listening skills and get them up and "moo-ving"—or oinking, or neighing! Arrange a class supply of carpet squares or placemats in a circle on the floor. Direct each child to sit on a mat. Make sure that each child is wearing her nametag. Review the sounds made by the animals pictured on the nametags. To play, say, "Cows in the barnyard. Moo, moo, moo," inserting a different animal name and sound each time. Each child whose nametag matches the named animal stands up and makes his animal's sound while finding a new mat to sit on. If you announce, "Animals in the barnyard," all of the children should stand up and make sounds while relocating. Sounds like a busy, noisy barnyard!

Daily Chores

It takes a whole lot of cooperation to keep a barnyard bustling! Prepare a helpers display by duplicating the same number of bucket patterns on page 11 as you have daily or weekly class jobs. Label each bucket with a different class job. Duplicate a class supply of the animal patterns on pages 11 and 12; then label each one with a different child's name. Color the patterns; then laminate them. Cut out the patterns. Arrange the buckets on a bulletin board. Store the animal patterns in a box decorated to resemble a barn.

Read aloud *Farmer Duck* by Martin Waddell (Candlewick Press) to help your little ones understand that everyone will need to help with the daily classroom chores. While reading through the first time, stop the story when the animals have come up with a plan. Have youngsters imagine that they are the duck's animal friends. How would they help the duck? After some discussion continue reading the story. Help your children understand the difference between one worker doing the work and several workers pooling their efforts. Then introduce your helpers display. Chances are, everyone will want to help today!

Ben

line leader

Victoria

Dalton

snack helper

table wiper

Cultivate Character

Plant the seeds of good behavior and watch your class grow with these good guidelines. Cut a different vegetable shape from a large sheet of construction paper for each of your classroom rules. Write a rule on each shape. Tape a paint stick to the back of each shape; then insert the sticks into a large piece of green Styrofoam®. As you need to introduce or review a rule, pick that vegetable from the garden and discuss it.

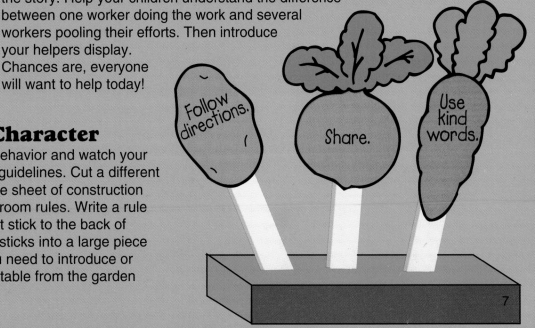

Follow directions.

Share.

Use kind words.

Hunting Our Way Around

Hunting for an "eggs-traspecial" way to introduce your little ones to your school? Farmer's hen can give you some help! In advance collect two plastic eggs for each child in your class. Just before the hunt, "hide" the eggs in strategic locations around your school. Make an egg basket for each child by poking each end of a pipe cleaner into opposite sides of a Styrofoam® bowl. Twist the pipe cleaner to secure the handle on the bowl. Explain to your children that Farmer's hen went strolling all around the school, leaving eggs in some unusual places. Lead your class to the areas you want to introduce them to. Invite the children to gather the eggs, making sure that each child has two eggs for her basket. When you return to your classroom, use the eggs for matching, counting, sorting, and graphing practice.

Something To Crow About

Send each child home with something to crow about—an award for being a first-rate farmhand down on the preschool farm! Program a copy of the award on page 13 with your name; then duplicate a class supply of the award onto red construction paper. Cut out the awards; then program each one with a different child's name. On one of your first days of school, have each child paint a white handprint onto his award. When the paint is dry, help him glue on construction-paper features as shown. Send the awards home. Cock-a-doodle-doo! I'm so proud of you!

Ms. Bunyan's
Farm

Cock-a-doodle-doo!
I'm so proud of you!

Carrie

is a first-rate farmhand...
and that's something
to crow about!

Farm News
For The Family

Be sure to use the open page (page 14) when corresponding with your little farmhands' families. "Yee haw!" There's a lot going on, y'all!

Animal Patterns

Use with "Who's In The Barnyard? Who's In The Barn?" on page 6 and "Barnyard Scramble" on page 7.

Animal Patterns
Use with "Daily Chores" on page 7.

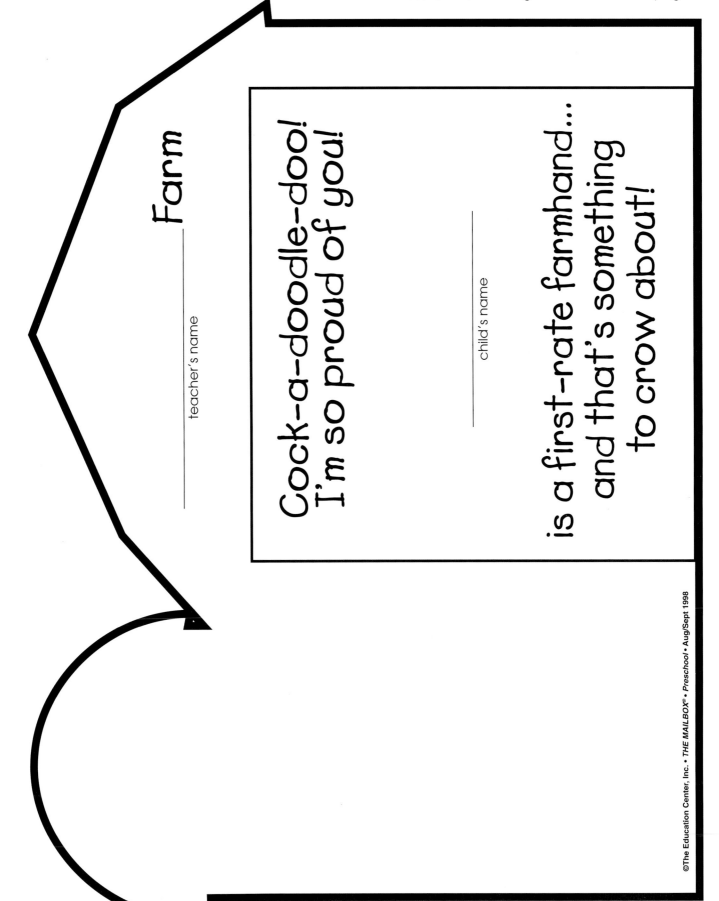

Farm

teacher's name

Cock-a-doodle-doo!
I'm so proud of you!

child's name

is a first-rate farmhand...
and that's something
to crow about!

Dear Parent,

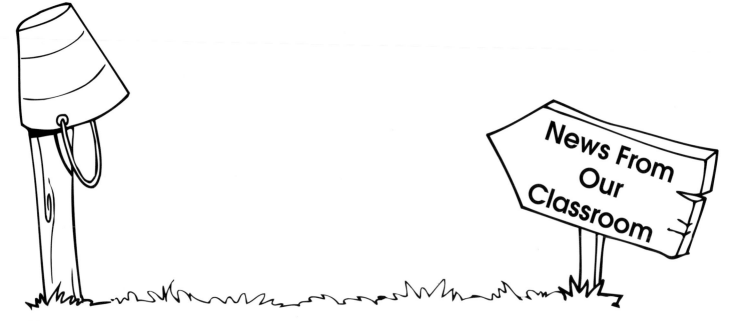

News From Our Classroom

Piggy-Bank Pattern
Use with "Peekaboo Piggy Banks" on page 16 and "Heads Or Tails?",
"Penny Pitches," and "Penny Pairs" on page 17.

©The Education Center, Inc. • *THE MAILBOX®* • *Preschool* • Feb/Mar1999

Penny-Wise Counting

We've coined a collection of "cents-able" counting ideas that you can bank on!

ideas by Mackie Rhodes

We're practicing counting—
one, two, three.
You can help us; you will see!

Put ten pennies in this piggy bank,
Then return it to school.
Many thanks!

Peekaboo Piggy Banks

To collect the pennies you'll need for the following counting activities, have youngsters prepare and take home these clever piggy banks. Duplicate a class supply of page 15 onto pink construction paper. Personalize a bank for each child; then invite each child to decorate her piggy bank with art materials, such as markers and stickers. Laminate the decorated banks for durability; then cut out the pigs along the bold lines. Staple one side of an unsealed, snack-sized resealable plastic bag—above the seal—to the back of each child's bank. Punch two holes near the top of the bank; then tie on a length of yarn to make the bank into a necklace. Before sending the banks home, insert a parent note—similar to the one shown—into each child's bank. Let the savings begin!

Pennies From Home

Once every child has returned her bank to school with ten pennies inside, begin your investment in counting skills with the song at the right. Direct youngsters to sit in a circle with their banks around their necks. Give each child a turn to sit in the center of the group. Have the child in the center remove her necklace, and then count out her pennies as the group slowly sings the song.

Piggy Pickings

Give youngsters chances to practice their counting skills with this snacktime idea. Pour individual servings of the same snack for students. Designate a penny amount for one serving. Then invite each child to wear his necklace over to your serving area so that he can count out the correct number of pennies to "purchase" his snack. After he cleans up, give him back his coins. Vary the snack and the penny amount each day for as many days as students are interested.

Ten Pennies In My Bank
(sung to the tune of "Ten Little Indians")

One little, two little, three little pennies;
Four little, five little, six little pennies;
Seven little, eight little, nine little pennies.
Ten pennies in my bank!

Penny-Wise Centers

Send your little ones with their piggy banks to these centers for some counting fun!

Heads Or Tails?

Student pairs are sure to make heads and tails out of this center. To prepare, duplicate a copy of page 15 onto pink construction paper; then laminate it for durability. To play, one of the partners empties his bank's pennies onto the piggy-bank sheet. Next he counts aloud as he takes each of the pennies that landed heads up. The second child then counts aloud as he takes the pennies that landed tails up. The children compare their totals. The first child puts all the pennies back in his bag; then the partners switch roles.

Penny Pitches

Pitch some more counting practice to students with this center. To prepare, duplicate five copies of page 15 onto pink construction paper; then laminate them for durability. Label each piggy-bank sheet with a different numeral from 1 to 5. Arrange these sheets in a row in an open area. To use this center, each child in a pair tosses a beanbag onto a piggy-bank sheet. Both children then count the corresponding number of their bank's pennies onto the mats that their beanbags landed on. The child who counts out the most pennies wins that round. The children put their pennies back in their banks before playing again.

Penny Pairs

Youngsters will improve their counting skills *and* their memories with this game of Concentration. Reduce the piggy-bank pattern (page 15) by 50%; then duplicate 10 copies of this pattern onto pink construction paper. Laminate the patterns; then cut them out. (Or, as a time-saver, obtain 10 index cards.) Label each pair of pigs or cards with a different numeral from 1 to 5. Tape the corresponding number of pennies to each card.

To play, a pair of children arranges the cards facedown. A child turns over two cards and then counts the number of pennies on each card. If he has found matching amounts, he keeps the cards. If not, he returns the cards facedown again. Play continues until the partners have found all the matching pairs.

A Cookie For You And A Cookie For Me

Who should take the cookies from the cookie jar? You should take the cookies from the cookie jar— and share them with your class! Find out how sweet sharing can be when you practice with cookies!

ideas contributed by Henry Fergus

Ding, Dong!

Did someone hear the doorbell ring? Introduce your sharing theme with the crowd-pleasing *The Doorbell Rang* by Pat Hutchins (Greenwillow Books). Bring a class supply of chocolate-chip cookies (plus a few extra) to your group area; then begin munching on a cookie or two in front of your class. When your children have figured out that you're up to something, state with surprise that you forgot to share! Then give each child a cookie to munch on while you read the story aloud. Pause to ask what the children in the story should do when all of the cookies have been shared and the doorbell rings *again*. Then share the surprise ending. More cookies, anyone?

One For You, And One For You, And One For You...

This activity will make your snacktime extrasweet and continue to teach the goodness of sharing. Put as many cookies in a jar as you have seats at a table. Ring a bell each time you invite a child to sit down and take a cookie from the jar. When the seats are filled and the cookies have been shared, invite everyone to eat. Vary the activity by substituting cookies with other single-serving items, such as crackers or flavored mini rice cakes. There's enough for everyone!

Let's Share

Sing this song during your snacktime or anytime you need to encourage sharing.

Share With Me

(sung to the tune of "This Old Man")

One for you; one for me.
Let's all sing this melody.
Come and share with me and I will share with you.
Sharing is so fun to do!

Who Shared The Cookie From The Cookie Jar?

Reinforce sharing with this tasty circle-time game based on a popular chant. Cut out a class supply of paper cookies; then label each one with a different child's name. Put the cookies in a cookie jar. During a group time, ask a volunteer to take a cookie from the jar; then identify the child's name on the cookie. Have the class join you in reciting the following chant, substituting the volunteer's name and the name on the cookie. Then have the volunteer give the cookie to the appropriate child. Invite that child to be the next person to take a cookie from the jar. Continue until each child has a cookie. To make the game even more fun, have each child give a real cookie to the child whose labeled cookie was selected.

Who shared a cookie from the cookie jar?
[Child's name] shared a cookie from the cookie jar.
[She/he] did? Yes, [she/he] did!
With whom?
With [name on cookie].

Shelly

A Cookie For You
And A Cookie For Me

Your little ones are sure to internalize the joy of sharing when they give away cookies they've decorated themselves. To prepare, duplicate a class supply of both labels on page 21; then cut them apart. Write each child's name on a separate pair of labels; then add a different child's name to each of the "A Cookie For You" labels. Tape each label to a separate resealable plastic bag. Set up a cookie-decorating center with two cookies for each child, different colors of frosting, plastic knives, a variety of candy decorations, and napkins. Invite each child to visit the center to use her choice of items to decorate two cookies. As she puts one cookie in each of her two bags, explain that she will keep one of her cookies and share the other one. She will also get a cookie from a friend. When everyone has decorated cookies, give them to the students with great ceremony; then direct them to take their bags home. Sharing is delicious!

A Cookie For
You!
This sweet treat was made by
Karen
for
Scott

A Cookie For
Me!
Karen

Pretend Cookies;
Real Sharing

Cook up some real sharing in your dramatic-play area by supplying just one of each different item needed to bake delicious imaginary cookies. Stock the center with a batch of cookie dough (play dough), one bowl, one spoon, one rolling pin, one cookie cutter, and one pan. Remind the children that in order to bake up a lot of cookies, they'll need to share the items. Sharing means more fun for everyone!

Please Share. Thank You!

Put social skills into practice with this tasty counting activity. For each child, duplicate the cookie-jar pattern on page 21 onto construction paper; then personalize it. Cut out the patterns. Working with a pair of children, give each child her jar and the same number of Cookie-Crisp® cereal pieces. To play, a child asks her partner for a number of cookies by saying, "May I please have [number] cookie(s)?" The second child then counts out that number of cookies from her jar and puts them onto her partner's jar. The first child says, "Thank you for sharing." The second child responds, "You're welcome." The second child then takes a turn. Continue until each child has had several turns; then provide each child with an individual bag of cereal pieces for snacking. Use the cookie jars with the incentive idea described in "Sharing Is So Sweet."

Sue

Sue shared the blocks at center time.

Sue

Sharing Is So Sweet

Use this display idea to share the good news of youngsters' social successes. When you observe a child sharing, record the circumstances on a paper cookie cutout. Glue the cookie to that child's jar. When each child's jar has one cookie, mount the jars on a display labeled "Sharing Is So Sweet!"

Celebrate Sharing

Celebrate your youngsters' success at sharing with a giant cookie. Follow the package directions on one or more refrigerated ready-to-bake pan cookies. When the cookie has cooled, divide it into pieces so that you have enough for each child and some extras to share with school staff or another class. *C* is for cookie. *C* is for celebration!

Sheila Krill

A Cookie For
You!

This sweet treat was made by

_____

for

_____

A Cookie For
Me!

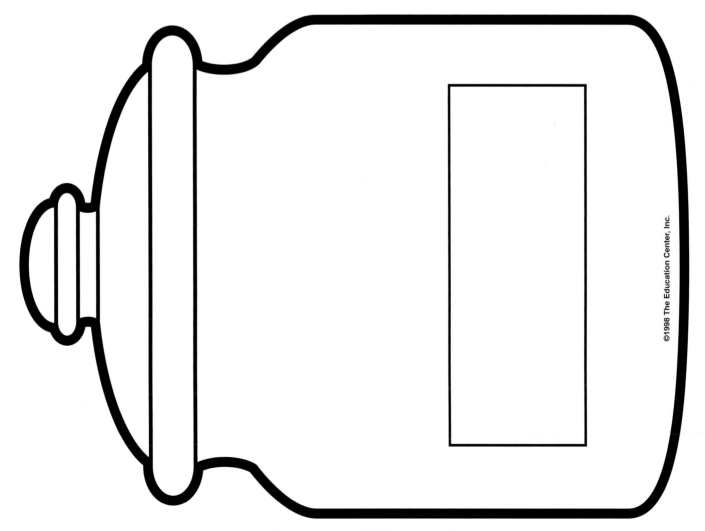

©1998 The Education Center, Inc.

Signs Of Fall

Colorful trees, falling leaves, acorns, squirrels—these signs tell us it must be fall! Use these "tree-mendous" activities to give your little ones learning fun as they discover this season.

by Suzanne Moore

Take A Walk

Before you announce your fall studies, duplicate a class supply of the leaf patterns (page 26) onto construction paper; then cut them out. Also prepare a large, bulletin-board-paper tree cutout. Mount the tree on a board along with the title "Signs Of Fall."

During a group time, introduce your students to the pleasures of fall by reading aloud *Fall* by Ron Hirschi (Cobblehill Books) or *When Autumn Comes* by Robert Maass (Henry Holt And Company, Inc.). After hearing the story and observing its photographs, youngsters are likely to be eager to head outdoors. Take a walk outside to give students a chance to search for signs of fall. When you return to your classroom, record an observation from each child on one of the leaf shapes. Then invite the child to attach his leaf to the tree display.

Tree Time

Here are some quick tips for teachable tree moments.

How Many Arms?

Measure the circumferences of several trees by having students hold hands while encircling each tree.

Outdoor Naptime

Develop patience by encouraging your little ones to lie still and quiet under a tree. I'm so still those squirrels don't see me!

Rubbings

Have youngsters make tree rubbings of various trees, then compare the bark designs.

It Is Autumn
(sung to the tune of "Skip To My Lou")

It is autumn up in a tree.
It is autumn up in a tree.
It is autumn up in a tree.
Up in a tree it's autumn.

Leaves are changing up in a tree...
Leaves are falling from that tree...
Squirrels are living up in a tree...
Acorns are growing up in a tree...

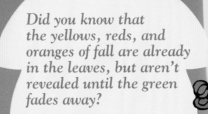

Did you know that the yellows, reds, and oranges of fall are already in the leaves, but aren't revealed until the green fades away?

Active Autumn Song

Practice color identification and listening skills with this active autumn song. In advance, duplicate the leaf patterns (page 26) onto yellow, orange, red, and brown construction paper so that you have a class supply. Laminate the leaves; then cut them out. Punch a hole near the top of each leaf; then string it onto a length of like-colored yarn to make a necklace.

During a group time, give each child a necklace. Have the group stand to sing this song. Direct each child to touch the floor when he hears the color of his leaf in the song.

Did You Ever See A Tree?
(sung to the tune of "Did You Ever See A Lassie?")

Did you ever see a tree,
A tree, a tree?
Did you ever see a tree,
A tree in the fall?

There are red leaves and orange leaves,
And yellow leaves and brown leaves.
Did you ever see a tree,
A tree in the fall?

Did you ever see the wind blow,
The wind blow, the wind blow?
Did you ever see the wind blow
A tree in the fall?

The [red] leaves all fall down.
They swirl down to the ground.
Did you ever see the wind blow
A tree in the fall?

The [yellow] leaves all fall down....
The [orange] leaves all fall down....
The [brown] leaves all fall down....

Let's Go Again!

Take a second outdoor walk so that youngsters not only look for signs of fall, but also pick some up to bring back to your discovery center. Prior to this walk, prepare a box for collecting the items. Have youngsters glue fall colors of crumpled tissue paper onto the branches of a large, brown tagboard tree cutout. Tape this tree to the inside back of a medium-sized brown box. Ask children what kinds of things they might find outside that are signs of fall. As students make suggestions, remind them to be careful to only choose leaves and other items that have fallen to the ground. When you return to the classroom, allow time for the children to explore the collection. As a group, sort the items by *object, color,* or *size.* Then put the box in your discovery area for independent exploration.

Preserving Leaves

Use these methods to preserve some of the most colorful fall leaves collected during your fall walks.

Press And Dry

Place leaves between the pages of an old phone book. Or put them between half-inch thicknesses of newspapers. Set bricks or weights atop the papers. Allow the leaves to dry for several days.

Leaf Dip

In a shallow pan, mix one pint of water with 13 ounces of glycerin (available in drugstores). Place up to 30 leaves in the pan, making sure each leaf is completely coated with the solution. Allow the leaves to soak overnight. The next day, remove the leaves and dry them between newspaper layers. Let the leaves dry for several days. Any leftover solution may be reused.

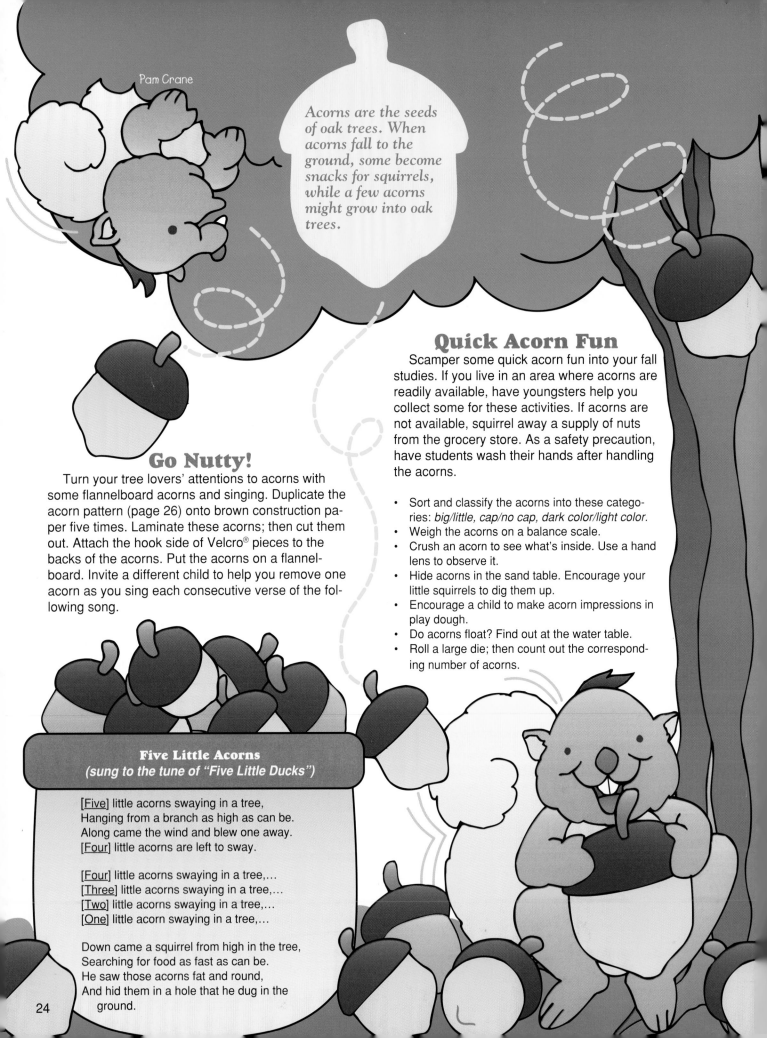

Pam Crane

Acorns are the seeds of oak trees. When acorns fall to the ground, some become snacks for squirrels, while a few acorns might grow into oak trees.

Quick Acorn Fun

Scamper some quick acorn fun into your fall studies. If you live in an area where acorns are readily available, have youngsters help you collect some for these activities. If acorns are not available, squirrel away a supply of nuts from the grocery store. As a safety precaution, have students wash their hands after handling the acorns.

- Sort and classify the acorns into these categories: *big/little, cap/no cap, dark color/light color.*
- Weigh the acorns on a balance scale.
- Crush an acorn to see what's inside. Use a hand lens to observe it.
- Hide acorns in the sand table. Encourage your little squirrels to dig them up.
- Encourage a child to make acorn impressions in play dough.
- Do acorns float? Find out at the water table.
- Roll a large die; then count out the corresponding number of acorns.

Go Nutty!

Turn your tree lovers' attentions to acorns with some flannelboard acorns and singing. Duplicate the acorn pattern (page 26) onto brown construction paper five times. Laminate these acorns; then cut them out. Attach the hook side of Velcro® pieces to the backs of the acorns. Put the acorns on a flannelboard. Invite a different child to help you remove one acorn as you sing each consecutive verse of the following song.

Five Little Acorns
(sung to the tune of "Five Little Ducks")

[Five] little acorns swaying in a tree,
Hanging from a branch as high as can be.
Along came the wind and blew one away.
[Four] little acorns are left to sway.

[Four] little acorns swaying in a tree,…
[Three] little acorns swaying in a tree,…
[Two] little acorns swaying in a tree,…
[One] little acorn swaying in a tree,…

Down came a squirrel from high in the tree,
Searching for food as fast as can be.
He saw those acorns fat and round,
And hid them in a hole that he dug in the ground.

Why do squirrels hide seeds? In the autumn seeds are plentiful. The squirrels come back to their hidden seeds in the winter when food is hard to find.

Squirrellin' Around

If your students have spent much time around trees, then they have probably seen some squirrels. To spark your students' curiosity about these cute little critters, read *Squirrels* by Brian Wildsmith (published by Oxford University Press, Inc.). After sharing the story, have youngsters try balancing like squirrels. Tape several strips of masking tape on the floor in an open area so that these strips connect and intersect similarly to the branches of a tree. Direct each child to try walking along a length first with his arms down, then with his arms outstretched at his sides. Which is easier? Lead students to realize that using their outstretched arms for balance is similar to how squirrels use their tails. Encourage youngsters to revisit this area to practice walking along the tape and jumping from tape branch to tape branch.

What Do You See?

Is it fun to climb trees like the squirrels? You bet! Here's a cute booklet with a surprise ending that is easy for youngsters to make and read. For each child, duplicate the booklet cover (page 27) once, and the booklet page (page 27) three times. Cut the pages apart; then program them as shown. To illustrate her book, have a child sponge-paint the cover and pages. When the paint is dry, have her write her name on the cover. Have her glue pieces of leaves and twigs to page 1. On page 2, have her use a Q-Tip® to paint brown acorns, and then use markers to decorate a fingerprint squirrel. To page 3, glue a trimmed photo or color copy of a photo. Sequence the cover and pages; then staple them together along the top. Practice reading the books together. Then encourage students to take them home to share with their families.

Branch Out— Read These Books About Fall

Why Do Leaves Change Color?
Written by Betsy Maestro
Illustrated by Loretta Krupinski
Published by HarperCollins Children's Books

Red Leaf, Yellow Leaf
Written & Illustrated by Lois Ehlert
Published by Harcourt Brace & Company

Autumn
Written by Nicola Baxter
Illustrated by Kim Woolley
Published by Children's Press®

Patterns

Use leaf patterns with "Take A Walk" on page 22 and "Active Autumn Song" on page 23.

Use acorn pattern with "Go Nutty!" on page 24.

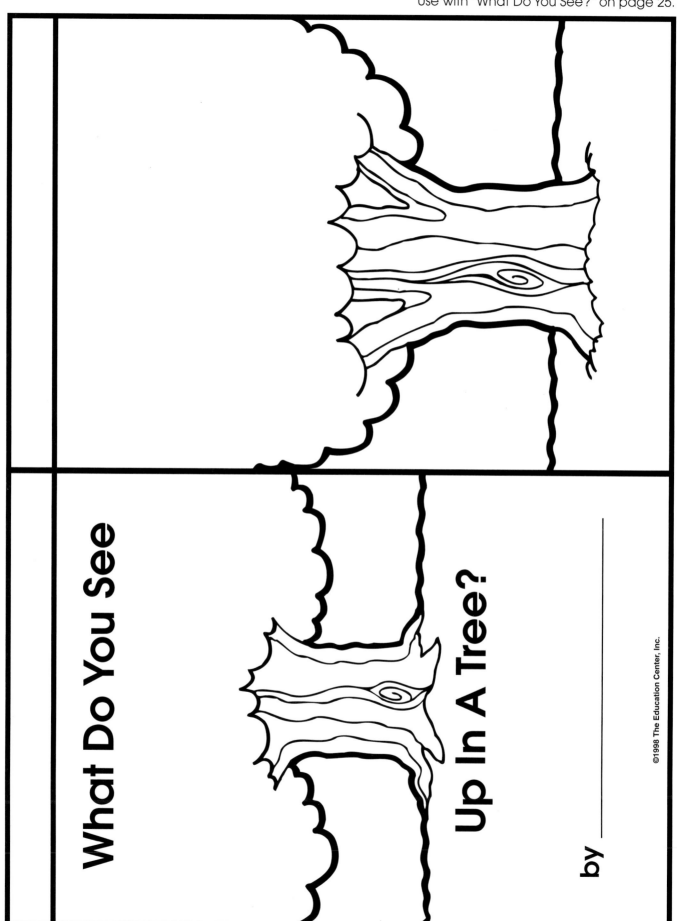

What Do You See

Up In A Tree?

by _____

Siblings Are Sensational!

Looking for ideas that your little ones can relate to? Oh boy! Here's a collection for you. Whether each child in your class is a big brother or sister, a little brother or sister, or an only child, these activities will help him or her understand and share common family experiences. Use the activities on pages 30–31 to honor youngsters who become new big brothers or sisters.

ideas by dayle timmons

The Scoop On Siblings

Since young preschoolers might have a difficult time articulating the ages and names of their siblings, contact parents to make sure you have accurate information. Duplicate a class supply of a parent note such as the one shown; then send them home. Soon you'll have information about every child and his brother—and sister!

How Many Brothers? How Many Sisters?

Sibling relationships can be puzzling, but all the pieces fit together nicely with these visual helps. Using the information from the returned parent notes (see "The Scoop On Siblings"), collect enough cardboard puzzle pieces (that resemble people shapes) so that you have one for each child and his or her correct number of siblings. To prepare, spray-paint the appropriate number of pieces one color to represent sisters and the remaining pieces a different color to represent brothers. When the paint is dry, use a black marker to add dot eyes to each piece. Have each child choose the pieces that represent the children in his family—a piece for himself and one for each of his siblings. Then have him glue the pieces on an index card. Write the siblings' names by the pieces.

During a group time, have the class look at each child's card as he tells about the children in his family. Spread the cards out in front of the group. Ask questions to help the children find similarities and differences. Which families have two brothers? Which families have three children? Are the numbers of brothers and sisters the same in those families? Which families have only one child? Finally, graph the cards by the number of children in each family.

Dear Parent,

We are learning what it's like to be a big brother or sister, a little brother or sister, or an only child. Please make sure we have the correct information.

My child's name _____.

His/her brothers' names and ages:

_____

His/her sisters' names and ages:

_____

If you are expecting a baby, when is it due?

_____

Thank you,
Mrs. Timmons

Ben   Beth

A Salute To Siblings

This song invites youngsters to stand up for "sibling-hood." Hooray!

Stand Up For Siblings
(sung to the tune of "If You're Happy And You Know It")

If you have a big [brother/sister], stand right up.
If you have a big [brother/sister], stand right up.
Big [brothers/sisters], it's true, are older than you.
If you have a big [brother/sister], stand right up.

If you have a little [brother/sister], stand right up.
If you have a little [brother/sister], stand right up.
Little [brothers/sisters], it's true, are younger than you.
If you have a little [brother/sister], stand right up.

If you're an only child, stand right up.
If you're an only child, stand right up.
In your own family, you are special—yes sirree!
If you're an only child, stand right up.

Super Siblings

Perhaps your little ones are so proud of their siblings that they want to show them off! If so, prepare a bulletin board titled "Super Siblings." Encourage students to display photos and illustrations on the board. Invite children without siblings to draw pictures of their friends with their siblings. Also invite children to cut out magazine pictures that show children who could be siblings; then help them attach these pictures to the board.

Bodacious Brothers And Super Sisters

Now that you know who has brothers and sisters, find out what your children think about them. On each of three different colors of bulletin-board paper, draw the outline shape of a child. Cut out these shapes; then label each one with one of the following phrases: "Big Brother Or Sister," "Little Brother Or Sister," and "Only Child." Display the cutouts on a wall. During a group time, ask volunteers to tell about children's big brothers or sisters or share stories about them. On the appropriate cutout, write the children's descriptions and one-sentence summaries. During another group time, similarly discuss little brothers and sisters. Next give only children a chance to share. Help children see the similarities and differences in their situations.

Sibling Stories

Since most of your children with brothers and sisters have probably had at least one good case of "sibling-itis," the situations in these stories will be familiar ones.

Geraldine First
Written & Illustrated by Holly Keller
Published by Greenwillow Books

I Love You The Purplest
Written by Barbara M. Joosse
Illustrated by Mary Whyte
Published by Chronicle Books

Bunny Cakes
Written & Illustrated by Rosemary Wells
Published by Dial Books For Young Readers

Ben and his sister.

29

"Rocka-My-Baby"

Every big brother and sister is sure to need to know how to rock a baby to sleep. Have youngsters share familiar lullabies that they already know, such as "Hush, Little Baby" and "Rock-A-Bye, Baby." Then continue your sibling training with this simple, but sweet, song.

Hush, Lil' Baby
(sung to the tune of "Mary Had A Little Lamb")

Hush, lil' baby, time to sleep,
Time to sleep, time to sleep.
Hush, lil' baby, time to sleep.
Rest quietly.

Hush, lil' baby, [brother/sister] loves you.
[Brother/sister] loves you. [Brother/sister] loves you.
Hush, lil' baby, [brother/sister] loves you.
Rest quietly.

Congratulations!

Chances are that one or more of your preschoolers will welcome the arrival of a new baby into her family. Honor the proud, new brother or sister with a crown and certificate. Duplicate the crown (page 32) and the certificate (page 33) onto construction paper; then cut them out. Color both items, if desired. Personalize the crown as shown; then tape a matching construction-paper strip to the crown so that it fits the child's head. Program the certificate; then mount it onto a larger piece of paper. Present the crown and certificate to the proud sibling during a group time; then invite her to tell about the most important baby in the world—her new brother or sister!

Nancy Goldberg—Three-Year-Olds, B'nai Israel Nursery School
Rockville, MD

Brothers And Sisters In Training

Set up a dramatic-play center that resembles a nursery so that the big brothers and sisters in your class can train their classmates in their new area of expertise. In addition to baby dolls, place items in the center such as empty baby-powder containers, bibs, empty baby-food containers (avoid glass jars), bottles, diapers, a lullaby cassette, and a rocking chair. My, what big helpers you all are!

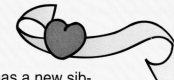

Books For The Big Brother Or Sister

Books abound for the child who is new in "sibling-hood." When a child has a new sibling, read aloud one of the following titles during storytime. Consider also preparing this thoughtful gift for the child to take home. Label a diaper bag "For Big Brothers And Big Sisters." Fill the bag with several of the following titles. Also include a note to the parents congratulating them on their new arrival, and encouraging them to use the books to spark discussion with their preschooler about the changes ahead. When the diaper bag is returned, record several words of advice from the child about taking care of a baby brother or sister. Put this advice in the bag before passing it to the next child.

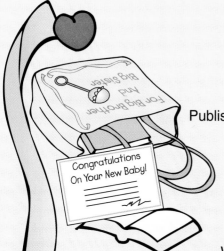

Cuddle And Read

I'm A Big Brother and
I'm A Big Sister
Written by Joanna Cole
Illustrated by Maxie Chambliss
Published by William Morrow And Company, Inc.

When The Teddy Bears Came
Written by Martin Waddell
Illustrated by Penny Dale
Published by Candlewick Press

The Baby Sister
Written & Illustrated by Tomie dePaola
Published by The Putnam Publishing Group

Something Special
Written by Nicola Moon
Illustrated by Alex Ayliffe
Published by Peachtree Publishers, Ltd.

Julius, The Baby Of The World
Written & Illustrated by Kevin Henkes
Published by Mulberry Books

Big Brother Dustin
Written by Alden R. Carter
Photographed by Dan Young with Carol Carter
Published by Albert Whitman & Company

We Have A Baby
Written & Illustrated by Cathryn Falwell
Published by Clarion Books

The New Baby: A Mister Rogers' Neighborhood®
First Experiences Book
Written by Fred Rogers
Photographed by Jim Judkis
Published by PaperStar

Ellen And Penguin And The New Baby
Written & Illustrated by Clara Vulliamy
Published by Candlewick Press

Crown

Use with "Congratulations!" on page 30.

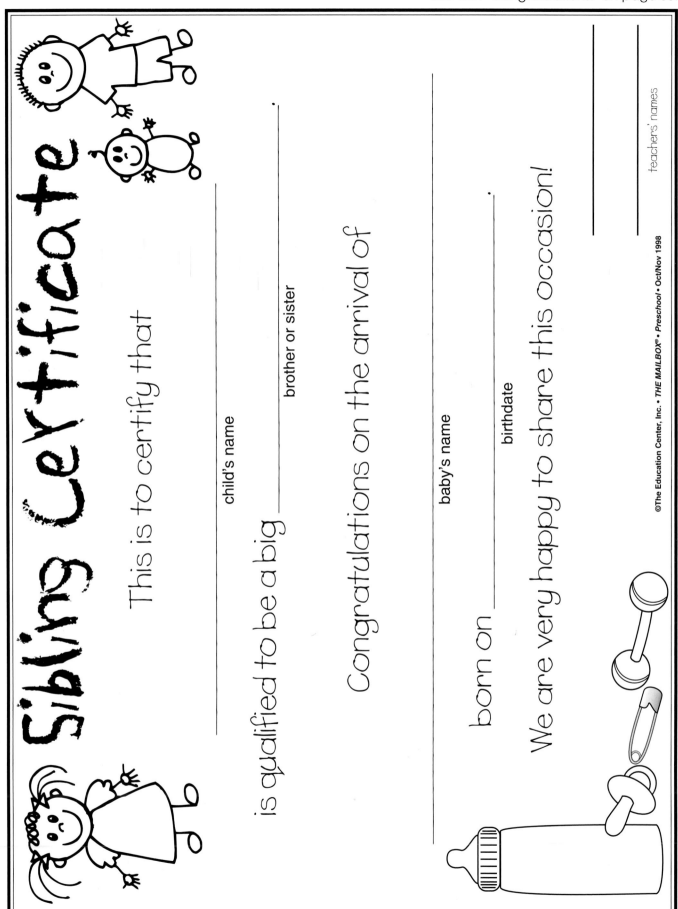

Sibling Certificate

This is to certify that

_____
child's name

is qualified to be a big _____
brother or sister

Congratulations on the arrival of

_____
baby's name

born on _____
birthdate

We are very happy to share this occasion!

_____
teachers' names

©The Education Center, Inc. • THE MAILBOX® • Preschool • Oct/Nov 1998

33

'Tis The Season For Shapes

'Tis the season to learn about shapes. Fa la la la la, la la la la!

by Lucia Kemp Henry

1 winter day I looked to see that
holiday shapes were all around me!

Winter Holidays Shapes Booklet

Center your shape studies around the making of these holiday booklets. Then, when your study is complete, each child will have a seasonal booklet to take home for holiday reading! To prepare, duplicate a class supply of the cover (page 39) and a class supply of the booklet text strips (page 40). Trim the covers and cut apart each set of strips. Glue the first text strip and the cover to a 9" x 12" piece of construction paper. For each child, precut the following construction-paper shapes so that their sizes correspond to the shapes on the cover: green triangle, yellow square, tan diamond, green circle with its center cut out, yellow star, blue rectangle, black rectangle.

As you study each shape, follow the directions (pages 34–38) for decorating the corresponding booklet page and portion of the cover. When each child has completed a page for each shape, sequence the pages; then bind them together. In time, each child will have a book of his own about the holidays *and* shapes of the season.

2 triangle trees standing in the snow.

Two Triangle Trees Standing In The Snow

Begin your seasonal shape studies with the terrific triangle. To make the first page of a holiday-shapes booklet, sponge-paint the bottom third of a sheet of blue construction paper white to resemble snow. Cut two green triangles; then glue them above the paint. To complete the page, glue two small, broken pieces of craft sticks below the triangles. Glue the appropriate text strip to the back of the booklet's cover.

34

Triangular Trees

Having youngsters make this forest of trees is a terrific way to teach them about triangles. Use an X-acto® knife to cut various sizes of triangles out of corrugated cardboard, making sure that the grain of the cardboard is vertical to the base of each triangle, not horizontal. Insert a craft stick into the cardboard layers of each triangle to create a trunk. Have each child sponge-paint both sides of a triangular tree green. Insert thestick into a ball of clay so that it remains upright while drying. When the paint is dry, invite each child to glue lengths of green rickrack, colorful beads, or decorative hole-punched paper shapes onto his tree. Display the trees together in a blocks center or manipulative area to create a faux forest just right for creative play.

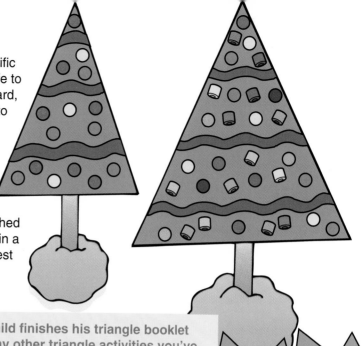

When each child finishes his triangle booklet page and any other triangle activities you've planned, have him glue a green triangle and a broken portion of a craft stick to his cover (shown on page 34).

Three Square Gifts With Christmas Bows

A trio of pretty square gifts decorates the next page of the holiday-shapes booklet. To decorate a page, sponge-paint three squares onto a sheet of construction paper. When the paint is dry, glue on three small gift-wrap bows or three hand-tied ribbon bows. Glue the appropriate text strip to the back of the triangle page.

Sorting Squares

These miniature wrapped presents give youngsters all sorts of ways to recognize squares. To prepare this center, cut a number of three-inch cardboard squares. Divide the squares into three or more groups. Wrap each group of squares in a different type of Hanukkah, Christmas, or Kwanzaa wrapping paper. Punch a hole near the top of one square in each group. Use curling ribbon to tie each of these three squares to the handle of a separate kraft bag. Place the tagged shopping bags and the wrapped squares in a center. To use the items, a child sorts the similarly wrapped squares into their matching shopping bags. Now that's all the fun of holiday shopping without the expense!

When each child finishes her square booklet page and any other square activities you've planned, have her glue a yellow square and a small bow to her booklet cover (shown on page 34).

Four Diamond Cookies Just Made To Eat

The next page of the shapes booklet includes a quartet of delicious-looking cookies to count. To make this page, cut four diamond shapes from tan construction paper; then glue them on a sheet of construction paper. Use a cotton swab to paint thick white acrylic paint onto each diamond to represent icing. While the paint is wet, shake on colored sugar sprinkles. Glue the appropriate text strip to the back of the square page.

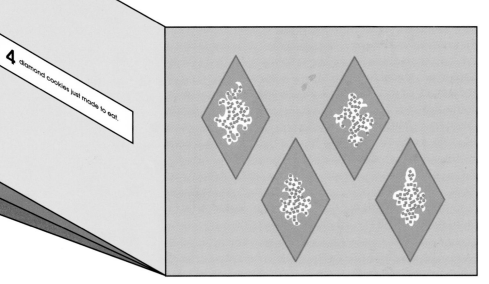

4 diamond cookies just made to eat.

Delicious Diamonds

After decorating booklet pages with paper cookies, your youngsters are sure to enjoy making some real diamond-shaped cookies. Prepare a batch of your favorite sugar-cookie dough; then roll it out on a cutting surface. For each child, use a permanent marker to personalize a piece of aluminum foil that is slightly larger than your diamond-shaped cookie cutter. Invite each child to cut a cookie from the dough, then put it on his piece of foil. When the cookies have baked and are cool, invite each child to use gel or icing in a tube to outline and decorate the shape of his cookie.

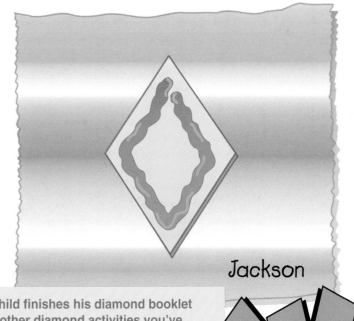

Jackson

When each child finishes his diamond booklet page and any other diamond activities you've planned, have him glue a tan diamond to his cover, then decorate it as described in "Four Diamond Cookies Just Made To Eat" (see cover on page 34).

Five Round Latkes For A Hanukkah Treat

Dish up latkes for the next page of the shapes booklet. For this page, paint a piece of finger-painting paper with brown or yellow fingerpaint. When the paint is dry, cut five circles out of the paper. Glue the circle latkes onto a sheet of construction paper. Complete the page by gluing on a plastic fork. Glue the appropriate text strip to the back of the diamond page.

5 round latkes for a Hanukkah treat.

Round Wreaths

Round out your circle studies with this wreath-painting project. In advance, collect a variety of containers—such as film containers with and without lids, thread spools, cardboard ribbon reels, yogurt containers, and small margarine tubs with and without lids—that would be useful for printing circles. Fill shallow pans with green tempera paint. Invite each child to discover circles by dipping his choice of items into the paint, then pressing them onto a large piece of newsprint. When the paint is dry, have him use glue that has been tinted red to add berries to the round wreath prints. Or have him glue on paper circles or red sequins. If desired, use the paper to gift wrap Christmas presents.

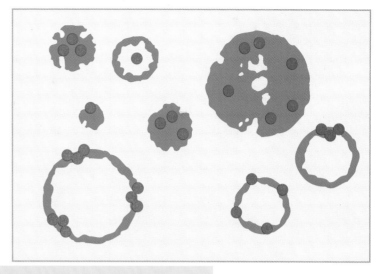

When each child finishes his circle booklet page and any other circle activities you've planned, have him glue a small, circular photo or color copy of a photo of himself to the cover. Then have him glue a green circle, with its center cut out, over the photo. Finally have him add red marker, glue, paper, or sequin berries (shown on page 34).

Six Star Shapes In The Winter Night

Youngsters are sure to be starry-eyed when making the next pages of their shapes booklets. To complete a page, sponge-paint six yellow stars onto a sheet of black construction paper. When the paint is dry, add a star sticker to the center of each painted star. Glue the appropriate text strip to the back of the circle page.

Shiny Star Sorting

This star-spangled center is just the place for youngsters' sorting skills to shine. To prepare the center, use a star-shaped cookie cutter to cut a number of star shapes from white Styrofoam®. Insert a craft stick into the edge of each star; then secure the sticks with Plaid® Tacky Glue. Divide the stars into the same number of groups as there are colors of glitter you would like to use. Using a paintbrush, completely cover each star with the Tacky Glue; then generously sprinkle it with glitter. When the glue is dry, place the stars in a container. Then put the stars and as many empty containers as you have colors of stars in a center. To use the items, a child sorts the stars by color into the containers.

When each child finishes her star booklet page and any other star activities you've planned, have her glue a yellow star to her cover, then decorate it with glue and glitter (shown on page 34).

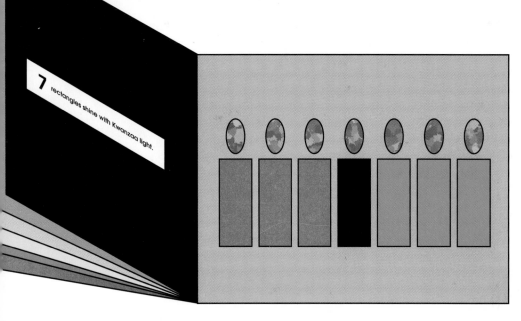

Seven Rectangles Shine With Kwanzaa Light

Light up the last page of the shapes booklet with Kwanzaa candles. Cut out three green construction-paper rectangles, one black rectangle, and three red rectangles. Glue the rectangles as shown to a sheet of construction paper to represent the candles in a *kinara,* or candleholder. Squeeze a flame-shaped amount of glue over each candle; then sprinkle on a generous amount of gold glitter. When the glue is dry, shake off the excess glitter. Glue the appropriate text strip to the back of the star page.

Rectangular Greeting Card

These greeting cards are the perfect way to add a glow to a loved one's day! And depending on the colors of construction paper, the card provides a greeting for the holiday of your choice! To make one, fold two pieces of construction paper in half along the width. Starting at the fold, cut two 2 1/2-inch long slits one inch apart in the center of one of the sheets. Gently fold the cut portion in to the inside of the sheet (as shown). Glue the second folded sheet to the outside of the cut sheet. Glue a 1" x 2 1/2" piece of construction paper to the inside of the card on the cut-out portion to represent the candle. Add a tissue-paper flame; then glue glitter onto the flame. On the outside of the card, write a message such as "Merry Christmas!" or "Happy Hanukkah!" Inside the card, include the message shown and the child's name.

Merry Christmas

See this little candle glow?

I made it just for you, you know!

Annie

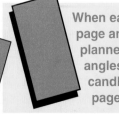

When each child finishes her rectangle booklet page and any other rectangle activities you've planned, have her glue the blue and black rectangles to her cover, then decorate the oval candle flames with glue and glitter (shown on page 34).

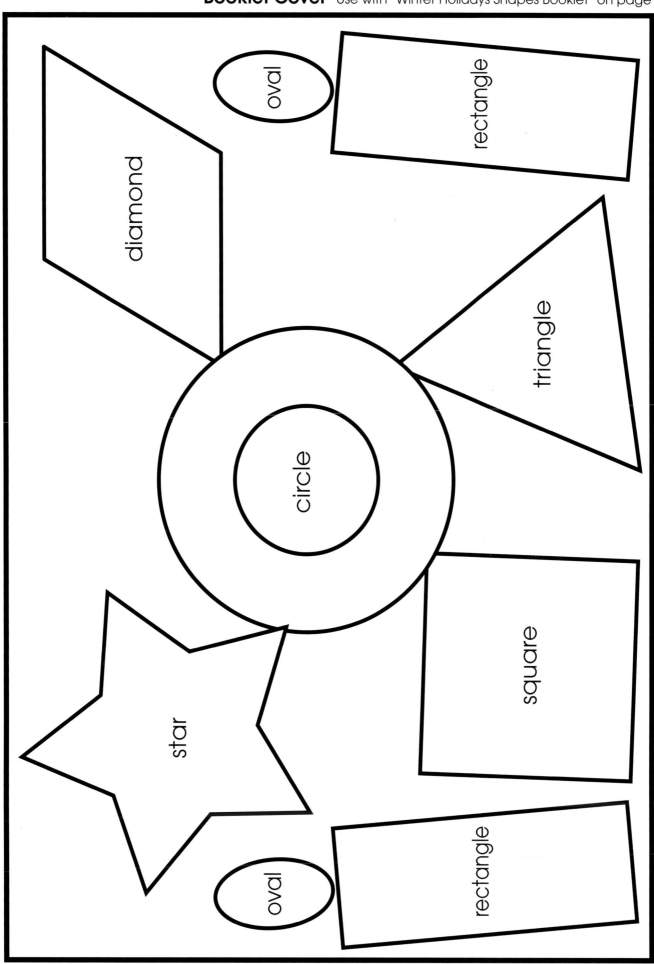

Booklet Text Strips

Use with "Winter Holidays Shapes Booklet" on page 34.

1 winter day I looked to see that holiday shapes were all around me!

2 triangle trees standing in the snow.

3 square gifts with Christmas bows.

4 diamond cookies just made to eat.

5 round latkes for a Hanukkah treat.

6 star shapes in the winter night.

7 rectangles shine with Kwanzaa light.

Discover The Five Senses

Preschoolers are natural explorers. When they explore, they discover. And when they discover, they *learn!* In this unit you'll find suggestions for setting up exploration centers that help children discover one of the five senses each week. You'll also find weekly notes that get families involved in the discoveries!

ideas by Katy Zoldak—Pre-K, Special Education, Metzenbaum School, Parma, OH

Hearing

Exploration Center

Hear, hear! Try adding these items to your center to help youngsters explore sound.

- tape recorder with headphones and cassette tapes
- musical instruments
- microphone with amplifier (Consider designating times when this can be used.)
- small, sealed boxes that you have filled with different items, such as beans, jingle bells, etc.
- tube telephone (To make one, use electrical tape to secure a plastic funnel to each end of a 15-foot-long plastic tube. The plastic tubes are available at home-supply stores.)

Family Activity

Prepare this family activity several weeks before beginning your study of the senses. Put a blank cassette tape in a battery-operated tape recorder. Put the recorder and a copy of the note below in a tote bag. Send the bag home with a different child each night. When every child has had an opportunity to record household sounds, play the tape during a group time. Make a list of all of the sounds that your class identifies. Then place the tape in your exploration center.

Dear Caregiver,

We're discovering the sense of sound! Would you please help us in our explorations? In this bag, you'll find a tape recorder with a tape in it. Please record your child's name; then help him/her record five household sounds, such as a baby crying or the television. (You do not need to rewind the tape before or after recording your sounds.) Return the bag to school tomorrow.

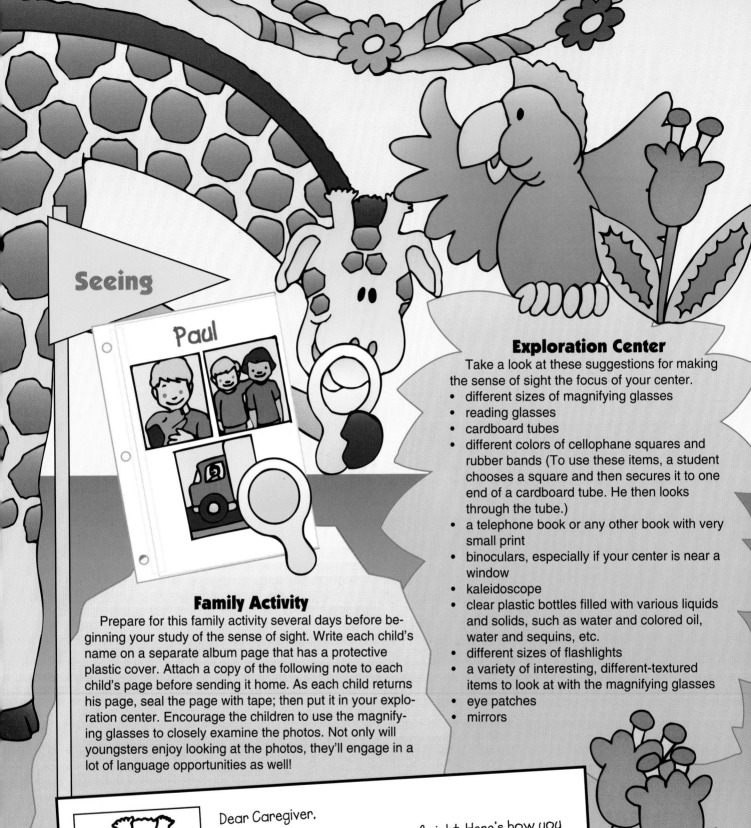

Seeing

Paul

Exploration Center

Take a look at these suggestions for making the sense of sight the focus of your center.
- different sizes of magnifying glasses
- reading glasses
- cardboard tubes
- different colors of cellophane squares and rubber bands (To use these items, a student chooses a square and then secures it to one end of a cardboard tube. He then looks through the tube.)
- a telephone book or any other book with very small print
- binoculars, especially if your center is near a window
- kaleidoscope
- clear plastic bottles filled with various liquids and solids, such as water and colored oil, water and sequins, etc.
- different sizes of flashlights
- a variety of interesting, different-textured items to look at with the magnifying glasses
- eye patches
- mirrors

Family Activity

Prepare for this family activity several days before beginning your study of the sense of sight. Write each child's name on a separate album page that has a protective plastic cover. Attach a copy of the following note to each child's page before sending it home. As each child returns his page, seal the page with tape; then put it in your exploration center. Encourage the children to use the magnifying glasses to closely examine the photos. Not only will youngsters enjoy looking at the photos, they'll engage in a lot of language opportunities as well!

Dear Caregiver,

We're discovering the sense of sight. Here's how you can help us take a closer look. With this note, you'll find a photo-album page with your child's name on it. Please help your child select three pictures to put on the page. (We will seal the plastic covering to the page with tape to ensure that the photos are returned without damage.) The photos will be placed in our exploration center along with magnifying glasses.

Exploration Center

Youngsters are sure to get a feel for the sense of touch when you add these items to your exploration center. (To avoid tactile messes, you may want to carefully consider the combination of items you put in the center at one time.)

- play dough
- ice packs and gel-filled ice packs
- plastic ice cubes in novelty shapes and colors
- zippered plastic bags filled with various liquids, such as tempera paint, fingerpaint, shampoo, etc. (Seal the bags closed with clear packing tape.)
- hot water bottle
- blindfolds
- a variety of other different-textured objects and materials, such as sandpaper, sponges, etc.

Family Activity

Use this activity to ask parents to help you during your study of the sense of touch. Personalize a paper lunch bag for each child; then attach a copy of the note below. Send the bags home. The next day collect the bags and bring them to your group time. Select a bag. Ask each child to put his hand in the bag and feel the object. When everyone has felt the item, have the group guess what it is. Then reveal the object and thank the child who brought it to school. Continue until all of the items have been discovered.

Dear Caregiver,

We're exploring the sense of touch. Here's how you can help us get a real feel for the topic! Please help your child find an item that has an interesting texture (such as a sponge or cotton ball) to put in the attached paper bag. Return the bag to school tomorrow. During a group time, we are going to try to guess what the item is just by using our sense of touch. Please indicate if you would like for the item to be returned after our activity.

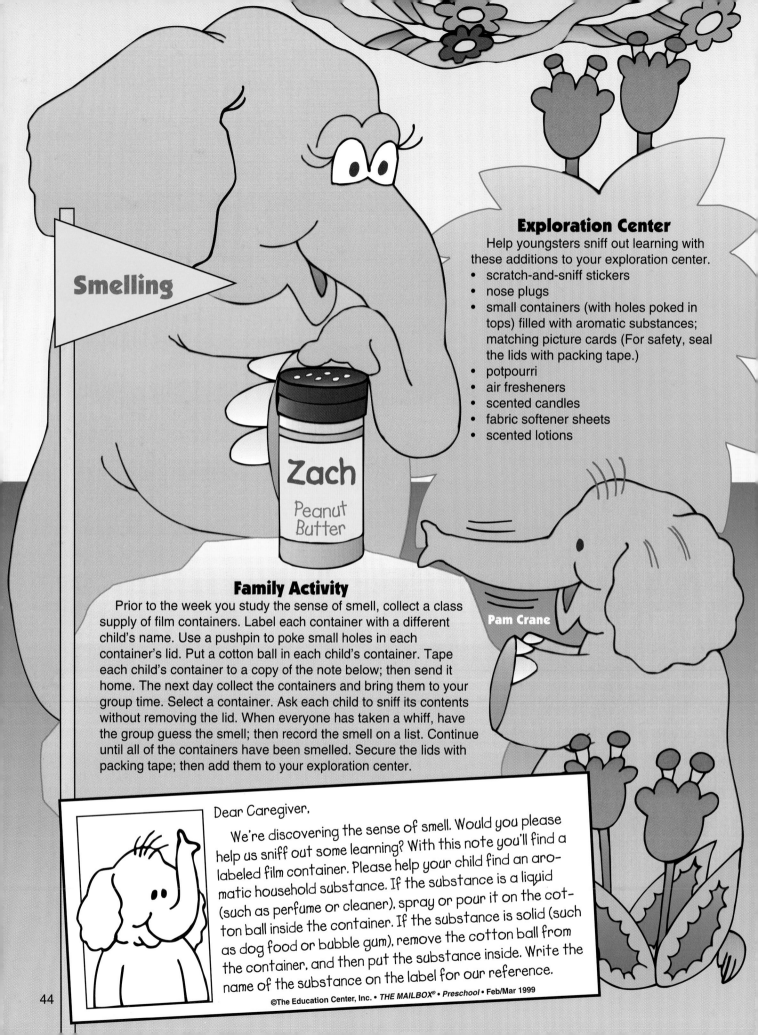

Smelling

Exploration Center
Help youngsters sniff out learning with these additions to your exploration center.
- scratch-and-sniff stickers
- nose plugs
- small containers (with holes poked in tops) filled with aromatic substances; matching picture cards (For safety, seal the lids with packing tape.)
- potpourri
- air fresheners
- scented candles
- fabric softener sheets
- scented lotions

Zach
Peanut Butter

Pam Crane

Family Activity
Prior to the week you study the sense of smell, collect a class supply of film containers. Label each container with a different child's name. Use a pushpin to poke small holes in each container's lid. Put a cotton ball in each child's container. Tape each child's container to a copy of the note below; then send it home. The next day collect the containers and bring them to your group time. Select a container. Ask each child to sniff its contents without removing the lid. When everyone has taken a whiff, have the group guess the smell; then record the smell on a list. Continue until all of the containers have been smelled. Secure the lids with packing tape; then add them to your exploration center.

Dear Caregiver,

We're discovering the sense of smell. Would you please help us sniff out some learning? With this note you'll find a labeled film container. Please help your child find an aromatic household substance. If the substance is a liquid (such as perfume or cleaner), spray or pour it on the cotton ball inside the container. If the substance is solid (such as dog food or bubble gum), remove the cotton ball from the container, and then put the substance inside. Write the name of the substance on the label for our reference.

Exploration Center

Each day that you study the sense of taste, set up a different tasting station at your exploration center using the ideas below. Provide napkins, cups, and a pitcher of water, if desired. Before students begin visiting the center, talk about good health habits, such as washing hands and not touching each other's food. Supervise the visits to the center more closely than in previous weeks.

- Provide individual portions of salty items in paper cups.
- Provide individual portions of sweet items in paper cups.
- Provide individual portions of fruit chunks in paper cups.
- Provide individual portions of vegetables in resealable plastic bags along with individual cups of dip.
- Provide a variety of sauces and spreads in bowls. Give each child a number of cracker pieces. Instruct him to dip each cracker piece once into a sauce or spread that he would like to try.

Tasting

Family Activity

To prepare for a group taste-testing activity, write each child's name on a separate resealable plastic bag. Put a copy of the following note in each child's bag; then send the bags home. The next day collect the bags and bring them to your group time. Select one of the bags and give every child a taste. Record whether the food was sweet, salty, spicy, sour, or bitter by making a simple graph like the one shown. Continue until all of the items have been tasted.

sweet	salty	spicy	sour	bitter
sugar	pretzels			
chocolate chips	potato chips		lemon juice	

Dear Caregiver,

We are discovering the sense of taste. Please help us have a taste-testing party. Assist your child in finding a food or sauce to put in this plastic resealable bag. We only need a very small portion for each child to taste. For example, include a quarter of a pickle for each child or enough sauce and small cracker pieces for each child to take a dip. Write the name of the food on the bag; then return it to school tomorrow. During our group time, we will taste the food. Then we will chart whether the food is sweet, salty, spicy, sour, or bitter.

All Aboard!

Now arriving at the station—thematic train activities to keep youngsters on track with learning. All aboard? It's full-steam fun ahead!

ideas contributed by Suzanne Moore

I've Been Working On The Railroad

At the end of the school day before you begin your train theme, distribute construction-paper train tickets to your children. Ask youngsters to bring these tickets with them when they return to school. Then get busy working on this door display that announces your train theme. Cover the door to your classroom with black construction paper; then mount a black paper smokestack above the door along with white paper smoke. Add colored paper plates for headlights and another plate personalized with your room information. Finally mount a red paper cowcatcher with black marker details.

As each child arrives at your door on the first day of your unit, collect his ticket and welcome him aboard. (Have extra tickets available for children who forget to bring theirs to school.) Toot, toot! Here we go!

Steamy Entertainment

Youngsters will jump aboard this circle-time train car for some steamy train entertainment. Arrange a class supply of chairs side by side in rows to resemble the passenger car of a train. Then get your unit off on the right track by showing *Choo Choo Trains: Close Up And Very Personal* (available from Stage Fright Productions: 1-800-979-6800). There's no narration—just the sounds of whistles blowing and the "clickety-clack" of the trains running down the tracks. Invite youngsters to make their own observations as they get an up close view of trains.

The Storytime Express

Leave your chairs in rows (see "Steamy Entertainment") for your storytimes. Then keep track of the train stories you read with this display idea. Cut out a black construction-paper engine using the outline shape of the pattern on page 50. Cut out various colors of train cars using the outline of the pattern on page 51. Mount the engine on a display. Each time you read a train-related story, record the book's title on one of the train cars; then display it to the right of the engine. See page 49 for a list of books to keep your storytimes chugging along.

Kathleen K. Padilla—Preschool Special Education
Elfers, FL

Freight Train by Donald Crews

The Train Ride by June Crebbin

Dramatic-Play Station

Provide lots of dramatic-play opportunities for your little travelers by setting up a train station, passenger car, dining car, and sleeping car. Here are some quick-and-easy suggestions. Create a ticket office by cutting a window from a trifold board (used for displays). Provide props, such as play money, paper tickets, and hole punchers. Near your housekeeping area, arrange a group of chairs in a row to represent the passenger car. Provide reading material about trains for the ride (see "Locomotive Literature" on page 49). For the child choosing to be the engineer, provide a hat, bandana, and flashlight (lantern). Label your kitchen area as the dining car. Finally label a resting area (a part of your room with several mats) as the sleeping car.

Exploration Station

Set up your blocks center as another center for train exploration. Use masking tape to create train tracks on the floor of your blocks area. Request that parents allow those children who have trains at home to bring them for display or use in the center. Encourage youngsters playing in this center to build train stations with the blocks as they explore railway transportation.

Creation Station

Youngsters can "choo-choo-choose" how to create their own trains at this art center. To prepare, cut out a number of colorful construction-paper rectangles, squares, and triangles. Then put the shapes in an art center along with black markers, glue, a shallow pan of black paint, and empty thread spools. Show a child how to use a black marker to draw tracks on a large sheet of white construction paper. Then allow her to choose the shapes she would like to glue on the paper to create a train. Invite the child to complete the project by using a spool and paint to print wheels below her train cars.

adapted from an idea by Martha Berry—Two-Year-Olds
Main Street Methodist Preschool
Kernersville, NC

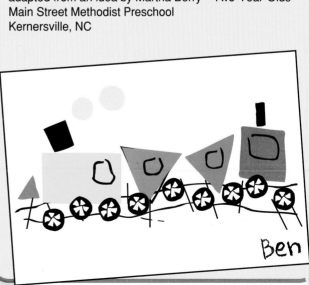

The Wheels On The Train

Invite your train gang to sing along to the tune of "The Wheels On The Bus."

The wheels on the train go round and round,
Round and round, round and round.
The wheels on the train go round and round,
All through the town.

The crossing gates go up and down,
Up and down, up and down.
The crossing gates go up and down,
All through the town.

The railroad cars go clickety-clack,
Clickety-clack, clickety-clack.
The railroad cars go clickety-clack,
All through the town.

The whistle on the train goes toot, toot, toot;
Toot, toot, toot; toot, toot, toot.
The whistle on the train goes toot, toot, toot,
All through the town.

Connie Walker
WICAP Head Start
Payette, ID

Bend arms at elbows and move in circular motion by sides.

Cross forearms in front of body; then move them up and down.

Clap hands.

Pull down on imaginary cord.

Stop And Go

Explain to your children that long ago lanterns were used by the conductor to tell a train's engineer whether to stop or go. A lantern swinging back and forth was the signal to stop. A lantern being raised and lowered was the signal to go. Dim the lights or close your shades; then use a flashlight to demonstrate these signals.

To play a stop-and-go game, have the group line up, side by side, at one end of your room. Have students chug from one side of your train yard (classroom) to the other as you repeatedly give the signals to stop and go.

Make-A-Train, Make-A-Train, Make-A-Train

Your train-loving youngsters will enjoy being a part of this cooperative train. Before playing, explain that sometimes more than one engine is needed to pull a group of railcars. Several engines work together until they have enough speed to pull the train. To play, have your group stand in a circle. Ask one child to be engine number one. Chant the first line of the following poem as that child chugs around the outside of the circle. After one trip around the circle, designate a second child to join him by placing his hands on the first child's hips. Chant the second line of the poem as the two children move around the circle. Continue in this manner until there are five engines. Then invite the remainder of the group to hook on. Choo, choo!

Five Big Engines

One big engine starts off slow.
Two big engines go, go, go.
Three big engines pick up speed.
Four big engines, yes indeed!
Five big engines down the track.
Clickety, clickety, clickety, clack!

"Chew-Chew" Trains

If all that train traveling has made you and your youngsters hungry, power up with these edible engines. To make one, break off one of the four sections of a graham cracker; then arrange the crackers as shown. Spread peanut butter on the crackers. Add two banana-slice wheels with raisins, a raisin headlight, and a few miniature marshmallows for smoke. Toot, toot! Puff, puff! Down they go!

Blowin' Smoke

Clear the tracks and save some time for this terrific outdoor train activity. During an outdoor-play time, invite several children to line up and "make a train." Give the first child in the train (the engine) a container of bubble solution and a bubble wand. As the train moves forward, have that child blow bubbles to represent smoke coming out of the train's smokestack. Offer each child in the group a chance to be the engine and blow bubbles. Full steam ahead!

Kathleen K. Padilla—Preschool Special Education
Elfers, FL

What Shall I See?

Take a journey on a train ride with this story that will have youngsters chugging and chanting along. As you read aloud the rhythmic text of *The Train Ride* by June Crebbin (Candlewick Press), invite youngsters to imitate a train by moving their arms in a circular motion at their sides to the rhythm. Then follow up your reading by making this class book. Duplicate the cover of the book (page 50) onto a light color of construction paper and a class supply of the book page (page 51) onto white construction paper. Cut out the cover and pages on the bold lines. For each child, cut out the window on the book page. Tape a different child's photo to the back of each page. (As an alternative, have the child draw his picture in the window.) Then have the child illustrate what he might see if he were riding on a train. Record his dictated text. Tape the cover and pages together to make a train; then accordion-fold the book. Share the book at storytime; then send it down the line for parents to enjoy.

Butterflies, butterflies _____,
That's what I see. That's what I see.

Locomotive Literature

Trains
Written & Illustrated by Byron Barton
Published by HarperCollins Children's Books

All Aboard ABC
Written by Doug Magee & Robert Newman
Published by Puffin Books

I've Been Working On The Railroad
Illustrated by Nadine Bernard Westcott
Published by Hyperion Books For Children

Tracks
Written by David Galef
Illustrated by Tedd Arnold
Published by William Morrow And Company, Inc.

The Caboose Who Got Loose
Written & Illustrated by Bill Peet
Published by Houghton Mifflin Company

Engine, Engine, Number Nine!
Written by Stephanie Calmenson
Illustrated by Paul Meisel
Published by Hyperion Books For Children

Freight Train
Written & Illustrated by Donald Crews
Published by Greenwillow Books
(See pages 108–110 for a unit of ideas featuring this book.)

Book Cover

Use with "The Storytime Express" on page 46 and "What Shall I See?" on page 49.

Riding on the train, What shall I see?

Book Page

Use with "The Storytime Express" on page 46 and "What Shall I See?" on page 49.

That's what I see. That's what I see.

SAY IT IN SIGN

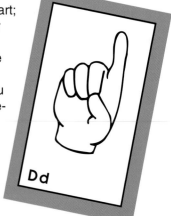

If you are looking for ideas that increase youngsters' vocabularies, promote their language development, and strengthen their fine-motor skills, all signs point this way! Using hand signs also fosters students' imitation skills and attention, and allows for creative expression. Sign-language activities are just right for your active preschoolers, especially your kinesthetic learners. And don't forget that you can use signs, too, in your daily routines and management strategies. Go ahead—say it in sign!

ideas by Terry Steinke and Mackie Rhodes

Remember that some signs may be difficult for children to imitate with accuracy. Be sure to accept youngsters' modified versions and offer praise for all their efforts to use signs.

Signing Sam

Use a stuffed-toy friend named Signing Sam to introduce your children to sign language. To prepare, remove the arms from a large (20 inches or taller) stuffed toy such as a bear; then stitch the openings at the torso closed. Next locate a long-sleeved sweatshirt that will fit over the toy loosely and that has sleeves large enough for you to put your arms into. Rip open the seams that join the sleeves to the back of the shirt, making sure that each opening is large enough to put your arm through. Reinforce the seams at the ends of both openings. Put the shirt on the toy.

During a group time, put on a pair of tight-fitting gloves; then insert your arms into the shirt sleeves. Put the toy in your lap so that it is facing your group. Introduce Signing Sam and explain that sign language is used by many people who are unable to hear or cannot speak and need a different way to communicate. Have Signing Sam join the group whenever you are using sign language or introducing new signs.

Alphabetically Speaking

Now that youngsters know a little about sign language, invite them to learn the hand signs for the alphabet. To prepare alphabet cards, use a duplicating machine to enlarge the letter hand signs on pages 55–57. Cut the cards apart; then glue them to slightly larger tagboard cards. Use the cards while teaching your children the signs for the letters. Then sing the alphabet song slowly as you practice the signs. For reinforcement, review each letter's sign as you focus on or introduce that letter during the year. *A, B,* "see" how much fun signing can be!

Signs For Self-Awareness

Develop self-awareness and self-esteem by helping each child create a hand sign to represent her name. Using the alphabet cards (see "Alphabetically Speaking"), review the hand sign for the first letter of a child's name. Then have that child name something she likes, or ask the group to think of something special about that child. Help the child make a new sign that combines her letter sign with a symbol for something about her. For example, if Chelsea likes dolls, do the *C* sign while pretending to hold a baby. Or if Wendy has pretty eyes, do the *W* sign near one eye. Be patient, as it may take a while to help each child make a sign. You'll see that the results are worth it!

Number Signs

Here's a signing idea designed to reinforce counting and number-sequencing skills. To make number cards, use a duplicating machine to enlarge the number signs on page 57. Cut the cards apart; then glue them to slightly larger tagboard cards. In each of ten resealable plastic bags, put one of the cards and a corresponding number of manipulatives. Give one of the bags to each child in a group of ten. Direct each child to count the manipulatives in her bag and then to form the finger sign for that quantity. Help the children sequence themselves by their numbers. Then chorally count to ten, having each child hold up her hand sign when her number is called. Afterward, have students exchange bags, and then repeat the activity.

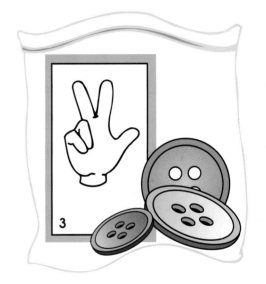

Sign-Along Sing-Alongs

Since signing and singing go hand in hand, this activity is bound to be a natural for your little ones. To begin, teach your class the animal signs shown. Then sing "Old MacDonald," including the sign name for the animals. In the same fashion, learn the signs for key words in other familiar tunes, such as "Twinkle, Twinkle, Little Star" and "Bingo." If desired, write the words of each song on a sheet of chart paper; then label the key words with pictures of their signs. For books on signing and singing in signs, refer to "Handy Resources" on page 54.

DOG **CHICKEN** **COW** **DUCK** **PIG**

Signs Of The Times

Encourage your class to fingerspell and sign throughout the year with this idea. Label a display area for signs of the week. Each week select new hand signs to teach your youngsters, and then post the signs on your display. You might choose signs that enrich your current unit of study or that reinforce basic concepts, such as letters, colors, and shapes.

Management Tools

If you'd like to increase youngsters' attention during transitions and decrease the noise level in the room, try this idea. First, teach youngsters the sign for each of your common directions and the signals for your transition times. Then use the signs to signal the change from one activity to the next or to give a nonverbal direction. Or have youngsters use the signs to signal a need such as going to the bathroom. Refer to the following signs for some examples; then add more signs to meet the needs of your class. For effectiveness, you might limit the number of signs to ten or fewer.

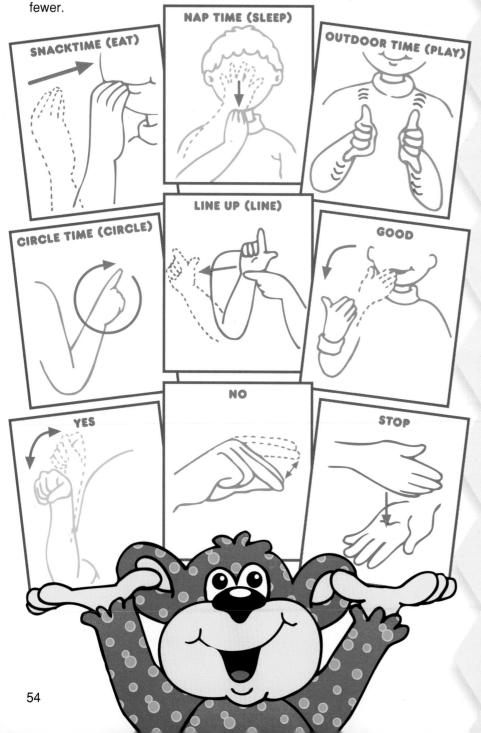

SNACKTIME (EAT)
NAP TIME (SLEEP)
OUTDOOR TIME (PLAY)
CIRCLE TIME (CIRCLE)
LINE UP (LINE)
GOOD
YES
NO
STOP

Handy Resources

Use some of these resources as references for teaching youngsters how to sign letters, words, songs, and phrases.

● *Simple Signs* and *More Simple Signs*
Written & Illustrated by
Cindy Wheeler
Published by Viking Children's Books

● *Sesame Street Sign Language ABC With Linda Bove*
Written by Linda Bove
Illustrated by Tom Cooke
Published by Random House Books For Young Readers

● *My ABC Signs Of Animal Friends*
Written by Ben Bahan and Joe Dannis
Illustrated by Patricia Pearson
Published by DawnSignPress

● Books in the *Handtalk* series
Written by Remy Charlip and Mary Beth Miller or George Ancona and Mary Beth Miller
Illustrated by George Ancona
Published by Simon & Schuster Children's Division

● *Handsigns: A Sign Language Alphabet*
Written & Illustrated by
Kathleen Fain
Published by Chronicle Books

● *The Handmade Alphabet*
Written & Illustrated by
Laura Rankin
Published by Viking Penguin

● *Songs In Sign*
Written by S. Harold Collins
Illustrated by Kathy Kifer and Dahna Solar
Published by Garlic Press

● *Signs For Me: Basic Sign Vocabulary For Children, Parents & Teachers*
Written by Ben Bahan and Joe Dannis
Published by DawnSignPress

Additional sign language resources are available through DawnSignPress. For more information, call 1-800-549-5350.

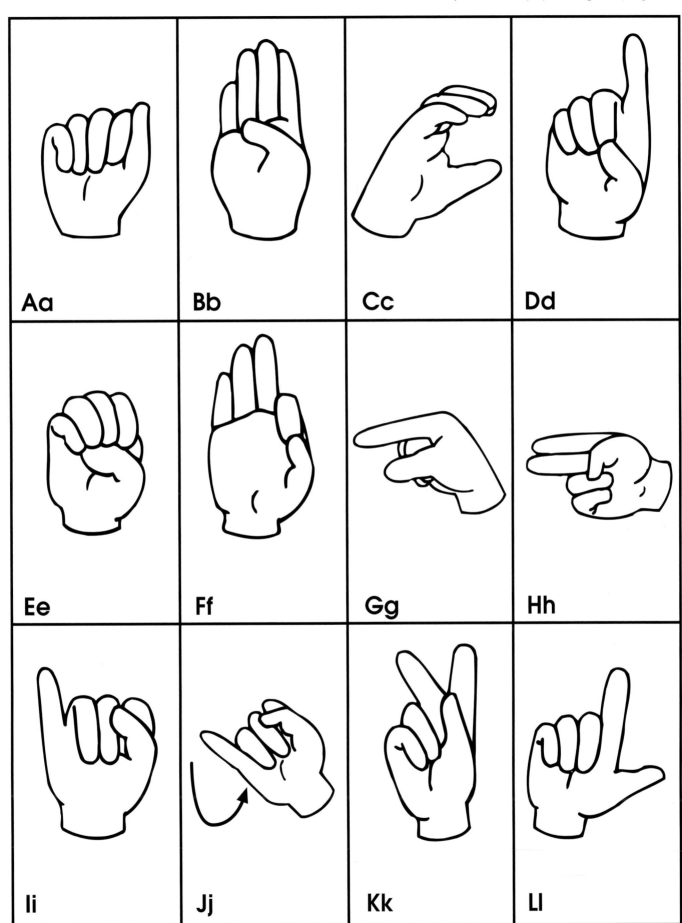

Aa Bb Cc Dd

Ee Ff Gg Hh

Ii Jj Kk Ll

Alphabet Hand Signs

Use with "Alphabetically Speaking" on page 52.

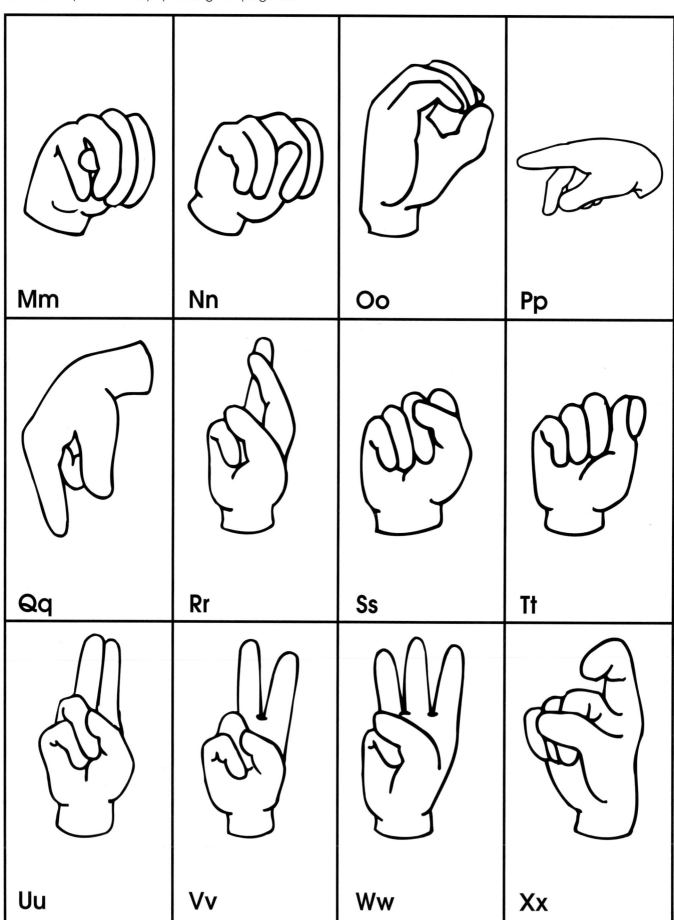

Mm   Nn   Oo   Pp

Qq   Rr   Ss   Tt

Uu   Vv   Ww   Xx

Use alphabet signs with "Alphabetically Speaking" on page 52. Use number signs with "Number Signs" on page 53.

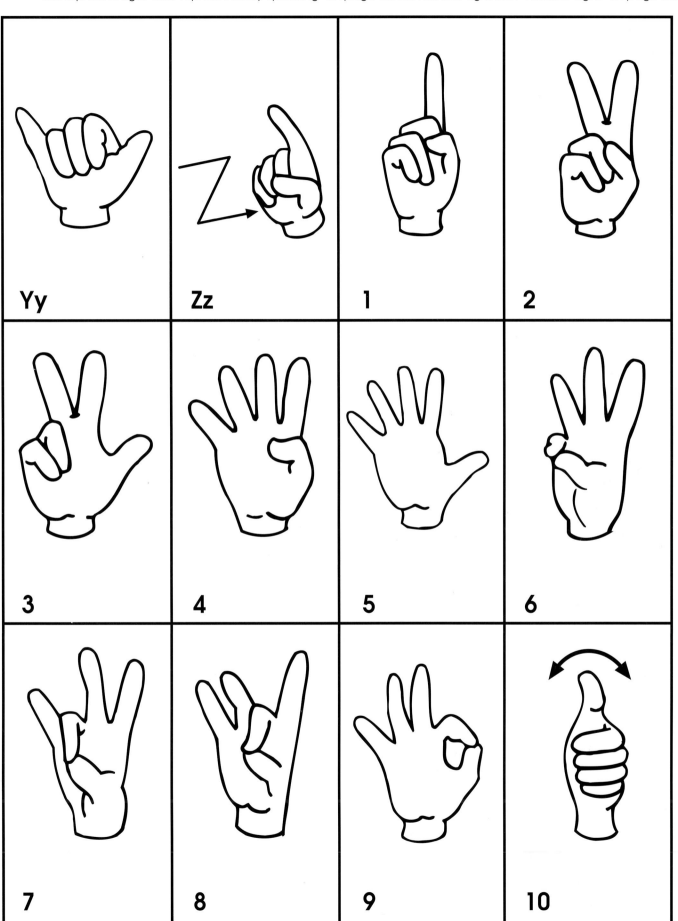

Yy

Zz

1

2

3

4

5

6

7

8

9

10

Let's Celebrate!

NAEYC's Week Of The Young Child
April 18–24, 1999

Celebrate Children

Paint a **banner** that announces the Week of the Young Child and that displays the handprints of each child in your program. Display the banner in front of your school or center.

Kick off the week with a **celebration at a local museum or library.**

Organize **hands-on activities for children** at an area mall.

With your students' input, plan a **breakfast for parents.** Have your children help prepare the food, decorations, and invitations. Invite parents to bring their children to school early on the designated day and to stay for a simple breakfast treat of muffins, doughnuts, and juice.

Encourage **parent visits** during this week. Invite each child's parent to visit your class to spend an extended amount of time with his/her child. Give the parent a badge to wear back to work that announces that he/she celebrated the Week of the Young Child.

Arrange for **local politicians to read to children** at area childcare centers. In advance, provide each participant with a book. Then ask that after the book is read, it is donated to the center. If the politician's schedule permits, encourage him/her to stay for lunch at the center. Or host a reception for the participants.

Educate parents about their children's learning with **photo displays.** In advance, take pictures of your children involved in learning activities, such as group games, storytimes, and centers. Arrange the pictures on walls or trifold project boards along with easy-to-read explanations of your curriculum, children's learning styles, and the learning outcomes of your daily activities.

The Week of the Young Child is an annual chance to celebrate young children, their families, and their teachers. In other words, it's a party—with a terrific purpose! Whether you are looking for new ideas or ideas to get started, check out these suggestions contributed from enthusiastic teachers.

Ideas contributed by:
Kathleen Harris, Chairperson, Ohio AEYC, Aurora, OH
Joyce Brison, Gaston County AEYC, Gaston County, NC
Cindy Lawson, Family Childcare Provider, Shell Lake, WI
Carrie Roberts Phelps, Child Advocacy Commission, Wilmington, NC

Celebrate Families

- Organize a **potluck lunch or dinner** for the families in your center. Decorate the eating area with students' art.

- Publish a **newsletter** to distribute to the families in your center or in your affiliation. Include highlights of the year, information about early-childhood education, students' art, names and numbers of agencies serving children and families, and more. To cover the printing costs, ask local companies to purchase inexpensive ads in the newsletter.

- Plan a **Family Fun Day** at a local mall. Invite local agencies to set up informative exhibits for parents and provide early-intervention screenings. Invite classes in your program or schools in your affiliation to perform songs. Show slide presentations featuring children engaged in learning activities.

- Ask local businesses to sponsor a free **concert** for families that features a local or national children's musician.

- Request that local **congregations** announce the week and any related community events in their **weekly bulletins**.

- Have a **parade** that leads to a **celebration** at a location such as a park. At the celebration, include children's activities, interactive group games, puppet shows, live music, and informative displays for parents.

Celebrate Teachers

Ask each parent with a child in your program to wear a **ribbon** to work in honor of his/her child's teachers.

Sponsor a **Teacher Appreciation Dinner** for the early-childhood professionals in your school or in your local NAEYC affiliate group. Here are some ideas for making the night an extra special one:

— Ask local businesses or parents to contribute items for goodie bags or door prizes. Request such items as gift certificates to discount stores, pencils, T-shirts, and more.

— Prepare a slide presentation featuring the teachers in attendance or highlighting the early-childhood programs in your community.

— Invite parents or local public-policy makers to attend the dinner. Better yet, encourage them to sponsor the event and prepare the meal!

— Read aloud quotes from children about their teachers.

— Honor teachers with both fun and meaningful awards. For example, award a retiree with a lounge chair, a straw hat, and a pair of sunglasses. Award an outstanding director with an engraved frame. Honor an especially committed teacher with a trip to your local or state AEYC conference.

— Invite local news media to the celebration, or provide them with pictures of the event for publication.

Ask local businesses to offer small **discounts** to teachers who shop in their stores during the week.

Open Newsletter
Program the open newsletter on page 61 with
— dates and times of the week's events
— announcements for use as miniposters
— information to parents concerning the purpose of the week
— information about early-childhood education
— letters to businesses or public-policy makers
— a photo and a thank-you message

For More Information
For more information about the Week of the Young Child, ideas for celebrating the week, and materials available for purchase, be sure to visit NAEYC's Web site: **www:naeyc.org/.**

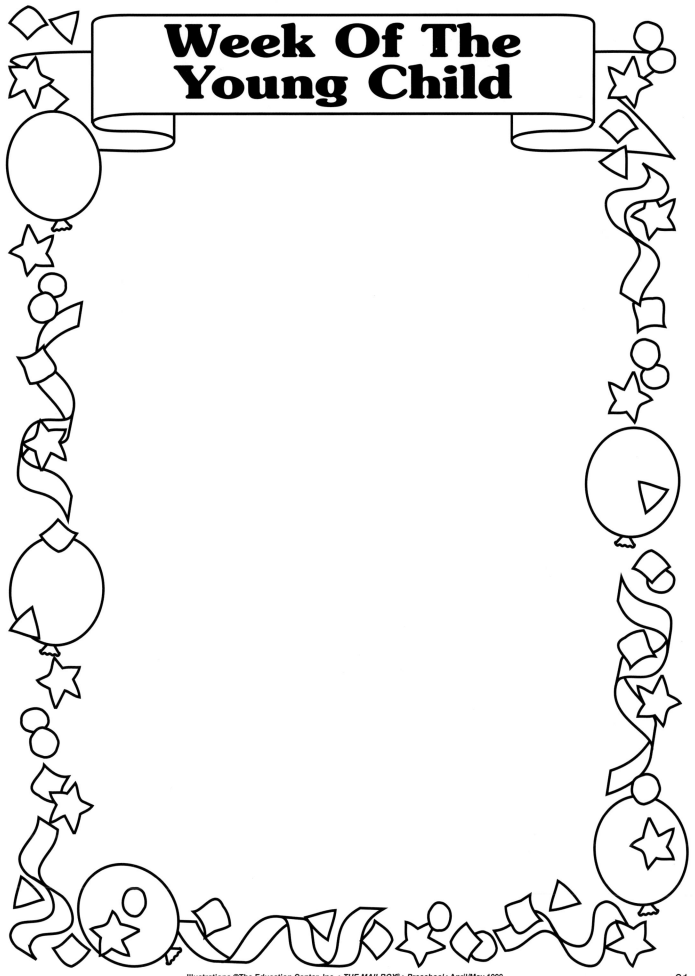

Week Of The Young Child

Pitter-Patter, Drip-Drop, Splish-Splash...Rain!

The forecast for this unit calls for showers of learning with frequent downpours of fun. Just pop open your umbrella and check out this flood of group-time and center-time activities.

Under The Weather

Create a storm of excitement when you use this idea to introduce youngsters to your rain theme. Prior to a group time, collect one umbrella for every two or three children. (Cover the umbrellas' tips with tape for safety.) Cover the floor of your group area with a plastic painting tarp or a plastic tablecloth. Put a bucket of water, a sponge, a raincoat, and the umbrellas near your chair. If desired, put an audiotape of rain sounds in a tape player that is also near your chair.

Begin the fun by putting on the raincoat, dimming your lights, and announcing that the weather forecast predicts rain. As the students take a seat on the plastic, give every two or three children an open umbrella to share. Turn on the audiotape; then quickly announce, "It's starting to rain!" Squeeze the water-filled sponge onto the umbrellas. Pitter-patter, hear the showers of laughter?

Henry Fergus—Preschool
Desert View Elementary
Phoenix, AZ

Reading In The Rain

After your surprise shower, wipe up the puddles and share any of these rainy-day stories that are just right for your preschool listeners.

Rain
Written by Robert Kalan
Illustrated by Donald Crews
Published by William Morrow And Company, Inc.

Wet World
Written by Norma Simon
Illustrated by Alexi Natchev
Published by Candlewick Press

In The Rain With Baby Duck
Written by Amy Hest
Illustrated by Jill Barton
Published by Candlewick Press

Listen To The Rain
Written by Bill Martin, Jr., and John Archambault
Illustrated by James Endicott
Published by Henry Holt And Company, Inc.

Noah's Ark
Written & Illustrated by Lucy Cousins
Published by Candlewick Press

Order books on-line.
www.themailbox.com

Cloudy With A Choice Of Centers

You'll have clear skies ahead when you use this system to help youngsters make learning center choices. To prepare, cut a poster-board cloud shape for each rain-themed center you set up in your classroom. (See pages 63–65 for center suggestions.) Label each cloud with a different center's name. To each cloud, attach the hook side of as many Velcro® pieces as you will allow children in that center at one time. Put each cloud in its corresponding center. From laminated construction paper, cut a raindrop shape for each child. Personalize each drop; then attach the loop side of a piece of Velcro® to the back of it. Store the raindrops in a bucket.

When it is time for your children to choose centers, toss the raindrops in the air so that they rain down over your group. Announce each child's name as you pick up his raindrop. Then direct that child to attach his drop to the cloud in the center of his choice.

Henry Fergus, Phoenix, AZ

Drip-Drop Dramatic Play

Grab your galoshes and get ready for a rain-stompin', puddle-hoppin' good time at this dramatic-play center. Fill a wading pool with water-soluble packing pieces. Above the area, hang crepe-paper or metallic streamers to represent rain. Near the center, place a box filled with rain gear, such as galoshes, raincoats, and umbrellas. To really give the area a rainy-day feel, play an audiotape of rain sounds. If desired, fill a bucket with the books listed on page 62 so that properly attired youngsters can settle in for some wet and wild reading.

Carla Arnouville, Bordelonville, LA

Just A Drop In The Bucket

Prepare this partner game for your math center, and soon it will be raining and pouring counting skills! Spray-paint both sides of 30 dried lima beans (plus some extra) blue. Divide the amount of beans in half; then store the halves in separate resealable plastic bags. Prepare a spinner, similar to the one shown, that displays numerals and matching numbers of rain-drops. (To match your students' abilities, increase or decrease the number of divisions and the numerals on the spinner.) Also put two cups in the center to represent buckets.

To play, each child in a pair receives a bucket and bag of raindrops. In turn, each child spins the spinner, and then counts a matching number of raindrops into her bucket. The winner is the first child to count all 15 raindrops into her bucket.

Ellen Van De Walle—Preschool Consultant
Hendersonville Childcare Resource and Referral, Hendersonville, NC

Water Table

Shower Power

The fun will go from a drizzle to a downpour at your water table when you add rainmaking items, such as colanders, strainers, sieves, watering cans, and sifters. If desired, invite visitors to this center to don raincoats and galoshes before reaching in to make it rain. And since the wet fun could get wild, keep some towels on hand as well.

Henry Fergus—Preschool, Desert View Elementary, Phoenix, AZ

Movement Area

Raindrops Keep Falling

Invite youngsters over to this movement center to do a rain dance, hop, skip, or jump! To prepare stuffed raindrops, fill five or more thin, blue children's socks with cotton balls; then knot the socks closed. On a length of blue bulletin-board paper, draw the outlines of five puddle shapes. Write a different numeral from 1 to 5 in each puddle. To use this center, a child tosses a raindrop into a puddle. He announces the numeral on that puddle; then he and his classmates at the center jump, hop, or clap the corresponding number of times. As a variation, draw ten puddles on the paper. Or challenge a child to throw the raindrops into the puddles in sequential order.

Ellen Van De Walle—Preschool Consultant
Hendersonville Childcare Resource and Referral, Hendersonville, NC

Sensory Center

April Showers Bring...Mud!

Invite youngsters to muddle around with these no-mess mud alternatives at your sensory center. Squirt brown liquid paint into several different sizes of sealable plastic bags. Seal the bags; then secure the seals with clear packing tape. Invite youngsters to use their fingers to create designs, shapes, or letters in the mud.

As another mud alternative, provide youngsters with this mushy mud dough for molding, mashing, and making mud pies. To make the mud dough, mix together 1/2 cup of cold water, one tablespoon of cooking oil, and two tablespoons of brown, washable liquid paint. Stir in 1/2 cup of salt; then add one tablespoon of cornstarch. Gradually add 1 1/2 cups of flour until the dough is soft and smooth. Store the dough in a container; then place it in a center along with plastic spatulas, plastic knives, and different sizes of aluminum tins. (If the dough gets sticky, add flour.) More mud, anyone?

Henry Fergus

Rainy-Day Blues, Reds, And Yellows

Add a splash of color to your rain unit with these umbrellas. To prepare this art center, cover a work surface with newspapers. Fill three small containers with water; then tint each container of water with a generous amount of either red, blue, or yellow food coloring. Place an eyedropper in each container. To make one project, provide a child with one good-quality white paper towel. Direct the child to drop the tinted water onto the paper towel until it is completely covered with color. When the towel is dry, cut out an umbrella shape. Have the child cut out a paper umbrella handle to glue to a large piece of construction paper. Then have him glue his umbrella onto the paper, over the handle. Let it rain!

Geri Covins, Rochester, MI

Rain Makes Rainbows!

Sunny smiles will pour out of your art center when your children create these magical rainbows of color. Cover a work surface with newspapers. For each child, cut a rainbow shape from a good quality white paper towel. Invite a child at the center to use water-based markers to draw wide stripes of different colors on one of the cutouts, leaving space between the stripes. Next have her use a paintbrush to apply water across the stripes. As the towel absorbs the water, the colors blend to create a beautiful rainbow!

Ellen Van De Walle—Preschool Consultant
Hendersonville Childcare Resource and Referral, Hendersonville, NC

Plop, Plop, Fizz, Fizz

After your weather watchers have visited your classroom rain centers, they're sure to enjoy Raindrop Fizzes from your cooking area. In advance, freeze ice cubes from water that has been tinted blue. (Freeze several ice cubes per child.) To make one drink, half-fill a plastic cup with a clear carbonated drink. Then drop several raindrops (ice cubes) into the drink. Plop, plop, fizz, fizz. Oh, what a fun drink this is!

Henry Fergus, Phoenix, AZ

Mud-Puddle Cookies

Invite your little ones to help make these "mud-licious" mud-puddle cookies to enjoy with their Raindrop Fizzes. To prepare the mud batter, beat one egg; then mix it into 2 1/2 cups of softened non-dairy topping. Fold in one package of devil's food moist cake mix (18.25 ounces). In a separate bowl, prepare the dirt mixture by combining 1/2 cup of confectioners' sugar with 1/2 cup cocoa. Plop a spoonful of the mud dough into the dirt mixture; then put the covered dough ball onto a greased cookie sheet. Bake at 350° for ten minutes. These mud puddles are mouthwateringly delicious!

adapted from an idea by Kimberli Carrier—Preschool, Wise Owl Preschool
Nashua, NH

Umbrella, Umbrella, Raindrops!

Save this version of the popular game Duck, Duck, Goose for a rainy day. Prior to playing, use a paper cutter to quickly prepare a supply of blue paper confetti to represent rain. To play, seat the class in a circle on the floor. Give a volunteer leader a small amount of the rain to hold in one hand. Direct the leader to walk around the outside of the circle while lightly tapping each seated child on the head and saying, "Umbrella." When desired, the leader drops the handful of rain over a child's head and announces, "Raindrops!" At that cue, the tapped child jumps up and chases the leader around the circle. The leader runs to sit in the open spot in the circle or the tapped child catches him and they both stop. Either way, the tapped child now becomes the leader. Play continues until each child has had a turn as the leader.

Kimberli Carrier—Preschool, Wise Owl Preschool, Nashua, NH

Pam Crane

Let's Make Mud

Your class is sure to have a thunderous time with this mud-making activity! Prior to this group project, pour a small box of instant chocolate pudding into a clear bowl. Use blue food coloring to tint two cups of milk blue; then pour the milk into a sanitized watering can. Tape a white cloud cutout to the can. Collect enough flashlights and small plastic containers for each child to have one. To begin, give each child either a flashlight or a tub. Let the rainstorm begin by having the children turn their flashlights on and off to represent lightning, or tap their containers to represent thunder. Pour the rain (milk) over the dirt (pudding). Stir until the mud is smooth. When the storm is over, direct each child to wash his hands; then put a dollop of mud on a piece of waxed paper for each child. How delighted your little ones will be when they find out that the mud tastes good, too!

Carla Arnouville, Bordelonville, LA

Balancing Raindrops

No one will take a rain check on the chance to participate in this movement activity! In advance, prepare a class supply of stuffed raindrops by filling thin, blue children's socks with cotton balls; then knot the socks closed (see "Raindrops Keep Falling" on page 64). Give each child a raindrop. As you sing the following song, challenge students to balance the raindrops on the named body part. Repeat the song, substituting a different body part each time.

(sung to the tune of "Frère Jacques")
Rain is falling, rain is falling,
On my [head], on my [head].
I can feel the raindrop, I can feel the raindrop,
On my [head], on my [head].

Ellen Van De Walle—Preschool Consultant
Hendersonville Childcare Resource and Referral, Hendersonville, NC

Singing In The Rain

Keep youngsters singing the rainy-day
blues to these familiar tunes.

I've Been Listening To The Rain Fall

*(sung to the tune of "I've Been Working
On The Railroad")*

I've been listening to the rain fall,
All the morning long.
I've been listening to the rain fall,
As I sing this little song.
Can't you hear the wind a-blowing,
Rustling through the trees?
Can't you hear the thunder rumbling?
Now sing this song with me.

Come out, Mr. Sun. Come out, Mr. Sun.
Come out, Mr. Sun, today and stay!
Come out, Mr. Sun. Come out, Mr. Sun.
So we can go out and play!

Melissa Pyles—Headstart
Carter St. Headstart of Childhood Development Services
Inverness, FL

Waiting For A Sunny Day

(sung to the tune of "This Old Man")

Drip, drop, drop. Drip, drop, drop.
Will these raindrops ever stop?
I guess we'll wait for another sunny day.
Then we'll go outside to play!

Deborah Garmon, Groton, CT

I'm A Little Raindrop

Introduce youngsters to the water cycle with this
simple song.

(sung to the tune of "I'm A Little Teapot")

I'm a little raindrop, wet and round,
Up in a cloud, far from the ground.

I'm a little raindrop, here I go,
Down to a puddle far below.

I'm a little raindrop, in the sun.
Changing to steam is so much fun!

I'm a little raindrop, rising in the heat.
Back to a cloud, isn't that neat?

I'm a little raindrop, wet and round,
Up in a cloud, far from the ground.

adapted from a song by Ronda Rasmussen—Preschool
Learning Ladder Preschool, La Mesa, CA

Out Pop The Raindrops!

(sung to the tune of "Pop! Goes The Weasel")

All around the sky today,
The clouds are full of raindrops.
They push and shove until they burst.
Out pop the raindrops!

Patricia Moeser—Toddlers
University of Wisconsin Preschool Laboratory
Madison, WI

67

Frog Follies

Jeepers creepers, take a look at these leapers! Turn your preschoolers into hopped-up herpetologists by introducing them to some fun facts about frogs: how they grow up, where they live, what they eat, and how they get around. You're never too young to leap into learning!

ideas contributed by Henry Fergus—Preschool,
Desert View Elementary, Phoenix, AZ

An Awesome Amphibian

"Ribbit" youngsters' attention to your frog theme with this friendly fellow. To make a beanbag frog, cut out two same-sized, five-inch-long ovals from green felt. Also cut out two webbed feet. Sandwich the feet and a two-inch length of red ribbon between the ovals as shown; then hot-glue the ovals together, leaving an opening. Fill the shape with beans; then hot-glue the opening closed. Finally, hot-glue on two white pom-poms and two wiggle eyes to complete the frog.

Use this frog to introduce a different froggie fact each day. In addition, seat him on your shoulder while reading frog-related stories or use him as a positive-behavior motivator by seating him on a child's shoulder. Also use him for the hopping game described in "Come On Over To My Pad" on page 69. Ribbit!

Froggie Facts

Frogs grow and change.
Tadpoles are frog babies. A tadpole has a tail and swims in the water. It grows back legs, then front legs. Next it climbs out of the water. Its tail gets smaller until it disappears. The tadpole has grown into a frog!

Fish Is Fish
Written & Illustrated by Leo Lionni
Published by Alfred A. Knopf, Inc.

Frog Song

Kids grow and change, and frogs do too! Simplify the text of an informative book such as Gail Gibbons's *Frogs* (Holiday House, Inc.) to introduce your little ones to a frog's growing pattern. Then invite them to sing the following song.

Frogs Grow And Change
(sung to the tune of "The Frog Went A-Courtin' ")

Did you know frogs grow and change? Uh-huh, uh-huh.
Did you know frogs grow and change? Uh-huh, uh-huh.
A tadpole is a baby frog. It moves its tail to swim along.
Now we know frogs grow and change. Uh-huh. Uh-huh.

Its back legs are the first to grow; then its front legs start to show.

It climbs onto the land that's near; now its tail can disappear.

The frog's back legs grow big and strong; it uses them to hop along.

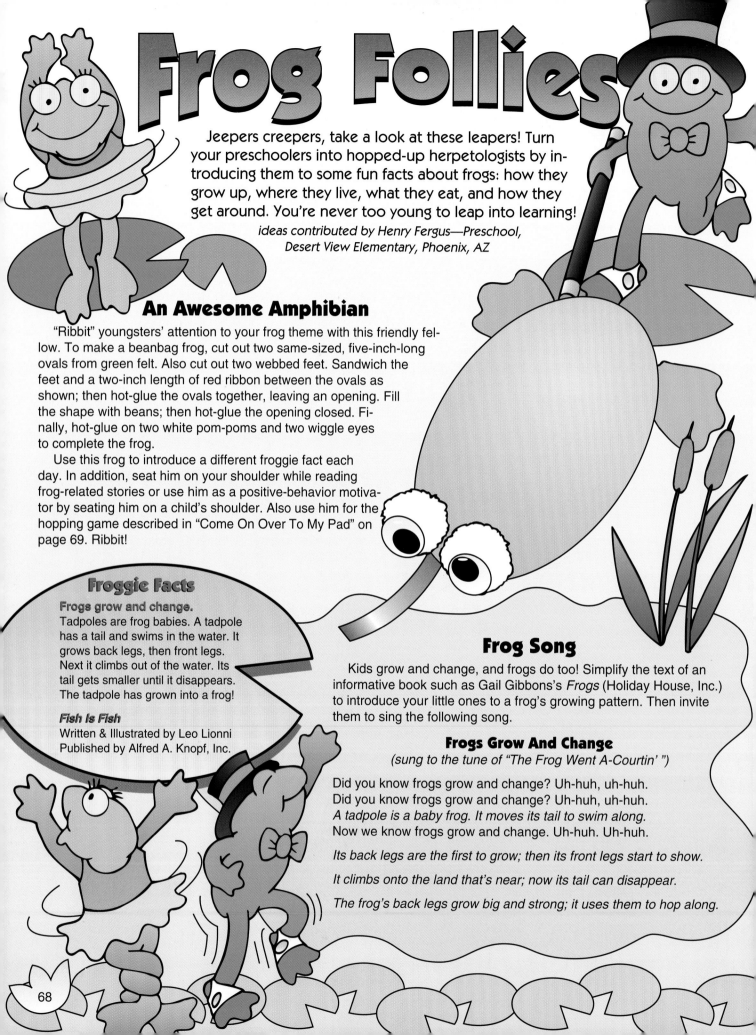

Froggie Facts

Frogs jump and swim. Frogs have long, strong back legs that make them good jumpers. Their webbed toes help them swim fast.

Hop Jump
Written & Illustrated by Ellen Stoll Walsh
Published by Harcourt Brace & Co.

April Showers
Written by George Shannon
Published by Greenwillow Books

Come On Over To My Pad

Prepare at least a class supply of laminated, green construction-paper lily pads. Then use them over and over as you leap from one of the following activities to the next.

- Arrange the lily pads in your group area to indicate seating spaces.

- Label one side of each pad with a colorful shape; then use the pads as a transition tool. For example, announce, "Everyone seated on a lily pad with a square, line up" or "Everyone seated on a lily pad with a yellow shape, pick a center."

- Arrange a number of lily pads in a path to make a giant gameboard. To play a counting game, invite several children to pretend to be frogs. On each child's turn, roll a large die. Have the child count the dots, then hop down the path that number of lily pads. Every child is a winner when he arrives at the end of the path and jumps onto the land.

- Use the lily pads to play a variation of Musical Chairs. As lily pads are removed, encourage your little frogs to share the remaining pads so that no frogs end up in the pond.

- Label one side of each pad with a numeral. Arrange the pads, numeral sides up, in an open area. Give a volunteer from the group the beanbag frog described in "An Awesome Amphibian" (page 68). Have the child toss the frog onto a pad, then announce that pad's numeral. Invite the children to hop that many times.

Leapfrogs

Inflate a number of green balloons; then use markers to draw a frog face on each one. As you throw the balloons into the air, encourage youngsters to keep the balloons hopping and not to let them land in the pond (on the ground). Play some lively music to accompany the fun.

Pond, Sweet Pond

"Pond-ering" how to teach youngsters about a frog's habitat? Here's a craft they'll jump at the chance to make. To make one, paint a rock green. When the paint is dry, glue on wiggle eyes. Next glue pieces of grass and twigs onto a white, sterilized Styrofoam® tray. When the glue is dry, cover the tray with blue plastic wrap, securing the wrap to the back of the tray with tape. Finally, glue the rock frog onto a construction-paper lily pad. Place the frog on top of the pond. Display each child's pond on a low surface along with his dictation of something he has learned about frogs or something he likes about frogs.

Frogs hop
really great!
Christopher

Pond Companions

Take a frog's-eye peek at pond life by reading aloud *In The Small, Small Pond* by Denise Fleming. Ask students to name as many animals as they can remember that share a frog's home. Then prepare this group-time graphing activity to plunge into over and over again. In advance, cut out ten each of yellow duck shapes, orange fish shapes, and green frog shapes. Also prepare a 3 square x 10 square graph on a length of bulletin-board paper. To begin, scatter several lily pads (see "Come On Over To My Pad" on page 69) and a number of the cutouts onto an open area. Ask how many of each animal are living in the pond. Collect, count, and then graph the cutouts. Each round, develop math skills by asking questions such as "Are there more frogs or ducks in this pond?" or "Is there a fish friend for every frog in our pond?" Now that's an activity that'll keep 'em pondering!

Frog Frolic

Transform your water table into a pond for your little ones' exploration. Simply tint the water blue and add aquarium plants and craft-foam lily-pad cutouts. If desired, spray-paint a number of Ping-Pong® balls green; then hot-glue wiggle eyes onto each one. Encourage a child to stand away from the water-table pond, then try to toss a frog onto a floating pad.

Froggie Facts

Frogs eat insects, spiders, worms, and tiny fish. A frog uses its long sticky tongue to catch food. Bugs, watch out—it flips in and out quickly!

Lickety-Split!

Your little ones will eat up the chance to find out what it's like to dine frog-style. For each child, you'll need a party blower that unrolls and a paper insect cutout. Gently unroll the blower to its full length; then attach the hook side of a piece of Velcro® to the bottom of the blower's tip. Attach the loop side of a piece of Velcro® to the top of the insect. To catch his dinner lickety-split, a child puts the insect on a surface in front of him, then blows the blower. If his aim is just right, he'll zap a bug delight!

Kim Pearson—Preschool
Newton Public School System
Boston, MA

Frog's Bag Of Bugs

Here's a snack full of a frog's favorites—bugs, worms, and tiny fish! Well maybe there's no fooling a frog with this snack, but the look-alike treats will please your little ones. To set up a frog buffet, fill each of four separate bowls with plain M&M's® (red and yellow ladybugs, green grass-hoppers, brown beetles), raisins (flies), chow mein noodles (worms), and Goldfish® crackers. Invite each child to fill a plastic bag with a scoop of each. If desired, serve up some frog grog (limeade) to wash down the treat.

More Frog Stories

Fill a wading pool with blue cellophane or tissue paper; then put it in your reading center. Fill this reading pond with the titles mentioned throughout this unit and below. Jump in—the reading's fine!

Tuesday
Written & Illustrated by David Wiesner
Published by Clarion Books

Jump, Frog, Jump!
Written by Robert Kalan
Published by Mulberry Books

Frog On His Own and *Frog Goes To Dinner*
Illustrated by Mercer Mayer
Published by E. P. Dutton Books and Dial Books For Young Readers

Order books on-line. www.themailbox.com

71

BIG Boxes, BIG Fun

We've received a box full of ideas from teachers for transforming big boxes into exciting dramatic-play props, so we're passing them on to you. It's time to think outside the box—or rather, *inside* the box! Have fun!

Freezer-Box Fire Truck

Great balls of fire! This fire truck is fun to make and "drive"! Cut off one long side of a large rectangular box; then position the box so that the open side is up. Invite your students to paint this box and a smaller, grocery store box red; two shoeboxes yellow; and four round pizza bases black. When the paint is dry, use nuts and bolts to attach the smaller box to one end of the larger box. In addition, bolt two plastic lids to the smaller box for headlights and the pizza bases to the larger box for tires (as shown). Similarly attach a plastic lid inside the truck for a steering wheel. Hot-glue the yellow boxes to the top of the smaller red box. Finally, cut doors in the sides of the truck.

Put a stool inside the box for youngsters to sit on and provide a vacuum-cleaner hose for use in dousing pretend fires. Don't forget to provide fire hats and boots, too!

Cindy Bormann—Preschool, Small World Preschool, West Bend, IA

In The Doghouse

To make a doghouse, cut an arched door in a box; then have students help paint the box, if desired. Invite youngsters to bring pictures of their dogs to attach to the outside or inside of the house. Or have youngsters cut out, draw, or paint pictures of dogs to glue onto the box. Encourage a child to pretend he is a dog, give himself a pet name, and then climb into the doghouse.

Karen Bryant—Pre-K
Miller Elementary School, Warner Robins, GA

Up, Up, And Away

Make a hot-air balloon for your classroom? Yes, you *can!* Borrow a parachute from your school's (or a local elementary school's) P.E. department. Secure the parachute to the ceiling by tying the handles along its edge to the ceiling. Below the parachute, place a large, square box from which one side has been removed. Attach a length of rope to each corner of the box, then to the ceiling. Stuff paper bags; then tie them to the sides of the box to represent ballasts. Inside the box, pack toy binoculars, a map, a canteen, a toy camera, and paper and crayons for recording the high-flying adventure!

Lorrie Hartnett—Pre-K
Canyon Lake, TX

Big Red Barn

Turn a corner of your classroom into a barnyard with these farm-fresh ideas using boxes. To make the barn, cut off the top and bottom of a cardboard box; then cut down one corner of the box to create one long strip of cardboard. Have students help you paint the cardboard red. When the paint is dry, cut the strip to resemble the barn shown. Place the strip against two walls in a corner of your room. Inside the barn, put a smaller box from which the top has been removed to serve as a horse stall. Arrange boxes outside the barn to represent chicken coops and pigpens. Invite students to help you fill the stalls, coops, and pens with hay, plastic eggs, and toy animals. Provide dress-up items—such as straw hats, overalls, boots, and flannel shirts—to get your little farmers in the "mooo-d"!

Christine E. Hansell—Preschool
Te-Lo-Ca Daycare, Campton, NH

Bank In A Box

This dramatic-play banking center is sure to yield high student interest! On a desk in the area, arrange supplies such as play money, notebooks, a phone book, a telephone, an adding machine or a calculator, scraps of paper, and writing utensils. Spray-paint a large box silver or gold to represent a vault. On the side that opens, use a long paper brad to attach a poster-board circle; then set the box in the center so that this side may be opened to store important items. Students are sure to check it out!

Leann Sommer—Preschool
Miriam's Basket Daycare
Muncie, IN

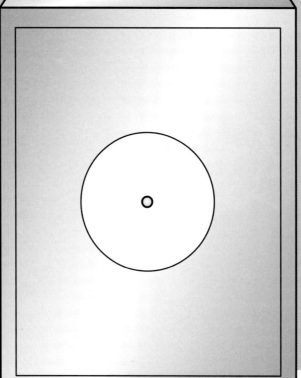

Snip, Snip, Snip

Convert a large box into a place where youngsters improve their fine-motor skills while snipping and clipping to their hearts' content. Cut a doorway in one side of a large box. Once the box is positioned so that the open side faces forward, put carpet squares in the bottom. Stock the area with baskets of paper scraps (greeting cards, junk mail, wrapping paper, magazines, construction paper, etc.) and scissors. If desired, also provide envelopes so that youngsters can take home the pictures and papers they cut.

Dianne Rawson—Preschool
Seven Dolors Child Care Center
Manhattan, KS

Going On A Bear Hunt

Try looking in this cave. If you don't find a bear, you're sure to find a child pretending to be one! Cut away one side of a large box; then position the box so that its open side is facing forward. To make the box resemble a cave, have students sponge-paint the sides and top with brown paint. When the paint is dry, hot-glue crushed paper bags to some areas of the box. Watch out for sleeping bears!

Susan Dzurovcik—Preschool
Valley Road School
Clark, NJ

Hop In The Bus!

Get your preschoolers ready to ride to kindergarten with this school bus. Ask your children to help you paint a long, rectangular box yellow. When the paint is dry, cut out front and side windows and a side door. If desired, tape clear cellophane inside the windows. Glue a poster-board circle to one end of a long cardboard tube to serve as a steering wheel; then make a hole in the front of the bus to insert the tube into. Add paper details, such as headlights, to the outside of the bus. Arrange several chairs inside the bus, including one for the driver. Use the bus to give students a lesson on bus safety and behavior, and they'll be ready to ride the real thing in the fall.

Christine E. Hansell—Preschool
Te-Lo-Ca Daycare, Campton, NH

Anchors

Ahoy there, mateys! Learn all about boats with these nifty nautical ideas.

Ideas contributed by LeeAnn Collins

All About Boats

Launch into learning all about boats by reading aloud any of these seaworthy books that introduce the many types of sailing vessels out on the deep blue sea. As you read, keep a list of different types of boats and invite youngsters to point out how they are alike and different.

I Love Boats
Written & Illustrated by
Flora McDonnell
Published by Candlewick Press

Boat Book
Written & Illustrated by Gail Gibbons
Published by Holiday House, Inc.

Harbor
Written & Illustrated by Donald Crews
Published by William Morrow And
Company, Inc.

Boats
(better for younger preschoolers)
Written & Illustrated by
Anne F. Rockwell
Published by
Dutton Children's Books

Boats
(better for older preschoolers)
Written by Ken Robbins
(Out of print. Check your library.)

Order books on-line.
www.themailbox.com

Nautical Knowledge

Get your little ones' knowledge of the different types of boats into shipshape with this movement activity and song. To prepare, duplicate pages 78 and 79 onto white construction paper so that you have one boat picture for each child in your class. Laminate the pages; then cut apart the squares. After punching a hole in each square, add a length of string to make a necklace. To begin the activity, have the class form a circle; then give each child a necklace to wear. Have the children move in a circle as you sing the first verse. Then, each time before singing the song again, review a type of boat and its uses. Instruct those children whose necklaces display that type of boat to move around in the center of the circle while the remainder of the group sings the song.

Boats Out In The Sea

**(sung to the tune of
"The Farmer In The Dell")**

[Boats] out in the sea.
[Boats] out in the sea.
Float up and down and all around.
[Boats] out in the sea.

A "Lotto" Boats

Invite your sailors to dock at your games center to play this lotto game that features the different types of boats. To prepare the game for one or two players, duplicate pages 78 and 79 onto white construction paper twice. Color the pages so that corresponding boats match. Laminate the pages; then cut apart the squares of one copy of each page to make playing cards. In a center, place the cards facedown in a stack along with the lotto boards. To play, a child takes a card from the stack. If he has a matching boat on his board, he puts the card on top of it. If he does not have a match, he returns his card to the bottom of the pile. He continues until he has filled his board. If two children are at the center, they take turns taking cards from the pile. The game continues until both players have filled their boards.

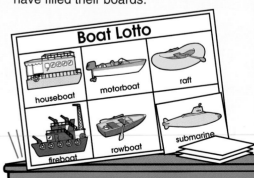

Aweigh!

Peeking At The Portholes

Here's another activity for your games center that will keep youngsters on the course to improved matching skills. To make this game, duplicate page 80 onto white construction paper. Program pairs of the portholes with matching stickers, colors, or symbols. Laminate the page for durability. Put the page in the center along with 14 milk-jug lids. To play a memory game, a child or pair of children covers the portholes with the jug lids, then removes the lids two at a time to find matching portholes. To keep score, a child keeps a pair of jug lids each time he finds matching portholes.

Boats For Sail

Set sail for some creativity with these crafty cruisers. For every four children, cut a paper plate into four pie-shaped pieces. To make a sailboat, invite a child to paint a plate-quarter as desired. When the paint is dry, have him fold a sturdy paper plate in half. Poke a hole near the fold on one half of the plate; then help the child use a brad to attach his sail to his boat. (If necessary, tape the sides of the plate together as shown.) Invite the child to give his boat a name, or label the boat with the child's name as shown. Dock the boats together on a flat surface; then add waves of crumpled blue tissue paper around the sailboats. Now that's a display that's sure to float your boat!

Hoist The Sails!

If those sailboats look like too much fun to display, invite students to use them as props as they cruise into singing the following song.

Have You Ever Seen A Sailboat?

(sung to the tune of "Did You Ever See A Lassie?")

Have you ever seen a sailboat,
A sailboat, a sailboat?
Have you ever seen a sailboat
Waving its sail?

Wave this way and that way,
Wave that way and this way.
Have you ever seen a sailboat
Waving its sail?

S.S. Jacob

Patterns

Use with "Nautical Knowledge" and "A 'Lotto' Boats" on page 76.

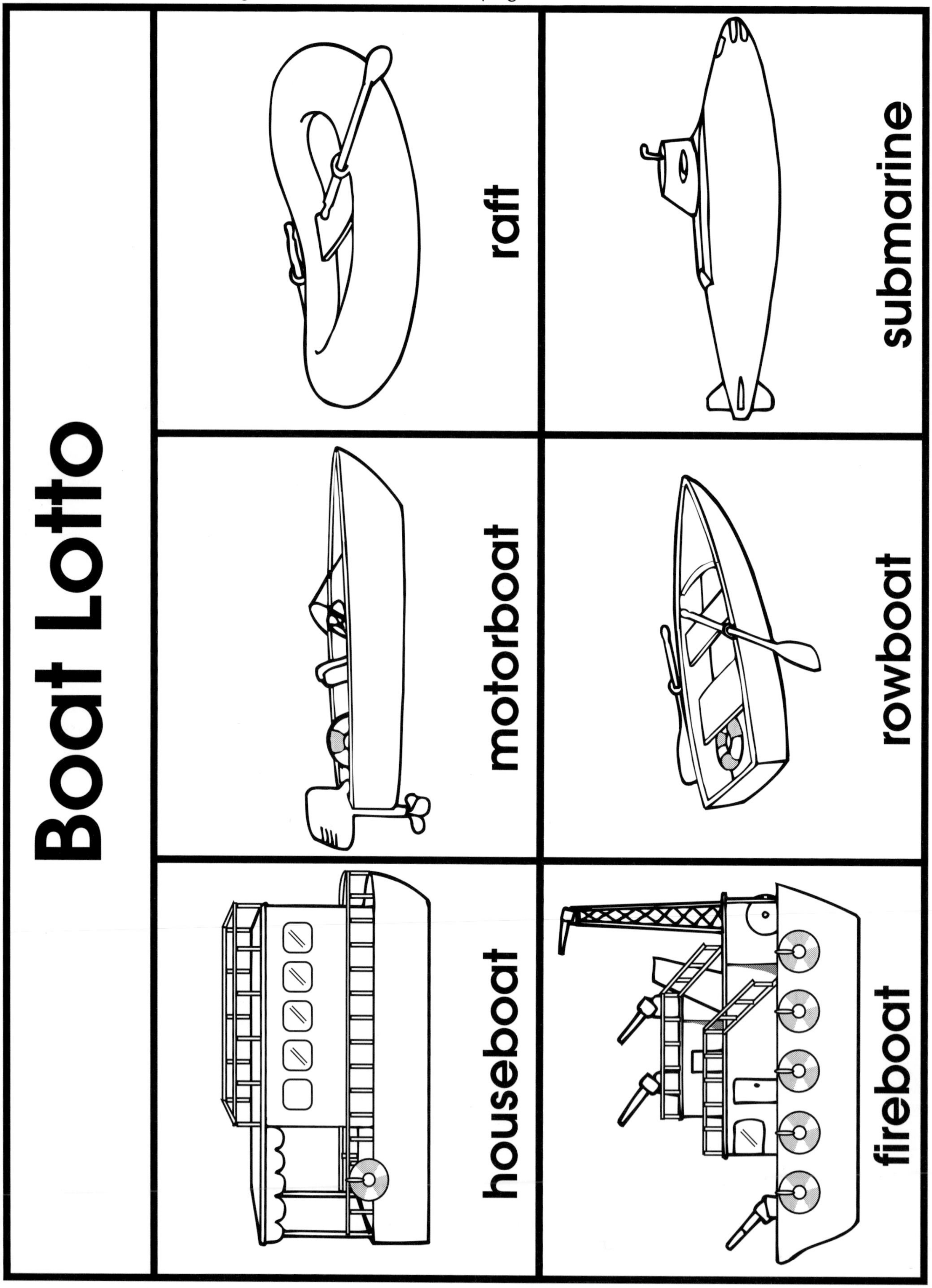

Boat Lotto

raft

submarine

motorboat

rowboat

houseboat

fireboat

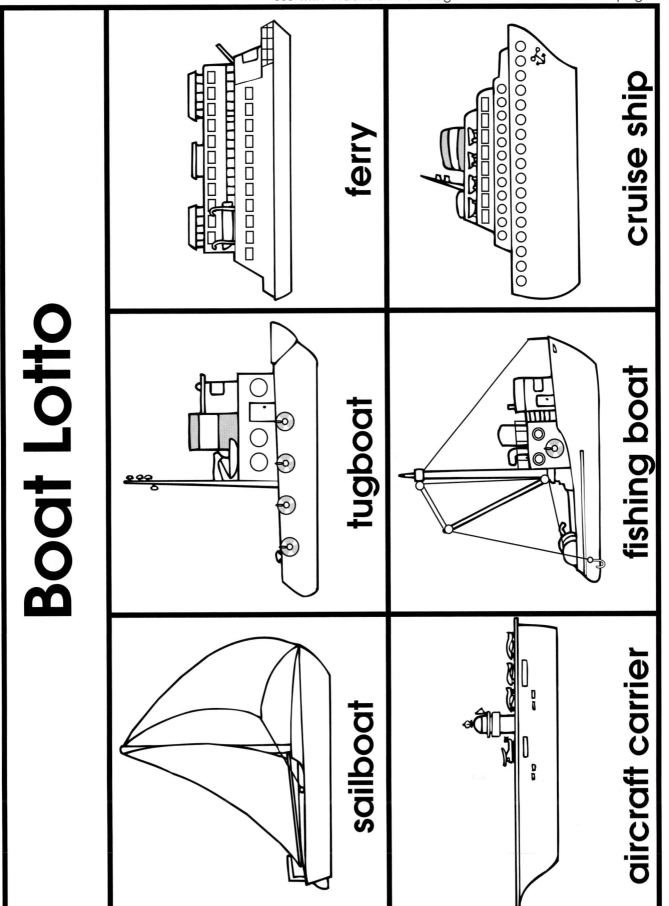

Boat Lotto

ferry

cruise ship

tugboat

fishing boat

sailboat

aircraft carrier

Patterns

Use with "Peeking At The Portholes" on page 77.

FIELD TRIP UNITS

Check Out The Library

Buddy Bookworm invites you and your little ones to visit the library. Use these ideas and handy reproducibles to make this trip an inspiring one from start to finish.

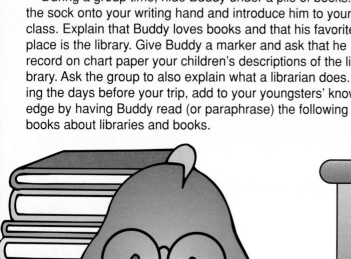

Buddy Bookworm

This library-loving character will worm his way into youngsters' hearts and get them excited about your trip to the library as well. To make a puppet, hot-glue wiggle eyes to a long green sock. Fashion a pair of glasses from a pipe cleaner; then secure them to the sock.

During a group time, hide Buddy under a pile of books. Slip the sock onto your writing hand and introduce him to your class. Explain that Buddy loves books and that his favorite place is the library. Give Buddy a marker and ask that he record on chart paper your children's descriptions of the library. Ask the group to also explain what a librarian does. During the days before your trip, add to your youngsters' knowledge by having Buddy read (or paraphrase) the following books about libraries and books.

Library Books

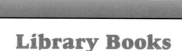

Red Light, Green Light, Mama And Me
Written by Cari Best
Illustrated by Niki Daly
Published by Orchard Books

I Took My Frog To The Library
Written by Eric A. Kimmel
Illustrated by Blanche Sims
Published by Puffin Books

I Like The Library
Written & Illustrated by Anne Rockwell
(This book is out of print. Check your library.)

My Hometown Library
Written by William Jaspersohn
Published by Houghton Mifflin Company

Check It Out! The Book About Libraries
Written & Illustrated by Gail Gibbons
Published by Harcourt Brace & Company

I Like Books
Written & Illustrated by Anthony Browne
Published by Alfred A. Knopf Books For Young Readers

Just Open A Book
Written & Illustrated by P. K. Hallinan
Published by Ideals Children's Books

Buddy Bookworm has invited our class to the library because he wants us to love books and become lifelong readers. We'll be checking out **Lakeview** *name of library* on **8/19/98** *date*.
Please sign here if your little bookworm can participate **Maggie Hunt** *child's name* **8/14/98** *date*
Amy Smith *caregiver's signature*

Additional Information:

Maggie Hunt *child's name*
Bookworm

Maggie Hunt *child's name*

Getting Ready To Go

Prior to your trip, prepare a class set of parent notes, nametags, and temporary library cards. To prepare the parent notes, duplicate a class supply of the pattern on page 85 onto white construction paper. Cut out the notes. For each child, round one end of a ten-inch green crepe-paper streamer. Have each child fold his note in half, then unfold it. Next have him glue the streamer to the back of his note. Last have him glue wiggle eyes on the streamer or use a marker to draw eyes on it to resemble Buddy Bookworm. Send the notes home.

To prepare nametags, divide your students into the same number of groups as you have chaperones. For each group and its chaperone, duplicate the nametag pattern on page 85 onto a different color of construction paper. Laminate if desired. Cut out the tags; then personalize them. Poke a five-inch chenille stem through the tag, twisting it to secure it. On field-trip day, twist the chenille-stem worm on each child's tag around a shirt button or shoelace hole. Or twist the top of the stem into a loop; then safety-pin the tag onto the child's clothing.

Duplicate a class supply of the library-card pattern on page 85. Personalize the cards. Invite each child to color his card. Use the cards as described in "Book Lovers Welcome Here" on page 84.

Bookworm Behavior

Using Buddy as your helper, discuss behaviors expected in the library. Explain that it is polite to walk slowly and talk softly so as not to disturb people who are reading. Remind youngsters that after looking at a book, it is important to put it back where it was found or to use a library card to check it out before taking it home. Then sing this action song to practice for your trip.

In The Library
(sung to the tune of "Bringing Home A Baby Bumblebee")

I'll walk very slowly in the library.
Won't Buddy Bookworm be so proud of me?
I'll walk very slowly in the library.
(Spoken) Ready? Let's tiptoe.

I'll talk very softly in the library.
Won't Buddy Bookworm be so proud of me?
I'll talk very softly in the library.
(Spoken) Shh. Let's whisper.

I'll put books on the shelf at the library.
Won't Buddy Bookworm be so proud of me?
I'll put books on the shelf at the library.
(Spoken) Okay, let's put our books away!

I'll check out a book at the library.
Won't Buddy Bookworm be so proud of me?
I'll check out a book at the library.
(Spoken) Now show me your library card.

Book Lovers Welcome Here

Make arrangements for a children's librarian to give your group a tour of the library and to lead a storytime with your group. Afterward give each child his library card (see "Getting Ready To Go" on page 83) and have him select one book to check out for your class library. Request that the librarian who checks out each child's book (with your personal card) stamp the back of his pretend card and place it in the book's pocket. (See "Buddy's New Home" for how to use the checked-out books.) Before you leave the library, take a group picture. Include the picture with the thank-you gesture described in "Book Donation."

Thanks for inviting us to check out the library.

Ms. Morris's Class
Sunshine Preschool

Book Donation

How can you show your appreciation to the librarians who helped make your trip successful? Why not give them something they're sure to appreciate—a book, of course! Write a message of thanks on the inside of a new, hardback book. Mount your class photo (see "Book Lovers Welcome Here") with your message. Then protect your message and photo with a piece of clear Con-Tact® covering. Be sure to let parents know of your donation, and encourage them to visit the library with their children to check it out!

Pam Crane

Buddy's New Home

After your trip, use a group time to take a look at the books that were checked out. Ask each child to share why she chose her book. Then encourage youngsters to role-play what they've experienced by transforming your reading center into a library. Invite students to set up the area with props, such as a table, the books your class checked out, stamps and stamp pads, pencils, and a basket for returning books. Duplicate another class supply of the library card on page 85; then cut them out and personalize them before adding them to the center. Buddy Bookworm is likely to want to move from the public library to your class library. Welcome, Buddy!

Library Card
Use also with "Book Lovers Welcome Here"
and "Buddy's New Home" on page 84.

Patterns
Use with "Getting Ready To Go" on page 83.

Nametag

child's name

child's name

Bookworm

Parent Note

Buddy Bookworm has invited our class to the library

because he wants us to love books and become lifelong

readers. We'll be checking out _____
name of library

on _____.
date

Please sign here if your little bookworm can participate

_____   _____   _____
caregiver's signature   child's name   date

Additional Information:

Fire-Station Field Trip

Using these guidelines to plan a field trip to the fire station won't require emergency measures. The ideas will, however, ensure a bell-ringing, lights-flashing learning experience for your little ones!

by Lucia Kemp Henry

Getting Fired Up For The Field Trip

Fire up interest for your trip with this hot center idea. In advance, cut a class supply or more of red, orange, and yellow construction-paper flame shapes. Put toy fire trucks, firefighter figures, fire hats, and other fire-fighting paraphernalia in your blocks center. While your youngsters are immersed in dramatic play, question them about what they might find at a fire station and what firefighters do. Ask them what they'd like to find out on your upcoming trip. Record youngsters' thoughts and questions on the flames; then display these flames on the walls or shelves in the center.

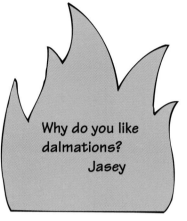

Why *do* you like dalmations? Jasey

Prepare With Picture Books

Share the photos in these books with your little ones, and they'll be ready to speed to the scene to see real firefighters and fire trucks.

I'm Going To Be A Fire Fighter
Written by Edith Kunhardt
Published by Scholastic Inc.

Community Helpers: *Fire Fighters*
Written by Dee Ready
Published by Bridgestone Books

Ready For Action

Once youngsters have dramatized and read about fire fighting, they'll jump at the chance to help you make these field-trip notes. In advance, duplicate the patterns on page 88 onto white construction paper so that you have one holder for each child. Also duplicate and program one copy of the field-trip notes at the bottom of page 89; then duplicate a class supply of this page onto red paper. Cut out the holders, notes, and nametags (save the nametags for later).

To complete a note for each child, use a craft knife to cut along the dotted lines on each dalmatian holder. Have a child press black fingerprints onto the dalmatian, then color its hat. Slip a field-trip note into the dog's mouth; then turn the holder over and tape the note on the back.

To prepare the fire-truck nametags for your trip, program each one with a different child's name or with your school name, if desired. If you'll be dividing your class into groups, designate these groups by putting different colors of dot stickers on the trucks' wheels.

Fire Station No. 1

We will visit the fire station on **Friday, Oct. 9**.

Call Ms. Henry if you have questions.

Miles

At The Firehouse

When you arrive at the fire station, have your little ones sing this song to start the tour.

Hello, Firefighters
(sung to the tune of "Frère Jacques")

Firefighters, firefighters,
How are you? How are you?
Would you like to tell us,
Would you like to tell us
What you do? What you do?

Photographic Memories

Be sure to take plenty of pictures on your trip, especially one of your class with your hosts (for use on a thank-you note). In addition, take pictures of parts of the fire station, the fire trucks, and individual pieces of equipment. When you return from your trip, display the developed pictures in a writing or reading center along with index cards programmed with the corresponding vocabulary words. Use these pictures and words to encourage follow-up discussion about the trip.

A Hero's Thanks

Thank your heroes at the fire station with this adorable dalmatian. Enlarge a dalmatian pattern (page 88) onto white construction paper or poster board. Invite each child to press a black thumbprint onto this dog and to write his name under the print. Mount the photo of your class (see "Photographic Memories") onto red construction paper; then have the class help you write a thank-you message on the paper. Cut along the dog's mouth. Slip the photo/note into its mouth; then turn the poster over and tape it. Firefighters might have to be tough folks to do their jobs, but they're sure to be touched when you deliver the class's thanks.

Field-Trip Note Holder

Use with "Ready For Action" on page 86 and "A Hero's Thanks" on page 87.

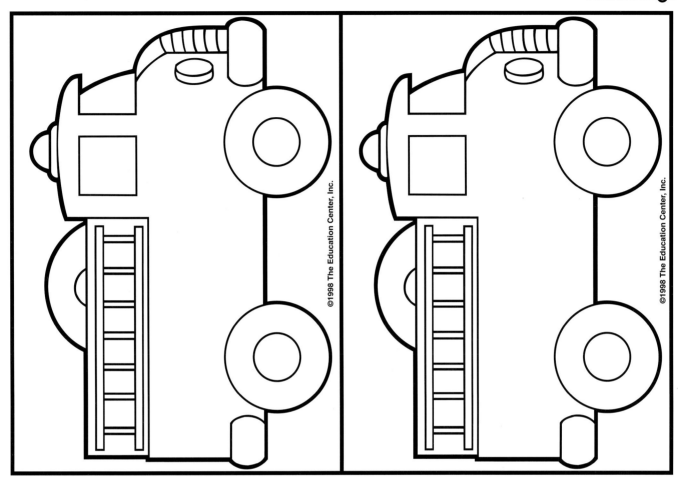

©1998 The Education Center, Inc.

©1998 The Education Center, Inc.

Field-Trip Notes

We will visit
the fire station
on

_____.

We will visit
the fire station
on

_____.

On Our Way To The Bakery

It only takes a few simple ingredients to make this bakery field trip a treat. Your little cupcakes are sure to have a great time!

by Lucia Kemp Henry

Muffin Memos

You'll want youngsters to take these field-trip memos home while they're still freshly made! Write or type a field-trip note containing the information you'd like parents to know about your trip. Duplicate a class supply onto white construction paper. For each child, cut out a tan construction-paper muffin shape. Have each child use crayons, confetti, or glitter glue to decorate a muffin. To complete each note, fold a cupcake liner in half; then glue its corners only to the note. Glue the child's muffin to the note so that it is behind the liner. These notes might just tempt every parent to come along!

Our class is taking
a trip to
Best Bakery
on
December 1st at 10:00.
Please call Ms. Henry if you would like to take the trip with us!

Before The Big Day

Roll into your bakery theme by brainstorming the kinds of food that your children might see at the bakery, such as cookies, bread, muffins, doughnuts, pies, cupcakes, and cakes. Then sing the following song, including a different type of baked good each time you repeat the verse.

(sung to the tune of "The Mulberry Bush")

What will you buy at the bakery,
The bakery, the bakery?
What will you buy at the bakery,
So early in the morning?

I'd like to buy some [bread] today,
[Bread] today, [bread] today.
I'd like to buy some [bread] today,
So early in the morning.

Bakery Books

Tempt your little ones' taste buds and get them ready for your trip by reading aloud these titles.

Mr. Cookie Baker
Written & Illustrated by Monica Wellington
Published by Dutton Children's Books

Walter The Baker
Written & Illustrated by Eric Carle
Published by Simon & Schuster Children's Division

Sofie's Role
Written by Amy Heath
Illustrated by Sheila Hamanaka
(This book is out of print. Check your library.)

Bread, Bread, Bread
Written by Ann Morris
Photographs by Ken Heyman
Published by Lothrop, Lee & Shepard Books

Muffin Nametags

Mix up a batch of nametag necklaces for your little ones to wear on your trip. Cut out a class supply (plus extras for your chaperones) of tan construction-paper muffin shapes. Fold half as many cupcake liners as you have nametags in half. Trim off the corners as shown; then trim the liners in half along the fold. To make one nametag, glue a liner piece to one side of a muffin cutout. Personalize the muffin; then invite a child to use a cotton swab to frost it with thick, white acrylic paint. While the paint is wet, have her sprinkle on candy decorations or confetti. When the paint is dry, reinforce the top back of the muffin with masking tape; then punch a hole through the muffin and tape. Tie on a length of yarn to complete the nametag necklace.

Our trip to the bakery was a treat!

Thank you, Mrs. Henry's class

Somi — Chocolate pie
Caroline — cherry tart
Frankie — strawberry cake
Ben — doughnut
Luke — brownie
Charles — chocolate chip cookie
Nick — cream puff
Danielle — cupcake
Rodney — raisin bread

At The Bakery

When you arrive at the bakery, have youngsters greet the workers with this chant.

Hello, Bakery Lady! Hello, Bakery Man!
Show us how to bake; we know you can.
Cookies and cakes we'd like to see.
Please introduce us to the bakery!

Thank-You Notes On A Platter

After returning from your trip, ask each child to tell which bakery goodie he liked best. Write each child's name and response on a separate, small paper plate. Direct each child to color a picture of the goodie in the center of the plate. Write a thank-you message in the center of a large bulletin-board-paper circle. Then glue the plates around the message.

Be sure to integrate the "Pat-A-Cake" nursery-rhyme ideas (pages 157–161) into your bakery studies. The combination of these ideas makes a thematic unit that really takes the cake!

SUPER-DUPER SUPERMARKET TOUR

Attention preschool shoppers! Check out these ideas for a field trip to the grocer's. There's a lot of fun in store!

by Lucia Kemp Henry

START WITH A GROCERY LIST

What do you need to make any trip to the grocery store successful? A list, of course! Study some full-color grocery store ad pages with your group, discussing the items available at the store, their prices, what youngsters would buy, and more. Then give each child a sale page from your paper. Ask each child to select and cut out one pictured item from his ad pages. Glue each child's picture on a large sheet of chart paper. Label the pictures. Then sing the following song, replacing the word *food* with one of the pictured items on the list each time you repeat the verse.

LET'S GO TO THE GROCERY STORE
(sung to the tune of "The Muffin Man")

Let's go to the grocery store,
The grocery store, the grocery store.
Let's go to the grocery store.
Let's buy some [food] today!

Our Grocery List

 apple

 noodles

 potatoes

 peanut butter

Katie's Grocery List

cereal

tomatoes

fruit candy

soup

MARKET MEMOS

Send this field trip memo and its little bag of goodies home, and you can count on speedy doorstep delivery. Duplicate a class supply of a note containing the information you'd like parents to know about your trip. For each child, use zigzag scissors to trim six inches off the top of a small brown paper bag; then attach the memo to the front of the bag. Ask each child to cut out pictures from a color grocery store ad, then glue the pictures to an 18" x 3" strip of white paper. With the child's input, write the name of each item next to its picture. Attach the bottom of the list to the inside of the bag. These grocery-bag bulletins are sure to have parents asking to be added to your field trip list!

Our class is taking a trip
to
Good Food Grocery
on
June 12 at 10:00.
Please call Mrs. Henry if
you can shop with us.

SHOPPING BAG NAMETAGS

To make these eye-catching tags for your trip, duplicate a receipt for each child from the store that you'll be visiting. Cut out the receipts and a class supply (plus some extra for chaperones) of brown construction-paper squares (about 3" x 3") to resemble bags. Personalize each bag; then glue on cutout pictures from food ads. Glue a receipt to the back of each bag. Reinforce the top of the receipt with tape; then punch a hole through it and add a loop of string to complete the nametag.

Our Grocery List
Mrs. Henry's Group

 hot dogs

grapes

 yogurt

 potatoes

TO MARKET, TO MARKET

This seek-and-find activity will really have your youngsters checking out the grocery store. Prepare a grocery list as shown for each group of children by gluing pictures of food from ads to a sheet of construction paper. After the grocery store staff has given your class a tour of the parts of the grocery store—such as the stock rooms, loading dock, bakery, and more—give each chaperone and her small group of students a list. Challenge each small group to search the store to find the items on its list, checking each one off with a marker when it is found.

THANKS ARE IN THE BAG

After your trip, ask each child to draw a small picture of a food she saw at the grocery store. Personalize and label the pictures before gluing them to a large paper grocery bag. Finally staple a thank-you message to the inside top of the bag.

Thank you for the
grocery store tour.
We think your market is
SUPER!
Mrs. Henry's class

CARTLOAD OF BOOKS

Do The Doors Open By Magic?:
And Other Supermarket Questions
Written by Catherine Ripley
Illustrated by Scot Ritchie
Published by Owl Books

A Busy Day At Mr. Kang's Grocery Store
Written by Alice K. Flanagan
Photographed by Christine Osinski
Published by Children's Press®

Feast For 10
Written & Illustrated by Cathryn Falwell
Published by Clarion Books

Make
Reservations
For A

Restaurant
Field Trip

Are you hungry for a tasty field-trip experience? Choose any local restaurant that's known for its child-friendly service; then use these ideas and reproducibles for a delicious trip!

by Lucia Kemp Henry

Culinary Clues

Whet youngsters' appetites for your upcoming field trip with a guessing game. In advance visit the restaurant you'll be touring and pick up a menu. Place the menu in a grocery bag, along with some of your own restaurant-related items, such as a pad and pencil, a small pan, a sponge, and toy food. Close the bag and bring it to a group time.

Tell your little ones that all the items in the bag are clues to your next field trip. Then remove one item at a time—saving the menu for last—and encourage youngsters to make guesses about your destination. After all the items have been removed from the bag and everyone has had a chance to guess, tell students about the field trip. Ask them to share what they know about restaurants. Then finish up by reading one or more of the following books.

Tasteful Selections

Chef Ki Is Serving Dinner!
Written by Jill D. Duvall
Photographed by Lili Duvall
Published by Children's Press®

Chop, Simmer, Season
Written & Illustrated by Alexa Brandenberg
Published by Harcourt Brace & Company

Dinner At The Panda Palace
Written by Stephanie Calmenson
Illustrated by Nadine Bernard Westcott
Published by HarperCollins
Children's Books

Chef ID

Prior to your field trip, help your young chefs make these adorable nametags. Duplicate a class supply (plus a few extras for yourself and your chaperones) of the nametag pattern on page 96. Have each youngster color and cut out his nametag, then glue it to a 4 1/2" x 6" piece of colorful construction paper. Provide food-themed stickers for decorating his nametag's border. For a final touch, have him glue wiggle eyes to the chef's face. Reinforce the top back of the nametag with masking tape; then punch a hole in the nametag. Thread it onto a yarn length, to be worn as a necklace.

Restaurant Rendezvous Reminder

This place-setting permission slip is sure to catch every parent's eye! In advance write or type the pertinent information about your trip, so that you can fit several copies of this note on a single sheet of copy paper. Duplicate a class supply of the note; then cut apart the permission slips. Assist each child in gluing his parent note to a 9" x 12" sheet of construction paper as shown. Then invite him to decorate the edges of his paper to resemble a placemat. Next, provide each child with a small paper plate, a folded paper napkin, and a plastic fork or spoon. Ask him to glue on these items to create a place setting above the parent note. As a final touch, have each child fill his plate with a serving of faux food rendered in crayon, or with a tasty photo cut from a magazine. This serving of takeout is set to take home!

Our class has an appetite for a tasty restaurant field trip! We have a reservation at

The Neighborhood Café on _2/10/99_
name of restaurant   date

Please sign here if your little gourmet can participate.

Mrs. Clay   _Samantha Clay_   _2/5/99_
caregiver's signature   child's name   date

Restaurant Responsibilities

One thing youngsters are sure to learn on their field trip is that there are different jobs at a restaurant. Acquaint them with various restaurant workers by teaching them this song before your trip. During the trip, snap a photo of each worker engaged in his job; then add these photos to a pocket-chart version of this song when you return to your classroom. Youngsters may think of additional verses after learning about other restaurant responsibilities.

Workers At The Restaurant
(sung to the tune of "The Farmer In The Dell")

The hostess says, "Hello."
The hostess says, "Hello."
Working at a restaurant,
The hostess says, "Hello."

The cook prepares the meal….
The waiter brings the food….
The busboy clears the table….
The dishwasher cleans up….

Mrs. Henry's class presents
the
Golden Spoon Award
to
The Neighborhood Café

Zach
Amber
Ty
Evan
Megan

Thank You!!

A Spoonful Of Thanks

After your field trip, seize this golden opportunity to say "thank you" to your host restaurant. Duplicate a class supply of the spoon pattern on page 96 onto yellow construction paper; then cut out the spoons. Write each child's name on a spoon's handle (or have children write their names if they are able). Have each child glue her choice of gold materials—such as glitter, pipe-cleaner pieces, or beads—to the bowl of her spoon.

To create the poster, sponge-print a checkerboard pattern on a large sheet of poster board to resemble a checkered tablecloth. Glue a class photo to the center of a paper plate; then glue this plate to the poster board. Glue each child's decorated spoon cutout to the poster board as well; then use a black permanent marker (and perhaps a glitter pen) to write a complimentary message similar to the one shown. That's a poster any café would be proud to display!

Nametag Patterns
Use with "Chef ID" on page 94.

Spoon Patterns
Use with "A Spoonful Of Thanks" on page 95.

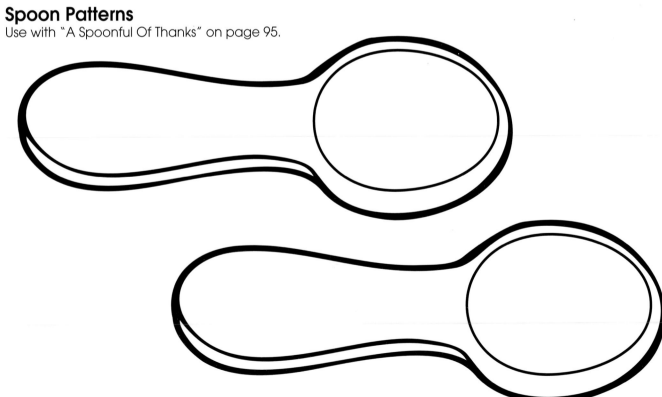

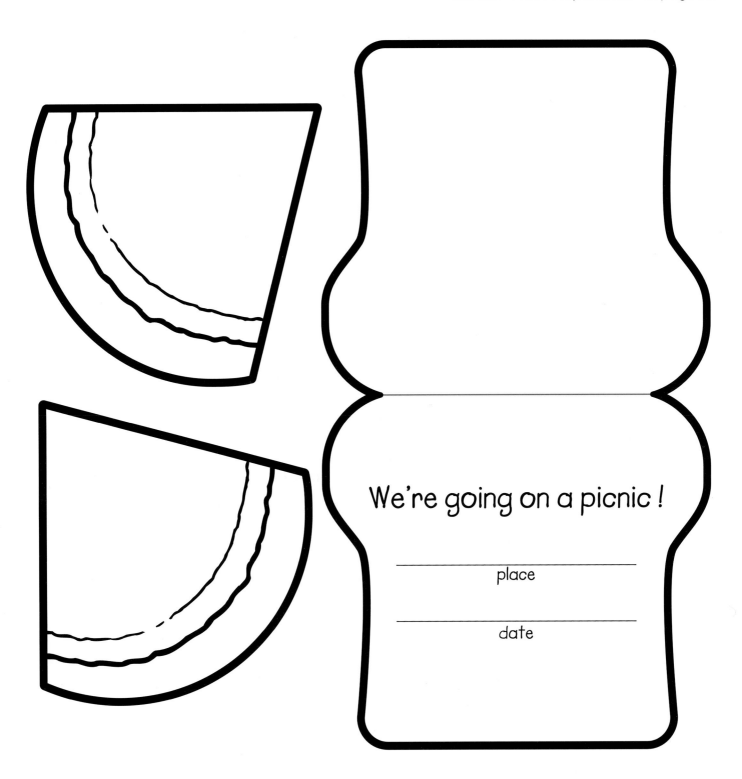

We're going on a picnic !

_____
place

_____
date

PICNIC IN THE PARK

Celebrate spring with a picnic in the park! Just follow this picnic plan, and there won't be anything to spoil your outing (except maybe a few friendly ants!).

by Lucia Kemp Henry

PACKING FOR A PICNIC

Packing for a pretend picnic will pique your youngsters' interest in the real thing! To prepare, collect items to represent things you might pack for a picnic, such as plastic utensils, clean food containers, empty juice boxes, plastic soda bottles, paper plates and cups, napkins, toy food, a blanket, and more. Bring the items in a paper bag—along with a picnic basket and a cooler—to a group time. Ask each child, in turn, to take an item out of the bag and put it into the basket or cooler to help you pack for a picnic. Then place the bag, basket, and cooler in a dramatic-play area to encourage indoor, pretend picnics before and after your outing.

To further whet youngsters' appetites for your trip, ask each child to name a food that he would take on a picnic. Write the child's suggestion on a small paper plate; then invite him to illustrate that food on the plate. When each child has illustrated his plate, add the plates to the picnic items in the dramatic-play area.

potato chips

BOOK PICKS

A-tisket, a-tasket, don't forget to pack some books in your picnic basket!

It's The Bear!
Written & Illustrated by Jez Alborough
Published by Candlewick Press

The Teddy Bears' Picnic
Written by Jimmy Kennedy
Illustrated by Michael Hague
Published by Owlet Paperbacks
    For Young Readers

Once Upon A Picnic
Written by John Prater
Illustrated by Vivian French
Published by Candlewick Press

This Is The Bear And The Picnic Lunch
Written by Sarah Hayes
Illustrated by Helen Craig
(This book is out of print. Check your library.)

Order books on-line.
www.themailbox.com

PICNIC PREPARATIONS

Get ready for your day in the great outdoors by preparing these field trip notes and nametags. Duplicate page 97; then program the bread pattern with your field trip information. Next duplicate a class supply of the page; then cut out the patterns. Also cut a class supply of three-inch yellow construction-paper squares. For each child, program a yellow square with additional information, such as an item that child should bring for the picnic or directions to bring a bag lunch.

To make a note, a child folds his bread, colors it, and then glues it onto a small paper plate. Next he glues torn construction-paper shapes to his bread to represent other items on a sandwich, such as meat and lettuce. He glues the yellow note inside the sandwich last. Finally, he glues a six-inch square of fabric to the back of the plate.

To make a nametag, have a child color two watermelon patterns, then glue them onto each side of a small paper plate. Punch a hole near the top of the plate; then add a length of yarn to make a necklace. Use markers (or dimensional paint) to write the child's name on one side of his tag and your school information on the other side. If you'll be dividing your class into groups, write each child's name on his tag using a different color for each group.

DON'T BE A LITTERBUG!

There won't be any litterbugs in your group when you practice park etiquette with this simple song. Each time you repeat the song, replace the word *litter* with a word such as *wrappers, boxes, paper, napkins, paper bags,* or another type of trash your youngsters suggest. Sing the song again at the park to remind your little ones not to litter.

PICK UP LITTER!

(sung to the tune of "London Bridge")

Don't throw [litter] on the ground,
On the ground, on the ground.
Don't throw [litter] on the ground.
Pick up [litter]!

A PICTURE-PERFECT DAY

Capture your picnic on film; then use the developed pictures to create this display that recaps your trip. Mount each photo onto a separate colorful paper plate. Use a marker to make a class supply of paper squares resemble napkins as shown. Ask each child to make a comment about the picnic for you to record on a separate square. Arrange the picture plates and comments on a tablecloth-covered background. Later, when you remove the display, put the pictures and comments in a picnic basket; then put the basket in a language or reading center to encourage tasty conversations.

BOOK FEATURES

IF YOU GIVE A MOUSE A COOKIE

Written by Laura Joffe Numeroff
Illustrated by Felicia Bond
Published by HarperCollins Children's Books, 1985

If you show youngsters this book, they'll want you to read it. If you read it, they'll love it. If they love it, they'll ask you to read it over and over again! The amusing mouse that starts the chain of events in this story is sure to start a chain of learning events in your classroom. Begin with the following ideas for extending the story; then, when youngsters beg for more, turn to "Mouse's Favorite Cookie Ideas" on pages 104–105.

MOUSE MANNERS

Invite youngsters to make these mice; then encourage them to use their puppets to improve their manners! To make a mouse puppet, glue a paper nose and paper eyes to the flap of a flat, brown paper lunch bag. Use a black crayon to add whiskers. Glue two brown paper circles to opposite sides of the back to represent ears. Tape a brown yarn tail to the back of the bag.

Have each child put his puppet on his hand. As you reread the story, pause to allow the mice to politely request each item. For example, after you read, "…he's going to ask for a glass of milk," encourage the children to ask in unison, "May I please have a glass of milk?" After your storytime, have youngsters take their mice home to find out what they'll politely ask for there!

Patricia Karatnytsky—Three-Year-Olds, St. Mary School, East Islip, NY

ONE THING LEADS TO ANOTHER

To get youngsters involved in retelling this story and to improve their listening skills, collect props that represent each of the mouse's requests (see the list below). Before reading the story, put the props around your room. Read the story without showing the pictures, pausing each time the mouse needs something new to encourage the children to recall the item(s). When the item is named, ask a child from the group to go find that item for the mouse. After your storytime, put these props in your reading center along with a copy of the book.

Henry Fergus—Preschool, Buckeye Elementary School District #33, Buckeye, AZ

Mouse's Requests

a cookie
milk (use a plastic cup)
a straw
a napkin
a mirror
a pair of nail scissors
a broom

a bed (use a small box, scrap of fabric, and powder puff)
a story (use a book)
paper and crayons
a pen
tape
a second glass of milk
a cookie

IF YOU MAKE A COOKIE THAT LOOKS LIKE A MOUSE,...

If your little ones make cookies that look like mice, they're sure to want some milk! To make a tasty mouse morsel, spread creamy peanut butter on a sugar cookie. Break a vanilla wafer in half; then put each half on the cookie to represent ears. Add candy-coated chocolate pieces for eyes and a nose. Then add pretzel-stick whiskers. Mmm...mice cookies!

If You Give A Mouse

If you give a mouse a donut, he will want some hot chocolate!

If You Give A Mouse

THE FUN HAS JUST BEGUN

Use this silly story to inspire your little ones to make up their own short stories for a class book. On separate large, white construction-paper circles, write each child's completion to the following sentence: "If you give a mouse a ___, he will ___." Have him illustrate his page. Bind the pages between same-sized, tan construction-paper covers. Add whiskers, facial features, and paper ears to the cover; then title the book "If You Give A Mouse." Now what might that mouse be up to next?

MORE, MORE, MORE!

Looking for more ways to enjoy this mouse tale? Visit the publisher's Web site at http://www.harperchildrens.com. You'll find information about related products, such as CD-ROMs, and a minibook and audiotape package. You'll also be able to print several free coloring pages!

103

MOUSE'S FAVORITE COOKIE IDEAS

TEXTURED COOKIES

Instead of for tasting, these cookies are for touching! To prepare textured paint, mix sand into brown, black, and tan paints until they have a thick consistency. Encourage children to paint tagboard circles to create cookie look-alikes. When these cookies are dry, have children compare the feel of these cookies to real cookies. Then put the painted cookies in a dramatic-play area. Invite youngsters to put the real cookies in their tummies!

Lori Parlier—Pre-K
Hubbard Elementary
Forsyth, GA

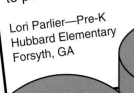

C IS FOR COOKIE

Youngsters will be quick to learn that *C* is for cookie with this hands-on idea. Cut a slit in the top of a cookie container. Cut a number of paper cookie shapes that are wider than the slit and a number of cookies that fit through the slit. Label the cookies that are too wide with different letters of the alphabet; then label all of the smaller cookies with the letter *C*. Put the container and the cookies in a center. To use the items, a child identifies the cookies labeled with the letter *C*, then drops them through the lid.

Sharon Warfuel—Pre-K
Tynes Elementary
Middleburg, FL

COOKIE POEM

Here's a delicious cookie poem for your cookie days.

Five round cookies as yummy as can be.
The first cookie said, "Please eat me!"
The second cookie said, "I have lots of chocolate chips."
The third cookie said, "I'll taste good on your lips!"
The fourth cookie said, "I'm right here on the pan."
The fifth cookie said, "Find me if you can!"
Then "Ding!" went the timer,
'Cause the cookies were done.
We ate all the cookies and had lots of fun!

Janet McGraw—Preschool
Abingdon Presbyterian Preschool
Abingdon, VA

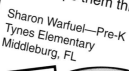

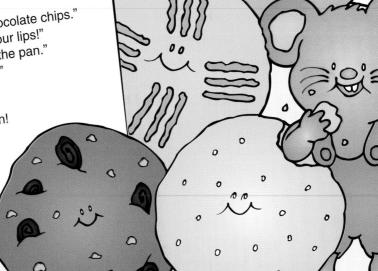

COOKIE KITCHEN BAND

This homemade band is sure to stir up some excitement! Collect items that can be used as rhythm instruments, such as wooden spoons, stainless-steel bowls, plastic bowls, beaters, wire whisks, cookie sheets, and toy rolling pins. Put chocolate chips in jars to make sweet-sounding shakers. Give each band member an instrument; then have the students march around the room to some lively marching music or the popular Sesame Street® song " 'C' Is For Cookie" (*Sing The Alphabet,* Sony Wonder).

Laurel Jonas, Portage, WI

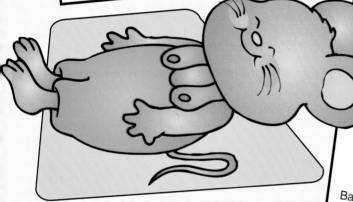

ROLLIN' IN DOUGH

Roll into gross-motor skills with this small-group idea. Spread a towel on the floor to represent cookie dough. Have a volunteer lie down across the towel so that her arms are at her sides and her legs are straight. Now you have a human rolling pin! Gently roll the child back and forth as the children in the group recite the following rhyme. When you say, "Again," gently pull the child to her feet. Then invite another child to roll out the dough!

Baker, Baker, roll that dough.
Roll it fast; roll it slow.
Roll it thick, roll it thin.
Roll it out and back again!

Barbara Kennedy, Carmel, IN

BOOGIE WHILE YOU BAKE

Why not mix up a batch of chocolate-chip cookies in your classroom? Can't remember the recipe? This song is sure to help you out!

THAT'S HOW WE MAKE OUR SNACK
(sung to the tune of "The Hokey Pokey")

We put some butter in.
We put white sugar in.
We put brown sugar in, and we stir it all around.
We make our cookie batter, and we stir it all around.
That's how we make our snack. Yum-yum!

We put some eggs in.
We put vanilla in.
We put some soda in, and we stir it all around.
We make our cookie batter, and we stir it all around.
That's how we make our snack. Yum-yum!

We put some flour in.
We put some chips in.
We scoop the spoon in; then we plop dough on the pan.
We put our cookies in the oven and we turn the timer on.
That's how we make our snack. Yum-yum!

Laurel Jonas, Portage, WI

CHANGES, CHANGES

Written & Illustrated by Pat Hutchins
Published by Simon & Schuster Children's Publishing Division

Combine a favorite center activity—blocks—with this classic book, and the result is sure to be a blockbuster hit! Introduce youngsters to this wordless, yet action-packed, book and build enthusiasm with these story-extension activities.

by Lisa Leonardi

Changes, Changes
By PAT HUTCHINS

A Framework For Storytime

Wondering where to begin with this wordless masterpiece? Here's a framework for success. Cover the flames in the cover illustration with a piece of paper before showing the book to your group. Ask if there are things on the cover that you also have in your classroom. When you have agreed that the answer is *blocks,* announce the title of the book and ask youngsters to predict what the story might be about. Ask volunteers to comment as to why the block people look frightened; then remove the paper to reveal the flames.

As you share each two-page spread in the story, build youngsters' curiosity by showing only one page at a time. (Cover each right page as you show the facing left page.) Invite children to predict what changes will be made on each following page. Or have them predict what the block people will build to solve each problem that arises. Have youngsters observe the block people's faces and describe what they might be thinking and feeling. At the end of the story, ask your little ones to think up some new adventures for the block people. After all, there are endless possibilities to explore with blocks!

Building Solutions

To build youngsters' problem-solving skills, divide a piece of chart paper into two columns. Label the first column "Problems" and the second column "Solutions." Review each of the roadblocks that the block people encountered; then discuss how they cleverly built their way out of trouble each time. Use rebus sentences to record both the problems and the solutions on the chart. Allow time for creative thinkers to share different ways that they would have triumphed over each tragedy.

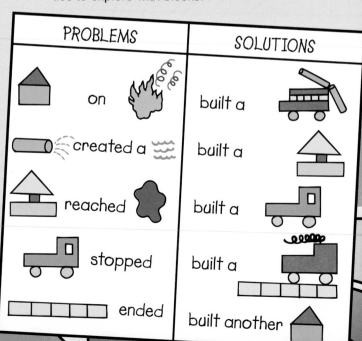

The Same But Different

Take a closer look at the first two pages of the story on which the blocks are displayed and the block people are standing side by side. Lead your group in counting and recording the number of each different color of blocks *(yellow, orange, red,* and *green)* in the set. To help your children realize that most of the same blocks are used in different ways to create each of the story's five structures, repeat these counting and recording steps while looking at each of the completed illustrations: *house, fire truck, boat, truck,* and *train.*

Under Construction

Follow up the discovery made in the previous idea by making this class book. Put a set of about 25 blocks of various shapes and sizes in a box. In turn, ask each child to build using only the blocks from the box. Take each child's picture near his completed structure. Feature these photos in a class book titled "Changes, Changes." It's a picture-perfect way to show that creativity comes in all shapes and sizes!

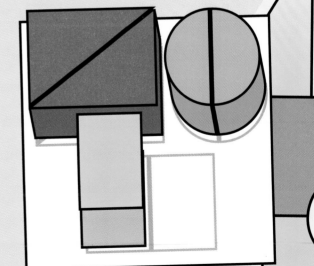

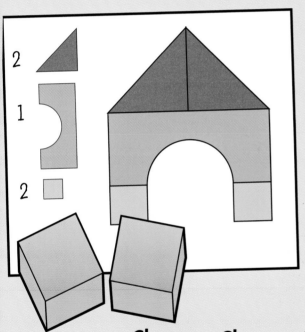

Have Plan, Will Build

Since youngsters can't replicate the exact designs in the book, make your own blueprints for students' building practice. To make a blueprint, build a simple block structure; then draw this structure on a piece of tagboard. If using colored blocks, color your illustration to match. Beside the illustration, draw a picture of each type of block used and write how many of each block are needed to build the structure. Put these blueprints in your block center. When a student has successfully copied a structure, talk with him about how he built his building, which types of blocks were used most, and which ones were used least.

Changes, Changes In Shapes

Math skills are sure to shape up as your little builders create new shapes from block pairs. Collect duplicates of the blocks—such as small triangles, large triangles, small squares, half circles, and arches—that can be joined in pairs to create new shapes. Seat an even number of children in a circle on the floor; then put a block in front of each child, making sure each child's block has a match. Ask a child to walk around the inside of the circle with his block until he finds a child with a matching block. Direct these two children to put their blocks together to form a new shape; then help them trace their blocks on paper to record their shape discovery. Continue until all of the block matches have been made and recorded.

107

FREIGHT TRAIN

Written & Illustrated by Donald Crews
Published by Greenwillow Books

With a series of brightly colored cars, Donald Crews's freight train travels past cities, through tunnels, and across trestles as it hurries on its way. It's going and going. So before it's gone, use *Freight Train* and the activities in this unit to reinforce colors. *Freight Train* is available in hardback, paperback, and big book versions.

Read And Review

Use this idea to review the types and colors of train cars as well as their order in the story. From large sheets of construction paper, cut out train cars that correspond in shape and color to each of the eight kinds of train cars in the book. (Refer to the cover.) Read the story aloud; then give each of eight children in the group one of the train cars. Ask the rest of the group to help those children holding cars to line up in the order of the cars in the story. Reread the story, pausing as you mention each type of car so that the child holding that car can find his place in the lineup. Have these children travel around your room together as you complete the story. Repeat this activity until each child has had a turn being a part of the freight train.

Deborah Ladd
Mustang, OK

Colorful Cargo

Use the train cars that you prepared for "Read And Review" to make this colorful display. Divide your class into seven groups: one group for each different color of car. Give each group one of the train cars, scissors, glue, and a stack of magazines. Direct each child in the group to cut out magazine pictures of things that are the same color as his group's car. Have the students glue the pictures to their car. (If you have a small class, have the whole group look for pictures for each different train car.) Display the completed cars along with the engine in the order of the train cars in the story.

Deborah Ladd

Paint A Freight Train

Have each child sponge-paint a freight train of his very own to take home. To prepare, fill each of seven shallow pans with a different color of tempera paint: red, orange, yellow, green, blue, purple, and black. Put a rectangular sponge in each pan. Include a circular item (such as a glue-bottle lid) near the black paint for painting train wheels. Provide each child with a length of white bulletin-board paper. To paint the engine, a child sponge-paints two black rectangles as shown. He then sponge-paints the remaining cars in the colors of his choice. He completes his train by painting wheels. When the paint is dry, label the child's train cars by color.

In the same manner, have children paint trains with cars that create a color pattern. For example, a child might paint an engine, then complete the train with cars that alternate between green and purple.

Kathleen K. Padilla—Preschool Special Education, Elfers, FL

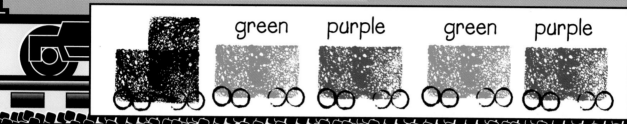
green   purple   green   purple

Train Game

Prepare this freight-train Memory game that will have players chugging along with color recognition. Duplicate a copy of the train-car game cards (pages 110-111) onto white construction paper two or four times. Color these train cars the appropriate colors; then cut them apart. To use the cards, a pair of children arranges them facedown, then plays a game of Memory or Concentration.

Connie Walker
Emmett, ID

Train Headband

Wrap up your focus on *Freight Train* by making these headbands that review colors and the types of train cars featured in the story. For each child, duplicate the headband patterns (page 111) onto white construction paper. Guide each child as he colors the train cars on the patterns. Have the child cut the patterns apart and then glue them, end-to-end, onto a sentence strip or tagboard strip that is long enough to wrap around a child's head. Finally, staple the ends of the strip together to fit the child's head. Parents are sure to ask about *Freight Train* when youngsters wear these colorful headbands home.

Deborah Ladd
Mustang, OK

Game Cards
Use with "Train Game" on page 109.

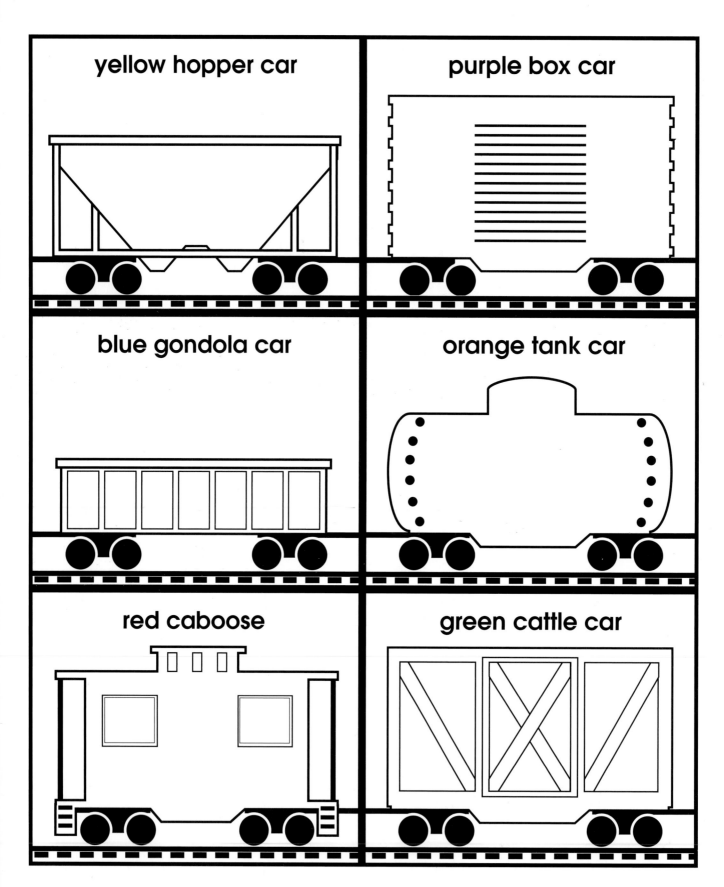

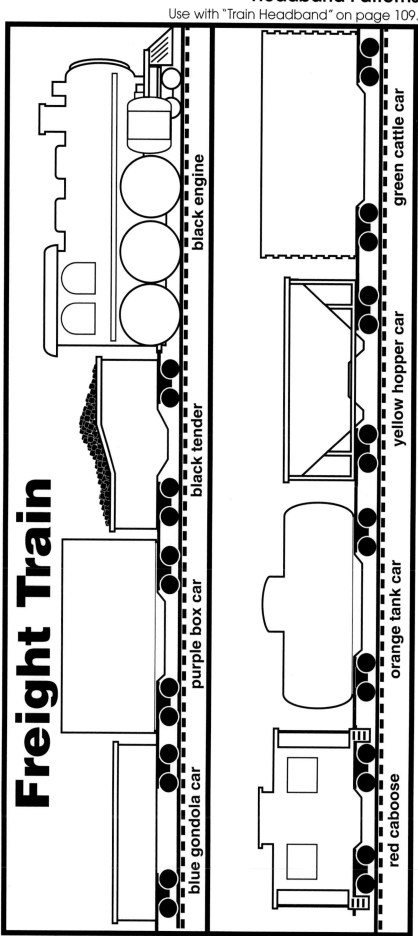

Freight Train

black engine

black tender

purple box car

blue gondola car

green cattle car

yellow hopper car

orange tank car

red caboose

Game Card
Use with "Train Game" on page 109.

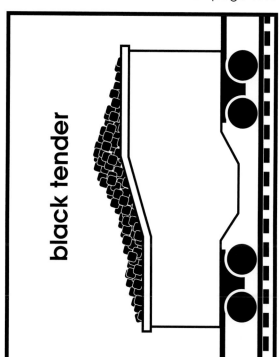

black tender

BIG FAT HEN

Illustrated by Keith Baker
Published by Harcourt Brace & Company

Let's meet at the barnyard for some counting fun with the big fat hen and her friends! Keith Baker's version of this traditional rhyme is sure to lead your class into a coop full of "egg-citing" storytime activities. Get a copy from your library, or order your own through our Web site: www.themailbox.com.

by dayle timmons—Kindergarten Inclusion
Alimacani Elementary, Jacksonville, FL

JEEPERS, CREEPERS, LET'S COUNT THOSE PEEPERS!

Read aloud *Big Fat Hen,* inviting any listeners who are familiar with the rhyme to join in. Next revisit each of the pages with numerals and invite your little ones to count the chicken, the eggs, and the other critters shown. Soon your youngsters will recognize a pattern in Baker's illustrations. Next have them compare the sets of eggs on each pair of numeral pages to the sets of chicks on the following pages. Who says you can't count your chickens before they hatch?

GET THE SCOOP AT THE COOP

Once your little ones have discovered Keith Baker's numeral-picture representations, turn your sensory table into a hands-on chicken coop of hatching eggs and counting fun. To prepare, fill the table with plastic Easter eggs, large yellow pom-poms to represent chicks, and an assortment of pretend worms, butterflies, and bugs (found at craft stores or educational toy stores). Also add sponge numerals or numerals die-cut from craft foam. To use the center, a child may practice one-to-one correspondence by putting one chick in each egg. She may count the bugs, worms, eggs, and chicks, or she may match a numeral to a set of objects. One, two, there's so much to do!

BIG FAT HEN AND HER FRIENDS...

Friends of a feather are sure to flock together at this art center! Have your children take a closer look at Keith Baker's colorful chickens, pointing out that their beautiful feathers are different shades of yellow, blue, green, purple, and pink. Next invite each child to use real feathers to paint his own big fat hen. To prepare, duplicate a copy of page 114 onto white construction paper for each child. Pour each different color of paint into a Styrofoam® tray. Also provide a large feather for each different color of paint, and orange and red markers.

To make one hen, have each child use markers to color the hen's crown, beak, and wattle. Then have him use his choice of colors to feather-paint the hen. When the paint is dry, cut out the hen; then glue on a wiggle eye. Display these fine-feathered friends with the caption "Big Fat Hen And Her Friends."

...AND ALL THEIR CHICKS

Now that your little ones have created some colorful hens, why not add the hens' chicks to the display as well? Prepare tagboard patterns for the chick (see shape on page 114) and the egg. To make one hatching chick, trace a chick shape onto yellow construction paper and an egg shape onto a large piece of white construction paper. Cut on the resulting outlines; then cut a jagged line across the top of the egg. To the chick, glue an orange paper diamond for a beak, wiggle eyes, and feathers (from an inexpensive feather duster). Display these chicks so that they can cluck right alongside their mother hens.

ONE, TWO, A BOOK FOR YOU

Three, four, read some more. Five, six, add the "pics." Seven, eight, this idea's great! Your little chicks are sure to enjoy reading their own *Big Fat Hen* books to their papa roosters and mama hens. To prepare a set of book pages for each child, duplicate page 115. Cut the pages apart for use as the cover and last page of the book. Cut nine additional sheets that are identical in size to the duplicated pages. Program each of four of the blank pages with a different poem line as indicated for pages 2, 4, 6, and 8 in the following directions. Assist each child in completing each page of his book as described. Numerals may be written, traced, sponge-printed, or glued on by the child. When the pages are complete, bind them together.

Cover:		Use watercolors to paint the hen.
Page 1:	*1, 2*	Add numerals.
Page 2:	*Buckle my shoe.*	Make a crayon rubbing of the bottom of the child's shoe.
Page 3:	*3,4*	Add numerals.
Page 4:	*Shut the door.*	Glue one long side of a 4" x 3" rectangle to resemble a door. Draw a knob; then fold the door open.
Page 5:	*5,6*	Add numerals.
Page 6:	*Pick up sticks.*	Randomly glue on craft sticks.
Page 7:	*7,8*	Add numerals.
Page 8:	*Lay them straight.*	Glue craft sticks on one above the other.
Page 9:	*9,10*	Add numerals.
Page 10:	*Big fat hen!*	Glue on a feather.

113

Hen Pattern
Use with "Big Fat Hen And Her Friends..." on page 113.

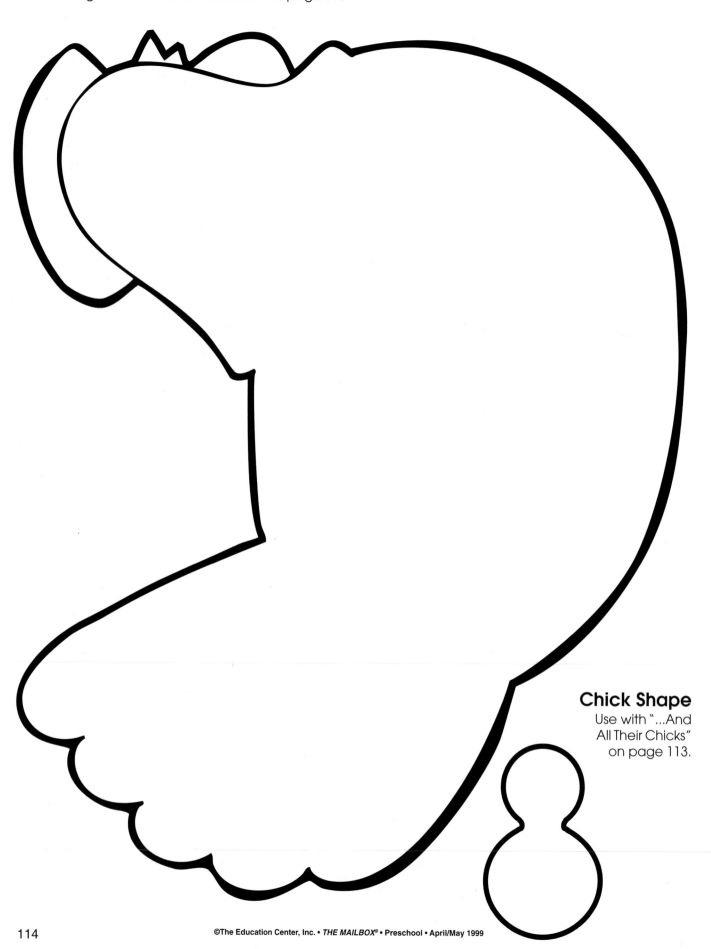

Chick Shape
Use with "...And
All Their Chicks"
on page 113.

Big Fat Hen

By

_____

Big fat hen!

LUNCH

Written & Illustrated by Denise Fleming
Published by Henry Holt And Company, Inc.

If your youngsters are hungry for a good book, nibble on the simple text and colorful illustrations of Denise Fleming's *Lunch* for a while. Here's a feast of story extensions that will fill your little ones up with learning fun. Get a copy from your library, or order the book through our Web site: www.themailbox.com.

by LeeAnn Collins—Director, Sunshine House Preschool, Lansing, MI

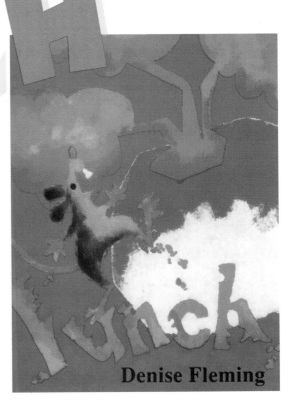

YUMMY IN HIS TUMMY

Share the story, allowing plenty of time for youngsters to digest the humorous illustrations of the mouse's munching marathon. Then, next time you present the book, inflate students' interest with this idea. Blow up a balloon, but do not tie it closed. Ask an adult helper to draw a simple mouse face on the balloon; then let the air out. Read the story, pausing each time the mouse eats a treat to inflate the balloon more and more. Soon your children will discover that the mouse on the balloon *and* the mouse in the story grow and grow as the lunch goes on.

That mouse just gets too much yummy in his tummy!

WHAT WOULD YOU MUNCH FOR LUNCH?

What messy munchies would the mice in your class choose to nibble on for lunch? Find out with this group activity. To prepare, tear simple construction-paper food shapes to match the foods in the story (white turnip, orange carrot, yellow corn, green peas, blue berries, purple grapes, red apple, pink melon); then glue each fruit shape onto a separate white paper plate. Label each plate with the food's name and color as shown. Gather a class number of some type of handy manipulative (such as gray pom-poms or gray paper ovals) to represent mice.

During a group time, arrange the plates on the floor; then give each child a manipulative. Ask each child to put his mouse on the plate of the food he would choose to munch for lunch. Then discuss the results. As a variation, ask youngsters to indicate which foods are their favorite colors or which foods they would have for breakfast instead of lunch.

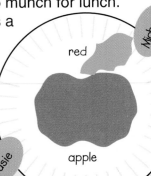

116

LUNCHTIME!

Shhh! Mouse doesn't want to be seen—so have your little ones whisper this fingerplay as you review the colorful foods he munched. Substitute a different food from the story (white turnips, orange carrots, yellow corn, green peas, blue berries, purple grapes, red apples, pink melons) each time you repeat the rhyme, using the plates prepared for "What Would You Munch For Lunch?" as visual reminders.

When the house is very quiet	*Put finger over lips.*
And it's time for some lunch,	*Rub tummy.*
A little gray mouse	*"Run" fingers like mouse.*
Looks for [white turnips] to munch.	*Pretend to eat.*

green beans

brown chocolate pie

red spaghetti sauce

Jodi

MESSY MOUSE PRINTS

On his way back to take a nap, Mouse left a trail of prints behind. Invite your children to pretend they are mice as they make this group mural. To prepare, fill a number of pans each with a different color of washable tempera paint. Also fill a tub with warm, soapy water (or use wet paper towels) and keep a towel nearby. Invite each child, in turn, to take off his shoes and socks and to step into the paint. Then have him scurry along a length of white bulletin-board paper. When the paint is dry, label each child's prints with a sentence that tells the child's name and the food of her choice that is the same color as her prints. Michele mouse ate red strawberries!

LET THE CRUMBS FALL

Youngsters are sure to notice that the mouse was a bit messy with his tasty treats. As a group, take a closer look at the last page of the book; then invite each child to make his own messy mouse. For each child, duplicate a copy of the mouse on page 119 onto gray construction paper. Have each child tear colorful tissue paper into small "food crumbs." Have him arrange the crumbs on his mouse and then brush over them with liquid starch. Label the mouse as shown, according to the child's description.

Jamie ate purple candy.

FEAST FOR A MOUSE

There is sure to be a bountiful banquet fit for any mouse when your class creates this cooperative mural. Cut out a large circle from white bulletin-board paper; then add details around the edge so it resembles a paper plate. Mount the plate to a wall near an art center. Encourage students who visit the area to cut out magazine pictures of food or to cut construction paper into food shapes and then glue the food to the plate. Just watch the feast flourish!

LUNCHEON MUNCHIN' PICNIC

Play this game with a small group of students to encourage some creative thinking and develop memory skills. Cut various colors of squares from construction paper, making sure you have one square per child; then put the squares in a basket. To play, pass the basket to each child, directing him to take one square, look at its color, and then name a food that is that color. Once everyone has taken a square, see if the group can remember all the foods named.

LUNCH LOGIC

Fill your preschoolers' plates with generous helpings of activities using the plastic food from your housekeeping center.

- Sort the foods by color.
- Classify the foods into two groups: a "yes" group if the food is in the book or a "no" group if the food is not in the book.
- Play a game of What's Missing? Name all of the foods; then put them in a box. Return all of the foods to the group's view except for one or two. Which food is missing?
- Play I Spy by supplying clues to the identity of one piece of food.

PIGGIES

Written by Don & Audrey Wood
Illustrated by Don Wood
Published by Harcourt Brace & Company

It's two hands up for *Piggies*! This award-winning, exuberant book has fat piggies, smart piggies, long piggies, silly piggies, and wee piggies—all sure to inspire your little ones to get their own fingers into the fun!

ideas by LeeAnn Collins

Cover of *Piggies* by Don and Audrey Wood. ©1991 by Don Wood.
By permission of Harcourt Brace & Company.

Get The "Pig-ture"?

It's guaranteed that one reading aloud of this perky pig tale won't be enough for your children. So use these ideas when you read the story again (and again) to help your little ones focus in on the piggy particulars of the illustrations. Instruct youngsters to get their peepers ready to look at the book again. Then as you introduce each pair of pigs, ask youngsters to look for ways that the pairs are alike as well as ways that they are different.

Next play a game of I Spy focusing on the hilarious details of the piggies' belongings and actions. Pick a spread of pages in the book for youngsters to look at. Then describe an object or a pig's behavior. Encourage each child to spy that object or pig. Continue during your group time until interest wanes. Then put the book in your reading center. Encourage pairs of children to play the game together during free times.

Piggies In The Mirror

Your little ones are still begging for more? Have them really pig out with this story-extension idea! As you read the story and show the pictures, encourage the children to copy the hand gestures. Next invite a volunteer to stand in front of the group. Direct the group to mirror that child's hand motions. After several children have led the group, pair youngsters for more practice with copying and coordination.

Five Times The Fun

If you've fallen in love with Don and Audrey Wood's piggies, then you're sure to love these finger puppets as well! A set of five plump piggy puppets is available from Innovative Educators Enterprises, Inc. (For price and ordering information, call toll-free 888-252-KIDS.) Use the puppets to retell the adventures in the story. Or challenge youngsters to find the matching piggies in the book; then invite them to use the puppets to make up their own stories. With these puppets, it's as if the piggies have come to life, leaped off the page, and arrived in your classroom for lots of piggy fun!

Ham It Up!

When you ask for volunteers for this dramatic activity, you're sure to have pigs aplenty! In advance, cut a giant hand shape from bulletin-board paper. If you'd like for youngsters to have props for their dramatics, prepare five sets of paper snouts and tails. To do so, cut ten 2-inch circles from pink construction paper. Draw nostrils on five of the circles for snouts, and spiral-cut five circles for tails. Put a loop of masking tape on the back of each snout and tail.

During a storytime, invite five volunteers to stand on the giant fingertips. Have each child wear a snout and tail if he desires. As you read the story, have each pig take a bow when you read the text that introduces him. Then encourage the pigs to act out the remainder of the story as read. For a variation, invite a group of five piggies to perform the actions for the following poem.

Five Little Piggies

Five little piggies standing in a row.
Five little piggies have curly tails to show.
Five little piggies have snouts for noses.
Five little piggies stand on their "toeses."
Five little piggies jump up and down.
Five little piggies turn round and round.
Five little piggies wink and blink their eyes.
Five little piggies all wave good-bye.

Porcine Portraits

Wind up your piggy escapades by making these porcine portraits that Don and Audrey Wood would surely be proud of! For each child, duplicate page 122 onto white construction paper. Paint one of each child's hands with the appropriate color of skin-toned paint. Then direct her to press her hand on the page so that each of her fingertips is beneath a pig. When the paint is dry, have the child color the pigs and use markers or stickers to add details to them. Now those are mighty fine swine!

Becky

Pattern
Use with "Porcine Portraits" on page 121.

ONCE UPON A STORY...

Once Upon A Story...

Color Farm

Mosey on into Lois Ehlert's *Color Farm* (HarperCollins Children's Books), and you'll find a menagerie of animals created by colorful shapes. After sharing the book with a small group, invite the students to identify the shapes used to create each different animal. Then, as a story extension, have your farmhands use precut construction-paper shapes, glue, and a little imagination to create their own versions of farm animals. Create labels for the animals. Mount the labels and creations on a bulletin board, complete with a barn and silo, for a "cock-a-doodle-dandy" display!

pig

Have You Seen My Cat?

This fun follow-up to a reading of *Have You Seen My Cat?* by Eric Carle (Simon & Schuster Books For Young Readers) is the "purr-fect" way to introduce your children to members of your school staff. Prior to your hunt, photocopy pictures or cut out magazine pictures of different kinds of cats. Make sure you have two copies of one of the pictures. Give each different staff member a picture, and give your teaching assistant one of the duplicate pictures. After reading the story, show your class the second duplicate picture; then explain that the group is going on a hunt to find that cat. As you approach each staff member involved, introduce him or her. Then have the students ask, "Have you seen our cat?" That person then shares his or her picture and asks, "Is this your cat?" Seeing that the cats do not match, the children say, "That is not our cat!" End your hunt by returning to your room to ask your assistant if she has seen the cat. When she shares the matching picture, celebrate by serving small cups of a cat favorite—milk! Meow!

Robin Pierce—Pre-K
Madison Oneida BOCES
Verona, NY

See the corresponding book notes on page 136.

A Busy Year

Observe the seasonal cycle of a tree with this hands-on project that is sure to keep your youngsters busy all year. Read aloud *A Busy Year* by Leo Lionni (Alfred A. Knopf Books For Young Readers) and discuss the changes in the tree through the seasons. To extend the story, make a tree in your classroom by taping several small tree branches securely to a structural floor-to-ceiling pole. Wrap brown crepe paper around the pole so that the tape is hidden and the pole resembles a tree. (As an alternative, use cement to secure one large branch in a bucket.) Invite students to decorate the tree's branches to correspond to seasonal changes. For example, attach fall leaf or apple projects, drape batting over the branches to resemble snow, hang ornaments on the tree, or tie on green crepe-paper lengths to resemble leaves. For added enjoyment invite students to join you by the tree for circle times or storytimes.

Alice M. Smith—Preschool
Delanco United Methodist Church
Delanco, NJ

I went walking. What did I see?

I saw purple flowers.

Sarah

I Went Walking

What will youngsters see when you share *I Went Walking* by Sue Williams (Harcourt Brace & Company)? They'll see a simple story about a young boy who encounters colorful animals as he takes a stroll. After reading invite your students to join you in a walk around your school. When you return trace each child's shoes onto construction paper. Have her cut out the shapes, then glue them to a large sheet of paper programmed with "I went walking. What did I see?" Write the child's response to the question. Then have her illustrate a sight from her walk. Ask each child to share her page with the class; then, if desired, assemble the pages into a book.

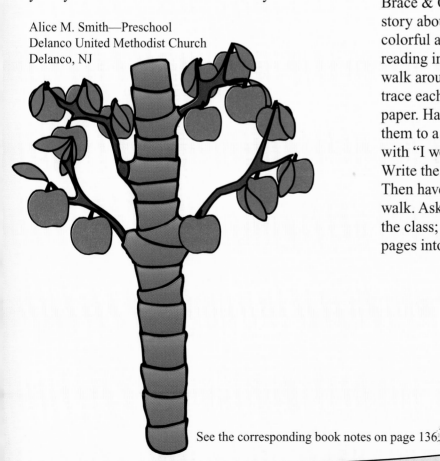

See the corresponding book notes on page 136.

Once Upon A Story...

Spider On The Floor

Even your most squeamish little ones will squeal with delight when they use these crafty spiders to follow along as you read *Spider On The Floor,* a Raffi Songs To Read® book (Crown Books For Young Readers). To make a spider, a child paints a small Styrofoam® ball black. When the paint is dry, she glues on wiggle eyes and sticks eight pipe-cleaner halves into the ball to represent the spider's legs. Have youngsters place their spiders on the floor and then on the appropriate body parts as you read the story. For added fun, listen to the recording from Raffi's album *Singable Songs For The Very Young* (Rounder Records). What creepy-crawly fun!

Carmen Carpenter—Pre-K
Highland Preschool
Raleigh, NC

Where The Wild Things Are

Since youngsters love the wild things in Maurice Sendak's classic *Where The Wild Things Are* (HarperCollins Children's Books), invite your group to create a wild thing to display in your classroom. Using an illustration in the book as a guide, cut large pieces of construction paper into simple shapes for the wild thing's body, arms, legs, and tail. Have youngsters cut or tear animal-print papers into pieces, and then glue these pieces to the wild thing's body. Assemble the cut-out pieces and add a head you've made from construction-paper shapes. Don't forget the sharp teeth, claws, and horns! Wild thing—we think we love you!

Nancy Barad—Four-Year-Olds
Bet-Yeladim Preschool And Kindergarten
Columbia, MD

See the corresponding book notes on page 137.

Henny Penny

Teach your little ones this lively song as a follow-up to reading Paul Galdone's version of *Henny Penny* (Houghton Mifflin Company). Then invite them to dramatize the story as they sing.

The Story Of Henny Penny
(sung to the tune of "The Mulberry Bush")

Henny Penny has a bump on her head,
Bump on her head, bump on her head.
Henny Penny has a bump on her head
And thinks the sky is falling.

Chorus:
The sky is falling on our heads,
On our heads, on our heads.
The sky is falling on our heads.
We must go tell the King!

Cocky Locky went along,
Went along, went along.
Cocky Locky went along.
Cock-a-doodle-doo!

Chorus

Ducky Lucky went along,….
Quack, quack, quack!

Chorus

Goosey Loosey went along,….
Honk, honk, honk!

Chorus

Turkey Lurkey went along,….
Gobble, gobble, gobble!

Chorus

Foxy Loxy tricked them all,
Tricked them all, tricked them all.
Foxy Loxy tricked them all
And took them to his cave.

Chorus

Foxes had a tasty lunch,
Tasty lunch, tasty lunch.
Foxes had a tasty lunch.
Yum! Yum! Yum!

Chorus

The King will never never know,
Never know, never know.
The King will never never know
That the sky is falling.

Peggy Moorefield and Linda Fogleman—Media Center
Gateway Education Center
Greensboro, NC

Go Away, Big Green Monster!

After a reading of *Go Away, Big Green Monster!* by Ed Emberley (Little, Brown And Company), invite youngsters to make their own portraits of the title character. Use the cut-out pages in the book to make tagboard stencils of the monster's facial features. Then have parent volunteers or an assistant help you cut out construction-paper pieces for each child. Give each child a set of the cutouts and a sheet of construction paper. Encourage students to assemble their pieces to create the monster's face, gluing each piece in place on the construction-paper background.

For a variation, cut the monster's facial features from colorful felt, and have little ones make the monster appear and disappear on your flannelboard. Your students won't want *this* activity to go away!

Patricia Harrison—Preschool
Playhouse Day Care Center
Stilwell, OK

See the corresponding book notes on page 137.

Once Upon A Story...

Jingle Bugs

Jingle all the way through this fun-filled, pop-up book by David A. Carter (Simon & Schuster Books For Young Readers). Then invite youngsters to ring in the season with their own jingle-bug ornament creations. After reading the story, turn back to the page with the envelope and remove the ornament bug. Point out the different parts of the bug: its shell, eyes, antennae, legs, and tail. Then invite each child to create an ornament bug from assorted craft items such as wiggle eyes, construction paper, and seasonal wrapping paper. Have her add a yarn-loop hanger to the bug. If desired, tie on a small jingle bell. Fold the bug; then insert it into an envelope. Encourage students to deliver the ornament bugs to their families as a holiday gift. Family members are sure to go "buggy" over these special decorations.

Mackie Rhodes
Greensboro, NC

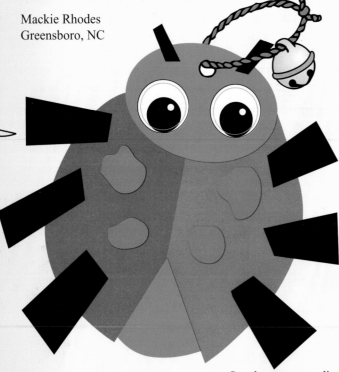

The M&M's® Brand Counting Book

This math-and-munch book will quickly become a "flavor-ite" with youngsters. Share *The M&M's® Brand Counting Book* by Barbara Barbieri McGrath (Charlesbridge Publishing, Inc.) with your class, omitting those pages that may exceed your students' understanding. Afterward have each child create a giant candy piece by stapling the rims of two paper plates together. Have the child paint the plates to correspond to his favorite color of M&M's®. When the paint is dry, glue a white lowercase *m* cutout to the center of one plate. Use the paper-plate candies for counting, sorting, and patterning activities.

Tricia O'Shea—Preschool
St. Mary's Early Childhood Center
Dumont, NJ

See the corresponding book notes on page 138.

Tacky The Penguin

Read Helen Lester's *Tacky The Penguin* (Houghton Mifflin Company) to discover that being unique has its advantages. Explain that Tacky is *unique*—he does not look or act exactly like any other penguin. Then discuss the similarities and differences between Tacky and the other penguins. Help each child name something unique about himself.

As a follow-up to your discussion, invite students to make unique penguins. Demonstrate how to make a penguin by using your fingers to spread thinned glue onto a plastic soda bottle, and then pressing torn construction-paper pieces onto the bottle to make a black-and-white penguin. Add wiggle eyes. Next brainstorm ways that each child could vary this method to make a unique penguin. For example, a child might add stickers to his penguin or choose unusual colors for his penguin's body.

Mackie Rhodes

Sebastian's Trumpet

"Try and try again" is the message of this charming story by Miko Imai (Candlewick Press). As you arrive at the end of the story, have youngsters raise imaginary trumpets to their lips and join Sebastian in tooting out the tune of "Happy Birthday." Discuss Sebastian's frustration—then elation—as he learned to blow his trumpet. Then provide time for volunteers to share their personal frustration-to-elation stories with the class.

See the corresponding book notes on page 138.

Once Upon A Story...

Sylvester And The Magic Pebble

Wishing for a story that appeals to older preschoolers? Read aloud *Sylvester And The Magic Pebble* by William Steig (Simon & Schuster Children's Division). After sharing this story about a young donkey who wishes on a magic pebble, invite youngsters to make their own magical-looking pebbles. Provide a bag of pebbles (from the landscaping department of your local home-improvement store). Invite each child to choose a pebble, and then decorate it with paint and glitter. Then use the class collection of magic pebbles for some magical math fun! Ask students to count the pebbles or sort them by size, color, or texture.

adapted from an idea by Patty Welsh Cox
Austin Elementary
Abilene, TX

The Teeny-Tiny Woman

After a reading of *The Teeny-Tiny Woman* by Paul Galdone (Clarion Books), engage in some great big fun with a Teeny-Tiny Day! Invite each child to bring a teeny-tiny object to school for show-and-tell. Serve teeny-tiny snacks (raisins, mini pretzels, and chocolate chips) with teeny-tiny beverages (juice in three-ounce paper cups). Walk everywhere taking teeny-tiny steps. Talk in teeny-tiny voices. Round out your Teeny-Tiny Day with a storytime that includes other books on the teeny-tiny theme, such as *George Shrinks* by William Joyce or *Thumbelina* by Hans Christian Andersen.

Debi Luke—Pre-K
Fairmount Nursery School
Syracuse, NY

See the corresponding book notes on page 139.

Saturday Night At The Dinosaur Stomp

Dance into storytime with a reading of *Saturday Night At The Dinosaur Stomp* by Carol Diggory Shields (Candlewick Press). Then follow up this energetic look at bebopping dinosaurs by holding a Dinosaur Stomp of your own! To prepare for this "dino-mite" musical sight, have each child create a pair of dinosaur feet to wear. Give each child two paper plates, cut as shown. Encourage her to color the tops of her paper feet and then glue a construction-paper triangle claw to each toe. Attach each child's dinosaur feet to the tops of her shoes with large pieces of rolled duct tape. Put on some lively music and let the Stomp begin!

Pancakes For Breakfast

Share the wordless book *Pancakes For Breakfast* by Tomie dePaola (Harcourt Brace & Company). Then follow up with some flapjack fun that will have your little ones practicing hand-eye coordination and balance. In advance cut an even number of identical circles from burlap; then sew or hot-glue two circles together to make each sturdy pancake. Provide a few spatulas, and encourage youngsters to take turns walking, tiptoeing, racing, or dancing while holding a burlap pancake on a spatula. For an added challenge, ask two classmates to pass a pancake back and forth on their spatulas.

Beth Marie Hagan—Three-Year-Olds
Jacksonville, FL

See the corresponding book notes on page 139.

Once Upon A Story...

The Little Mouse, The Red Ripe Strawberry, And The Big Hungry Bear

Oh, what's a mouse to do when there's a hungry bear just waiting to eat his strawberry? Share it, of course! After sharing this charming story by Don and Audrey Wood (Child's Play [International] Ltd.), ask your little ones to help make a giant strawberry for your class. Have the children take turns sponge-painting a large bulletin-board-paper or poster-board strawberry shape. When the paint is dry, add a paper stem; then ask youngsters to glue black buttons to the strawberry. Next ask your group how they would hide such a giant strawberry from a hungry bear. Record their ideas and display them with the berry. Don't forget to serve some real red, ripe strawberries for a snack!

Cindy Lawson—Preschool
The Children's Educare Center
Ft. Wayne, IN

I can stomp my feet. Can you?

Tobias

From Head To Toe

Get ready to move from head to toe with this busy book by Eric Carle (HarperCollins Juvenile Books). It won't be an ordinary storytime when you read this story! That's because you'll want to invite your little ones to improve not just their listening skills but their motor skills also as they move along. After your storytime, keep the learning moving by making a class book based on the text. To make the book, ask each child to think of a movement; then take his picture moving in that way. Mount each child's developed photo onto a piece of construction paper. Program the page as shown with the child's name and movement. Laminate the pages to protect the photos; then bind the pages between covers. Get ready to move again with your new *Head To Toe* title!

Karen Bryant—Pre-K
Miller Elementary School
Warner Robins, GA

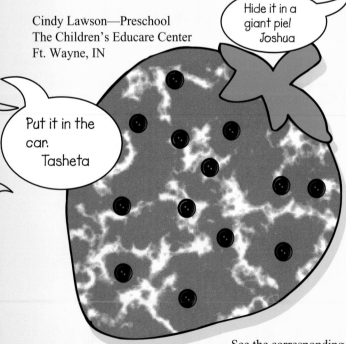

Hide it in a giant pie! Joshua

Put it in the car. Tasheta

See the corresponding book notes on page 140.

Inch By Inch

Invite your little ones to inch over to your group area for this classic story by Leo Lionni (Mulberry Books). Prior to your storytime, collect a class supply (plus extras) of worm-shaped Styrofoam® packing pieces. Use a marker to add two dot eyes to one piece so that it resembles a worm. Introduce your class to the inchworm; then read aloud the story. After the story, demonstrate how to use the worm to measure objects. Give each child a worm; then allow time for the children to explore the lengths of classroom items. Later invite each child to dip his worm in green paint and to print worm shapes over a paper letter *I* or over a paper worm shape.

Jill Beattie—Four- And Five-Year-Olds
Apple Place Nursery School
Chambersburg, PA

Noah's Ark

Your little ones are sure to enjoy Lucy Cousins's colorful illustrations in this easy-to-understand version of the story of Noah and the flood (Candlewick Press). After sharing the story, invite youngsters to visit a center to match animal pairs just like Noah does. To prepare the center, collect a variety of animal-shaped cookie cutters. Trace each shape onto craft foam twice; then cut the shapes out. Use a permanent marker to label each shape. Put the shapes in a center along with a box that has been cut to resemble an ark. Chances are good—especially on rainy days—that youngsters will visit the center two by two to match the animal pairs and put them in the ark!

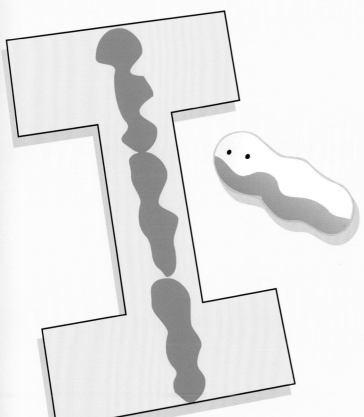

See the corresponding book notes on page 140.

Once Upon A Story...

Mouse Count

Ten little mice *almost* become a snake's dinner in this mathematical tale by Ellen Stoll Walsh (Voyager Picture Book). After sharing this book, follow up with a numeral-recognition and counting activity. Bring in a clear glass jar and ten toy mice (or mice cut from construction paper or felt). On each index card in a class set, print a numeral from 1 to 10; then pass out the cards. Ask a child to role-play the hungry snake from the story. Have her identify the numeral printed on her card. Then encourage her to come up and count the corresponding number of mice into the jar. Continue until each child has had a turn. S-s-s-s-simply s-s-s-super!

Jaime Latimer—Four-Year-Olds
Carousel Of Children Day Care Center
Monticello, NY

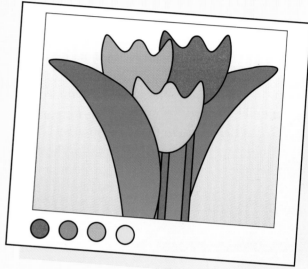

See the corresponding book notes on page 141.

Is It Red? Is It Yellow? Is It Blue?

Your little ones will be seeing red—and lots of other colors—with this extension of Tana Hoban's photo-illustrated book *Is It Red? Is It Yellow? Is It Blue?* (William Morrow And Company, Inc.). To prepare, purchase as many different colors of sticky dots as possible; then gather a class supply of white paper. Have each child find and then cut out a magazine picture of his choice. Have him glue the picture to a sheet of white paper. Then invite him to identify the colors he sees in the picture and affix the corresponding sticky dots below it. Display the finished projects on a bulletin board, or bind them together and add a cover to make your own version of Tana Hoban's book.

Cindi Zsittnik
Surrey Child Care Center
Hagerstown, MD

Order books on-line.
www.themailbox.com

The Very Lonely Firefly

Before sharing *The Very Lonely Firefly* by Eric Carle (The Putnam Publishing Group), make this storytime prop to invite your youngsters to listen to this delightful story. To make a firefly, hot-glue a white or yellow bulb from a string of outdoor Christmas lights to one end of a wide craft stick. Hot-glue three same-colored pom-poms to the center of the craft stick (to make the firefly's body); then add one different-colored pom-pom at the end (to make the firefly's head). Glue on two wiggle eyes, a pair of pipe-cleaner antennae, and six short pipe-cleaner legs. Cut two ovals from cellophane; then glue them to the back of the craft stick to make the firefly's wings.

At storytime, introduce youngsters to your firefly. Have the firefly invite the children to listen to a story about a time when he was very lonely. Afterward, place the firefly in your art center. Invite students to use the craft materials of their choice to create their own fireflies. Display their creations with the title "Not-So-Lonely Fireflies."

Bonnie Elizabeth Vontz
Ansonia, CT

Whose Shoe?

Hockey skates, ballet slippers, cleats—find them all in Margaret Miller's *Whose Shoe?* (Greenwillow Books). After reading this book, invite your youngsters to wear their own favorite footwear to school one day. Have a camera handy so you can make a class book titled "Whose Shoes?" Simply take a photo of each child's feet clad in her fancy footwear. Then take a photo of each child's face. (Or use school photos instead).

To make each page of the book, cut out a large shoe shape from construction paper. Print the question "Whose shoes?" on the toe portion of the shoe cutout. Glue a photo of a child's footwear onto a slightly larger piece of construction paper. Then tape the top edge only of the paper next to the question. Flip the paper up and glue the picture of the child underneath. Bind all the shoe-shaped pages together and add a cover. A book about our feet? Neat!

Sheryl Banser—Early Childhood
   Special Education
Julia S. Molloy Center
Morton Grove, IL

See the corresponding book notes on page 141.

Book Notes

After reading each of the books mentioned below and on pages 124 and 125, send home copies of the corresponding note.

I looked for shapes in

Color Farm
by Lois Ehlert.

What shapes do you see?

Have you seen

Have You Seen My Cat?

by Eric Carle?

Let's go to the library to look for another book by Eric Carle.

Two mice learn about the seasons when they spend a year with their tree friend, Woody.

Our story today was **A Busy Year** by Leo Lionni.

Let's go look at trees. Ask me to tell you how they change.

We read
I Went Walking
by Sue Williams.

I saw a black cat,
a brown horse,
a red cow,
a green duck,
a pink pig,
and a yellow dog.

Let's go walking.
I wonder what we'll see!

Book Notes

After reading each of the books mentioned below and on pages 126 and 127, send home copies of the corresponding note.

Today we read

Spider On The Floor.

I'll show you my spider—but watch out!

It likes to climb!

We went wild over

Where The Wild Things Are.

Let's go to the library and find more books by Maurice Sendak.

Do you know the story of

Henny Penny?

Today we sang a song about it and pretended we were the characters.

Maybe we could act out another favorite story together!

Do you like scary things?

Let me tell you about

Go Away, Big Green Monster!

by Ed Emberley.

(It's OK. This monster isn't too scary, and it goes away when you tell it to!)

Book Notes

After reading each of the books mentioned below and on pages 128 and 129, send home copies of the corresponding note.

We went "buggy" over the pop-up book

JINGLE BUGS

by
David A. Carter.

Let's sing a round of "Jingle Bells" on our way to the library to find more pop-up books.

©1998 The Education Center, Inc.

Mmm, Mmmm!

THE M&M's®
BRAND
COUNTING
BOOK

by
Barbara Barbieri McGrath
is tasty!

Let's count, sort, and pattern the candies in a small bag of M&M's®.

©1998 The Education Center, Inc.

We read
Tacky The Penguin
by Helen Lester.

It's pretty neat to be unique. Let's talk about what makes me special.

©1998 The Education Center, Inc.

In
Sebastian's
Trumpet

by Miko Imai,
a little bear practices and practices until he can blow his trumpet.
Let me toot my own horn—ask me to tell you about something I do well!

©1998 The Education Center, Inc.

Book Notes

After reading each of the books mentioned below and on pages 130 and 131, send home copies of the corresponding note.

If I had a magic wishing pebble—like the donkey in

Sylvester And The Magic Pebble

by William Steig—

I would wish for you to read me a story!

Today we read

The Teeny-Tiny Woman

by Paul Galdone.

Let's look for something teeny-tiny that I can take to school for show-and-tell.

The dinosaurs danced the bump and the twist in

Saturday Night At The Dinosaur Stomp

by Carol Diggory Shields.

Let's put on some music and dance like dinosaurs!

Pancakes For Breakfast

by Tomie dePaola

is a story without any words. Ask me to tell you what happens in the pictures.

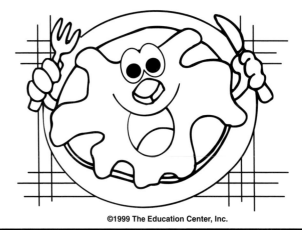

Book Notes

After reading each of the books mentioned below and on pages 132 and 133, send home copies of the corresponding note.

Our story today was

The Little Mouse, The Red Ripe Strawberry, And The Big Hungry Bear

by Don and Audrey Wood.

Ask me what the mouse does with his strawberry.

Let's cut a snack in half and share it!

We got moving today when we read

FROM HEAD TO TOE

by Eric Carle.

I can stomp my feet. Can you?

I can spin around. Can you?

How can you move? I can do it, too!

Inch By Inch

is a story about a smart inchworm.

Let's inch down to the library to find more stories by Leo Lionni.

Today we read

Noah's Ark

with pictures by Lucy Cousins.

Noah finds pairs of animals. I bet I can find pairs of things, too!

Book Notes

After reading each of the books mentioned below and on pages 134 and 135, send home copies of the corresponding note.

Today we read

MOUSE COUNT

by Ellen Stoll Walsh.

Ask me how the mice got away from the snake!

We found lots of colors when we read

Is It Red? Is It Yellow? Is It Blue?

by Tana Hoban.

Let's look for colors on our way to the library to find another book with pictures by Tana Hoban.

Whose Shoe?

by Margaret Miller

is a neat book with pictures of shoes.

Let's count how many shoes I have, then count how many you have.

There's a happy surprise at the end of

The Very Lonely Firefly

by Eric Carle.

Let's look for fireflies this evening, and I'll tell you all about the story.

Magical Ideas For Using Book Notes

Capture parents' attention with these bright ideas for using the notes that accompany the books featured in "Once Upon A Story."

by Lori Kent

Now Reading:

We read
I Went Walking
by Sue Williams.

I saw a black cat,
a brown horse,
a red cow,
a green duck,
a pink pig,
and a yellow dog.

Let's go walking.
I wonder what we'll see!

Make a journal for each child by stapling a number of blank pages between construction-paper covers. Each time a featured book is read, invite each child to color a copy of the corresponding book note, then glue it onto a blank page in his journal. If desired write in each child's journal as he dictates something about the story, such as a description of his favorite part or his favorite character. Send the journal home as each new page is completed, along with a request that a parent initial the page and return the journal the following day.

Keep parents posted on the books you are reading in class with these book-note posters. Enlarge a book note to poster size; then color it. Display the poster in your hallway or on the door of your classroom with a sign titled "Now Reading." Parents are sure to take a look at this literary marquee.

Create a necklace for each child by punching a hole just below the resealable zipper on each side of a small plastic bag. Thread a length of ribbon through the holes; then tie the ends together to create a necklace. Personalize the bags. After reading a story, have each child color a copy of the corresponding book note. Put the note in the bag of the child's necklace; then reseal the top. Have each child wear his necklace home. Request that a parent sign the back of each child's book note, then return it to the necklace so that the child can wear it to school the next day. If desired reward each child who returns his note with a small prize or sticker.

Parents are sure to ask about the book of the day when youngsters wear these headbands. After reading a featured story, have each child color a copy of the corresponding note. Then have her glue the note to the center of a construction-paper headband. Staple the band to fit the child's head.

This book-note story line provides a visual way for parents and children to keep track of the books you've read. Attach a length of adding-machine tape or a strip of bulletin-board paper to a wall in an area of your room or hallway that parents pass by often. Each time you read a book, glue a copy of the corresponding book note to the story line; then record the date.

NURSERY-RHYME UNITS

Little Boy Blue

Hire your youngsters to help this classic nursery-rhyme napper round up some wandering farm animals. In the process, they'll learn about the opposites *in* and *out* quicker than you can say, "Little Boy Blue!"

by Lucia Kemp Henry

Little Boy Blue, come blow your horn!
The sheep's in the meadow; the cow's in the corn.
Where is the boy who looks after the sheep?
He's under the haystack, fast asleep.

A Sleepy Farmhand

Why is this sleepy boy feeling blue? It's because his nap has kept him from doing his farm chores! In advance of a group time, duplicate the animal patterns on pages 146–147. Color and cut out the patterns. Fold each pattern on the lines; then use tape to secure the short side to the labeled side.

As you introduce this rhyme, show the sheep and the cow. Ask youngsters to explain in their own words what the problem is in this rhyme and then suggest how the situation could be resolved. When your listeners are familiar with the original rhyme, introduce new animals to the rhyme. Each time you show a different combination of animals, invite youngsters to join you in modifying the original rhyme as follows:

Little Boy Blue, come blow your horn!
The [animal]'s in the meadow; the
[animal]'s in the corn.

The Ins And Outs Of Farm Life

Little Boy Blue may be sleeping, but your group won't be when it's their turn to let the animals in and out of the barn. To prepare for this singing game, use masking tape to make the outline of a square on the floor. Make sure that the square is large enough for your class to line up on its four sides to form the walls of a barn. Direct the children to stand on the tape; then give one child a plastic farm animal. As the group sings the first verse of the following song, the child walks around the outside of the barn. As the group sings the second verse, the child walks inside the barn. To continue, give another child a different animal, and have the group sing more about the ins and outs of farm life.

In And Out Of The Barn
(sung to the tune of "The Farmer In The Dell")

The [animal]'s out of the barn.
The [animal]'s out of the barn.
Heigh-ho, the derry-o;
The [animal]'s out of the barn.

The [animal] is in the barn.
The [animal] is in the barn.
Heigh-ho, the derry-o;
The [animal] is in the barn.

144

Sheep In The Meadow, Cows In The Corn

Wake up, Boy Blue! It's time to sound your horn and round up some animals! To play this outdoor game of tag, divide your class into two groups: sheep and cows. Direct both groups to stand on opposite sides of the playing area. Designate a small area to the side of the playing area as the barn. Demonstrate how to pretend to blow a toy horn or cardboard tube to announce that it's time for the animals to come home. Ask a volunteer to stand in the center of the playing area and to be Boy Blue; then give that child the horn. To play, Boy Blue "blows" his horn. On that signal, the sheep run to the meadow (the opposite side from their area) and the cows run to the corn (the opposite side from their area). Any animals tagged by Boy Blue go to the barn for one round of play. Select a new Boy Blue for each round. No sleeping on this job, Boy Blue!

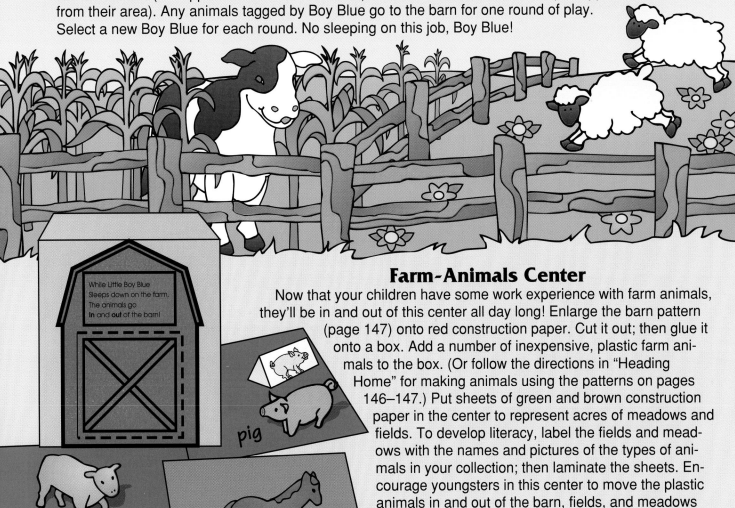

Farm-Animals Center

Now that your children have some work experience with farm animals, they'll be in and out of this center all day long! Enlarge the barn pattern (page 147) onto red construction paper. Cut it out; then glue it onto a box. Add a number of inexpensive, plastic farm animals to the box. (Or follow the directions in "Heading Home" for making animals using the patterns on pages 146–147.) Put sheets of green and brown construction paper in the center to represent acres of meadows and fields. To develop literacy, label the fields and meadows with the names and pictures of the types of animals in your collection; then laminate the sheets. Encourage youngsters in this center to move the plastic animals in and out of the barn, fields, and meadows as they play.

Heading Home

Learning at home won't be a farm chore with this game. Duplicate a class supply of the patterns on pages 146–147. Have each child color a set of the patterns; then cut them out. To make one take-home game, glue a child's barn pattern to a personalized paper lunch bag, making sure that the barn door is completely glued to the bag. Cut through the bag and pattern along the dotted lines. Insert a brad through the bag to make a latch for the barn door. Fold each animal pattern on the lines; then use tape to secure the short side to the labeled side. Tuck the animals and parent note inside the bag. This "*out*-standing" activity will remind parents that learning at home is the *in* thing to do!

Patterns

Use with "A Sleepy Farmhand" on page 144 and "Farm-Animals Center" and "Heading Home" on page 145.

Parent Letter

Dear Parent,

While Little Boy Blue sleeps down on the farm, the animals go in and out of the barn! Review the nursery rhyme below with your child. Then use the barn, the animals, and the sample directions to develop your child's problem-solving skills, language skills, and math skills. When you're finished, don't forget to let your child blow his/her own horn with pride!

Sample directions:

- How many animals are in the barn? How many are out of the barn?
- Take one animal out of the barn. Take one more. How many animals are left in the barn?
- Put the animal whose name starts with the *p* sound in the barn.
- I put one animal back in the barn. Guess which one is missing from the meadow.
- Put the animals in the barn; then take one out. Can you remember which animals are still in the barn?
- The animal I put in the barn says, "Moo." Which animal is it?

Little Boy Blue, come blow your horn!
The sheep's in the meadow; the cow's in the corn.
Where is the boy who looks after the sheep?
He's under the haystack, fast asleep.

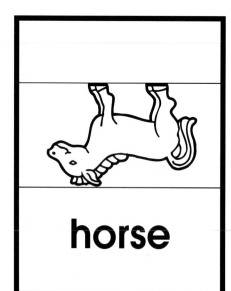

horse

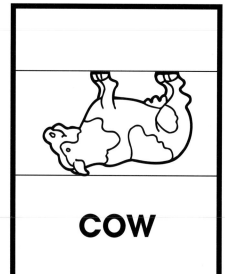

cow

cat

Use with "A Sleepy Farmhand" on page 144 and "Farm-Animals Center" and "Heading Home" on page 145.

sheep

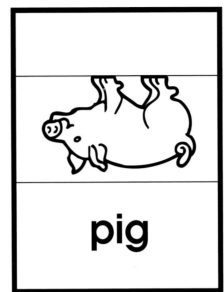

pig

chicken

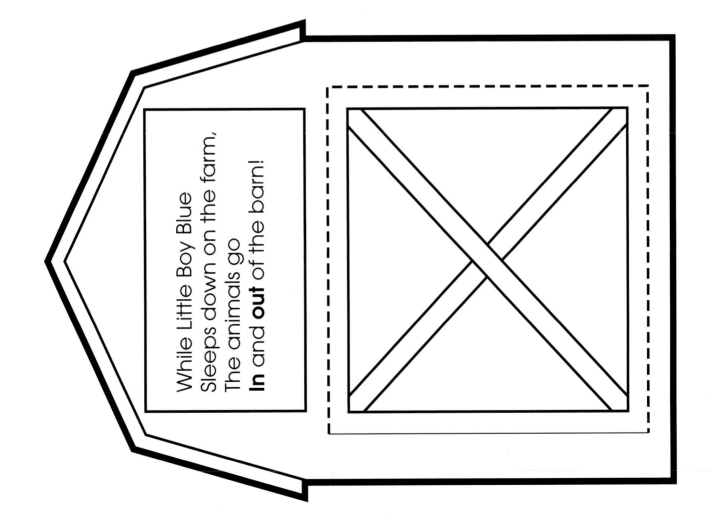

While Little Boy Blue
Sleeps down on the farm,
The animals go
In and **out** of the barn!

Hey Diddle, Diddle!

Hey diddle, diddle!
The cat and the fiddle;
The cow jumped over the moon.
The little dog laughed
To see such sport,
And the dish ran away with the spoon.

What's more likely to capture your youngsters' imaginations than a curiously musical cat, a fantastically high-flying cow, a laughing dog, and a pair of unlikely tableware runaways? It's a fact—this fantasy provides lots of learning fun!

by Lucia Kemp Henry

Fantastic Fantasy Pairs

Your youngsters are sure to detect some make-believe as they meet the characters in "Hey Diddle, Diddle." Prior to introducing the rhyme, duplicate the patterns on page 150. Color them and then cut them out on both the solid and dotted lines. During a group time, give each cutout to a different student. Recite Lines One and Two of the rhyme; then ask the children holding the cat and fiddle pieces to put them together. Repeat these steps for Line Three *(cow, moon)*. After reciting Lines Four and Five, explain that the dog needs the telescope in order to see all the fun; then ask the children holding those items to put them together. Finally repeat the steps for Line Six *(dish, spoon)*. When you've finished the rhyme, ask volunteers to tell why they think the characters are more make-believe than real.

Fact Or Fantasy?

Continue your investigation of real and make-believe with this up-and-down listening game. Read each of the questions below. Direct your children to stand up to answer a question "yes" and to sit down to indicate "no."

Can a cat meow?
Can a cat play a fiddle?

Can a cow eat grass?
Can a cow jump over the moon?

Can a dog wag its tail?
Can a dog laugh?

Can a dish and a spoon be washed?
Can a dish and a spoon run away?

Hey Diddle, Diddle; The Cat And The Fiddle

Through this activity, your youngsters will discover that music and art make great partners. Invite each child to fingerpaint while listening to country-fiddle or classical-violin music. When each child's fiddle-inspired painting is dry, have her further decorate it with cat stickers. Fiddling around with paint and music is the cat's meow!

The Cow Jumped Over The Moon

Watch your little ones jump for joy when you invite them to make moon-shaped cookies. In advance bake a batch of crescent moon–shaped cookies. (Use a cookie cutter and your favorite sugar-cookie recipe. Or cut refrigerated cookie dough into slices; then cut away a portion of one side of each slice.) To prepare a cookie treat, a child spreads white frosting onto a cookie, then adds yellow sugar sprinkles. Finally he adds a candy-corn nose and a mini-chocolate-chip eye.

The Little Dog Laughed To See Such Sport

Ask your children what the little dog saw that made him laugh out loud, and they'll quickly remind you of the cow making a moon shot. Then expand children's thinking by asking them to think of scenes involving an animal other than the cow that would tickle the little dog's funny bone—scenes such as a pig in a bubble bath or an elephant on the slide. Direct each child to draw his own silly scene; then have him dictate a sentence to describe the laughable action. Enlarge the dog character and his telescope (page 150); then mount it along with the children's pictures and the caption "The little dog laughed to see such sport!" Your youngsters are sure to laugh, as well, when they see the sights they've imagined!

The Dish Ran Away With The Spoon

Invite students to pair up at this center to match the dishes and spoons that would be most likely to run away together. To make this matching game, program a number of plastic-plate and plastic-spoon pairs with matching stickers. Store the programmed tableware in a dish rack in the center along with a colorful tablecloth so that youngsters are inspired to set a table with all the dish-and-spoon duos they can find.

Real Partners In Learning

Both parent and child will have a fantastic time when paired up to play this take-home game. Duplicate two copies of page 150 and one copy of page 151 for each child. Have each child color his shape patterns, then cut them out. Cut each of the eight shapes in half where indicated. Have the child glue the poem to a personalized, colorful paper bag and then attach star stickers. Tuck the 16 shape patterns and the parent note/directions inside the bag. Families and learning fun—now that's a match!

Patterns

Use with "Fantastic Fantasy Pairs" on page 148 and "Real Partners In Learning" on page 149.

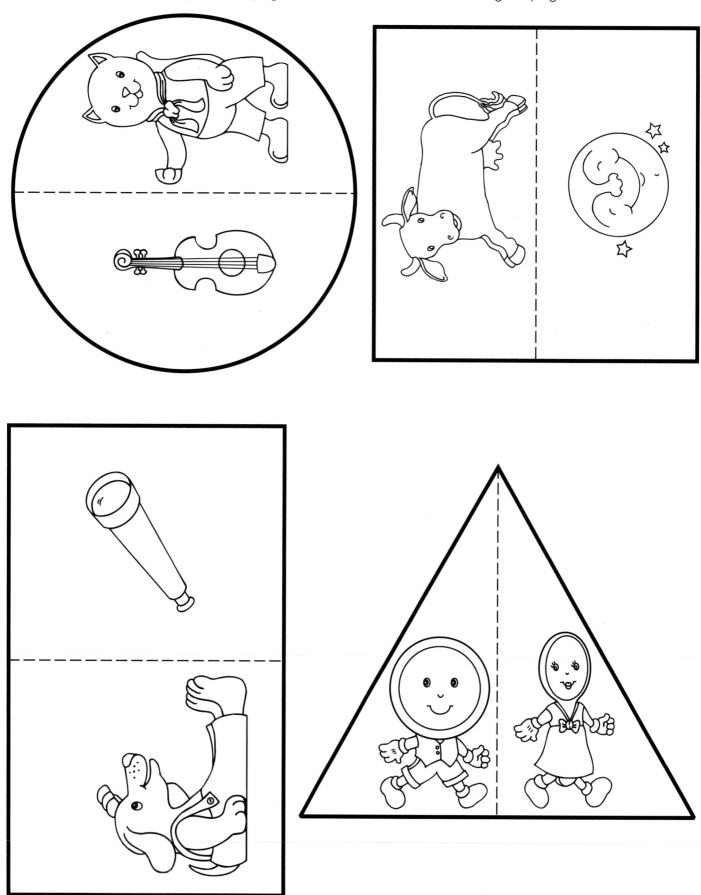

Dear Parent,

Both you and your child will have a fantastic time when you pair up to play this game. First review the nursery rhyme on the bag. Then put the bag with the 16 game pieces inside between you and your child.

To begin play, take one game piece out of the bag and put it faceup in front of you. Have your child do the same. Then take out a second piece. If that piece is *not* a shape match to your first piece, put it back in the bag. If the piece *is* a shape match, keep it. Have your child take a second piece in the same manner. Continue in this manner until either you or your child has four pairs of different shapes. The first person to have a complete set of four pairs recites the rhyme.

Hey diddle, diddle!

The cat and the fiddle;

The cow jumped over the moon.

The little dog laughed

To see such sport,

And the dish ran away with the spoon.

Humpty Dumpty

All the king's horses and all the king's men couldn't keep your youngsters from having fun with these nursery-rhyme activities that reinforce teamwork!

ideas contributed by Lucia Kemp Henry

Getting Humpty Together Again

Recite the traditional rhyme. Then pause to allow youngsters to suggest ways that they would try to mend Humpty. Next introduce the new, happier ending at the left. How's that for a quick fix?

Teamwork

When each child does his part in this activity, a whole lot of cooperative learning is sure to take place! For every four children in your class, copy the puzzle on page 154 onto a different color of construction paper. Cut the puzzles apart; then put all of the pieces into a bag. To begin the teamwork, ask each child to take a puzzle piece out of the bag. Then direct each child to find those classmates who have the same color pieces and to work with his team members to put their puzzle together. Praise every group for their cooperative work. For added fun, repeat the activity as many times as desired, challenging the children to complete the task faster and faster each time. The more you practice teamwork, the easier it gets!

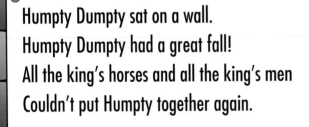

Humpty Dumpty sat on a wall.
Humpty Dumpty had a great fall!
All the king's horses and all the king's men
Couldn't put Humpty together again.

So all the king's horses and all the king's men
Went right back to the castle again,
To find a bandage, some tape, and some glue,
So they could make Humpty as good as new!

Humpty Goes Home

There'll be no sitting down on the job for Humpty when you send him home to help with learning. Once students have enjoyed the team-work activity that uses the reproducible on page 154, copy a class supply of the puzzle onto white construction paper. Give each child a copy to color and cut apart. Next have her paint a bag in which to take the puzzle home. To paint a bag, have a child use a small, rectangular block of Styrofoam® to paint red bricks onto a brown bag or gray bricks onto a white bag. When the paint is dry, have the child put her puzzle into the bag and take it home.

Humpty's Fix-It Center

Give your little ones some hands-on practice taking things apart and putting them together again at Humpty's Fix-It Center. First ask your students to help you collect items from your classroom—such as manipulatives, puzzles, and building toys—that can be "broken" (taken apart) and "fixed" (put together). Put the items in the center. Next label several self-adhesive nametags "Humpty's Fix-It Center." Attach each label to a separate apron or man's shirt. Encourage each child who takes a shift at the center to put on a uniform and to cooperate with his co-workers to put everything back together again.

All Cracked Up

Oh, no! Humpty Dumpty really *is* cracked up and needs your youngsters' help with this small-group craft project to put him back together again! To prepare for the repair, have students tear a supply of white tissue paper into pieces to resemble egg-shells. Store the torn pieces in a bowl. Next cut a large egg shape from clear Con-Tact® covering for every group of about four children. Use markers to draw a face on the slick side of each egg. For each group, remove the paper backing from the egg; then tape the egg—sticky-side up—to a table. Direct the children in each group to cover their egg with the tissue-paper eggshells. When their work is complete, remove the egg from the table; then trim around the edge. Arrange the happy Humpties on a paper brick-wall display. Hooray! Our teamwork saved the day!

Stories They'll Fall For

Little Lumpty
Written & Illustrated by Miko Imai
Published by Candlewick Press

Eggbert: The Slightly Cracked Egg
Written by Tom Ross
Illustrated by Rex Barron
Published by Paperstar

Order books on-line. www.themailbox.com

Puzzle Pattern

Use with "Teamwork" on page 152 and "Humpty Goes Home" on page 153.

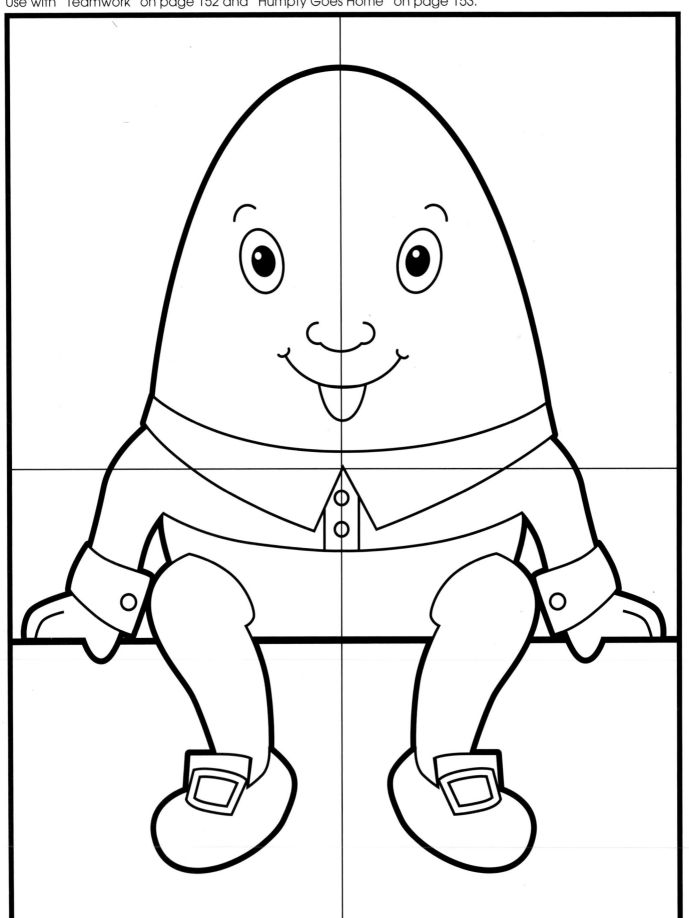

THIS LITTLE PIGGY

This little unit about these nursery-rhyme piggies will have
your youngsters saying, "We, we, we had fun" all the way home!

ideas by Lucia Kemp Henry

This little piggy went to market.
This little piggy stayed home.
This little piggy had roast beef.
This little piggy had none.
This little piggy cried,
"Wee, wee, wee" all the way home!

Busy Little Piggies

Introduce the rhyme during a group time by asking a volunteer to
remove a shoe and sock. Then gently pull on each of his toes from
largest to smallest as you recite each line of the rhyme. When the
giggling subsides, assure every child that you will find a time during
the day to demonstrate the rhyme on her toes as well.

Next invite the class to recite the rhyme with you. Stretch youngsters' thinking by asking questions about each little pig, such as,
"Why did the little pig go to market, and what did he buy there?",
"Why did this pig stay home?", and "Why did this pig cry all the way
home?" For one author's opinion of the *real* story about these pigs,
read aloud *Five Little Piggies* by David Martin (Candlewick Press).

Little Piggy Puppets

You'll hear squeals of delight from your little piggies when you invite them to make
these perky puppets. To make one, paint the bottom sides of two small paper plates
pink. Also paint a one-inch thick, circular piece of Styrofoam® pink. When the paint is
dry, staple the plates together, sandwiching two pink paper triangles between the plates
for the pig's ears. Fold down the ears. Trim off a portion of the plates as shown to create an opening. Glue the Styrofoam® nose and two wiggle eyes onto the puppet. Complete the puppet by gluing two black paper circles onto the nose.

When each child has made a puppet, incorporate them into your group-time review
of the rhyme. Invite five children to sit with their puppets in front of the group. As the
remainder of the class chants the rhyme, have a different child hold up his puppet for
each line of the poem. Encourage the fifth child to run with his puppet away from the
group. As a variation, modify the rhyme to include the children's names. For example,
"Joshua's little piggy went to market. Margaret's little piggy stayed home."

155

"Piggly Wigglies"

With their piggy puppets in hand (see "Little Piggy Puppets"), youngsters are sure to go hog-wild over this playful action poem.

The Piggy Wiggle

This little piggy shakes a wiggle, waggle, wiggy.
This little piggy sways to and fro.

This little piggy jumps a jiggle, jaggle, jiggy.
This little piggy claps high and low.

This little piggy hops a higgle, haggle, higgy.
This little piggy touches knees and toes.

This little piggy turns a tiggle, taggle, tiggy.
This little piggy bows down so low.

Pass The Piggy

Continue the movement fun with one of the piggy puppets (see "Little Piggy Puppets") and this game idea. Seat youngsters in a circle. Give one of the puppets (or any toy pig you have on hand) to one child. To play one round, the group recites the traditional rhyme. As each line is recited, the pig is passed from one child to the next. When the last line is said, replace the word *cried* with an action word such as *ran* or *tiptoed*. The child who receives the pig on the last pass gets up and moves accordingly once around the circle.

Read, Read, Read All The Way Home

This class book adapted from the original rhyme goes all the way home so that parents can participate in the piggy fun. To prepare the pages, cut a class supply of white paper circles plus two extra. Program one circle with the traditional rhyme. Program another with the phrase "These little piggies said, 'Read, read, read' all the way home!" Also include on this page directions to parents to read the class book and return it the next day. To complete each of the remaining pages, write as each child dictates his completion to the phrase, "This little piggie…" Then have him illustrate his sentence. Bind the pages—rhyme first, student-illustrated pages next, and parent directions last—between same-sized pink construction-paper circles. Title the cover; then add paper ears and a foam-board nose covered with pink paper. Add details to the cover with markers. Parents and children are sure to enjoy looking at the "pig-tures" and reading the book together!

"Pig-ture" Books

This Little Piggy
This book is shaped like a foot, and when you wiggle the toes, up pop piggies!
Illustrated by Jane Manning
Published by HarperCollins Juvenile Books

This Little Piggy
Written by Nicholas Heller
Illustrated by Sonja Lamut
Published by Greenwillow Books

Pat-A-Cake, Pat-A-Cake, Baker's Man

Pat-a-cake, pat-a-cake, baker's man.
Bake me some skills as fast as you can.
Let's sort and sequence and learn the letter B.
Learning is fun for you and me!

by Lucia Kemp Henry

Pat-a-cake, pat-a-cake, baker's man.
Bake me a cake as fast as you can.
Pat it and prick it and mark it with a *B*.
Put it in the oven for baby and me!

Bakery Cakes

The batch of sorting, patterning, and sequencing opportunities that the patterns on page 161 provide really take the cake! To prepare, duplicate page 161. Choose three colors of crayons; then color one cake on each row with each different color of crayon. Cut apart the cards.

During a group time, arrange the cakes in random fashion. Ask a volunteer to be your partner; then chant and pat hands with the child in traditional pat-a-cake fashion. Invite the children to recite the rhyme with you as they also clap and tap their thighs in a repetitive rhythm. Once your group is familiar with the rhyme, ask them to first help you sort the cakes into those with the uppercase *B*, the lowercase *b*, and no letter. Then sort the cakes by color, size, or type. Pattern the cakes by color. Finally, sequence the cakes by size. You're really baking up basic skills now!

One, Two, Three, Eat!

This song will help your little bakers see that making a cake is as easy as one, two, three! Pat it, prick it, and mark it with a *B?* No, just mix, bake, and frost. A scrumptious sequence!

Baking Cakes
(sung to the tune of "Short'nin' Bread")

Every little baker loves [mixing, mixing].
Every little baker loves [mixing] cakes.

I can make a cake! You can, too.
Listen and you'll know just what to do.

Repeat the song three times, replacing the action word with baking, frosting, *and then* eating.

Take-Home Cakes

This take-home activity reinforces your group-time sorting and sequencing experiences. For each child, duplicate the parent note and cake patterns (pages 160–161). Have each child color his parent note, cut it out, and then glue it to a paper bag as shown. Have each child choose three different colors of crayons. Direct him to color one cake on each row with each different color of crayon. Cut out the cards. Have each child put his cards in his bag; then fold the bag and tape it closed. Send the materials home for each child and his parent to enjoy together. It doesn't take a baker's dozen to complete a recipe in home learning—it only takes two!

Cake-Baking Aprons

Prepare several of these aprons; then "cut the apron strings" and send youngsters off to bake some imaginary and real cakes of their own (as described in the following ideas). To make one apron, fold two corners of a 26" x 18" kitchen towel toward (but not completely to) the towel's center. Then fold the towel down as shown. Stitch the folded towel edges in place. Center a piece of 28" ribbon across the top; then fold the ribbon upward at the edges of the apron. Stitch the ribbon in place on the apron; then stitch the ends of the ribbon in place to create a neck band. Stitch a 43" piece of ribbon across the middle of the towel to create a waistband tie for the apron. Encourage each child to wear an apron while completing the remaining activities described in this unit.

Playtime Baking

Here's the recipe for a dramatic-play center that has many layers of fun. To prepare your housekeeping kitchen for cake baking, fill the area with baking gear and gadgets, such as plastic mixing bowls, spoons, rolling pins, measuring cups, empty frosting containers, spreading knives, and circular cake pans. Next, cut several Styrofoam® circles to fit inside each of the cake pans; then cut circles the same size as the Styrofoam® circles from various colors of felt. Encourage youngsters to use the foam cake layers and felt frosting to create fabulous faux cakes.

Basic-Skills Baking Center

Now that you've created a dramatic-play center for baking, you'll want to add spice to your math center as well with these ideas.

Sorting

Have youngsters sort empty cake-mix boxes, frosting containers, and round and square pans.

Patterning

Glue paper cupcake liners to tagboard strips to create patterns. Provide an additional supply of liners for youngsters to use to copy and extend the patterns.

Size Sequencing

Provide cake pans, spoons, and measuring cups for youngsters to sequence by size. For novice sequencers, trace the outlines of the equipment in sequential order onto tagboard.

Mark It With A *B*

Mark these cakes with the letters of the alphabet; then bake up letter recognition in a language center. To prepare, use correction fluid to mask the letters on a copy of page 161. Then make six copies of the cake patterns on various colors of construction paper. Label the cards with different uppercase and lowercase letters of the alphabet. Cut the cards apart; then store them in an empty cake-mix box. Place the box and a baking pan in a language center. Encourage some of these tasty ideas:

- Sort the cakes into the pan by uppercase and lowercase letters.
- Match the cakes by letter. Then recite the traditional rhyme, inserting the selected letter.
- Sequence the cakes.

Icing On The Cake

Complete your unit with a hands-on review of the steps in baking a cake–or in this case, cakes! Invite your group to carefully examine a box of cake mix to find the name, flavor, and most important, the directions. Then ask them to help you mix the batter, and then pour it into cupcake liners. Bake according to the directions. When the cupcakes have cooled, have each child frost one. Help her use her finger to trace the initial of her first name into the frosting. Recite the traditional rhyme again, this time inserting the child's name and initial. Don't forget the last step— eating!

Parent Note

Use with "Take-Home Cakes" on page 158.

Dear Parent,

It doesn't take a baker's dozen to complete a recipe in home learning. It only takes two—you and your child! Ask your child to join you in reciting the traditional rhyme "Pat-A-Cake," shown on this bag. Then take the cake cards out of the bag. Help your child with these activities:

- Sort the cakes by size, color, type, and uppercase/lowercase/no letter.
- Pattern the cakes by color.
- Sequence the cakes by size from smallest to largest or largest to smallest.

You'll be baking up a batch of basic skills in no time!

Pat-a-cake, pat-a-cake, baker's man.

Bake me a cake as fast as you can.

Pat it and prick it and mark it with a _B_.

Put it in the oven for baby and me!

©The Education Center, Inc. • THE MAILBOX® • Preschool • Dec/Jan 1998–99

Use with "Bakery Cakes" on page 157, "Take-Home Cakes" on page 158, and "Mark It With A *B*" on page 159.

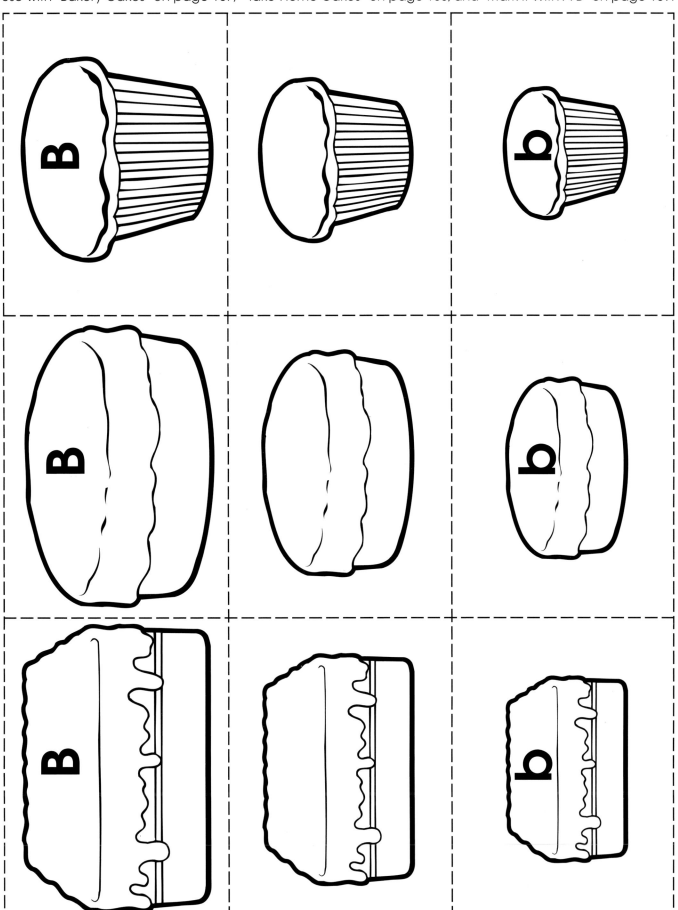

Rub-A-Dub-Dub

Rub-a-dub-dub,
Three men in a tub;
And who do you think they be?
The butcher, the baker,
The candlestick maker;
And all of them gone to sea.

Adventures in nursery rhyme land, whether on land or sea, are always just right for preschool scholars. Set sail on a voyage of learning about careers and counting with the butcher, the baker, and the candlestick maker.

by Lucia Kemp Henry

Three At Sea

Invite your classroom crew to help you launch an oceangoing tub with a career-minded trio aboard. In advance, duplicate the patterns on page 166 onto white construction paper. Color the patterns; then cut them out. As you introduce the rhyme, have three children put the butcher, the baker, and the candlestick maker inside a small plastic tub. Once your group is familiar with the rhyme, remove the original trio from the tub; then introduce three new seaworthy workers. As you recite the rhyme again, change the word *men* to *helpers,* and introduce the flagger, the sailor, and the furniture maker. Repeat the rhyme again as you introduce the doctor, the painter, and the ice-cream maker. Finally, show all nine characters at once. Invite three children at a time to each select a helper to put in the tub. Have the group say the new rhyme. Anchors aweigh!

Rub-A-Dub, A Sailing Tub!

Your little mates are sure to jump aboard this fantasy sailing ship. Transform a large tub or plastic wading pool into a ship by duct-taping a long cardboard tube (from a roll of wrapping paper) to the side. Attach a bulletin-board-paper sail to the mast. Float the boat in an open area of your classroom; then fill it with a number of career-themed hats and outfits. Encourage trios of youngsters to choose a career and board the boat. Wish them "bon voyage" and send them out to sea!

Three Friends In The Tub

Use the fantasy ship described in "Rub-A-Dub, A Sailing Tub!" as the centerpiece for this activity. (If you did not make the ship, put a hoop or circular piece of bulletin-board paper on the floor to represent the sailing tub.) To begin, seat the class in a circle around the boat; then ask a trio of volunteer sailors to stand inside the boat. Have the group recite the variation of the traditional rhyme (right) to include the names of the three onboard buddies. Continue with new sets of sailors until every child has gone out to sea.

Rub-a-dub-dub,
Three friends in a tub;
And who do you think they be?
There's [child's name], and
    [child's name], and [child's name], too;
And all of them gone to sea!

Sailors On A Water-Table Sea

Give your water table a nautical twist that promotes counting skills and numeral recognition. Gather a supply of small plastic people figures and different-sized plastic food tubs. Use a permanent marker to write a numeral on each tub. Encourage youngsters to count the correct number of plastic people into the tubs. Which tubs have more? Which have less? Which have the same? Rub-a-dub-dub, counting is fun!

Sail Away Home

Count on this take-home activity to launch some number practice. To make one for a child to take home, duplicate pages 164 and 165. Have the child color the patterns. Cut them out. Trim the flap off a legal-sized envelope; then glue the tub to the front of the envelope. Tuck the parent note and game pieces inside. Send the materials home so that the parent and child can set out on a voyage of learning together.

Dear Parent,
    Rub-a-dub-dub! It's fun to count sailors...
your child to help you recite the tradi...
put the sailors, flags, and tub o...
• Ask your child to pick a fl...
• Put a number of sailors in t...
find...
• Have...
count...
tak...
Or h...
...nting.

Rub-a-dub-dub,
Three men in a tub;
And who do you think they be?
The butcher, the baker,
The candlestick maker;
And all of them gone to sea.

163

Patterns
Use with "Sail Away Home" on page 163.

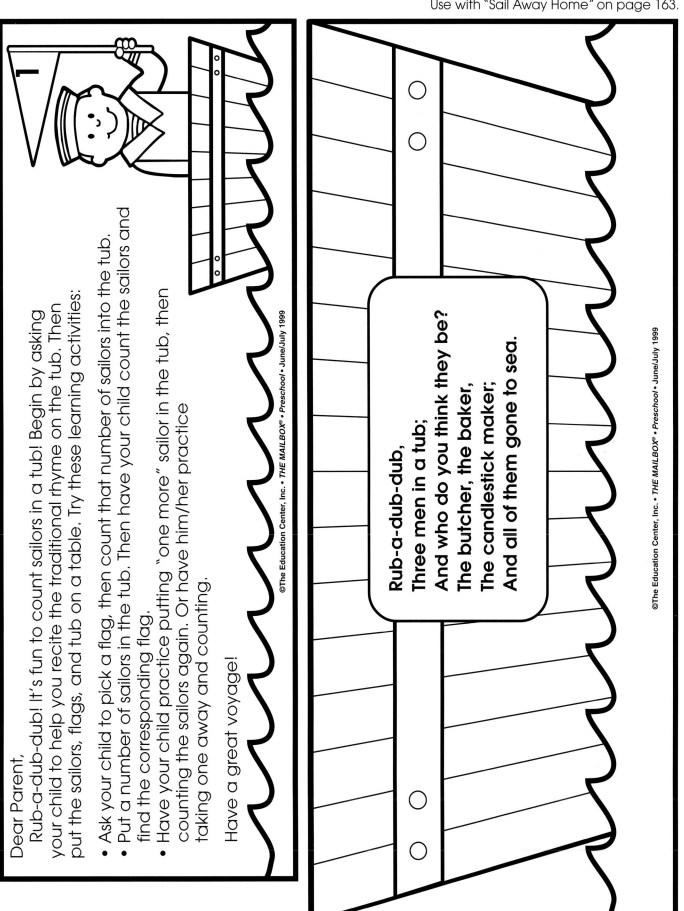

Dear Parent,
Rub-a-dub-dub! It's fun to count sailors in a tub! Begin by asking your child to help you recite the traditional rhyme on the tub. Then put the sailors, flags, and tub on a table. Try these learning activities:

• Ask your child to pick a flag, then count that number of sailors into the tub.
• Put a number of sailors in the tub. Then have your child count the sailors and find the corresponding flag.
• Have your child practice putting "one more" sailor in the tub, then counting the sailors again. Or have him/her practice taking one away and counting.

Have a great voyage!

©The Education Center, Inc. • *THE MAILBOX®* • *Preschool* • June/July 1999

Rub-a-dub-dub,
Three men in a tub;
And who do you think they be?
The butcher, the baker,
The candlestick maker;
And all of them gone to sea.

©The Education Center, Inc. • *THE MAILBOX®* • *Preschool* • June/July 1999

Patterns

Use with "Three At Sea" on page 162.

butcher

baker

candlestick maker

flagger

sailor

furniture maker

doctor

painter

ice-cream maker

It's Circle Time!

IT'S CIRCLE TIME!

Birthday Whoop-De-Do!

Have a birthday to celebrate? Then start the day out on a happy note with this birthday song. In advance personalize a party horn for each child. During a group time, give each child a horn; then invite the birthday child to stand in front of the class. Lead your little ones in singing the following song; then have them blow their horns at the end of the song. Collect the horns; then store them in a gift-wrapped box for use during future birthday celebrations.

Today's A Special Day
(sung to the tune of
"Head, Shoulders, Knees, And Toes")

Today's a special day for you.
Just for you!
Today's a special day for you.
Just for you!
You're one year older.
Whoop-de, whoop-de-do!
Happy birthday!
Hooray for you!
Whoop-de-do!   *(Blow horn.)*

Lisa Leonardi
Norfolk, MA

Ten Red Apples

Seeing a worm on one of these apples won't spoil the fun of this fingerplay and numeral-recognition activity. To prepare, tape one apple-shaped cutout to each of ten craft sticks. Write a different numeral from 1 to 10 on each of the apples. Then write the corresponding number word on each craft stick. Bend a green pipe cleaner to resemble a worm. Tape the worm to the back of an apple so that it is hidden. During a group time, ask ten volunteers to each hold an apple. Have the remaining children join you in reciting the following fingerplay; then have them guess the apple that has the worm by naming its number.

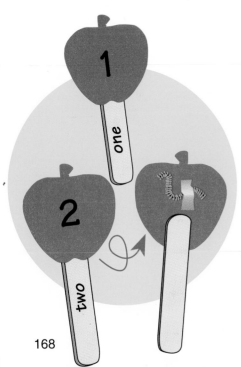

Ten red apples growing on a tree.   *(Hold up ten fingers.)*
Five for you and five for me.   *(Show one hand; then the other.)*
There's one little worm that you can't see. *(Wiggle one finger.)*
Where, oh where, could that little worm be? *(Hold hands out questioning.)*

Karen Eiben—Three- And Four-Year-Olds
The Kids' Place Child Development Center, LaSalle, IL

Colorful Sheep

Your little lambs will enjoy reviewing colors as they sing about Baa, Baa, Black Sheep and his colorful friends. To prepare, cut a sheep shape from black and other colors of felt. Also cut three bag shapes from felt. Display the black sheep and the three bags on your flannelboard. Lead students in singing "Baa, Baa, Black Sheep" to the tune of "Twinkle, Twinkle, Little Star." Repeat the song, displaying a different-colored sheep and substituting the corresponding color word each time you sing.

Kathleen Soman—Two-Year-Olds & Pre–K
Kids World, Holiday, FL

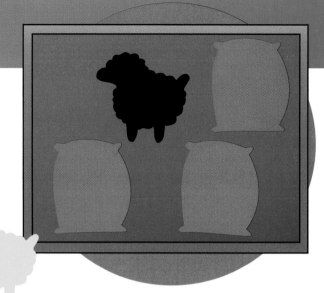

Birthday Pies

These birthday pies may not tickle the birthday child's taste buds, but they are sure to tickle her fancy! Stock your sand table with small pie tins, a few spray bottles filled with water, birthday candles, and some plastic flowers. During center time, invite students at the sand table to make birthday pies for the birthday child. Encourage students to put a number of birthday candles equal to the birthday child's age in each of the pies. Then, during your circle time, have the students present their pies to the birthday child while reciting the following poem.

Close your eyes.
Make a wish or two.
Blow out the candles.
May all your wishes come true!

Lisa Leonardi, Norfolk, MA

Hungry Puppy

This circle-time game will have your little ones howling with delight as they feed bones to a hungry pup! To make a puppy prop, tape together a shoebox and its lid; then cover the entire box with brown bulletin-board paper or a cut paper bag. Stand the box on one end; then decorate it to resemble a puppy by gluing on construction-paper eyes, ears, and whiskers, and a construction-paper nose. Cut an opening in the box to resemble a mouth; then cut an opening in the back of the box that is large enough to fit your hand through. Cut out at least a class supply of different-colored construction-paper bones.

To play, give one or more bones to each child in the group. Lead students in chanting, "Puppy, puppy wants a treat. What kind of bones will he eat?" Designate a color; then direct those children holding bones of that color to "feed" them to the puppy. Continue until each child has fed his bones to the hungry pup. For a variation, program the bones with letters, numerals, or shapes. Woof!

Michelle Crosby—Pre-K, ESE
E. H. Miller School, Palatka, FL

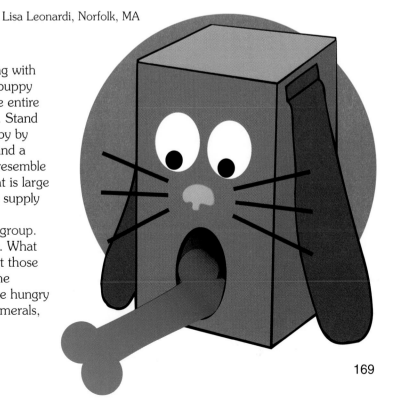

IT'S CIRCLE TIME!

Wiggle Your Fingers, Stomp Your Feet

Use this movement poem to invite youngsters to wiggle and stomp right into your morning circle time.

Wiggle your fingers in the air.
Wiggle them, wiggle them everywhere!

Stomp your feet upon the ground.
Stomp them, stomp them all around!

Now sit down and cross your feet.
Hands in laps all nice and neat.

Now we're ready to start our day.
We'll listen first, and then we'll play!

Sandy Curtis—Pre-K
Browncraft Day Care Center
Rochester, NY

Chinese New Year Parade

Turn your group time into a celebration by planning a parade. To follow this Chinese New Year's custom, you'll need a dragon, of course. To make one, use fabric paints to paint colorful designs or Chinese symbols on a white sheet. Cover a shoebox, the shoebox lid, and a medium-sized box with bulletin-board paper. Turn the larger box upside down; then cut eyeholes in it. Hot-glue the shoebox and lid below the eyeholes for a mouth. Use markers, crepe-paper streamers, and paper to decorate the boxes to resemble a dragon. Lastly, hot-glue the sheet to the box.

Invite several children to stand under the dragon; then provide the remaining children with rhythm sticks. Lead the group in a parade as you shout Happy New Year in Chinese: *"Gung-Hey-Fat-Choy!"*

Sam Ferguson—Four- And Five-Year-Olds
St. Joseph Child Development Center
Louisville, KY

170

Flannelboard Gingerbread Men

Catch these gingerbread men for your flannelboard and you'll have a fun way to reinforce shapes and colors. To prepare, cut four large gingerbread-man shapes from brown felt. Use wiggle eyes and a marker or felt to add facial features to the cutouts; then glue a different color of ricrac around the edge of each one. For each gingerbread cutout, cut three felt buttons that are the same color as the cutout's ricrac, making sure that each set of buttons is a different geometric shape. Following a telling of the Gingerbread Man story, invite youngsters to match the buttons to the flannelboard gingerbread men. Your group will catch on to counting, colors, and shapes as fast as they can!

Lucille Ann Ingrassia—Two-Year-Olds Integrated,
    Special Education/Day Care
Just Kids Learning Center
Middle Island, NY

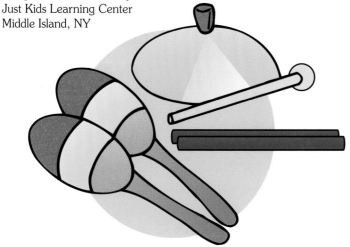

Musical Patterns

Need a quick circle-time activity? Pull out your supply of rhythm instruments. Ask two volunteers at a time to each choose an instrument. Have the two children stand in front of the group. Then suggest a musical pattern for them to play. Tap, ding! Tap, ding! Tap, ding! Now that's a pattern that's music to your ears!

The Baker Says

This adaptation of Simon Says bakes up a batch of youngsters who are great at following directions. To play, you'll need a tagboard cookie cutout for each child and one baker's hat. (Use a real hat, or make one by stapling white tissue paper to a sentence-strip headband.) Don the hat; then give each child a cookie cutout. Remind students that all directions preceded by the phrase "The baker says" should be followed. Then begin the game by giving directions involving the cutouts. For example, you might say, "The baker says put your cookie on the ground," or "The baker says tap your cookie with your left foot." Invite group members to don the hat and take turns being the baker. Just for fun, give youngsters real cookies. The baker says *eat your cookies!*

Henry Fergus—Preschool
Buckeye Elementary School District #33
Buckeye, AZ

IT'S CIRCLE TIME!

Cupid, Cupid

Here's a lovely valentine's game for your preschoolers! Choose a student to be Cupid and give him a Cupid's headband. Ask Cupid to hide his eyes while you give another child a valentine card to hide in her lap. When the card is out of sight, have Cupid uncover his eyes while his classmates say, "Cupid, Cupid, where's your valentine?" Help Cupid guess who has his valentine. Then have the child hiding the valentine become the next Cupid.

Cracker-Crumb Dance

This action song is sure to get enthusiastic reviews from your little snackers! After a cracker snack for everyone, get rid of those pesky crumbs by singin' and movin' to the beat. Crunch and munch—we love crackers, crumbs and all!

(sung to the tune of "Frère Jacques")

Graham crackers,
Animal crackers,
Soda crackers too.
Soda crackers too.
They make such a crumbly mess. *(Brush hands together.)*
They make such a crumbly mess.
What to do? *(Turn palms up.)*
What to do?

Brush your shirt off, *(Brush imaginary crumbs off clothing.)*
Dust your pants off,
Stomp your feet! *(Stomp feet.)*
Stomp your feet!
Do the cracker-crumb dance. *(Dance in place.)*
Do the cracker-crumb dance.
Shimmy and shake! *(Shimmy and shake.)*
Shimmy and shake!

adapted from an idea by Diane Z. Shore
Marietta, GA

172

Bear, Bear, Spring Is Here!

If you're ready for spring, play this group game with all of your little cubs! Use blankets over a couple of chairs to create a bear cave. Have the children sit in a circle near the cave's opening. Ask one child to be a bear, sleeping in the cave. As soon as the bear is slumbering, give another child a bunch of berries (pom-poms or beads) to hide in her lap. When the berries are hidden, have the children call out, "Bear, bear, spring is here!" Encourage the bear to wake up and come out of the cave, then guess who is hiding the berries. Have the child caught with the berries become the bear and continue play. Who's ready for spring?

Diane DiMarco—Preschool
Country Kids Preschool And Child Care Center
Groton, MA

Cattle Roundup

During Western Days or a farm unit, corral a small group of your aspiring cowhands for this cow-counting card game. To prepare, die-cut up to 80 cow cutouts. Glue one, two, or three cutouts on each of 15 cards. In the center of a circle of three or four children, place the cards facedown—along with the remaining cow cutouts. Give each player a piece of twine or yarn to loop into a corral for his cattle. To play, have each cowpoke in turn take a card, then put a matching number of cow cutouts in his corral. Continue play for four or more rounds. At the end of the game, have each cowpoke count the number of cows in his corral. Get along, little dogies!

adapted from an idea by Charlet Keller—Pre-K
ICC Elementary Preschool, Violet Hill, AR

Alphabet Walk

Put a little rhythm into letter recognition with this musical game. In advance, fill a bag with initial-sound cards. Place alphabet letters in a circle on the floor. Instruct the children to walk or dance around the circle when the music plays and stop immediately beside a letter when the music stops. Start some lively music, stopping it when the children least expect it. Draw a card from the bag, show it to the children, and say the picture word and the name of its initial letter. Ask the children to identify the child standing by the matching letter in the circle. When the music stops next time and it's time to pull another card from the bag, invite that child to do the honors. Here we go again. Listen carefully!

Beth Walker—Four- And Five-Year-Olds
BCC Child Development Center, Melbourne, FL

173

The Easter-Egg Patch

Sing this spunky song with your youngsters to reinforce their color-recognition skills. To prepare, fill a basket with a class supply of different colors of plastic eggs. Have students sit in a circle. As you sing the first verse, walk around the circle and invite each child to take an egg from the basket. Put the empty basket in the center of the circle. As the second verse is sung, have each child holding that color egg place it in the basket. Continue singing the second verse, substituting different color words until each child has placed his egg in the basket.

(sung to the tune of "Paw-Paw Patch")

Where, oh, where are the Easter eggs?
Where, oh, where are the Easter eggs?
Where, oh, where are the Easter eggs?
Take one from the basket.

If you have a [blue] egg, put it in the basket.
If you have a [blue] egg, put it in the basket.
If you have a [blue] egg, put it in the basket.
Way down yonder in the Easter-egg patch!

Dayle Timmons—Kindergarten Inclusion
Alimacani Elementary School
Jacksonville, FL

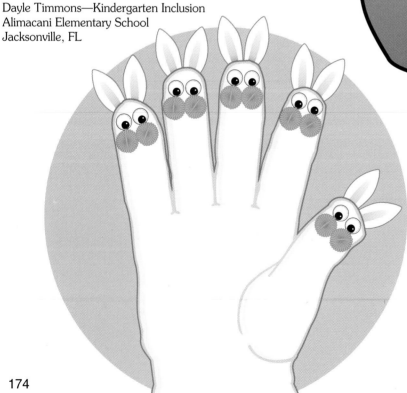

Bunny Mitt

Imagine how your children's eyes will light up when you produce five or ten bunnies for a circle-time fingerplay! To make one mitt, obtain a white fabric glove. Cut out ten bunny ears from white craft foam. Add a pink streak to the center of each ear with a cotton swab that has been dipped in cosmetic blush. Hot-glue two ears to the back of each fingertip. Next hot-glue two wiggle eyes to the front of each finger-tip. Complete the mitt by hot-gluing two small pink pom-poms directly underneath each pair of eyes. Now you're ready to perform to your hand's content!

Dayle Timmons—Kindergarten Inclusion

A Basket Of Names

Here's a sweet way for youngsters to practice name recognition. In advance, write each child's name on a slip of paper. (Or use a permanent marker to personalize a plastic egg for each child.) Tuck a name slip and a candy treat inside each egg; then place it in a basket. During circle time, have a child close her eyes and choose one egg. After the child opens the egg, help her identify the name on the slip. Then have her give the candy to that child. The child receiving the candy takes the next turn. Play until every child has had a chance to crack open an egg.

Dana Smith—Noncategorical Preschool, Special Education
Donaldsonville Elementary
Donaldsonville, LA

Once Upon A Pea

Searching for a pesky pea under a mound of mattresses will be so much fun children are unlikely to notice they're working on color identification. From felt, cut a brown bed shape, a number of different-colored strips for the bed's mattresses, and one small pea. During circle time, introduce this activity by asking students to recall the story of *The Princess And The Pea*. Place the bed and mattresses on your flannelboard. Show the children the pea; then have them close their eyes while you hide it under a mattress. Invite youngsters to open their eyes and guess under which color mattress the pea is hidden. Remove mattresses as they are guessed until the pea is found. What royal guessers your preschoolers are!

Leslie Madalinski—Preschool
Weekday Children's Center
Naperville, IL

Carpet Colors

Have youngsters link their efforts in this small-group sorting activity. To prepare, pour out a tub of Unifix® cubes; then set out one carpet square for each different color of cube. Place a different-colored cube on each carpet square. Invite the same number of students as you have colors of cubes to the group area. Assign each student a color to find and place on the matching carpet square.

If interest allows, extend this idea by next putting the carpet squares in a line. Have each child start at the beginning of the line and stack one cube from each carpet square to make a stick. Encourage children to compare their sticks with other children's to find matching colors. You're really stacking up fun now!

Debbie Thompson—Pre-K, Handicapped Class
East Robeson School
Lumberton, NC

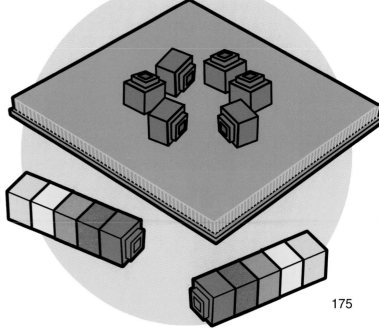

Raindrops On Roses

This flowery movement activity will help your children's spatial awareness bloom! Cut a class supply of laminated construction-paper flower shapes; then tape them in a large circle on the floor. Have the children imagine they are raindrops that must water the flowers. Instruct them to walk around the circle as you play a lively musical selection. Stop the music and direct each little raindrop to "water" a flower by standing on it and wiggling her fingers or whole body. After each child has found a flower to stand on, begin the music again and repeat the activity.

Sharla Park—Three-, Four-, And Five-Year-Olds
Friends And Neighbors Preschool
Lehi, UT

Spot 'em; Then Swat 'em!

Use this activity to hone your youngsters' eye-hand coordination while reinforcing color and shape recognition. From tagboard, cut out a number of different-colored geometric shapes; then draw a fly on each shape. Arrange the shapes in an open area on the floor. Give a volunteer a flyswatter; then direct her to swat one of the flies. For example, say, "Swat the fly on the red circle." Once she spies the correct bug, have the remaining students help her sing the song below, saying, "Splat!" as she swats the bug. Next have her give the swatter to another child, and then direct that child to swat a specific bug.

(sung to the tune of "Row, Row, Row Your Boat")

> Bug, bug, on the shape,
> Afraid of you I'm not!
> I see you, I see you!
> Now I'm going to swat!
> Splat!

Jeanine Trofholz—Three-Year-Olds
St. Luke's Rainbow Preschool
Columbus, NE

Jumping Waves

Refine your youngsters' muscle control and create a wave of giggles with this lively game. Hold one end of a jump rope and have another adult hold the opposite end so that the rope is stretched out between you and is close to the ground. Make waves by gently shaking the rope up and down. Next challenge each child, in turn, to jump over the waves, being careful not to "wipe out" by touching the rope. After each child has had a turn, raise the rope slightly higher than before. This game is sure to have your little ones jumping with joy!

Lori Kent
Hood River, OR

Skill-Building Aquariums

There's nothing fishy about this activity that has youngsters following directions while sharpening their color-recognition and counting skills. Give each child in a small group a sterilized, blue Styrofoam® tray (aquarium) and ten colorful paper fish. Next give the group various directions to follow, such as "Place three fish in your aquarium" or "If you have a yellow fish or a blue fish, put it in your aquarium." Encourage your little ones to take their fish and aquariums home, then share this activity with their families.

Susan Luengen—Preschool Special Education
Makalapa School
Honolulu, HI

Transition Chant

For a smooth transition into circle time, have your little ones perform this charming chant.

Sit like a butterfly.   (Sit with legs crossed.)
Buzz like a bee.   (Make buzzing noises.)
Shake your head like a monkey in a tree.   (Shake head.)
Put your hands down on your knees.   (Put hands on knees.)
Make your mouth like a fish in the sea.   (Pucker lips.)

Wanda Odom—Pre-K
Waller Elementary
Youngstown, FL

SONGS & SUCH

SONGS & SUCH

Moving Hands

(sung to the tune of "Turkey In The Straw")

I can clap my hands,
Clap high, clap low.
I can clap my hands,
Clap fast, clap slow.
I can clap my hands to the left and the right.
I can clap my hands 'til I say, "Good night!"

I can wiggle my fingers,
Wiggle high, wiggle low.
I can wiggle my fingers,
Wiggle fast, wiggle slow.
I can wiggle my fingers to the left and the right.
I can wiggle my hands 'til I say, "Good night!"

I can snap my fingers,
Snap high, snap low.
I can snap my fingers,
Snap fast, snap slow.
I can snap my fingers to the left and the right.
I can snap my fingers 'til I say, "Good night!"

I can wave my hands,
Wave high, wave low.
I can wave my hands,
Wave fast, wave slow.
I can wave my hands to the left and the right.
I can wave my hands 'til I say, "Good night!"

Suzanne Moore

Welcome To Preschool

(sung to the tune of "Up On The Housetop")

We made some friends today, today.
We had lots of fun, I'd say.
Blocks, puzzles, and other games to play.
Welcome to preschool. Hooray! Hooray!

Mary Summers—Parent/Toddler Class
Hobbitts Preschool
Richfield, OH

SONGS & SUCH

Nighttime Noises

Who's poking around outside when night falls? Bats and owls and raccoons—that's who! As you sing this lively tune, invite youngsters to add the sound effects to each verse.

(sung to the tune of "This Little Light Of Mine")

I hear a noise outside.
It's a flapping bat. Whoosh!
I hear a noise outside.
It's a flapping bat. Whoosh!
What's it doin' outside?
It's chasing a bug.
Hear it flap, hear it flap, hear it flap!

I hear a noise outside.
It's an old hoot owl. Hoot!
I hear a noise outside.
It's an old hoot owl. Hoot!
What's it doin' outside?
It's chasing a mouse.
Hear it hoot, hear it hoot, hear it hoot!

I hear a noise outside.
It's an old raccoon. Splash!
I hear a noise outside.
It's an old raccoon. Splash!
What's it doin' outside?
It's chasing a fish.
Hear it splash, hear it splash, hear it splash!

adapted from an idea by Linda Blassingame
JUST 4 & 5 Developmental Laboratory, Mobile, AL

Halloween Dress-Up

Invite your little ones to tell you about their Halloween costumes. After they share their disguises, teach them this tune, substituting the costumes your children have named.

(sung to the tune of "Twinkle, Twinkle, Little Star")

I'm dressed up for Halloween—
Best little [cat] you've ever seen!
Here I am in my disguise.
I have changed before your eyes.
I'm dressed up for Halloween—
Best little [cat] you've ever seen.

Lucia Kemp Henry

182

The Pumpkin In The Patch

Teach little ones this version of "The Farmer In The Dell" and have youngsters act it out accordingly.

The pumpkin's in the patch.
The pumpkin's in the patch.
Boo! Boo! It's Halloween.
The pumpkin's in the patch.

The pumpkin takes the cat…

The cat takes the bat…

The bat takes the ghost…

The ghost takes the treats…

We all say, "Trick or treat"…

Scarecrow Song

(sung to the tune of "Up On The Housetop")

Out in the field in a row of corn,
Stands a scarecrow so forlorn.
Crows on his head and crows at his feet,
He's the saddest scarecrow you'll ever meet.

Can't scare the crows,
Oh, no, no!
Can't scare the crows,
Oh, no, no!
Out in the field in a row of corn,
Stands a scarecrow so forlorn.

LeeAnn Collins—Director
Sunshine House Preschool
Lansing, MI

The Turkey Bird

(sung to the tune of "The Silliest Goat I Ever Saw")

The silliest bird; *The silliest bird;*
I ever met; *I ever met;*
Is the turkey bird; *Is the turkey bird;*
My barnyard pet. *My barnyard pet.*
The silliest bird I ever met
Is the turkey bird, my barnyard pet.

LeeAnn Collins

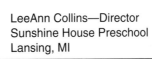

SONGS & SUCH

Hey, Mr. Groundhog!

Teach little ones about the tradition of Groundhog Day (February 2) with a song and this adorable tissue-box puppet. To make a puppet, cover the sides of a tall tissue box with brown construction paper. Cut a one-inch slit in the center of the bottom of the box. Fringe one long side of a 10" x 3" piece of brown construction paper; then crease the paper slightly at the base of the fringe. Glue the ends of the strip together; then insert the fringed circle into the opening of the tissue box as shown. Cut out and color a small groundhog pattern; then glue it to one end of a large craft stick. Push the free end of the craft stick into the tissue box until it goes through the slit in the bottom.

Add this fun tune to your lesson, inviting youngsters to take turns sliding the craft stick up and down in the box to make Mr. Groundhog appear at just the right moment!

(sung to the tune of "Where Is Thumbkin?")

Sleeping groundhog, sleeping groundhog,
Today's the day; today's the day!
Tell us please if spring's near. Or will winter stay here?
Come out and say! Come out and say!

puppet idea by Sue McClimans—Three-Year-Olds
Edward's School, Davenport, IA

song by LeeAnn Collins—Director
Sunshine House Preschool, Lansing, MI

Pickin' Out Valentines

Here's a musical activity that's sure to make your little ones feel loved! In advance, cut out a paper heart for each child. Gather your youngsters and have them form a circle. Scatter the supply of paper hearts around the outside of the circle. Teach youngsters the following song. As they sing, designate one child to walk around the outside of the circle, select a paper heart, and then hand it to one of her classmates. In the last line of the song, fill in the name of the child who receives the heart. Then have the class sing the verse again as the recipient walks around the circle, chooses a heart, and then gives it to another child. Continue until everyone has received a valentine heart.

(sung to the tune of "The Paw Paw Patch")

Pickin' out valentines to give to all my friends,
Pickin' out valentines to give to all my friends,
Pickin' out valentines to give to all my friends,
Look! Here's one for [child's name]!

LeeAnn Collins

Use Your Toothbrush

(sung to the tune of "Where Is Thumbkin?")

Use your toothbrush.
Use your toothbrush.
Every day,
Every day.
Keep your smile shining bright
Morning, noon, and every night.
Brush, brush, brush.
Brush, brush, brush.

LeeAnn Collins—Director
Sunshine House Preschool, Lansing, MI

A Pretty Valentine

(sung to the tune of "Did You Ever See A Lassie?")

I have a pretty valentine,
A valentine, a valentine.
I have a pretty valentine
I'm sending to you.

It's red and it's lacy!
I made it so fancy!

I have a pretty valentine
I'm sending to you.

LeeAnn Collins

Welcome, Spring!

Seat your children in a circle; then teach them this seasonal song and its accompanying motions.

(sung to the tune of "Christmas Is Coming")

Up come the flowers.	*Raise hands.*
Out comes the sun.	*Form arms into circle above head.*
Hear the bees buzzing.	*Cup one hand behind ear.*
Springtime has begun!	*Fold hands together.*
Up in the treetops	*Raise arms above head like treebranches.*
The birds are all here.	*Open and close hands like birds chirping.*
Now we know it's springtime.	*All join hands.*
Let's give a great big cheer!	*All stand and raise arms in a cheer.*

Lori Maiello and Beth Klidonas—Four-Year-Olds, First Step Preschool, Niagara Falls, NY

SONGS & SUCH

When Spring Comes Rolling In

(sung to the tune of "When The Saints Go Marching In")

Oh, when spring
Comes rolling in,
Oh, when spring comes rolling in,
[The flowers will all start blooming]
When spring comes rolling in.

Repeat, substituting the phrases below for the underlined words.

The plants will all start growing...

The birds will all start nesting...

The bees will all start buzzing...

LeeAnn Collins—Director, Sunshine House Preschool
Lansing, MI

Bug Song

(sung to the tune of "If You're Happy And You Know It")

Oh, I wish I were an eensy-weensy spider.
Yes, I wish I were an eensy-weensy spider.
I'd go "creepy-creepy-crawly" down your hall and up your "wall-y"!
Oh, I wish I were an eensy-weensy spider.

Oh, I wish I were a yellow honeybee.
Yes, I wish I were a yellow honeybee.
I'd go "buzzy-buzzy-buzzy" and my stripes would be all fuzzy!
Oh, I wish I were a yellow honeybee.

Oh, I wish I were a wiggly caterpillar.
Yes, I wish I were a wiggly caterpillar.
I'd go "munchy-munchy-munchy." All the leaves would be my "lunch-y"!
Oh, I wish I were a wiggly caterpillar.

Oh, I wish I were a small red army ant.
Yes, I wish I were a small red army ant.
I'd go "trompy-trompy-trompy" over hills and through the "swamp-y"!
Oh, I wish I were a small red army ant.

Oh, I wish I were a hungry little skeeter.
Yes, I wish I were a hungry little skeeter.
I'd go "bitey-bitey-bitey" when you went outside at "night-y"!
Oh, I wish I were a hungry little skeeter.

Vicki Widman—Pre-K, A.J. Stepansky Early Childhood Center
Waterford, MI

In The Farmyard

Animal noises abound in this lively tune! Have your young farmhands sing it several times, substituting other animals and animal noises for the underlined words.

(sung to the tune of "My Bonnie Lies Over The Ocean")

The [cow] lives out in the farmyard.
She's an animal I go to see.
The [cow] lives out in the farmyard
And sometimes she says things to me.
["Moo, moo, moo, moo."]
That's what the [cow] says to me, to me.
["Moo, moo, moo, moo."]
That's what the [cow] says to me!

adapted from a song by LeeAnn Collins—Director
Sunshine House Preschool, Lansing, MI

Flitter, Flutter, Butterfly

Invite youngsters to make fluttering finger puppets to accompany this song. To make a puppet, cut a simple butterfly shape from construction paper. Attach a strip of wide masking tape to the center of one side of the cutout. Then fold the cutout in half and cut two slits, about 3/4" apart, through both the paper and the tape. Unfold the cutout. A child may slip one or two fingers through the slits to operate the puppet.

(sung to the tune of "Twinkle, Twinkle, Little Star")

Flitter, flutter, butterfly,
Flying in the big blue sky.
Flutter high and flutter low.
Flutter fast and flutter slow.
Flitter, flutter, butterfly,
Flying in the big blue sky.

puppet idea by Diane White—Preschool, Rotary Youth Centre Preschool Program
City Of Burlington, Burlington, Ontario, Canada

The Itsy-Bitsy Seed

Teach little ones the accompanying motions to this tune. It'll grow on you!

(sung to the tune of "The Itsy-Bitsy Spider")

The itsy-bitsy seed was planted in a hole.   (Pretend to plant seed in palm.)
Down came the rain and a sprout began to grow.   (Wiggle fingers downward.)
Out came the sun and shone down on the leaves.   (Place arms in circle overhead.)
Now the itsy-bitsy seed is a great big grown-up tree!   (Raise hands above head, fingers spread wide.)

Kimberly Boston—Preschool, Brooklyn Blue Feather Early Learning Center, Brooklyn, NY

SONGS & SUCH

How Do Bugs Move?

What's the buzz on insect movement? Find out when you point your antennae toward this active tune. As students sing the following song, have them move like the insects named. For added fun, provide your little bugs with headband antennae or paper wings. Students will buzz and float their way through this six-legged song!

(sung to the tune of "Bingo")

There was a little bumblebee,
Who buzzed around the garden.
Buzz, buzz, bumblebee.
Buzz, buzz, bumblebee.
Buzz, buzz, bumblebee.
Buzz around the garden.

There was a little ladybug,
Who crawled around the garden....

There was a little butterfly,
Who floated 'round the garden....

There was a little pesky fly,
Who zipped around the garden....

There was a little grasshopper,
Who jumped around the garden....

Dawn Spurck, Omaha, NE

Take Me Out To The Circus

Delight your little ones with this circus idea! Use stickers or cut-outs to create a class supply of stick puppets that match the animals named in the song. Have the children stand in a circle; then give each child a puppet to raise when his animal is named.

(sung to the tune of "Take Me Out To The Ball Game")

Take me out to the circus.
Take me to the big top.
Show me some horses and lions and clowns,
Monkeys and elephants dancing around.
Can you hear the band playing loudly?
We're ready and set to go!
Oh, I love, love, love the big top,
And the circus show!

LeeAnn Collins—Preschool/Director
Sunshine House Preschool, Lansing, MI

This Fabulous Year

(sung to the tune of "We Wish You A Merry Christmas")

We did a lot of playing,
We did a lot of building,
We did a lot of singing,
This fabulous year.

We did a lot of cooking,
We did a lot of eating,
We did a lot of sharing,
This fabulous year.

We did a lot of reading,
We did a lot of listening,
We did a lot of talking,
This fabulous year.

We did a lot of learning,
We did a lot of thinking,
We did a lot of growing,
This fabulous year!

Karen Hoover—Four-Year-Olds
Asbury Preschool, Raleigh, NC

This Little Ladybug

Youngsters are sure to enjoy "flying" these lovely ladybug finger puppets while singing the following song. To make one, cut a 2 1/2" circle from red craft foam; then cut the circle in half to form wings. Use a black marker to add spots. Next hot-glue the wings, a bent four-inch length of black pipe cleaner, and wiggle eyes to a film canister as shown. Ladybug, ladybug, fly away home!

(sung to the tune of "This Little Light Of Mine")

This little ladybug,
I'm gonna let it fly.
This little ladybug,
I'm gonna let it fly.
This little ladybug,
I'm gonna let it fly.
Let it fly, let it fly, let it fly.

Janis Woods—Four-Year-Olds, Ridgeland Elementary School, Ridgeland, SC

Five Dandelions

We're not "lion"! Youngsters are sure to have fun as they count down the verses of this dandy song.

(sung to the tune of "Five Little Ducks")

[Five] dandelions in the grass so green.
Little yellow flowers as pretty as you've seen.
One turned to fluff and then it blew away.
[Four] dandelions were left that day.

Show five fingers.
Make fist.
Pop hand open; then flutter fingers away.
Show four fingers.

LeeAnn Collins—Preschool/Director, Sunshine House Preschool, Lansing, MI

SONGS & SUCH

Ten Little Latkes

(sung to the tune of "Pawpaw Patch")

One little, two little, three little latkes;
Four little, five little, six little latkes;
Seven little, eight little, nine little latkes;
Ten little latkes for a Hanukkah treat!

We peeled and chopped and grated our potatoes.
Peeled and chopped and grated our potatoes.
We peeled and chopped and grated our potatoes.
Ten little latkes for a Hanukkah treat!

We put them in the pan and fried them in the oil.
Put them in the pan and fried them in the oil.
We put them in the pan and fried them in the oil.
Ten little latkes for a Hanukkah treat!

They fried and sizzled until they were brown.
Fried and sizzled until they were brown.
They fried and sizzled until they were brown.
Ten little latkes for a Hanukkah treat!

We smelled them, ate them—mmm…how delicious!
Smelled them, ate them—mmm…how delicious!
We smelled them, ate them—mmm…how delicious!
No more latkes for a Hanukkah treat!

Kathy Cotton—Preschool
Stepping Stones Preschool, Westport, CT

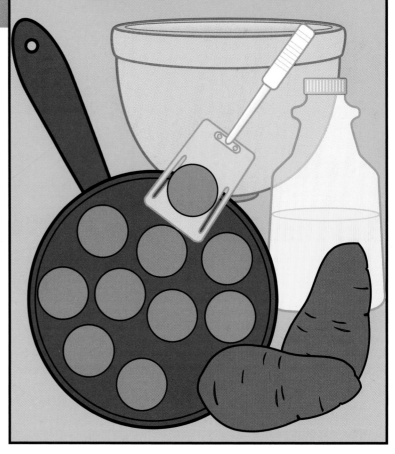

Little Pine Tree

(sung to the tune of "Clementine")

Little pine tree, little pine tree,
You have branches green and wide.   *Stretch arms out to sides.*
Little pine tree, little pine tree,
Gently sway from side to side.   *Sway body from side to side.*

Little pine tree, little pine tree,
In the winter woods you grow.   *Hold arms above head.*
Little pine tree, little pine tree,
Stand so bravely in the snow.   *Stand on tiptoes; stretch arms up.*

Little pine tree, little pine tree,
You have snowflakes in your hair!   *Wiggle fingers above head.*
Little pine tree, little pine tree,
Welcome birds to shelter there.   *Make a welcoming motion.*

Lucia Kemp Henry

CRAFTS FOR LITTLE HANDS

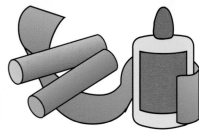

Crafts For Little Hands

Shiny Shakers

Add a little polish to craft time with these shiny apple shakers. To make a shaker, paint the backs of two small paper plates red. When the paint is dry, brush a mixture of two parts glue and one part water on the painted side of each plate to create a polished look. Allow the glue mixture to dry. Bend a brown pipe cleaner in half; then tape it to the rim of the unpainted side of one plate. Glue a green construction-paper leaf near the stem. Position the plates together so that the unpainted sides face each other. Staple the plates together, leaving an opening near the stem. Insert approximately ten dried beans in the opening; then staple the opening closed. Complete the shaker by squeezing a happy face on one side using a mixture of two teaspoons black powdered-tempera paint and four tablespoons white glue.

Melba Clendenin—Preschool, Chester Elementary School, Chester, IL

Pretty As A Peacock

The plumage on this pretty peacock is sure to please your preschoolers. To make a giant peacock, use large droppers to randomly drop yellow, blue, and purple tempera paints onto a piece of white bulletin-board paper. Dip a trim roller into a meat tray filled with green or blue paint; then roll it over the dots in an outward motion, creating a fan shape. When the paint is dry, complete the peacock by gluing a construction-paper body to the base of the painting as shown.

Pat Johnson—Three-Year-Olds
Church of the Redeemer
Columbus, OH

Beautiful Bovine

Your little ones will think this handsome holstein is simply "moo-velous." To make a cow, paint black spots on a large paper plate. Paint one small paper plate pink and another yellow. When the paint is dry, staple the pink plate near the bottom of the large plate to make a nose. Use a black marker to draw eyes, nostrils, and a mouth on the two plates. Cut the yellow plate in half; then trim the pieces to resemble horns. Staple the horns to the top back of the cow's head. Staple black construction-paper ears to the front of the plate; then bend them forward.

Pam Selby—Preschool: Developmentally Delayed, Walls Elementary, Walls, MS

Bag Buddies

Be prepared for giggles when youngsters make these bag buddies using recycled materials. To make a buddy, use markers and scraps of material or paper to decorate a paper grocery bag. Stuff the bag with newspaper; then staple it closed to create a body. To make a face, use markers and recycled materials—such as bottle caps, yarn, and cellophane grass—to decorate a paper plate. Then staple the face to the body. Next color four toilet-paper tubes and two paper-towel tubes. Trace a pair of hands and a pair of feet onto construction paper; then cut them out. Punch a hole at the base of each hand and at the heel of each foot. Punch a hole near the top and bottom of each tube. Punch a hole on each side of the bag, and two holes in the front bottom of the bag. To assemble each arm, use pipe cleaners to attach a hand and two toilet-paper tubes together; then attach the arm to the bag. To assemble a leg, similarly attach a foot to a paper-towel tube before attaching the tube to the bag.

Dorothy Ewing—Four-Year-Olds
Future Stars Preschool, South Plainfield, NJ

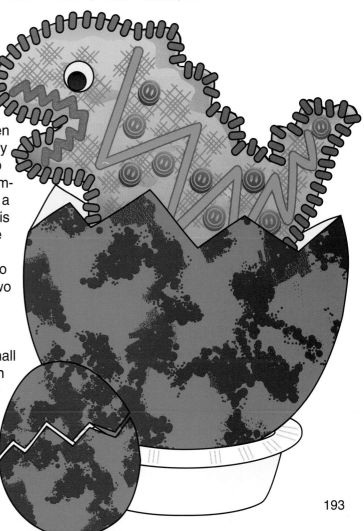

I'm Bringing Home A Baby Dinosaur

To make a papier-mâché dinosaur egg, dip newspaper strips into a soupy mixture of flour and water; then press the strips onto a large balloon until it is completely covered. Apply several layers of strips. Allow the egg to dry for one or more days. Then apply a base coat of tempera paint to the egg. Next sponge-paint the egg using a second and even a third color of paint. When the paint is dry, use a utility knife to cut the egg as shown. Remove the balloon.

To make a dinosaur baby, use a permanent marker to trace a simple dinosaur shape onto a piece of burlap two times. Trace the resulting outlines with glue to prevent the burlap from fraying when cut. When the glue is dry, cut around the outlines. Use yarn and a large, blunt-tipped needle to sew the shapes together, leaving a small opening for stuffing. Stuff the dinosaur with fiberfill; then sew the opening closed. Decorate the dinosaur with dimensional paints, buttons, yarn, and wiggle eyes. Complete this project by placing the baby dinosaur inside the egg. To display this prehistoric pet, set the egg in a Styrofoam® bowl.

Theresa Knapp—Preschool
Asbury Day Care Center, Rochester, NY

Crafts For Little Hands

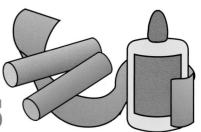

Winter Preparations

Squirrel away a class supply of brown paper-towel tubes in preparation for this project. To make one tree, cut a hole out of the center of the tube as shown. Also cut slits from the top of the tube toward the center. Bend the tube's sections downward to resemble tree branches. Crumple small pieces of orange, yellow, and red tissue paper; then glue them to the branches. Color a copy of one of the squirrel patterns (page 196) red, brown, or gray; then cut it out. Put glue on the back of the pattern; then insert it into the tube so that the squirrel's face can be seen through the hole. Press the pattern in place. Looking for nuts? Look in this tree!

Virginia Nickelsen—Preschool, YAI/NYC Early Child Learning
William O'Conner School, Brooklyn, NY

Haunted House

There's nothing scary about making this Halloween house! In fact, it's "spookily" easy for your little spirits to create. Use the pattern on page 197 to prepare oaktag tracers. To make one house, use white chalk to trace one of the patterns onto black construction paper; then cut along the resulting outlines. To embellish this house, glue on cotton-ball spirits and dried lima-bean ghosts. If desired, add die-cut pumpkins or pumpkin stickers. Arrange the completed houses together on a display to create a spooky neighborhood.

Mary Hilditch—Preschool
Relax Children's Center, Baltimore, MD

Flipped Over Bats

Everyone is sure to have a good "bat-itude" when making these creatures. To make one bat, paint a cardboard tube black or brown. Set the tube aside to dry. Using the wings pattern on page 196, make an oaktag tracer. Use white chalk to trace the wings onto black or brown construction paper; then cut them out. Also cut out two small triangles from black or brown paper to represent the ears. Glue the wings, the ears, and a pair of wiggle eyes to the tube as shown. Feeling batty? Display these projects upside down!

Laura Castro—Three-Year-Olds, Vallco Child Development Center
San Jose, CA

194

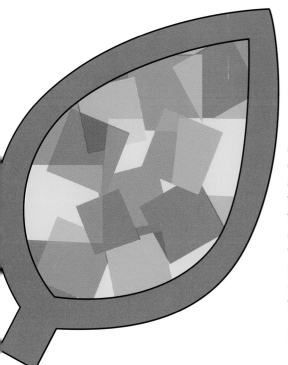

Falling For Leaves

Have youngsters create colorful fall foliage to hang in front of a sunny window. To make one leaf, fold a piece of red, yellow, brown, or orange construction paper in half. Cut out one half of a simple, symmetrical leaf shape starting at the fold. Then cut out the center of this shape, leaving an outline about 1/2 inch wide. Unfold the outline; then lay it on a slightly larger piece of waxed paper. Drizzle a generous amount of glue along the shape's outline and in the center of the waxed paper. Press tissue-paper squares onto the glue. When the glue is dry, peel the leaf off the waxed paper. Trim around the leaf's edges. Use monofilament line to hang the leaf from the ceiling in front of a window.

Betsy Ruggiano—Three-Year-Olds, Featherbed Lane School, Clark, NJ

Thanksgiving Placemat

Prepare these placemats for your Thanksgiving feasts; then send them home as gifts along with Happy Thanksgiving wishes. Write or type the poem (shown on the placemat); then duplicate a copy for each child. To decorate one placemat, glue a copy of the poem onto a large piece of construction paper. Use washable paint to paint the palm and thumb of a child's hand brown. Paint her fingers various colors. Have the child press her hand onto the construction paper. When the paints are dry, have her use markers to add legs and feet, eyes, and a wattle to her print. Have her also personalize the poem. Laminate the placemat for durability.

Shelly Dohogne—Early Childhood Special Education
Scott County Central
Sikeston, MO

This isn't just a turkey,
As anyone can see.
This very special turkey
Was made by hand by me!
Happy Thanksgiving!

Katy

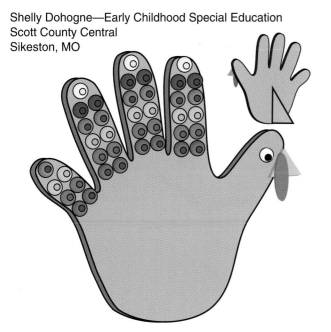

Beaded Turkey

This turkey project makes a gobbling good activity because it improves fine-motor skills, reinforces color recognition, and teaches patterning! Trace a child's hand onto cardboard; then use an X-acto® knife to cut out the shape. Have the child squeeze a generous amount of Plaid® Tacky Glue onto the fingers. Starting at the tops of the fingers and working toward the palm, have him press on colorful beads to create a pattern. Then have him glue on a wiggle eye, a felt beak, and a felt wattle. Use a hot glue gun to attach a cardboard right triangle to the back of the turkey so that it is freestanding. A flock of compliments will follow wherever these precious projects go.

Gayle J. Vergara—Preschool
Willowbend Preschool
Murrieta, CA

195

Squirrel Pattern
Use with "Winter Preparations" on page 194.

Wings Pattern
Use with "Flipped Over Bats" on page 194.

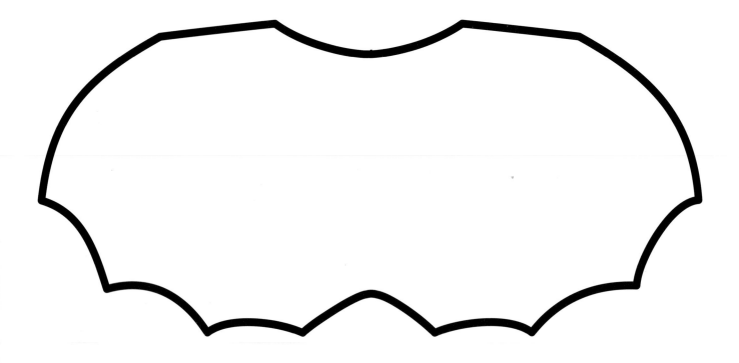

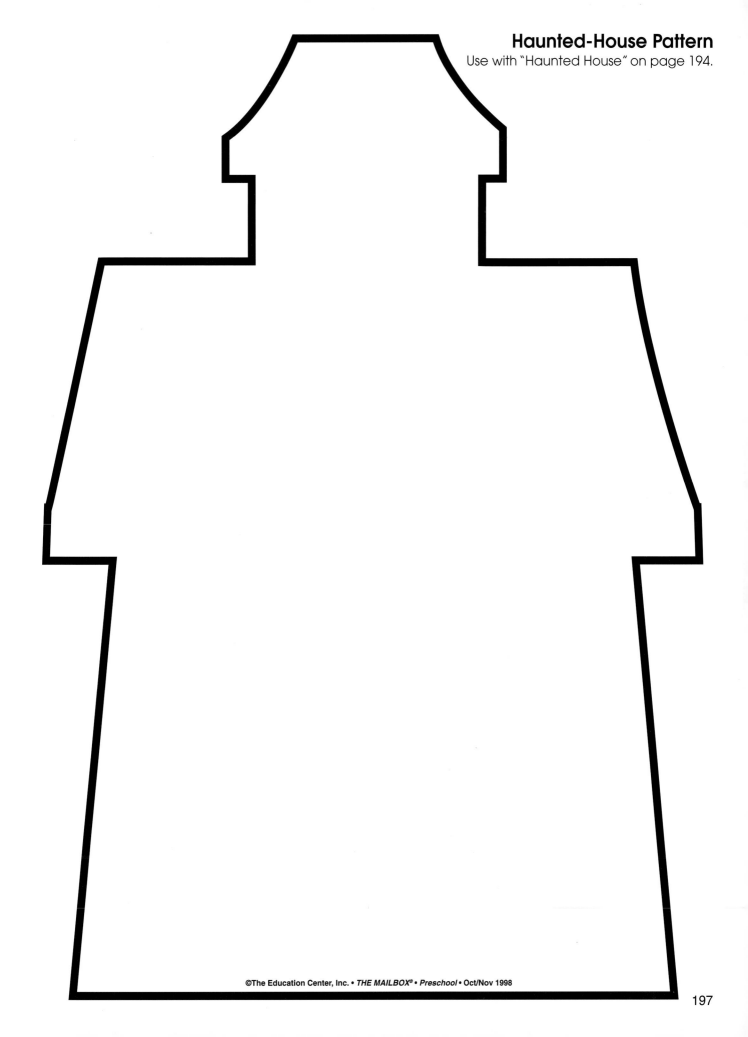

Crafts For Little Hands

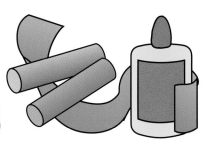

Painted Poinsettias

These painted poinsettias are a pretty way to add color to your classroom decorations. To prepare to paint one, use an X-acto® knife to cut a 2" x 10" strip of corrugated cardboard. Bend the strip in half; then bend two inches of each end toward the center. Tape the ends together to make a kite shape. Dip the shape into a shallow pan of white paint, and then press the shape onto the center of a sheet of red construction paper. Continue printing in a circular fashion, making sure the bottom point of the shape remains in the center. When the paint is dry, glue crumpled yellow tissue-paper pieces to the center of the prints. Trim around the poinsettia shape; then add a construction-paper leaf.

Lisa Desrosiers—Preschool, Special Needs
Gates Lane School Of International Studies
Worcester, MA

Christmas Bells

Ring out the good news. These bells make adorable gifts! To make one bell, sponge-paint a two-inch clay flowerpot red, green, or white. Sprinkle glitter onto the wet paint, or glue on sequins when the paint is dry. Then glue a child's picture onto the bell and outline the picture with dimensional fabric paint. Allow the paint to dry. Next thread an 18″ piece of ribbon through a jingle bell's loop. With the ends of the ribbon even, tie a large knot in the ribbon about one inch above the jingle bell. Starting from inside the pot, thread the ribbon's ends through the drain hole. Pull the ends upward until the knot reaches the drain hole. Tie a second knot just above the hole. Tie the ribbon's ends together.

Peggy Witman—Four- And Five-Year-Olds, Willow Creek Learning Center, Poland, OH

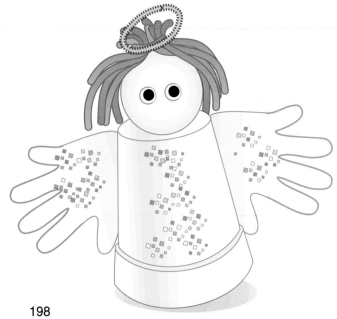

Celestial Sensations

These sweet angels are a craft sent from heaven. To make one, trace a child's hands onto white construction paper; then cut them out. Spread glue onto both hand shapes and a Styrofoam® cup; then sprinkle on silver glitter. When the glue is dry, invert the cup and glue the hand shapes to it to represent wings. Insert a craft stick into the bottom of the cup, leaving about one inch sticking out of the cup. Press a 2 1/2-inch Styrofoam® ball onto the stick for the angel's head. Glue wiggle eyes and yarn hair onto the ball. Top the angel with a glittery pipe-cleaner halo.

Sandra Anzaldi—Three-Year-Olds
Noah's Ark Day Care and Kindergarten Haverhill, MA

Candy Dish

This sweet treat makes a perfect gift for Hanukkah, Christmas, Valentine's Day, or any other special holiday. To make one candy dish, use pinking shears to cut a nine-inch fabric circle. Place the circle, printed-side down, onto a piece of waxed paper. Next put one hand into an inverted, plastic punch cup. Using a paintbrush, completely coat the sides and bottom of the cup with Mod Podge®. Set the bottom of the cup onto the center of the circle. Bring the edges of the circle toward the top of the cup, smoothing the fabric against the cup. Generously apply a second coat of Mod Podge® to the fabric. Allow the cup to dry. Finally, fill the cup with a plastic bag of candies and a special wish.

Karen Eiben—Preschool, The Kids' Place Child Development Center, LaSalle, IL

A Troupe In Tuxedos

These perky little penguins are all dressed up for winter. To make a penguin, cut off the top of a cardboard egg carton; then paint it black. (Discard the bottom of the carton.) When the paint is dry, glue on an oval construction-paper tummy and feet. Fold a seven-inch strip of orange construction paper in half. Insert the ends of the strip into one of the lid's holes above the penguin's tummy. Tape the ends of the strip to the back of the penguin. Finally add adhesive hole reinforcements for eyes. If desired, glue a folded tagboard square to the back of the penguin so that it is freestanding.

Alma Kay Borgen—Preschool, Amherst Own Child Care, Amherst, WI

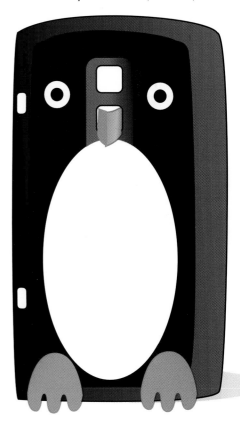

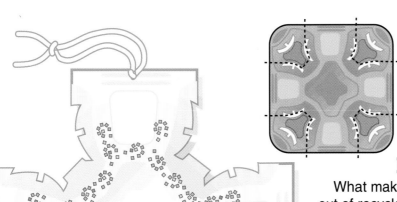

Recycled Snowflakes

What makes these snowflakes unique? They're made out of recycled soft-drink holders from fast-food restaurants! Begin by cutting off the cup compartments in the four corners of the holder (as shown). Paint the resulting snowflake white; then sprinkle on glitter. When the paint is dry, punch a hole in the snowflake and tie on a length of white yarn for hanging. Look up—it looks like snow!

April Eastman—Preschool, Kampus Kids Daycare, Concord, NH

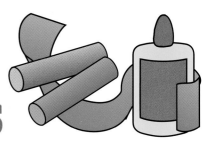

Crafts For Little Hands

Attractive Valentine Bags

Spread the love around with these magnetic valentine-collection bags that can be displayed on your filing cabinets or magnetic boards. In advance, prepare tracers for the cupcake and icing shapes shown. Also cut a supply of construction-paper hearts. To make one bag, a child traces the shapes onto construction paper in the colors of his choice, coloring the shapes, if desired. He then cuts out the shapes and glues them onto one side of a paper bag. Next he writes each letter of his name onto a different heart. (Complete this step for younger preschoolers.) He then glues the hearts to his cupcake. To complete each bag, attach a strip of magnetic tape to the top of the back of the bag. After displaying these bags on Valentine's Day, how about decorating real cupcakes with candy hearts for a sweet treat?

Deborah Lockhart
Scotia, NY

"Some-bunny" Loves You!

These valentine magnets are really "thumb-thing" special! To make one, cut two hearts from white card stock. Cut out the center of one heart, leaving a 1/2-inch border. (Use a die-cutting machine if available to save time.) Have a child paint red thumbprints around the heart border; then have him paint one pink thumbprint near the center of the solid heart. When the paint is dry, have the child use a permanent marker to add details to the pink thumbprint so that it resembles a bunny. Glue the border on top of the solid heart. Write the message shown, the child's name, and the date. Finally attach a strip of magnetic tape to the back of the heart.

Martha Berry—Two-Year-Olds
Main Street Methodist Preschool, Kernersville, NC

Valentine Vases

My, won't your little ones be proud when they present these lovely vases to their loved ones? To make one vase, completely cover a clean, 16-ounce plastic soda bottle with strips of masking tape. Sponge-paint the bottle. Then, when the paint is dry, fill it with colored water and add a white carnation. As each child's sweetheart enjoys this gift, the flower will become more colorful every day!

Donna McConkey—Toddlers and Preschool
Kids Kare Daycare
Ozark, MO

Western Wear

Yahoo! Your little ones are sure to have a rootin'-tootin' good time making these cowpoke hats. For each child, use an opaque projector to enlarge the hat pattern (page 208) onto tagboard. Direct each child to use markers to color his hat. Then cut out the hat as indicated on the pattern. Invite each child to embellish his hat with feathers or sequins, if desired. To complete the hat, staple a sentence-strip headband to fit the child's head. Then staple the hat onto the band as shown so that the narrow strips at the bottom of the hat are toward the back of the headband. How about those hats!

Carol Pochert—Four- And Five-Year-Olds
ABC Kids Care
Grafton, WI

"Giddyup!"

Nothing's more valuable to a cowpoke than her own horse! Before youngsters make these horses, use an opaque projector to enlarge the pattern on page 208 onto tagboard. Cut the pattern out to make a tracer. To make one horse, trace the pattern onto one side of a large, folded piece of brown kraft paper. Cut along the outline through both thicknesses. Attach lengths of yarn to a masking-tape strip; then attach the strip to one of the horse shapes for the mane. Glue the shapes together along the edges, leaving the bottom of the neck open and making sure that the yarn is on the outside. Use markers to add details to both sides of the horse shape. Slide a wrapping-paper roll into the neck opening; then glue it closed. Finally attach a length of yarn to the horse for a rein. Ride 'em, cowpoke!

Carol Pochert—Four- And Five-Year-Olds

Precious Puppies

Think these dogs are cute? It must be puppy love! To make one, paint the bottom of a child's foot the color of his choice, such as white, brown, black, or gray. Have the child press a footprint onto a sheet of construction paper. When the paint is dry, provide the child with paper scraps, markers, and wiggle eyes for decorating his dog as he desires. Display these canine crafts so that everyone can "paws" to admire them!

Stephanie Adkison
Stillwater, OK

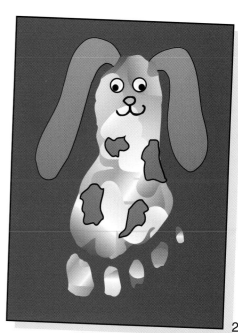

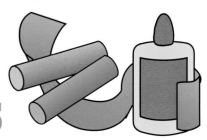

Crafts For Little Hands

Bunny Frame

You bet your whiskers! This frame should be given to "somebunny" special! To make one project, take a close-up picture of a child; then trim the developed photo into a circle. Mount the photo onto the center of a small paper plate. Glue white cotton balls around the photo. Glue pink cotton balls onto two poster-board bunny-ear shapes. Staple the ears to the top of the plate. Write an Easter message on a construction-paper bow-tie shape; then staple the tie to the front of the plate. If desired, attach a strip of self-adhesive magnetic tape to the back of the frame. Adorable!

Diane DiMarco—Preschool
Country Kids Preschool
Groton, MA

Handy Bunnies

Hippity, hoppity! This craft is sure to be a hands-down favorite! To make one bunny, paint a child's hand (excluding the thumb) white. Help the child separate her fingers into a V shape; then press her hand onto a sheet of construction paper. When the child's hand is clean and the paint is dry, direct the child to glue on wiggle eyes and a pom-pom nose. Next have her use markers to add whiskers and a smile. Have her also add pink paint to the bunny's ears. Finally, have the child twist the center of a tissue-paper rectangle, then glue it to the bunny to represent a bow tie.

Leigh Ann Clark—Four-Year-Olds
First Baptist Kindergarten, Eufaula, AL

Look What Hatched!

Feathers will be flying in your classroom when youngsters make this fun craft project. To make one chick, trace a pear shape onto a large sheet of yellow construction paper. Next use an X-acto® knife to cut about 15 one-half-inch slits in the bottom part of the shape. Cut out the shape; then glue on wiggle eyes or paper eyes and a beak. Slide a yellow feather into each slot. (Feather dusters are a cheap source of feathers.) Turn the chick over; then tape each feather to the back. To really cause a hullabaloo, display these chicks together in a nest created by weaving together strips of brown paper.

Lisa Marie Bouldry—Four-Year-Olds
McLean Child Care Center
Belmont, MA

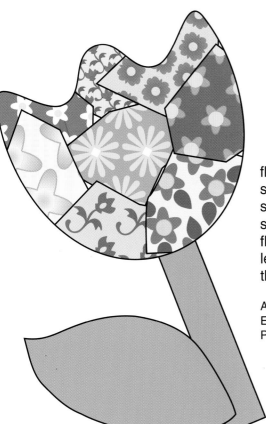

Floral Fabric Posies

Aren't these flowers just fabulous? To prepare to make these floral creations, cut scraps of several different floral fabrics into small pieces. Next trace a flower shape onto a sheet of white construction paper. To decorate a posy, use a paintbrush to glue the scraps over the flower shape. When the glue is dry, cut out the flower; then glue the flower to a green construction-paper stem with leaves. Display these flowers together to create a garden of flowers that will delight every eye!

Alison Link—Pre-K
Englewood Elementary
Port Charlotte, FL

Handfuls Of Flowers

A tisket, a tasket, fill a basket with handfuls of flowers! Make two green handprints on light green construction paper. For each different color blossom, dip a Q-tip® or cotton ball into paint; then press it onto the fingers of the handprints. When the paint is dry, cut around the handprints. Cut out a construction-paper basket shape. Glue the palms of the handprints onto the back of the basket so that the fingers are on top of the handle as shown.

Bettye King—Three-Year-Olds
Pleasant Hill Nursery School
Owings Mills, MD

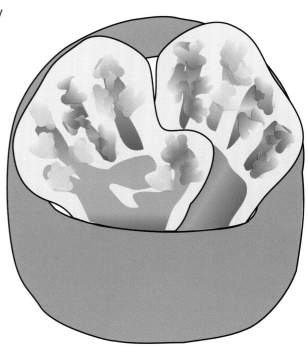

Fashionable Flowers

Youngsters can fashion these one-of-a-kind necklaces to wear during spring. Working atop waxed paper, roll out an individual portion of self-hardening clay to a thickness of approximately one-quarter inch. Use a cookie cutter to cut a flower shape from the clay. Use a drinking straw to cut a hole in the shape for hanging. Allow the clay to completely harden, turning it occasionally. Add touches of color to the hardened clay with acrylic paint. Finally, thread the flower onto a length of ribbon or yarn. Tie the ribbon or yarn ends, and the necklace is ready to wear!

Fly, Butterfly!

These unique butterflies will grace your room with color. To make one butterfly, paint a paper plate as desired. Paint a cardboard tube black. When the paint is dry, cut the plate in half; then trim the straight sides as shown to resemble the outer edges of the wings. Glue the round edges to the tube. To complete the butterfly, tape two pipe cleaners in the top of the tube for antennae. To display these butterflies, hang them from your ceiling or near a window.

Michelle Pendley—Three-Year-Olds
The Children's Corner
Orange Park, FL

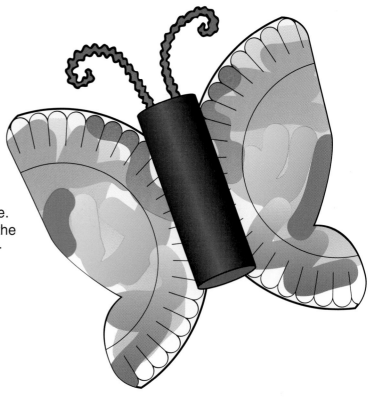

Winged Wonders

Wandering around in search of a simple and fun spring craft? These butterflies are wonderful for any of your preschoolers! Make a butterfly by using water-based markers to color two coffee filters. Spray the filters with water so that the colors blend. When the filters are dry, fold them in half. With the round edges together, slightly overlap the filters; then pinch them together in the center. Twist a pipe cleaner around the filters as shown. Curve the ends of the pipe cleaner to create the antennae. Surprise your little ones by using clear fishing line to dangle these butterflies in unusual places throughout your school or center.

Amy Jenkins—Preschool
Children's Country Day School
Mendota Heights, MN

Flannelboard Butterflies

Have your little ones make these beautiful butterflies; then use them on your flannelboard for counting practice and language activities. In advance, tint small amounts of water with food coloring. For each child, cut out a Pellon® butterfly shape; then use a permanent marker to add the child's initials. To add color to one shape, dampen it; then put it in a pie pan. Use an eyedropper to put small amounts of the tinted water onto the shape until no white is visible. Remove the shape from the pan to allow it to dry. Flannelboard fun takes flight with these beauties!

Kevin F. Humphrey—Head Start
Oxon Hill, MD

204

Flowers For A Special Lady

Each of your children can present a bouquet of long-lasting posies to his mom for Mother's Day. To make one bouquet, decorate a paper lunch bag with any of a variety of art materials, such as crayons, paint, flower stickers, flower stamps, or cut-out magazine pictures of flowers. Open the bag; then fold the top of the bag down about one inch. After putting the stems of several artificial flowers in the bag, squeeze the bag together just below the fold. Secure the flowers in the bag by tying a length of ribbon around the top of the bag. Flowers—for you!

Margaret Watts
15th Street Church Of God
Centralia, IL

An Expression Of Love

The love that fills this Mother's Day greeting keeps growing and growing and growing! To make one card, fold a sheet of construction paper in half. Write the message shown on the front and inside of the card. To decorate the front, glue on groups of scrunched tissue-paper squares to resemble flowers; then use a marker to add stems. As a special surprise, tape a package of marigold seeds to the inside of the card. If desired, send along planting instructions with a suggestion that mother and child spend some quality time together planting the seeds.

Debi Luke—Preschool
Fairmount Nursery School
Syracuse, NY

My love for you...

...grows and grows and grows!

MARIGOLD SEEDS

Happy Mother's Day!
Love, Stephen

My mom is "berry" special! Here's why!

My mom looks very pretty when she brushes her hair.

My mom's favorite thing to do is talk on the phone.

I love my mom because she sings to me.

Shelly

"Berry" Special Card

Here's a "berry" special card for a very special mom! Fold a large sheet of construction paper in half. To decorate the outside of the card, paint one side of a plastic berry basket green. Press the basket on the card to leave a print. Next sponge-paint red heart shapes above the basket to resemble strawberries. Dip a toothpick in white or black paint to add seeds to the berries. Finally, use a small piece of sponge to paint green leaves on the berries. To complete the inside of the card, write the message shown on the top of a white page. Ask a child to complete several sentence starters such as those shown. Record his answers. When the paint on the front of the card is dry, glue the page to the inside of the card.

Cheryl Cicioni—Preschool
Kindernook Preschool
Lancaster, PA

Crafts For Little Hands

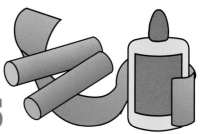

We're Talkin' Turtles!

Don't be a slowpoke to try out this turtle craft! To get started, collect soft cardboard produce separators found in boxes of apples at your local grocer. Cut the cardboard apart so that you have a class supply of shapes to serve as turtle shells. To make one turtle, use tempera paint to paint a shell green or brown. From construction paper, cut out four turtle legs, a head, and a tail; then glue the shapes to the underside of the dry shell. Use markers and wiggle eyes to add details to the legs and head. Display the projects on a bulletin-board-paper pond along with rocks and a collection of Franklin books by Paulette Bourgeois.

Barbara Meyers
Fort Worth Country Day
Fort Worth, TX

Dazzling Dragonflies

Dazzle 'em with these easy-to-make dragonflies! To make one, use markers to add eyes and some color to an old-fashioned wooden clothespin. Next tie a ten-inch length of monofilament line into a loop. Also cut two rectangles (about 5" x 8") from different colors of cellophane. Holding the clothespin with the open end up, slide the loop, then the two cellophane pieces into the clothespin. Dangle these dainty insects in front of a sunny window.

Sharon M. Coulter
Park Place Children's Center
Muncie, IN

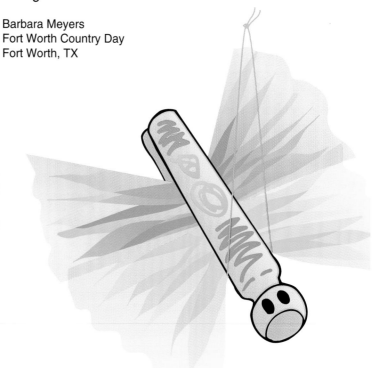

Pretty Polka-Dotted Ladies

Youngsters will scurry over to make one of these ladybugs. To make one, cut a pair of same-sized circles from waxed paper. Place one of the circles, waxed side up, on a newspaper-covered surface. Sprinkle red crayon shavings over the circle; then add black construction-paper circles and antennae. Place the remaining circle on top of the first. Cover the layers with a second piece of newspaper; then use an iron (on a low heat setting) to melt the wax. Are you seeing spots yet?

Kimberli Carrier—Preschool
Wise Owl Preschool
Nashua, NH

Fine-Feathered Friends

These birds look so "tweet" tucked into nests of plastic grass. To make one, cut a cardboard tube into two pieces—one shorter than the other. Paint both pieces. When the glue is dry, glue the shorter piece to the longer piece as shown, clipping them together while the glue is drying. Remove the clips; then glue on feathers, wiggle eyes, and a paper beak. Display these birds in nests (boxes of plastic grass) tucked in quiet corners of your classroom or throughout your school.

Kimberli Carrier—Preschool
Wise Owl Preschool, Nashua, NH

Here's The Scoop

Briskly fold two parts nonmenthol shaving cream with one part white glue. Add food coloring, if desired. When the mixture is slightly stiff and shiny, get ready for a "scooper-duper" art activity! On a large sheet of construction paper, draw an ice-cream cone. Drop a dollop of the mixture onto the paper above the cone and then spread it around with a craft stick until it resembles a scoop of ice cream. While the mixture is wet, sprinkle on sequins or glitter.

Debbie Clark—Preschool
Little Red Caboose Preschool
Virden, IL

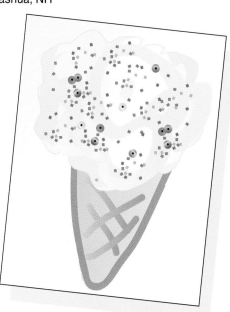

A Holder And A Hug, Too

Dad is sure to find this gift amusing *and* handy! To make one pencil holder, cut a piece of construction paper to match the height and circumference of a plastic container (such as a powdered-drink container). Label the center of the paper with the child's name and the date. Add a picture of the child. Next trace the child's hands and feet onto construction paper. Cut out the hand and foot shapes along with an 11" x 1" strip of construction paper that is the same color as the hand cutouts. If desired, laminate all of the pieces.

To assemble the gift, use tape to secure the labeled paper around the container. Use an X-acto® knife to cut a vertical 1 1/2" slit on opposite sides of the container. Slide the construction-paper strip into the slits so that it is extended; then slide the center of the strip into the container so that it folds inside the can. Glue one hand cutout to the end of each strip and the feet cutouts to the bottom of the container. Give Dad the holder to fill with pens and pencils. Then, when he needs a hug, he can just give the hands a tug!

Carol L. Hammill—Two- And Three-Year-Olds
Community Christian Preschool, Fountain Valley, CA

Patterns

Use with "Western Wear" and " 'Giddyup!' " on page 201.

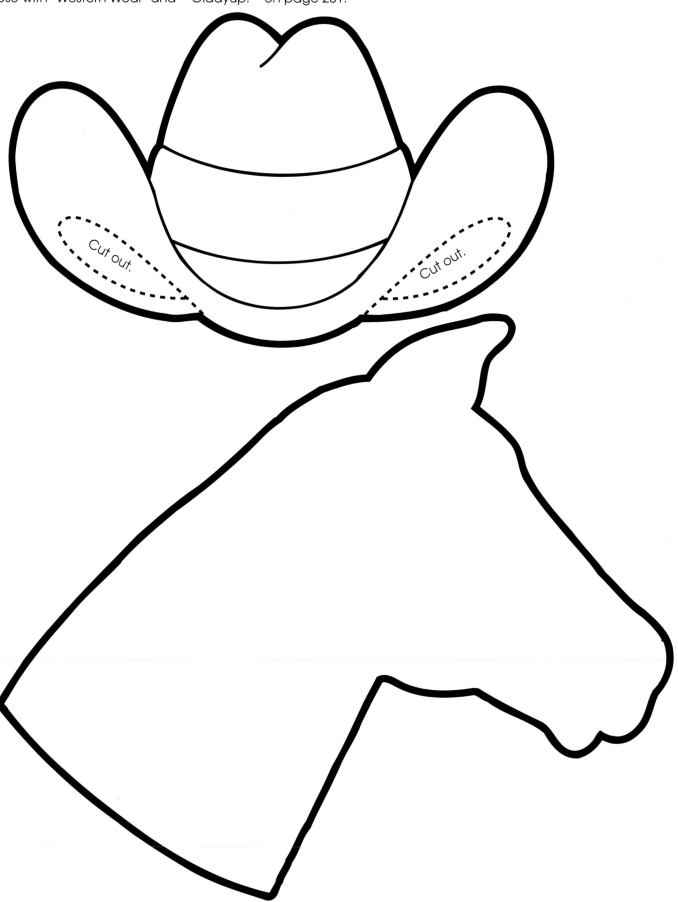

Cut out.

Cut out.

SETTING THE STAGE

Setting The Stage:

Block Center

A House For Me

These charming additions to your block area will help youngsters learn their addresses as well as develop the concept of community. Purchase a class supply plus some extra of freestanding wooden house shapes (available at craft stores). Invite each child to paint a house; then allow the paint to dry. Use a permanent marker to write each child's name and address on her house; then coat each house with nontoxic varnish. When the varnish is dry, add the houses and a supply of toy vehicles to your block area. Encourage youngsters to build neighborhoods; then, as the children play, point out the names and addresses on the houses. Later add additional houses painted to resemble other familiar places, such as your preschool, stores, and fast-food restaurants. What a busy neighborhood!

Liz Novak—Preschool, Pumpkin Patch Preschool And Playcare, Davenport, IA

Sensory Table

Road Construction

Your sensory area will be humming with the sounds of bulldozers and backhoes when you add some road-construction props. Fill your sensory table with soil. Add some small rocks and sticks, along with a supply of toy construction vehicles. Spray the soil with water to keep it moist and pliable; then watch your crew of workers dig in.

Claudia V. Tábora—Preschool
Como Community Child Care, Minneapolis, MN

Literacy Center

Alpha-Boards

These personalized workmats and plaster letters spell out fun at your literacy center. Cut the fronts and backs from cereal boxes so that you have a class supply of cardboard mats. Personalize the blank side of a mat for each child. Laminate the mats. Using Faster Plaster™ and alphabet-shaped candy molds, make enough letters so that each child has the letters needed to spell his name. Store each child's set of letters in a separate, labeled berry basket. Put the workmats and baskets in a center. At the center, a child chooses a workmat and the corresponding set of letters. He then matches the letters to the letters on the mat to spell his name or a classmate's name.

Bonnie McKenzie—Pre-K And Gr. K
Cheshire Country Day School, Cheshire, CT

Interest Areas And Centers

Water Table

Getting The Worm

Youngsters are sure to wiggle right over to your water center when they discover that it has been inhabited by worms—rubber worms that is! Purchase a number of rubber worms from the fishing department of a discount store. Put the worms in your table; then fill it with water and a squirt or two of washable brown paint so that the water looks muddy. Add buckets, small fishnets, and paper towels to the center. Invite youngsters to reach in and have a slimy good time!

Cindy Lawson—Toddlers And Preschool
Shell Lake, WI

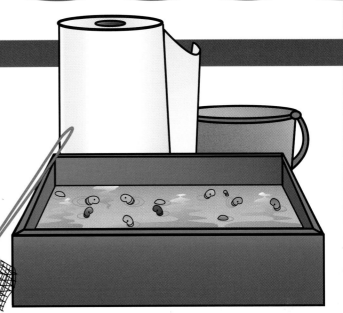

Manipulatives Center

Tabletop Flannelboard

Transform an unused table into an instant flannelboard with this handy idea. Cut a piece of felt to match the dimensions of a small tabletop. Use double-sided tape to attach the piece to the tabletop. Place the flannelboard table in a center along with a variety of felt shapes, numerals, and letters.

Nancy Wolfgram—Two-Year-Olds
KinderCare Learning Center #1111
Lincoln, NE

Games Center

Farm Animal Slapjack

Bring the farmyard to your games center with this variation of the card game Slapjack. To prepare a game for two players, attach a different farm-animal sticker on each of eight index cards. Laminate the cards if desired.

To play, a pair of children sit facing each other with the cards faceup between them. The teacher names a color, characteristic, or type of animal, or makes the sound of an animal. Each partner then tries to be the first to slap the appropriate card. The first child to slap the correct animal card keeps the card. Continue the game until all the cards have been slapped. The partners then count their cards to determine a winner.

Jeri Ashford, Granite School District, Salt Lake City, UT

Setting The Stage:

Dramatic Play Area

Indoor Snow Trek

Bring winter inside with this sensory walk that provides the crunch and bounce of snow. Open a number of empty Styrofoam® egg cartons; then use clear packing tape to attach the cartons upside down to the floor in your center. Place a box of winter dress-up clothes beside the egg cartons. Invite a child who visits this center to put on a winter outfit. Then encourage him to walk over the egg cartons to get the sensation of stepping on newly packed snow. Crunch, crunch, crunch—sounds just like snow!

Sherry McClure—Three-Year-Olds
Western School
North Lauderdale, FL

Games Center

"Alpha-Cookies"

Cook up some fun with this tasty alphabet-matching game! Using permanent markers, color 26 round foam makeup-remover pads to look like cookies. Hot-glue a different foam uppercase letter (or write one with a permanent marker) on each cookie. Store your cookies in a cookie tin labeled " 'Alpha-Cookies.' " Tape paper uppercase letters to a cookie sheet; then cover the sheet with clear Con-Tact® covering. To use the items, a child uses a spatula to slide each cookie onto its matching cookie-sheet letter.

As a variation, program a second set of cookies with lowercase letters. Have a child similarly match the cookies to the uppercase letters on the pan.

Donna Allen—Three-, Four-, And Five-Year-Olds
A-Is-For-Apple Preschool
Glen Dale, WV

Play-Dough Center

Peppy Play Dough

It's holiday time and sweet scents fill the air. Why not add an exciting aroma to your play dough, too? Just add a few drops of peppermint oil or extract (and red food coloring, if desired) to your favorite play-dough recipe. When children go to this center, encourage them to identify the new smell. Provide rolling pins and candy cane–shaped cookie cutters to cut out the peppermint dough. Mmmm—smells sweet!

Interest Areas And Centers

Water Table

Reflecting Pool

Reflecting on a way to add excitement to your water table? Line your empty water table with aluminum foil; then fill it with water. Stock this center with various metallic objects, such as keys, spoons, aluminum pie pans, and silver coins. Also provide flashlights and handheld mirrors. Encourage youngsters to put the items—but not the flashlights or mirrors—in the water. Have them then use the flashlights to shine light into the water and the mirrors to reflect the light of the metallic objects in different directions and angles. What a bright idea!

Dawn Hurley—Preschool
CUMC Child Care Center
Bethel Park, PA

Sand Table

Frosty The Sandman

Start the new year off with sandy "snow" in your sensory table! Add enough water to the sand to make it stick together like snow. Complete the center with ice-cream scoops, melon ballers, bowls, and other nifty circular objects. Students will develop their fine-motor skills as they make snowballs, mold snowpeople, and create snow sculptures in the sand. The best part about this tactile experience is that nothing melts!

Betty Silkunas
Lansdale, PA

Housekeeping Area

O Christmas Tree

Children are sure to have a ball practicing fine-motor skills as they decorate a Christmas tree in your housekeeping area. Place a small, artificial Christmas tree in the center. Fill an open, gift-wrapped box with unbreakable ornaments that have loops for hanging; then put it near the tree. Encourage little ones to visit the center and trim the tree to their hearts' content!

Pat Smith—Pre-K
Bells Elementary
Bells, TX

Setting The Stage:

Literacy Center

Mini-Eraser Alphabet

Novelty erasers make motivating manipulatives in this center that focuses on alphabet skills. To prepare, purchase a large quantity of miniature, shaped erasers to coordinate with your current thematic or seasonal unit. For each alphabet letter you'd like students to practice, make a letter mat by printing the letter on an individual sheet of construction paper. Laminate the letter mats if desired. Place the letter mats and mini erasers in a center.

To use the center, a child chooses a letter mat, then places the erasers along the lines to form the letter. Keep this center fresh by adding more (or different) letter mats and erasers throughout the year.

Janet Witmer—Pre-K And Kindergarten
Learn And Grow Preschool, Harrisburg, PA

Games Center

Don't Forget To Brush!

Your students will rush to brush at this center that emphasizes good dental hygiene. To prepare, cut a few large tooth shapes from white construction paper. Glue each tooth cutout to a different piece of poster board; then laminate them. Place the boards in your games center, along with a basket of dry-erase markers and a few old toothbrushes. To use this center, a child uses a dry-erase marker to draw "food stains" on a tooth. (Encourage youngsters to imagine that the red marker makes a cherry stain, the blue marker a blueberry stain, and so on.) Then the child uses a toothbrush to brush the food away. Brush, brush, brush—clean as a whistle!

Karen Poccia—Four-Year-Olds
Scituate Early Learning Center, Scituate, RI

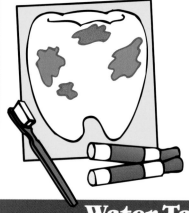

Water Table

A Balancing Act

Here's a "weigh-cool" idea for your water table! Fill each of several zippered plastic bags with a different material, such as rice, water, cotton balls, sand, air, popcorn kernels, or popped popcorn. Seal each bag and add a strip of clear packing tape to prevent leakage. Place the filled bags and a balance scale on a table near your water table. Invite children to explore and compare the weights of the various materials, both on the balance scale and in the water.

Esther S. Wert
Children's Place Preschool
Sayre, PA

Interest Areas And Centers

Play-Dough Center

A Box Of Chocolates

Treat yourself (or your sweetie) to the candies in a heart-shaped box; then place the empty box and candy wrappers in your play-dough center. Add a batch of this luscious-looking play dough and watch your little ones use their fine-motor skills to roll out some confections! Encourage children to count aloud as they put one play-dough chocolate in each wrapper. (Make sure youngsters know that this dough is *not* edible!)

Rosalie Sumsion
Monument Valley, UT

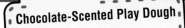

Chocolate-Scented Play Dough

1 1/4 cups flour
1/2 cup cocoa powder
1/2 cup salt
1/2 tablespoon cream of tartar
1 1/2 tablespoons cooking oil
1 cup boiling water

Mix the dry ingredients. Add the oil and boiling water. Stir quickly, mixing well. When cool, mix with your hands. Store in an airtight container.

Art Center

Magnet Madness

If you have a plexiglass fingerpainting table or a sand table with a clear plastic liner, you'll love this attractive idea! Cover the floor around the table with newspaper; then set out shallow trays of tempera paint, a powerful magnet, and a few magnetic objects—such as washers, paper clips, or bolts. Invite a child to dip a magnetic object into the paint color of her choice, then place it on (or in) the clear table. Have her sit beneath the table and move the magnet against the plastic or plexiglass, causing the magnetic object to move and create a paint design visible from below. Once she has delighted in viewing her design, wash it away to prepare the table for the next magnet painter. Or invite her to make a more permanent design by placing a sheet of art paper on (or in) the table before she magnet-paints.

Sandra J. Patane, ABC Preschool, Fulton, NY

Dramatic-Play Center

Happy Trails To You!

Saddle up and head for the Wild West—it's just across the room in your dramatic-play center! Cover the furniture in your housekeeping area with green fabric to resemble bushes. Then add some costume items and props, such as cowboy hats, vests, boots, sleeping bags, sticks (for making a campfire), and metal camping dishes. And—since every cowpoke needs a horse—add a rocking horse or spring horse, too. Yee-haa!

Rhonda Dominguez—Pre-K
Downs Preschool
Bishop, GA

Setting The Stage:

Art Center

Stamp Bunnies

Youngsters can count and stamp to their hearts' content with this adaptable activity. To prepare, duplicate a supply of bunny patterns, or die-cut a quantity of bunny shapes. Program each bunny with a numeral; then place all the bunnies in a center along with several Easter-related rubber stamps and an inkpad. To use this center, a child chooses a bunny, identifies the numeral, and then stamps the corresponding number of designs. Encourage each child to repeat the activity as desired.

To adapt this center, do not program the bunnies with numerals. Invite younger children to stamp as desired. Have older children write numerals on the bunnies before stamping the corresponding number of designs. Ready, set, stamp!

Samita Arora—Pre-K
Rainbows United, Inc.
Wichita, KS

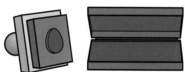

Games Center

Abracadabra!

It won't take much hocus-pocus to entice students to practice numeral-recognition and counting skills at this center! To prepare the center, program a spinner with numerals; then mount it on top of a plastic top hat (available at party stores). Cut out a simple bunny shape. Prepare a number of gameboards similar to the one shown, tracing the number of bunnies to match the highest numeral on the spinner. For each gameboard, cut a corresponding number of bunny shapes; then program the bunnies numerically. Laminate the gameboards and bunnies for durability. Store each set of bunnies in a resealable plastic bag; then store the bags in the top hat.

To play, each child at the center takes a gameboard and a set of bunnies. In turn, each child spins the spinner, then puts the bunny with the matching numeral on his gameboard. Play continues until each child's gameboard is covered with bunnies. Pulling rabbits from a hat for numeral-recognition practice works like magic every time!

Debra L. Erickson
Milan-Dummer Area Kindergarten
Milan, NH

Sensory Table

Sensory Seeds

Bring spring inside by filling the sensory table with birdseed and plastic eggs of various sizes. Encourage youngsters to feel the hard, slippery seeds, hear the sounds seeds make when they are shaken and poured, and examine the many different types of seeds. Encourage your little ones to visit this multisensory center to scoop, pour, and explore!

Betsy Ruggiano—Three-Year-Olds
Featherbed Lane School
Clark, NJ

Interest Areas And Centers

Water Table

Alphabet Quackers

Make a big splash with your little ones with this simple, yet fun, addition to your water table. Program the bottoms of a number of rubber-duck bath toys with numerals or letters. Float the ducks in your water table; then invite your little ones to take turns selecting a duck from the table and identifying the symbol written on it. As a challenge, have youngsters sequence the ducks by numeral or find ducks programmed with matching upper- and lowercase letters. Be sure to invite the children to enjoy some free water play, too!

Lonnie Murphy
Sarasota, FL

Manipulatives Area

Building Table

Put your LEGO® and DUPLO® blocks up on a pedestal with this unique idea. Glue LEGO® or DUPLO® building plates to the top of folding television tray tables. This sturdy, defined workspace makes it easy for little builders to create masterpieces. Storage is a snap—simply put the blocks in a container, and then fold up the table!

Amy Flori—Two- And Three-Year-Olds
Christ Methodist Child Development Center
Venice, FL

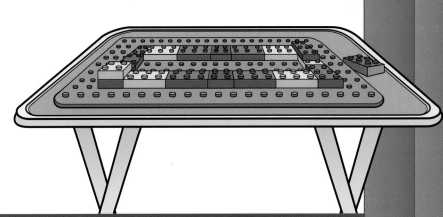

Dramatic-Play Area

Preschool Posy Shop

Your children's color-recognition, sorting, and counting skills are sure to bloom when you transform your dramatic-play area into a posy shop! Ask parents to donate old artificial flowers, vases, and flowerpots; then place the items in your center along with seed packets, paper, markers, and play money. Encourage children playing in the center to count the flowers and sort them by color. Also encourage literacy by having workers make price tags and signs for the store. Now that's some bloomin' good fun!

Colleen Keller—Preschool And Pre-K
Clarion-Goldfield Elementary
Clarion, IA

Setting The Stage:

Sensory Area

Desert Dig

Sharpen your students' senses and skills by creating this simple, yet exciting, classroom desert. Hide an assortment of rocks, plastic lizards, and toy snakes in your sand table or in a large plastic tub filled with sand. If desired, add colored sand to the table or tub. Encourage your youngsters to research desert life by placing in the area several reference books about deserts, lizards, and snakes. Add magnifying glasses, small shovels, and sand sifters to help your little ones search the sand. Stock the area with crayons and paper so that students can draw pictures of their desert discoveries. After informing your little ones of the buried items, invite them to visit the area and use the provided materials.

Kathy Valeri—Preschool
Spaulding Memorial, Townsend, MA

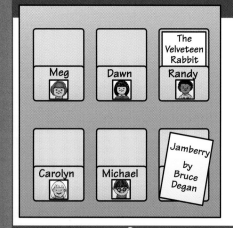

Reading Area

Check It Out!

Summer is the perfect time to begin transforming your reading center into a class library. Write each book's title and author on a small index card; then slip the card and the book into a large, resealable plastic bag. When the school year begins, label each of a class supply of library pockets with a different child's name and photo; then glue the pockets to a piece of poster board. When a child wishes to check out a book, she removes the card from the bag, then places it in her pocket on the chart. When she returns the book, she places the card back in the bag. What a great home-school connection!

Janina Savala—Bilingual Pre-K And Gr. K
West Birdville, Fort Worth, TX

Discovery Center

Sink Or Float: It's In The Bag!

Your little ones will delight in this adaptation of a sink-or-float experiment! Gather a number of objects small enough to fit inside resealable plastic bags. Be sure to gather some that will float—such as a cork, a Ping-Pong® ball, or a small piece of Styrofoam®— and some that will sink, such as a penny, a small stone, or a marble. Drop each item into a separate resealable plastic bag; then half-fill each bag with water. For added fun, mix a little glitter with the water. Seal the bags; then secure them with duct tape to prevent accidental spills. Place the bags in a large plastic tub; then put the tub in a center along with two more tubs—one labeled "Float" and the other labeled "Sink." Instruct your students to observe the item in each bag to determine whether it is a floater or a sinker and then put the bag in the corresponding tub. Your little ones will love feeling the squishy bags, observing the items inside, and sorting the bags into the tubs. Who said science was dry?

Geri Covins, St. Anne School, Warren, MI

Interest Areas And Centers

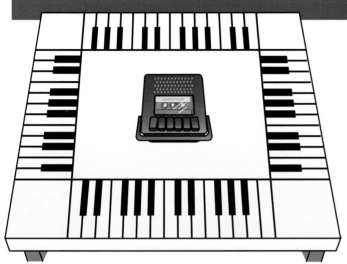

Listening Center

Ticklin' The Ivories

Get your youngsters in tune with their musical talents by turning one of your tables into a pretend piano. Use masking tape to secure a sheet of white bulletin-board paper to a tabletop. Next draw a large piano keyboard around the table as shown. Put an audiotape of piano music in a cordless tape recorder; then place it in the center of the table. As the music plays, invite your students to pretend to play the piano. Soon your room will be full of baby Beethovens!

Patricia Moeser—Preschool
U. W. Preschool Lab Site 1
Madison, WI

Manipulatives Center

String 'em Up

Have your youngsters exercise their problem-solving and fine-motor skills with this beaded brainteaser. Tie several lacing strings to the top of an empty chart stand; then clip a clothespin to the bottom of each string. Place a tub of large wooden beads below the stand. Challenge visitors to this center to string the beads *up* the strands. Be sure to give a lot of encouragement, but avoid giving specific directions. Your little Einsteins will beam proudly when they have discovered their own ways to string the beads.

Nancy M. Lotzer—Four-Year-Olds
Hillcrest Academy
Dallas, TX

Dramatic-Play Area

Fly Me To The Moon

If you have a play loft in your classroom, turn it into a rocket ship with these out-of-this-world ideas. First cover the walls near the loft with black vinyl tablecloths or bulletin-board paper; then tape cut-out stars and planets onto the walls. Next enclose the loft with several silver automobile sunshades. (If the cost of the shades is prohibitive, ask parents for donations.) To make space helmets, cut off the top halves of several plastic milk jugs. Create moon rocks by painting several large stones silver. If you have access to a broken computer, add it to the area as mission control. Encourage your little astronauts to hop aboard the loft. You'll see their language skills and imaginations blast off!

Sharon Otto—Preschool
Gallup Child Development Center
Lincoln, NE

THE MAGIC OF MANIPULATIVES

The Magic Of Manipulatives

Pipe Cleaners

Gather an assortment of pipe cleaners; then try these ideas with new twists to teach basic concepts.

by Mackie Rhodes

Twist several pipe cleaners into rings. Have students use them along with large manipulatives in a game of ringtoss.

Twist together several sparkly pipe cleaners to create a magic wand. Invite a child to use the wand as a pointer for counting, for identifying letters, or as part of her imaginary-play activities.

Invite each child to create pipe-cleaner letters and numerals by forming them over printed symbols.

Use separate pipe cleaners to measure around different body parts, such as a finger, a wrist, an ankle, and a leg. Compare the pipe-cleaner lengths.

Have each child loop and link together short lengths of various colors of pipe cleaners to create a pattern. Invite the child to wear the chain as a belt, headband, or necklace.

Have a child sequence different lengths of pipe cleaners from shortest to longest.

Show youngsters a pipe cleaner with a simple bend, twist, or curve in it. Challenge them to imitate the shape of the pipe cleaner with their bodies.

The Magic Of Manipulatives

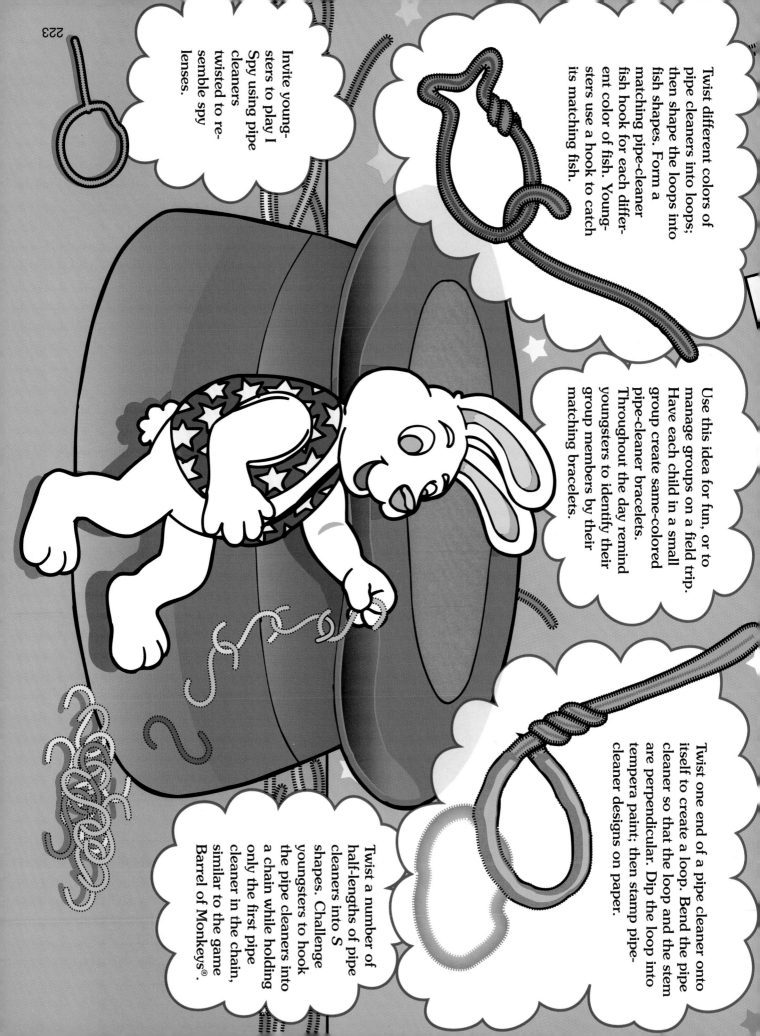

Twist different colors of pipe cleaners into loops; then shape the loops into fish shapes. Form a matching pipe-cleaner fish hook for each different color of fish. Youngsters use a hook to catch its matching fish.

Invite youngsters to play I Spy using pipe cleaners twisted to resemble spy lenses.

Use this idea for fun, or to manage groups on a field trip. Have each child in a small group create same-colored pipe-cleaners bracelets. Throughout the day remind youngsters to identify their group members by their matching bracelets.

Twist one end of a pipe cleaner onto itself to create a loop. Bend the pipe cleaner so that the loop and the stem are perpendicular. Dip the loop into tempera paint; then stamp pipe-cleaner designs on paper.

Twist a number of half-lengths of pipe cleaners into S shapes. Challenge youngsters to hook the pipe cleaners into a chain while holding only the first pipe cleaner in the chain, similar to the game Barrel of Monkeys®.

The Magic Of Manipulatives

Plastic Animals

Create some magical learning opportunities with an assortment of plastic animals and these curriculum-related ideas.

by Mackie Rhodes

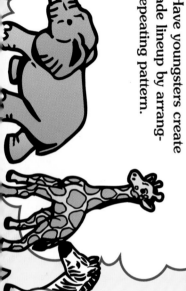

Fur, feathers, or fins? Invite youngsters to sort the collection of animals according to the body coverings and body parts found on the real animals.

Give each child an animal. Have a student secretly choose a classmate's animal, then describe it to the class without naming it. Invite the children to guess the animal and who has it. The child with the correct guess may then choose and describe a different animal.

It's parade time! Have youngsters create an imaginary parade lineup by arranging animals in a repeating pattern.

Arrange a set of animals with similar characteristics on a table, adding one animal that does not fit the description of the set. Challenge youngsters to find the out-of-place animal, then to explain why it does not belong.

Before a transition time, give each child a plastic farm animal. Direct students through the transition—such as lining up or washing their hands—by having them respond when you create the sounds made by their animals.

Give a child several different animals. Ask him to tell an imaginary story about these animals.

To play a modified version of Duck, Duck, Goose, give each child seated in the circle an animal. To play, a child secretly picks another child's animal. He then walks around the outside of the circle, tapping each child on the head and saying the name of his own animal. When he taps the head of the child with his chosen animal, he says that animal's name instead. The child with that animal chases him around the circle. Whether or not the first child is caught, the children trade animals and places.

Appoint a child to count the animals in a small set, then to distribute them to the same number of classmates. On that child's signal, each of those students pretends to be the animal he holds.

Invite youngsters to arrange the animals to create simple shapes, letters, and numerals.

Challenge youngsters to sort solid-colored animals onto construction-paper pens that correspond to the animals' colors.

Hide an animal in your classroom. Give a child directional cues—such as "Walk to the sink" and "Look below the tape player"—to help her find the animal.

The Magic of Manipulatives

Toy Vehicles

Move youngsters through these curriculum-related activities using a variety of toy vehicles. Vroom. Vroom. Zoom!

by Mackie Rhodes

Wings or wheels? Invite students to group the vehicles according to the different modes of travel such as in the air, on land, or in the water.

Mark a piece of tagboard with evenly spaced lines to create a row of parking spaces. Have a child park the vehicles to create color, size, or vehicle-type patterns.

Use a paint pen to label each vehicle in a set with a different numeral; then invite students to send them rolling in numerical sequence.

Seat youngsters in a circle; then have them pass a solid-colored vehicle in Hot Potato fashion. When the music stops, ask the child holding the vehicle to find that color on her clothing or another child's clothing.

Use a wide marker to write each letter of the alphabet on a separate sheet of construction paper. Have a child arrange a set of small, same-sized cars on each of the letters in his name.

Give each child a vehicle to manipulate on her body according to your directions. For example, have her roll a car down her leg, around her ankle, and across her foot.

Arrange a row of ramps so that each ramp is at a different angle. Ask a child to roll a different car down each of the ramps, then compare the cars' traveling distances.

Invite a child to roll a toy vehicle through tempera paint, then over large printed symbols to "track" shapes, numerals, or letters.

Ask students to create a road system with blocks. Invite each child to maneuver a toy vehicle on the roadway, naming the various directions and positions his vehicle takes.

If you labeled vehicles with numerals, try using them for turn taking and during line-up time. Simply have each child take a vehicle from a bag; then invite youngsters to join the activity in numerical sequence.

Invite youngsters on an imaginary adventure with this idea. Begin a story about a trip taken on or in a specific vehicle. In turn, pass that toy vehicle to each child, encouraging him to add an event to the story. Afterward, invite each child to illustrate an event from the class adventure.

Have students measure items in the classroom using a number of same-sized vehicles.

The Magic Of Manipulatives

Crackers

Is the search for new manipulatives making you feel "crumb-y"? Try this tasty assortment of ideas at group time or at snacktime. Your youngsters are sure to go "crackers"!

ideas contributed by Chrissy Yuhouse

For each child, prepare a paper bag with an assortment of various shapes of crackers. Have a child repeatedly reach inside his bag, feel a cracker, and then guess its shape. Then give him the bag of crackers to enjoy.

Arrange a set of crackers that vary in size and shape on a tray. Working with a small group of students, talk about how the crackers are alike and different. Sort the crackers onto two plates. Then put the crackers together and sort them again using different characteristics. After several rounds, invite the children to eat the crackers.

Give each child a zippered bag of two different shapes of crackers. Encourage her to make a pattern with the crackers.

Challenge the class to guess the number of crackers in a bag or box. Record their guesses. Count the total together; then give each child a cracker to eat.

Arrange a set of crackers that vary in size and shape on a tray. Have a small group of children describe each of the crackers; then cover the tray with a napkin. Remove one of the crackers. Remove the napkin. Have the children guess which cracker is missing. After several rounds of play, invite the children to each take a cracker to eat.

Carefully break a variety of crackers in half. Challenge youngsters to match the correct halves together.

Trace a fishbowl pattern onto ten different sheets of paper. Label each fishbowl with a different numeral from 1 to 10. Put these sheets and a separate bag of ten fish-shaped crackers for each child in a center. To use this center, a child counts the corresponding number of fish-shaped crackers from his bag onto each fishbowl. Then he eats his crackers!

Give each child a bag of various types of crackers. Have her sort the crackers by type. Then challenge her to count each type and decide which group has the most and the least. Are any groups equal? Next help her arrange the crackers in rows to create a graph.

Use animal crackers to practice ordinal numbers. Give a child four different crackers; then have her put them in order according to your directions. After several rounds, offer to switch roles with the child. Then give her the crackers for a treat.

Select a set of five to ten crackers that vary in size and shape. Then make a number of different parquetry boards for use at snacktime. To make each board, arrange the set of crackers on tagboard and trace them. Prepare a zippered bag for each child that contains a matching set of crackers. Give each child in a small group a board and a bag of crackers. Have him arrange his crackers on the board. Then have him return his crackers to his bag and trade boards with a friend. After several rounds, invite the children to eat their crackers.

Reminder: Clean hands are a must for most of these activities.

229

The Magic Of Manipulatives

Die-Cut Shapes

If you have access to a die-cutting machine, use it to cut out oodles of inexpensive class manipulatives. These ideas for using die-cut shapes are truly a cut above! ideas contributed by Betty Silkunas

These dominoes improve visual discrimination and matching skills. To make a set, visually divide a number of large index cards in half as shown. Die-cut three to four different shapes from the same color of paper. Glue one die-cut to each index-card half. Or cut the different shapes from different colors. Laminate the dominoes for durability. Let the matching fun begin!

Use die-cut shapes to play an "everybody wins" version of Pin The Tail On The Donkey. For example, in autumn, play by attaching leaf shapes to a paper tree. In winter, attach candy shapes on a paper gingerbread house. In spring, attach birds to a paper tree. In summer, attach boat shapes to a paper ocean.

To make sturdy stencils for your art center, die-cut shapes from placemats, plastic lids, or tagboard. Provide youngsters with the stencils and the die-cut shapes for use as tracers.

Play a game of musical shapes. Label a class supply of seasonal die-cut shapes with numerals or letters. Scatter the shapes on the floor in an open area. Play lively music as the children move around the shapes. When the music stops, direct each child to pick up the shape closest to his feet. In each round, ask several different students to identify the numeral or letter on their shapes.

Invite a child to make a bookmark to make a give as a gift. To make one, decorate a die-cut shape; then laminate it. Hot-glue the shape to one end of a craft stick.

Have a scavenger hunt! For each child, cut a specific number of each of several different shapes. Hide the shapes in your room. Prepare a chart (similar to the one shown) that indicates the number of each different shape that should be found. When each child has found the correct number of each of the shapes, invite him to decorate them as desired.

Play a game of Simon Says with die-cut shapes. Provide each child with a shape; then give directions such as "Put the shape on your head" and "Hold the shape in your right hand."

Periodically fill a clear container with a number of seasonal die-cut shapes. After allowing time for observation, invite children to estimate the number of shapes in the container. As a group, count aloud the shapes.

Improve visual memory with this quick game. Identify several different die-cut shapes displayed together. Have the children close their eyes as you remove one shape. Ask the children to identify the missing shape. As play continues, increase the number of shapes on display.

Make simple puzzles by die-cutting large shapes from laminated paper. Cut each shape into several puzzle pieces.

For gross-motor fun, scatter die-cut shapes on the floor around an open area. Encourage youngsters to walk, hop, run, or otherwise move around the shapes.

The Magic Of Manipulatives

Paper Plates

White paper plates and leftover party plates make wonderful, yet inexpensive, manipulatives. Use these ideas to sharpen your youngsters' skills while dishing out platefuls of fun!

by Michele Dare

Invite students to measure the length or width of the room using large paper plates, then to count the plates used. Have them repeat the activity using smaller paper plates; then have them compare the two findings.

Have your little ones sequence a variety of plates from smallest to largest.

Punch holes around the edges of the plates to create inexpensive lacing cards.

Use dimensional fabric paint to create tactile alphabet cards. Paint an uppercase letter on each of 26 large paper plates. Paint a lowercase letter on each of 26 small paper plates. Have your youngsters feel the shapes of the letters, match uppercase and lowercase letters, or practice spelling their names.

To make a memory game, program pairs of plates with matching stickers, colors, letters, or shapes.

Challenge your students to sort a collection of party plates in several different ways—by color, holiday, or size.

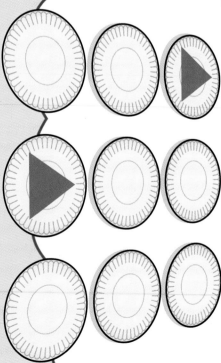

Label ten plates, each with a different numeral from 1 to 10. Challenge students to arrange the plates in numerical order.

Cut an assortment of plates into large interlocking pieces. Place all the pieces in a tub; then challenge your little ones to put the plates back together.

To make a paper-plate stencil, cut out a shape from the center of the plate. Invite students to practice drawing shapes using these stencils.

Place a variety of paper plates and cardboard tubes in your block area to add interest to structures.

Invite your youngsters to complete or create a pattern with a supply of colorful plates.

Place a stack of white paper plates and pictures of china patterns near your painting easel. Encourage your youngsters to examine the pictures, then copy or create their own china patterns by painting the paper plates.

233

EXPLORATIONS

Explorations

Just Add Water

Science concepts will soak in quite naturally with this absorbing activity. How? Just add water!

STEP 1

Direct youngsters to close their eyes and cup their hands in front of them. Put a "mystery item" (a lima bean) in each child's hands.

STEP 2

Before students peek at the mystery objects, ask questions:
Is your object big or small? Hard or soft? Smooth or rough?
What color do you think your object is?
What do you think your object is?

It is hard.
It is smooth.
It would hurt your teeth if you tried to eat it!

Have each student open his hands and examine his bean. Does it have an odor? Is it edible?
Record students' observations on chart paper.

STEP 5

The next day, remove any floating beans. Remove a half-cup of soaked beans for use in Step 6. Transfer the water and remaining beans to a slow cooker, and then cook them until they are tender.

Sing the next verse of the song from Step 4.

Now add some heat, now add some heat,
To the beans, to the beans.
Cook the beans in water, cook the beans in water,
So we can eat a bean treat!

STEP 6

On three separate plates, put the half-cup of dried beans, the half-cup of soaked beans, and a half-cup of the cooked beans. Encourage students to each examine the beans with a hand lens, then compare them. How are the beans alike or different? How did the water change the beans? How did the heat change the beans? Which beans can be eaten? Add the observations to the chart. Then dish up some cooked beans for a tasty treat.

Science You Can Do *by Suzanne Moore*

To investigate the effects of water on dried beans, you will need:

—1 package of large, dried lima beans
—chart paper (lima bean shaped, if desired)
—marker
—measuring cup
—large glass bowl
—water
—slow cooker
—plastic wrap
—hand lenses
—3 plates
—serving spoon
—1 plastic spoon per child
—1 Styrofoam® bowl per child

STEP 3

Explain that the beans have been dried: all of the water has been removed so that the beans can be stored. Collect the students' dried beans, but reserve a half-cup for use in Step 6; then pour the remainder into a large glass bowl. Ask, "How can we get water back into the beans so we can eat them?" After discussing youngsters' ideas, suggest soaking the beans in water.

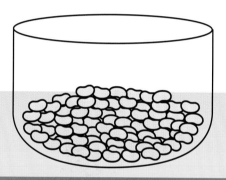

STEP 4

Have the class join you in singing the following song as several students help you cover the beans with water. Cover the bowl with plastic wrap and allow the beans to soak overnight.

Just Add Water
(sung to the tune of "Frère Jacques")

Just add water, just add water,
To the beans, to the beans.
Soak them in the water, soak them in the water,
So we can eat a bean treat!

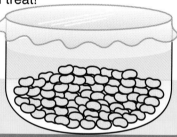

Did You Know?

- Removing the water from a bean is called *dehydration.* When a bean is dried, the bean's walls stay rigid. Even though the bean is smaller than when fresh, its original shape remains.
- Beans double in size when soaked. The beans swell because the starch inside absorbs water.
- When the beans are cooked, their walls break. When heat breaks the walls, the starch can come out. This makes the beans soft.

What Now?

Try adding water to other items, such as those listed. Will any of these items expand like the dried beans, or will something else happen?

cornstarch	oil
powdered soup mix	ice cubes
raisins	grits
tea bags	sugar
cereal	pasta
lemonade mix	dehydrated potatoes
salt	
oatmeal	

Explorations

Magic Paint

Sometimes a science experiment seems like magic—until you find out why the experiment worked! Say, "Abracadabra" and have youngsters try out this science activity that involves a chemical reaction.

STEP 1

Give each child in a small group a quarter of a lemon and a bowl. Direct the students to squeeze their lemons over their bowls, extracting as much juice as possible. Use the moist towelettes for easy cleanup.

STEP 2

With dramatic flair, produce a cotton swab for each child. Announce that the swabs are magic paint-brushes, the lemon juice is magic paint, and the children are magicians! Use the pencil to write each child's name on a piece of construction paper. Direct each child to use her swab to paint a lemon-juice design on her paper.

STEP 5

Have the children examine their dried paintings. Is it easy to see the lemon juice? In turn, have each child say the magic words, then dip her entire sheet of paper into the iodine-water mixture.

"Presto, chang-o!
Abracadabra, too!
My magic paint will soon appear,
When my paper turns purply blue!"

Have each child put her wet paper on a newspaper-lined surface, then wash her hands. Allow the papers to dry.

STEP 6

When the pictures are dry, provide time for group sharing. As each child shows her painting, ask some questions.

What made the lemon-juice paint appear?
Since the iodine mixture was brown,
*   why did the paper turn purply blue?*

If desired, share the information in "This Is Why" with the children, adapting it to meet their ability levels.

Science You Can Do

by *Suzanne Moore*

To find out about the magic of lemon juice, you will need:

—one-quarter of a lemon per child
—1 bowl per child
—moist towelettes
—1 cotton swab per child, plus extras
—foil pie pan
—1 piece of white construction paper per child, cut slightly smaller than the size of the pie pan

—pencil
—tincture of iodine
—measuring cup
—water
—1/2 teaspoon measuring spoon
—several sheets of newspaper

STEP 3

As your magicians are painting, encourage them to observe and to make comments about the juice. Ask some questions:

What color is a lemon? What color is the lemon juice?

Can you see the juice when you paint it on the paper?

Do you think you'll be able to see the juice when it dries?

Allow the paintings to dry.

STEP 4

In the foil pie pan, mix together another magic potion—one cup of water and 1/2 teaspoon tincture of iodine. Have students take note of its yellowish brown color.

This Is Why

- If the iodine mixture is brown, why did the paper turn purple? There is a substance in the paper called *starch*. There is a substance in the mixture called *iodine*. When the two substances are together, the color of the paper and the liquid are changed to purply blue.

- Why did the lemon-juice design stay white? The lemon juice has vitamin C. After the juice is painted on the paper, the vitamin C in the lemon juice separates the starch in the paper from the iodine in the mixture.

What Now?

Try another magical science activity. Have students paint lemon juice on additional sheets of white construction paper. When the paintings are dry, heat them with a warm iron. (The iron's heat will slightly burn the natural sugar in the juice.) Abracadabra! The invisible juice paintings appear like magic!

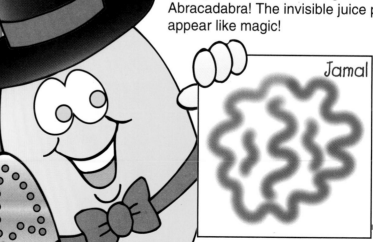

239

Explorations

Run, Spot, Run!

In this simple experiment, a black spot separates into a band of colors.

STEP 1

Give each child in a small group a paper-towel strip. Have her use the marker to draw a spot at one end of the strip.

STEP 2

Assist each child in taping the end of the strip to the middle of a craft stick.

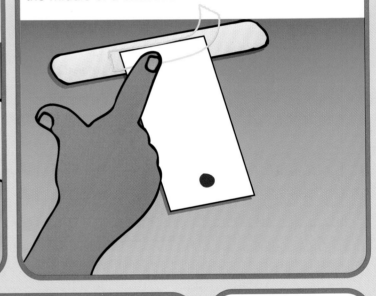

STEP 5

Encourage students to verbalize their observations as the water moves through the spot, separating the colors. (Be sure to allow time for this step. Some ink will move more slowly up the strip.) After several minutes, ask some questions:

What happened when the paper-towel strips touched the water?
What happened to the black dots?
Are all of the splotches of color the same size?

Remove the strips from the cups; then place them on trays to dry.

This Is Why

Darker colors of soluble ink, such as black or brown, are made of many colors of dye. As the water is absorbed by the towel, it travels through the ink spot. The ink begins to dissolve and separate into other colors. The color splotches are different sizes because some dyes making up the spot are more water soluble than others.

Science You Can Do *by Suzanne Moore*

To conduct this color-separation experiment, you will need:
—one 2" x 3 1/2" strip of white paper towel per child
—black water-soluble marker
—1 jumbo craft stick per child
—clear tape
—1 clear, plastic 10-ounce cup per child, marked 1" from the bottom
—room-temperature water
—trays for drying the strips

STEP 3

For each child, fill a cup to its one-inch mark with water. Ask students to predict what will happen if a paper-towel strip touches the water.

STEP 4

Have each child balance her craft stick on top of her cup so that the bottom of the paper-towel strip just barely touches the water. Encourage students to watch closely through their cups as the water begins traveling up the strip toward, then through, the spot.

Prepare a science center so that your little scientists can experiment with additional colors of water-soluble markers. Tape a number of paper-towel strips to craft sticks as before. Place the strips, a supply of markers, and the cups used in the experiment in the center. To use the center, a child chooses a marker. He then completes the experiment as described in Steps 1–5. If desired, also stock the center with crayons and paper so that youngsters can record their discoveries.

What Now?

Test the effect of water temperature with this experiment. Put cold water in one cup, room-temperature water in a second cup, and warm water in a third cup. Use a marker to draw a spot on each of three paper-towel strips that have been taped to sticks. Put each strip in a separate cup at the same time. Observe the changes. The ink suspended over the warm water will separate more quickly because water and dye move faster when warmer.

Explorations

The Eyes Have It!

Take a look and you'll find that potato eyes have buds that grow into sprouts that grow into plants!

STEP 1

Give each group of about three children a potato. Have the groups observe their potatoes. Ask questions:

What color is your potato?
What shape is your potato—round or oval-shaped?
How does it feel? Are there lumps on your potato?
How does it smell?
Could you find your potato if all of them were piled into a group? What makes your potato different?

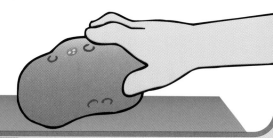

STEP 2

Point out the indentions on a potato. Explain that these are potato eyes. Next direct each group of youngsters to use a hand lens to take a closer look at its potato. Ask more questions:

How many eyes does your potato have?
How many eyes do you have?
Can potatoes see with their eyes?
Why do you think potatoes have eyes?

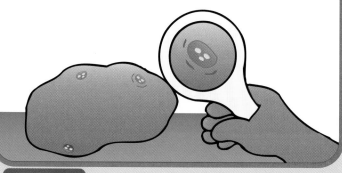

STEP 5

The next day, invite each child to plant his potato sprout in soil, making sure that the eye is facing up. (Have each child wash his hands after handling potting soil.) Keep the soil moist and in a warm area of your classroom.

STEP 6

Invite youngsters to sing this song while they are waiting for their sprouts to grow into plants—10 to 14 days.

(sung to the tune of "She'll Be Coming Round The Mountain")

Oh, we'll plant potato eyes in the ground.
Oh, we'll plant potato eyes in the ground.
Oh, we'll plant potato eyes,
And we'll get a big surprise!
Oh, we'll plant potato eyes in the ground.

Oh, the eyes have sprouts and they'll begin to grow.
Oh, the eyes have sprouts and they'll begin to grow.
Oh, the eyes have sprouts that grow,
Leaves above and roots below.
Oh, the eyes have sprouts and they'll begin to grow.

Oh, those plants can grow potatoes underground.
Oh, those plants can grow potatoes underground.
Oh, those plants can grow potatoes,
No, not carrots or tomatoes.
Oh, those plants can grow potatoes underground.

Science You Can Do by *Suzanne Moore*

To grow potato plants, you will need:
—1 potato for every three to four children
—hand magnifying lenses
—masking tape
—permanent marker
—sharp knife (for adult use only)
—1 personalized waxed-paper square per child
—1 personalized,10-ounce clear plastic cup per child
—potting soil

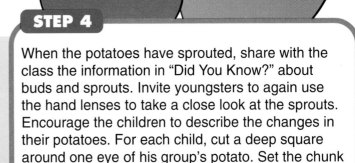

STEP 3

Ask youngsters to predict what will happen if the potatoes are hidden in a dark place. Label each group's potato by writing the children's initials on masking tape; then attach the tape to the potato. Store the potatoes in a dark place. Invite each group to check on its potato periodically during the next one to three weeks.

STEP 4

When the potatoes have sprouted, share with the class the information in "Did You Know?" about buds and sprouts. Invite youngsters to again use the hand lenses to take a close look at the sprouts. Encourage the children to describe the changes in their potatoes. For each child, cut a deep square around one eye of his group's potato. Set the chunk on his waxed paper, and allow it to dry overnight.

Did You Know?

- Here's a new word for your little scientists—*propagation*. That means that a new plant can grow from part of an old plant.

- Believe it or not, the curved part over each potato eye is called an eyebrow.

- Inside each potato eye are several buds. Each bud will grow into a white sprout that has leaves. The sprout will grow into the stem and leaves of a new potato plant.

- A potato can also be called a *tuber*. A tuber is part of a potato plant's underground stem.

What Now?

Try another spud-related experiment. Cut a potato into chunks, making sure that each chunk has an eye. Put some water in a shallow bowl; then put the fleshy part of the potato in the water. Watch for about a week. What happens?

Try planting parts of other plants in wet sand. Carrot tops will soon sprout new green leaves and stems. Pineapple tops will grow new roots.

Explorations

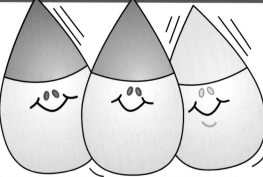

Color Swirl

Science concepts flow naturally out of this colorful science activity.

STEP 1

Just prior to trying this experiment with a small group, set out a pan and jar lid for each child. Pour enough milk into each pan to cover the bottom of the pan. Pour a small amount of liquid dish detergent in each lid.

STEP 2

Help each child squeeze one drop of four different food colorings into his milk near the edge of the pan. Encourage the children to observe the drops of food coloring, being careful not to touch or move the pans. After allowing time for comments, ask some questions:

What happened when the drops of food coloring touched the milk?
Did the whole pan of milk change color?

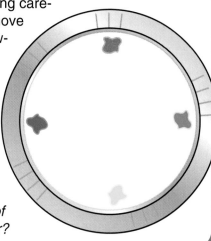

STEP 5

Direct each child to pour his milk into a sink, then use a paper towel to wipe his pan dry. Again pour milk into each child's pan. Ask students to predict what will happen if the detergent is added first and the food colorings are added second. Help each child squeeze a drop or two of the detergent in the center of the milk in his pan; then help him add a few drops of different colors of food coloring on top of the detergent. (Be sure not to stir the milk.) Discuss how the colors swirl at a slower pace.

STEP 6

Help each child recall the experiments by asking some questions:

The soap and the colors dance together in the milk.
Jason

What do you think makes the food coloring swirl in the milk? What happened when the detergent-covered toothpick touched the food coloring?

Record each child's observations and explanations.

Science You Can Do *by Suzanne Moore*

To conduct color-swirling experiments, you will need:
—1 aluminum pie pan per child in a small group
—whole milk, enough to cover the bottom of each child's pan twice
—1 jar lid per child
—liquid dish detergent in a squeeze bottle
—food coloring (red, blue, green, yellow)
—1 toothpick per child

—paper towels
—chart paper
—marker

STEP 3

Assist each child in squeezing a drop of liquid dish detergent into the center of the milk in his pan. Allow time for youngsters to verbalize their observations as the food coloring swirls together to create unique designs.

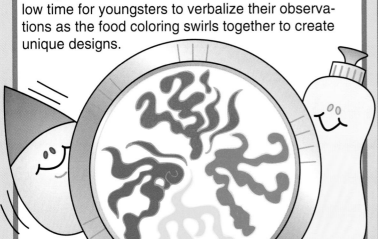

STEP 4

Direct each child to dip a toothpick into the jar lid of dish detergent, then into the milk. Remind him to dip the toothpick into the milk or color without stirring it. Again, invite the children to make observations as new color patterns are created. (If the swirling in a child's pan stops, add more food coloring and/or dish detergent.)

This Is Why

Milk is mostly water. The water in the milk forms an invisible "skin" on the surface of the milk. This skin is created by *surface tension.* When the food coloring is added to the milk, the skin supports it. But when the detergent touches the milk, the surface tension breaks, pulling the skin to the edge of the pan. This causes the colors to swirl!

What Now?

Try another experiment with milk and soap. Again pour milk into a pan. This time, shake some cinnamon on the milk. Then dip the corner of a bar of soap into the center of the milk in the pan. What happens to the cinnamon? Encourage careful observation; then discuss the results.

Explorations

Hot Dog!

Heat got you down? Perk up the dog days of summer with this activity that combines science with cooking.

STEP 1

Invite a small group of children to help you measure the cooking-dough ingredients into the bowl. Give each child a turn stirring the dough, mixing until it is smooth. (If the dough seems sticky, add more flour.)

STEP 2

Direct each child in the group to wash her hands. Give each child a hot dog on a piece of aluminum foil. Demonstrate how to roll the hot dog in the foil, then crimp the ends of the foil to seal it. (Be sure to check each child's efforts to make sure that her hot dog has been totally covered with foil.)

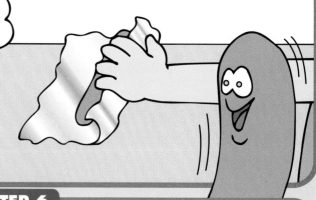

STEP 5

After removing the dough dogs from the oven, allow them to cool about an hour. Ask some questions:

How does the dough dog feel different?
What do you think made the dough change?
What do you think happened to the hot dog? How can you find out?

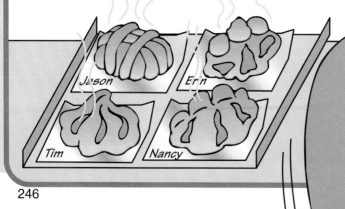

STEP 6

Give a resealable plastic freezer bag to each child; then direct her to put her dough dog inside. Seal the bag. Have each child break the dough with a block. After she has removed the foil-wrapped dog from her bag, have her discard the clay. Next have her unwrap the hot dog to find that it is completely cooked. Provide the plates, buns, and condiments so that the children can eat these tasty science projects!

Science You Can Do *by Suzanne Moore*

To cook hot dogs in clay, you will need:
—1 hot dog per child (turkey and tofu franks also work)
—2 strips of aluminum foil per child (wide enough to wrap a hot dog)
—1 batch of cooking dough (3 cups flour, 1 1/2 cups water, 3/4 cup salt) for every 4–6 children
—extra flour
—large mixing bowl
—large stirring spoon
—1 plastic tray per child in a small group
—baking sheets
—permanent marker
—1 resealable plastic freezer bag per child
—building block (from your construction center)
—1 hot-dog bun per child
—1 paper plate per child
—condiments such as ketchup, mustard, etc.

STEP 3

Give each child a tray. Have her dust the tray and her hands with flour (to prevent the dough from sticking); then give her a portion of the dough. Direct each student to use her hands to flatten the dough, then cover her foil-wrapped hot dog with it. Encourage students to embellish their dough dogs with extra dough to create sculptures, if desired.

STEP 4

Use a permanent marker to personalize each child's second strip of aluminum foil. Place the strip on a baking sheet; then place the child's dough dog on it. Ask students to predict what will happen to the dough dogs in the oven. Bake the dough dogs at 350° for about 1 1/2 hours or until the dough is completely dry.

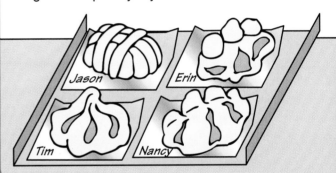

This Is Why

Cooking a dough dog is similar to cooking in a clay pot. When placed in a hot oven, the dough heats up. The dough dries as the water in it slowly turns to steam. The hot dog cooks in its own juices because it is completely trapped inside the steaming hot dough. When the dough dries, the hot dog is cooked!

What Next?

Try this experiment to help children understand that the oven's heat cooks the hot dog. Make one dough dog by following Steps 1 through 3. Allow the dough dog to air-dry. (Depending on the humidity and the thickness of the dough, the drying process will take one to three days.) Crack the clay, peel back the foil, and then invite youngsters to look at and smell the hot dog. Did it cook? Guide the children to determine that the hot dog did not cook even though the clay dried out. (Also point out that nobody would want to eat a hot dog that has been left at room temperature for several days!)

247

BUILDING BRIDGES BETWEEN HOME AND SCHOOL

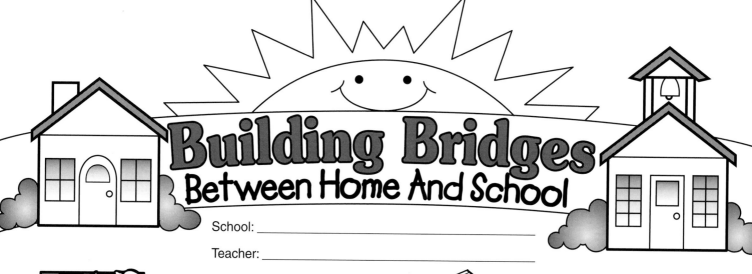

Building Bridges
Between Home And School

School: _____

Teacher: _____

Date: _____

Sharing

"It's mine!" Oh, the challenges of sharing when you've just learned what belongs to you and what belongs to others! Sharing is indeed difficult for toddlers. Fortunately between the ages of three and four, sharing becomes easier. Watch for these social developments in your preschooler.

- **Three-year-olds** begin experimenting with various sharing techniques, such as taking turns and trading toys, for short periods of time.
- **Older three-year-olds** begin to cooperate. They understand that giving doesn't mean giving up, and are more willing to give and take freely with friends.
- **Four-year-olds** grasp the concept of sharing very well. They play cooperatively with their friends and are willing to share their possessions.

What can you do to help your preschooler's transition from a possessive toddler into a caring sharer?

- **Encourage sharing; don't force it.** A reluctant sharer may feel that his/her needs are less important than the other child's needs. Forcing a child to comply is not the same as teaching him/her to be generous.
- **Acknowledge that sometimes it's hard to share.** Use empathy rather than scolding to encourage sharing.
- **Applaud sharing.** Notice times when your child shares willingly with a sibling or friend; then compliment his/her efforts.
- **Share with your child.** Be a role-model for the behaviors you wish your child to exhibit. Share food, books, and small articles of clothing to reinforce the benefits of sharing.

The Book Corner

Books About Sharing

It's Mine!
Three selfish frogs fuss over their pond home. Then they realize the fun of sharing.
Written & Illustrated by Leo Lionni
Published by Random House, Inc.

Peter's Chair
Many of Peter's baby things are given to his younger sister. He resents having to share, until he realizes he doesn't need those things anymore.
Written & Illustrated by Ezra Jack Keats
Published by HarperCollins Children's Books

The Little Mouse, The Red Ripe Strawberry, And The Big Hungry Bear
How do you keep a bear from finding your strawberry? Share it!
Written & Illustrated by Don & Audrey Wood
Published by Child's Play (International) Ltd.

My New Sandbox
A little boy has a sandbox that is just the right size for him—and him alone. Eventually he realizes how lonely he is in his sandbox and invites some guests to join him.
Written by Donna Jakob
Published by Hyperion Books For Children

One Of Each
Oliver Tolliver lives alone in his house that is perfect for one. Then Oliver finds out how he can make his house welcoming for more.
Written by Mary Ann Hoberman
Published by Little, Brown And Company

To The Teacher: Duplicate a copy of pages 251 and 252. Complete the information at the top of page 251; then add class-related news to page 252. Trim away these instructions. Duplicate a copy for each child on the front and back sides of a colorful piece of paper.

Together Time

Kitchen Capers

Check It Out!

Check out this idea that will give your little one practice sharing. Ask each member of your family to think of one thing he/she would like to borrow from one other member, or one thing he/she would loan to other members. Display the items. Prepare a checkout card for each member of the family. Designate a borrowing time, such as 30 minutes. Ask each family member to select one item he/she wishes to check out. Then have that person present his/her card to you so that you can note on the card what was borrowed and when it is due back. Repeat the borrowing and lending process several times. Soon your child will understand that sharing is all about giving and taking!

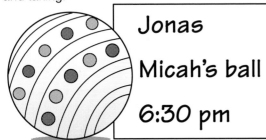

Jonas

Micah's ball

6:30 pm

Share A Pear

Follow these easy directions to make a healthful snack that you can share with someone special. Wash a pear. Cut two thick slices from opposite sides of the pear. Share the pear by giving your cooking partner a slice. Spread flavored yogurt or peanut butter onto your slice. Invite your partner to spread one of the toppings on his/her slice. Decorate your slice with dried fruit and cereal pieces. Exchange your pear slice with your partner. Share smiles as you enjoy the snacks!

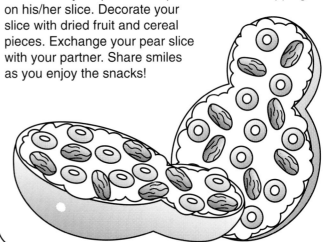

Read All About It!
Our Class News

The ideas in this newsletter are contributed by Jan Brennan.

Building Bridges
Between Home And School

School: _____

Teacher: _____

Date: _____

Thankfulness

"Thank you for picking up your toys." "Thank you for sharing." Did you realize that your frequent expressions of gratitude to your child not only model good manners for him/her but also foster thankfulness in him/her? If your child is three or four years old, you have another thing to be grateful for: it's the prime time to develop this virtue!

- A preschooler's ability to reason is expanding, so he/she is better able to understand right and wrong.
- Other people's feelings are becoming important to the young child.
- Three- and four-year-olds have the desire to please their parents and caregivers.

With these developments in mind, use these tips to foster thankfulness in your child.

- Talk with your child about things that you and he/she are happy to have, people you are happy to know, and situations that you are happy have happened.
- Teach your child to say "Thank you" in appropriate situations.
- Explain why it is important to say "Thank you"—emphasizing the consideration of other people's feelings.
- Continue to model gratitude in your words and actions. Imitation is an important way for youngsters to learn social skills and values.
- Read stories in which the characters are grateful. (Visit your library to check out some of the books listed at the right.)

The Book Corner

Books About Thankfulness

Find out what the characters in these stories are thankful for!

The Relatives Came
When the relatives come for their yearly visit, their sincere thankfulness for one another is evident in their exuberant fun and shared love.
Written by Cynthia Rylant
Published by Simon & Schuster Children's Books

Giving Thanks: A Native American Good Morning Message
A beautifully illustrated book that details the glorious gifts from Mother Earth for which we can all be thankful.
Written by Chief Jake Swamp
Published by Lee & Low Books, Inc.

I'm Thankful Each Day!
A collection in rhyme of blessings and gifts given to us each day.
Written & Illustrated by P. K. Hallinan
Published by Ideals Children's Books

The Child's World Of Thankfulness
This straightforward book asks what thankfulness is, then answers with many different examples.
Written by Janet McDonnell
Published by The Child's World®, Inc.

To The Teacher: Duplicate a copy of pages 253 and 254. Complete the information at the top of page 253; then add class-related news to page 254. Trim away these instructions. Duplicate a copy for each child on the front and back sides of a colorful piece of paper.

Thankful-Thoughts Game

This version of the game Mother, May I? will have your family giving thanks. To play, one family member is asked to be Mother. Mother stands on one side of an open space or room, and the remaining family members stand on the opposite side. Mother asks each player in turn, "For what are you thankful?", to which the player responds, "I am thankful for [person, place, or thing]." Mother then gives the player a command such as "Take two baby steps" or "Hop five times." The player completes the command, moving toward Mother. The game continues in the same manner until each player reaches Mother.

Count Your Blessings

This cooking activity will have your child counting his/her blessings on one hand—one hand-shaped sandwich, that is! Assist your child as he/she makes a peanut-butter sandwich. Have your child gently lay one hand on top of the sandwich. Use a butter knife to cut out the shape of his/her hand. Ask your child to name one thing he/she is thankful for before he/she eats each finger of the sandwich.

Read All About It!
Our Class News

The ideas in this newsletter are contributed by Jan Brennan.

©The Education Center, Inc. • *THE MAILBOX®* • *Preschool* • Oct/Nov 1998

Building Bridges
Between Home And School

School: _____

Teacher: _____

Date: _____

Holiday Traveling

If your holiday plans involve traveling with your preschooler, be of good cheer! The holiday merriment *can* continue right into your trip, and you can pack some learning into the journey as well. Use these easy-to-play games to help pass the time and stretch your little one's thinking. Are we there yet?

- Since you can't stretch your muscles, stretch your imaginations with a game of **What's Their Story?** Observe the people you see in passing vehicles. Help your child make up a story about them by asking him/her questions such as "What are their names? Where are they going? Why are they going there?"

- Play a game of **What If?** to let your child's imagination run wild. Ask questions such as "What if you were the queen or king?" or "If you could invent a new holiday, what would you celebrate?"

- To play a game of **Cars Like Ours,** study a nearby car to see how many similarities it has to yours. For example, is the car the same color? How many people are in the car? Is that number more or less than in your car?

- Here's a way to add new fun to the traditional **"Eye" Spy** game. Have your child look out the window or around the plane to find a specific item. When he/she spies it, reward him/her with one small snack item. Allow him/her to collect the treats in a plastic bag or munch as he/she collects.

Don't forget to pack some books! Your traveling time together is the perfect time to improve your child's listening and reading skills. (Visit your library or a bookstore to check out some of the books listed at the right.)

The Book Corner
Books About Traveling

First Flight
Fly along with this little boy, and you'll note the differences between his good manners and those of his traveling companion.
Written & Illustrated by David McPhail
Published by Little, Brown And Company

The Bag I'm Taking To Grandma's
Youngsters enjoy reading along with the rebus pictures in this book about a boy packing—or rather stuffing—a bag to take to grandma's.
Written by Shirley Neitzel
Published by Greenwillow Books

Round Trip
Follow this black-and-white journey from the country to the city and back again in this incredibly clever book.
Written & Illustrated by Ann Jonas
Published by Mulberry Books

Counting Our Way To Maine
Count along with this family as they pack one baby, two dogs, and three bikes for their vacation in Maine.
Written & Illustrated by Maggie Smith
Published by Orchard Books

Dinosaurs Travel: A Guide For Families On The Go
Lively text and funny illustrations make this the perfect traveling guide for your youngster.
Written & Illustrated by Laurie Krasny Brown and Marc Brown
Published by Little, Brown And Company

To The Teacher: Duplicate a copy of pages 255 and 256. Complete the information at the top of page 255; then add class-related news to page 256. Trim away these instructions. Duplicate a copy for each child on the front and back sides of a colorful piece of paper.

Together Time

Pack Your Sack!

Foster your child's independence with some problem-solving packing. Before your departure, invite your child to pack a sack to take along with him/her. Give him/her an appropriately sized bag—not too large for the space available and not too small for a satisfying amount of goodies. Together decide what is important when choosing items. For example, you may decide that some art supplies could spill or be messy, or that other items—such as small action figures—provide lots of fun for a long time. However, allow your child as much freedom to choose the items as possible.

If desired, have your child decorate a tag to identify his/her own special bag. Then help him/her attach the tag to the bag with a length of ribbon.

Kitchen Capers

Edible Jewelry

Your child will improve his/her fine-motor skills when making this snack to take along for the ride. In advance of the trip, provide your child with a variety of snacks that have holes, such as Cheerios®, Froot Loops®, pretzels, and LifeSavers®. Have him/her string the items onto a clean shoelace or length of yarn that is long enough to make a necklace. Tie the ends of the lace together. Put it in a resealable bag; then pack it for a special moment on the trip.

Read All About It!
Our Class News

The ideas in this newsletter are contributed by Jan Brennan.

Building Bridges
Between Home And School

School: _____

Teacher: _____

Date: _____

Math At Home

Do you feel "at home" guiding your child's understanding of math? You can—it's as easy as 1, 2, 3! First you need to understand your child's developmental level—what your child can understand and learn.

- **Three-year-olds** can count aloud to five. They can touch and count up to three objects. They can match shapes, but they may not be able to name them. They can also sort things by their color or size.

- **Four-year-olds** are learning to count the objects in a set of up to five or ten and to create sets of up to five objects. They can match shapes and are beginning to identify them.

Preschoolers learn best when they can count, match, sort, or group *real* objects rather than pictures. Keep this in mind and you'll find lots of math opportunities at home. Here are some ideas to get you started!

- Have your child set the table. He/She will practice sorting objects, counting, and following a pattern.
- Invite your child to help you sort clothes when you do the laundry. Shirts over here, socks over there!
- When making a phone call, invite your child to press the buttons for you. Point out each button and say its number.
- Be brave when you are baking! Invite your child to count/measure some of the ingredients.
- Read books together that reinforce math concepts. Look for the books on the list (at the right) in your library or bookstore.

The Book Corner

Books You Can Count On

Five Little Monkeys Jumping On The Bed
This story will have your own little monkey jumping with delight as he/she counts five falling monkeys.
Written & Illustrated by Eileen Christelow
Published by Clarion Books

Ten Black Dots
You and your child will be amazed at all the things you can do with ten black dots.
Written & Illustrated by Donald Crews
Published by Greenwillow Books

One Was Johnny: A Counting Book
As Johnny's tale is told, your child can join in the rhyme by counting up to ten, then back down again.
Written & Illustrated by Maurice Sendak
Published by HarperTrophy

Numbears: A Counting Book
Pleasant rhymes and endearing paintings of teddy bears make this counting book a treasure.
Written by Kathleen Hague
Published by Henry Holt And Company, Inc.

The M&M's® Brand Chocolate Candies Counting Book
Older preschoolers will enjoy this tasteful book. Get your own pack of M&M's® so your child can count along and sample the candies as well!
Written by Barbara Barbieri McGrath
Published by Charlesbridge Publishing, Inc.

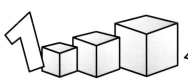

©The Education Center, Inc. • THE MAILBOX® • Preschool • Feb/Mar 1999

To The Teacher: Duplicate a copy of pages 257 and 258. Complete the information at the top of page 257; then add class-related news to page 258. Trim away these instructions. Duplicate a copy for each child on the front and back sides of a colorful piece of paper.

Together Time

Kitchen Capers

"Math-magic" Bag

This bag of tricks provides magic math moments whenever you need a time filler. Take a few moments to gather the following items and put them into a bag: a ball of string; a zippered plastic bag containing several pennies, nickels, dimes, and quarters; a deck of cards; and plastic forks, knives, and spoons. Here are some ideas for instant math fun:

- Use the **ball of string** to measure different parts of your child's body. (No numbers are needed; just compare the lengths of string.) Let him/her measure you as well. Move on to measuring household objects, siblings, and even pets!

- Spread out all of the **coins.** Ask your child to find ways that they are alike and different. Sort the coins by size and color. Play a guessing game: Tell your child you've picked out one of the coins. Then give him/her hints to figure out which one. Reverse roles.

- Help your child sort the **deck of cards** by number and symbol. Find all of the ones, twos, and threes; then arrange those cards facedown. Tell your child to flip over two cards. Do they match? Keep flipping pairs until you find all the matches.

- Have your child sort and count the **forks, knives, and spoons.** Help him/her make a simple pattern, such as fork, knife, fork, knife, and so on.

Shapely Snacks

Challenge your child to start pointing out the foods that you eat that are circles, squares, triangles, rectangles, or ovals. Why not have a special shape of the day? Here are some shapely food suggestions:

Circles
pancakes
banana slices
bagels

Squares
cheese slices
saltine crackers
Chex® cereal

Triangles
Doritos® tortilla chips
sandwich halves
slice of cake or pie

Read All About It!
Our Class News

The ideas in this newsletter are contributed by Jan Brennan.

Building Bridges
Between Home And School

School: _____

Teacher: _____

Date: _____

Rainy-Day Fun

It's raining, it's pouring, but your day doesn't have to be boring! Chase away the rainy-day, stay-in-the-house blues with these simple activities. Not only will these ideas keep your little one busy, but they'll promote learning, too!

- **Go on a treasure hunt.** Wrap up a simple surprise treat (such as candy or a sticker); then hide it. Lead your child through the hunt with a series of verbal directions. Or draw picture clues to the object's location. A treasure hunt is a great way for three-year-olds to practice following two- or three-step directions. Picture clues also help develop prereading skills in four-year-olds.

- **Play dress-up.** Develop creativity by playing dress-up (it's not just for girls, you know!). Playing dress-up is also a fun way for your child to practice dressing skills and strengthen his/her small-muscle control. In addition, this is a good time to listen to your child and discover his/her observations of the grown-up world around him/her.

- **Create a maze.** Make a maze to help your child release indoor energy. Move furniture around to create a crawling, climbing, balancing maze. Or arrange a set of small objects in an open space for your child to hop over or tiptoe between.

- **Set up a crafts table.** Simply provide your child with scissors, glue, markers, and any scrap paper you can recycle, such as junk mail or magazines. Give your child the freedom to create unique artwork.

- **Read stories.** Learning benefits of reading together include improved listening, thinking skills, new vocabulary, and, of course, a love of reading. Next time you have a rainy day, visit a library to check out some of the books suggested at the right.

The Book Corner

A Shower Of Stories About Rain

Peter Spier's Rain
In this wordless picture book, a brother and sister frolic through their neighborhood during a rainstorm.
Illustrated by Peter Spier
Published by Picture Yearling

Rain
Rain falls on many colorful things, then ends with a rainbow. A simple book that even the youngest listeners will want to join in reading.
Written by Robert Kalan
Published by William Morrow & Company

Listen To The Rain
Simple paintings and descriptive words bring out the beauty of a rainstorm. Read this one over and over again.
Written by Bill Martin, Jr., and John Archambault
Published by Henry Holt & Company, Inc.

In The Rain With Baby Duck
Grandpa Duck empathizes when Baby Duck doesn't like the rain. Then he solves the problem with love and understanding.
Written by Amy Hest
Published by Candlewick Press

Cat And Mouse In The Rain
Through the help of a little frog, Cat and Mouse find out how much fun the rain can be.
Written by Tomek Bogacki
Published by Farrar Straus & Giroux

To The Teacher: Duplicate a copy of pages 259 and 260. Complete the information at the top of page 259; then add class-related news to page 260. Trim away these instructions. Duplicate a copy for each child on the front and back sides of a colorful piece of paper.

Together Time

Wet-Weather Walk

Don't let the weather rain on your parade. Instead, parade right out into the rain with your child to make some wet discoveries. Here are some questions you can ask your child.

Why do you think it rains?
What does the rain do when it hits the ground?
   A puddle? Your hand?
If you were an animal, where would you hide?
Where do you think the flowing water will go?
Where did the sun go?
Why do we need rain?
What do you think makes puddles?
How do we know when it is going to rain?

Kitchen Capers

Rainy-Day Tea

A tea party can brighten any rainy day! Enjoy making hot cross buns and tea with your little one; then sit down for a fancy treat.

Hot Cross Buns

Have your child arrange refrigerator dinner biscuits on a pan. Next have him/her use a knife to make a criss-cross on each biscuit. Help your child measure and mix together one tablespoon of sugar, one teaspoon of cinnamon, and one tablespoon of melted butter. Have your child brush the mixture on top of each roll. Bake the biscuits according to the package directions. The smell will be as good as the taste!

Rainy-Day "Tea"

To make two servings, help your child pour two cups of fruit juice and one-half cup of water into a small pan. Add one cinnamon stick to the liquid before heating it. Serve with a smile.

Read All About It!
Our Class News

The ideas in this newsletter are contributed by Jan Brennan.

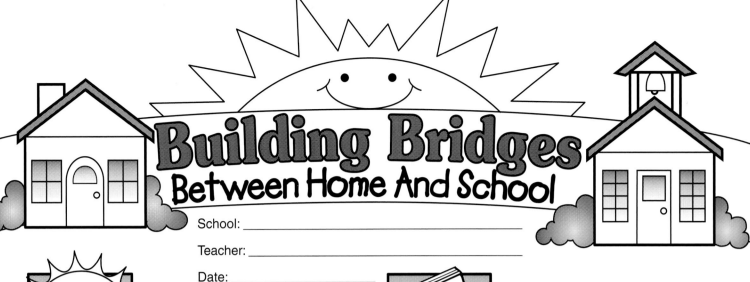

Building Bridges
Between Home And School

School: _____

Teacher: _____

Date: _____

Summer
A Hot Time For Some Cool Learning!

It's summertime—and the learning is easy! Since your preschooler is ready to soak in learning opportunities no matter what the season, here are some ideas to help you plan some meaningful summer fun for your child.

- **Outdoor Art**—Pack up the art supplies your child already has and encourage him/her to take them outside. Mess isn't much of a problem outdoors, so pull out the paint and fingerpaint. Or try painting with water. And don't forget an old favorite, colorful chalk.

- **Water Play**—Whether indoors or outdoors, water play is just plain fun. Keeping your child occupied, exploring, and discovering is as easy as filling a sink or tub with water and providing a variety of containers and kitchen gadgets. Outdoors, tint tubs of water with food coloring or add dish soap.

- **Excursions**—Anything from a quick walk around a block to a planned outing offers opportunities for conversations, questions, and discoveries. Why not take along a video camera and make your child the star? Or ask your child to spend some time after an outing drawing pictures of the trip.

- **Read**—Take a few of your child's favorite books outside and read. Or make a weekly treat of visiting the library. (Many libraries offer fun summer reading programs.) For starters, check out the titles at the right.

The Book Corner
Summer Selections

One Hot Summer Day
This book invites you to experience a hot summer day in the city through the eyes of an energetic, fun-loving girl.
Written by Nina Crews
Published by Greenwillow Books

Sophie's Bucket
Sophie takes a memorable excursion to the beach with her mom and dad.
Written & Illustrated by Catherine Stock
Published by Harcourt Brace & Company

When Daddy Took Us Camping
A father takes two of his children camping and they all love every minute of their experience.
Written & Illustrated by Julie Brillhart
Published by Albert Whitman & Company

The Best Vacation Ever
A little girl helps her family decide where to go on vacation by asking family members questions and using the information to make a compromising choice.
Written by Stuart J. Murphy
Published by HarperTrophy

When Summer Comes
Discuss the many activities of summer as you look at these photos with your child.
Written by Robert Maass
Published by Henry Holt And Company, Inc.

Fireflies For Nathan
Nathan spends a magical evening catching fireflies with his grandparents.
Written by Shulamith Levey Oppenheim
Published by Puffin Books

To The Teacher: Duplicate a copy of pages 261 and 262. Complete the information at the top of page 261; then add class-related news to page 262. Trim away these instructions. Duplicate a copy for each child on the front and back sides of a colorful piece of paper.

Summer Memories

Whether it's simply playing outside or taking a trip to the shore, record your child's summer fun on film. Later glue a picture of each experience on a separate large index card. Date the card. Ask your child to tell you a sentence or two about the picture to write on the card. At the end of the summer, sequence the pictures; then bind them together with a shower-curtain ring, keyring, or length of string to make a booklet. Your child will learn from this project now and remember the glory days of summer later.

July 7

Jobie came over to play in my pool!

Citrus Slush

Blend together one of these Citrus Slushes for a refreshing taste of summer! Just blend the following ingredients together until you have a thick, pulpy drink. If desired, add some orange juice or water.

1 peeled and seeded lemon
1 peeled and seeded orange
5 ice cubes
1 tablespoon sugar

Refreshing!

Read All About It!
Our Class News

The ideas in this newsletter are contributed by Jan Brennan.

PEEK-A-BOO

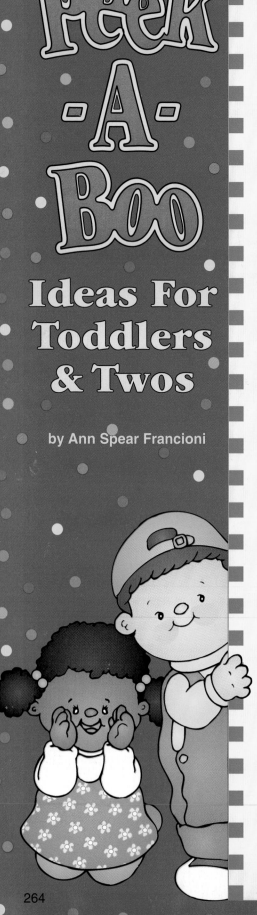

Peek -A- Boo

Ideas For Toddlers & Twos

by Ann Spear Francioni

Fine-Motor Skills

- Fine-motor activities help your tiny tots gain control over their small-muscle movements.

- From a toddler's head down to his toes, fine-motor activities encourage a child to wiggle his fingers and wrists, practice hand-eye coordination, and even move his feet.

- Fine-motor activities help a toddler gain independence by increasing her ability to use her hands to manipulate her environment.

Hide-And-Seek

This idea uses a toddler's natural curiosity as a motivational tool for learning. Fill a small tub with large, dried lima beans. Put the tub and several objects (such as beads, cubes, or toy cars) on the floor in front of a child. Begin by choosing one item and pushing it down into the beans so that it is hidden from view. Invite the child to put his hand in the tub to find the object. Ask him what he hears and feels, supplying words such as *cold, slippery,* and *hard,* if necessary. Gradually increase the number of items you put into the tub at one time. The look of delight on the child's face when his hand disappears into the beans will let you know he's having fun and learning, too!

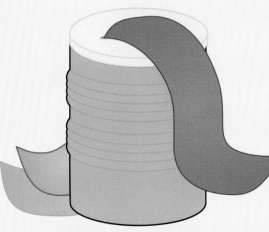

Toddler Magic

"You can do it!" are the only magic words you'll need to encourage a child to give this scarf trick a try. To prepare for this magical learning experience, cover a large can that has a tight-fitting lid (such as a coffee can) with colorful Con-Tact® covering. Cut an *X* in the lid to create an opening that is large enough for a toddler to put her hand through. Trim the sharp points of the lid. Have a child observe as you put a number of colorful scarves into the can through the lid. Then pull out one of the scarves and wave it in the air with great excitement. Pull out the tip of another scarf before offering the can to the child. For younger toddlers, tie the scarves together to make them easier to pull out. Forget Houdini! You're looking at the great "Two-dini"!

Who Took The Cookie From The Cookie Jar?

Toddlers can take the cookies from the cookie jar. Who, twos? Yes, twos! Remove the labels from a number of clean, large, clear plastic jars (such as peanut-butter containers). Put an edible treat—such as a cookie or cracker—inside each jar; then loosely screw on the lid. Demonstrate how to unscrew the lid from a jar, take out the cookie inside, and screw the lid back on. (As children gain proficiency at this task, screw the lids on tighter.) Give each child a jar and encourage him to give the jar a twist to get his treat.

Shake Things Up

Learning to pick up and hold objects is an exciting accomplishment. To help your younger toddlers develop this skill, fill containers—such as potato-chip cans and spice bottles—with dried beans, beads, or bells. Tightly screw on the lids. First provide large shakers that need to be held with two hands; then gradually decrease the size of the containers to those that can be easily held by one hand. If you really want to shake things up in your toddler classroom, give each child a shaker and play some lively music. Who would have thought that working on fine-motor skills would be so noisy and fun?

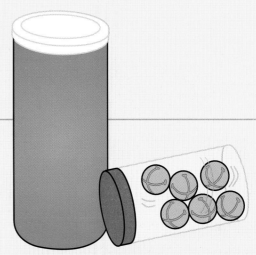

Drop Everything!

Once toddlers get the hang of picking up objects, the next task is to learn how to release the objects at will. This activity develops imaginations and language skills, provides releasing practice, and builds self-esteem. Make a game out of picking up a group of like toys and dropping them into a tub by pretending that the tub is something different that relates to the items. For example, with a collection of plastic food, pretend the tub is a soup pot. Repeatedly encourage a child to pick up a piece and drop it in the soup pot (tub). During the fun, describe the items and emphasize how they relate. Clap and lavish verbal praise on the child each time she drops an object in the tub. Let's go now…grab and release, grab and release…

This Game's A Ringer

When it comes to developing hand-eye coordination, this activity is a ringer! Borrow a clean baby-bottle drainer from the infant room in your center. Collect a number of plastic rings and plastic bracelets. (Make sure that the rings are too large to be swallowed.) Encourage children to put the rings on the drainer's posts. As a challenge, ask a child to put on two rings at a time. Encouraging children to put the rings on their wrists is yet another quick way to develop small-muscle coordination.

Peek -A- Boo

Ideas For Toddlers & Twos

by Ann Spear Francioni

Tidbits
Gross-Motor Skills

Looking for a way to boost a toddler's self-esteem? Help him improve his gross-motor abilities! Here's why:

- A child builds self-esteem as each new skill is mastered. Large movements are some of the most obvious to see and evaluate.

- The more independence a young child has, the more self-confident he feels. Gross-motor skills help a child manipulate and control his surroundings.

Spooky Parade

Learning to balance can be tricky! So give your little goblins practice by having a spooky parade. Prepare a masking-tape trail on the floor in an open area. Have your toddlers follow you in parade fashion as you walk on the trail. Enhance the fun by making spooky "oohs" and "aahs" as you go. Or travel to the beat of a lively selection of music. Ask an adult volunteer to stop the music to cue your group to freeze. Be sure to observe and take note of how well each of your toddlers balance on the line, both while walking and standing still.

Step-By-Step

Here's another quick way to have toddlers follow your lead to improve their walking skills. With a small number of youngsters behind you, take *giant steps, tiny steps, soft steps, stomping steps, skating steps,* and more. With every small step a toddler takes, there's a giant step toward gross-motor development!

Dot-To-Dot

Once your little ones get pretty good at moving around, prepare this game to help them learn to control their movements. For each child, secure a colorful, laminated construction-paper circle to the floor in an open area. Direct each child in your group to stand on a circle. On your sound cue (such as a ringing bell or buzzer), challenge each child to move off his circle, then onto a different circle by the time you give the cue a second time. Speed up the game or slow it down to match your children's ability and interest levels.

Climbing The Wall

Work out little ones' shoulders and arms with this creative painting activity. Vertically attach a length of bulletin-board paper to a wall so that the base of the paper is even with the base of the wall. Spread additional paper on the floor to protect it from paint. Have a child dip her hands into a shallow pan of washable paint. Direct the child to squat in front of the paper on the wall and to press her hands on the paper directly in front of her. Then challenge her to "walk" her hands up the paper as far as she can reach, leaving handprints that show her path.

Tunnel Tubes

Keep youngsters' hands busy with this tunnel-tube challenge. Invite each child to use markers and seasonal stickers to decorate a personalized cardboard tube. Have the child use one hand to hold the tube horizontally and at one end. Put a Ping-Pong® ball in the tube; then challenge the child to balance his tube so that the ball does not roll out. As the child becomes better at managing this trick, have him gradually move his hands toward the center of the tube.

Strike!

This bowling game is inexpensive to prepare and is sure to have each of your toddlers on a roll toward improving large-motor movement *and* eye-hand coordination. Use markers to draw silly faces or jack-o'-lantern grins on six to eight empty, large, plastic soda bottles. Arrange these bottles in a close line or in a group. Challenge a child to roll a ball toward the bottles to see how many he can knock down. Take away one bottle at a time so that the child must roll more accurately in order to hit the remaining bottles.

Peek -A- Boo

Ideas For Toddlers & Twos

by Ann Spear Francioni

Tidbits

Language Skills

● Looking for signs of a toddler's intellectual development? Listen to her language! Language is one of the greatest indicators you'll have of her mental growth.

● Language helps a toddler communicate with the world around him. Using new vocabulary makes him feel capable and independent.

● Language is more than talking—it's listening and thinking, too.

Name That Noise

Guess what this game encourages? Listening and speaking, of course. Invite your children to watch and listen as you repeatedly record familiar sounds (such as a door closing and blocks falling), then play the sounds back again. When you have completed making the tape, replay it and have the children take turns naming the sounds. Very soon you'll hear the results of their increased listening skills.

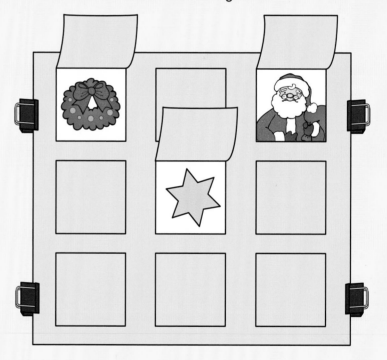

Surprise Me

Don't be surprised how much this game improves your little ones' language skills. It's simple to make and it helps youngsters guess, describe, and remember. To make a guessing game, use a utility knife to cut nine or more square flaps in a sheet of poster board, making sure that the flaps are spaced apart evenly. Lift each flap and fold it along the uncut side. Clip the sheet of cut poster board on top of a second sheet of poster board. Beneath each flap, tape a different magazine picture, clip art image, or photo to the bottom sheet of poster board. To use the game, invite a child to look under each flap and describe what he sees. Then have him close the flaps and guess what is under a flap before lifting it again. Vary the pictures by season, holiday, or theme.

Landmarks For Language

Here's a decorating tip that helps youngsters use their language skills and reinforces colors and shapes at the same time. In each area of your classroom, secure a large shape of a different color to the floor. For example, attach a blue star to the floor in your block area and a yellow star to the floor in your group area. Refer to these shapes when giving directions to your toddlers. For example, you might say, "Sit near the yellow star for storytime" or "Wait by the red star to go outside." Change the shapes periodically to keep your little ones listening, looking, and learning!

Telephone A Toddler

If you want to increase a child's verbal skills, give him a call! For this quick activity, keep two toy phones available (or remove the cords from real phone receivers). When you'd like to have a conversation with a child, ask him to pretend that he is talking with you on the phone. Use this technique just for fun, to ask diagnostic questions, or to inquire about his activity choice during free time. When the child understands the concept of phone-talking, offer to pretend to call someone he knows, such as a parent. "Dial" the number; then model talking to that person. When it is the child's turn to talk, prompt him with phrases to use, such as "How are you?" or "What are you having for lunch?"

Pack In The Language Skills

Put on your thinking cap and get toddlers talking with this small-group activity. Show the group a container, such as a basket, a tote bag, or a small suitcase. Pose a situation, such as "We're going on a picnic" or "We're going to Grandma's house." Begin by naming an item you would like to take; then pretend to put it in the container. Then invite each child, in turn, to name something she would like to pack and to tell why. Have her pretend to bring it to the container. Sounds like you're ready to go!

Quiet-Time Imagination

Even your quiet resting times can be learning times for toddlers. While youngsters rest, reread a familiar story. Instead of showing the illustrations, describe them. Softly tell your listening resters what the characters are wearing, what they are doing, and what their facial expressions look like. Your little ones will not only hear the story; they'll imagine it, too!

Peek -A- Boo

Ideas For Toddlers & Twos

by Ann Spear Francioni

Emotional Development

● The feelings of sadness, joy, anger, and fear aren't new to your toddlers. What may be new, however, is that a toddler may now want—or be expected—to control his feelings.

● Since so much of a toddler's success in learning can depend on being able to control herself and her environment, learning to appropriately express her emotions can develop a child's self-esteem.

● Emotions can be scary to toddlers. Toddlers sometimes feel emotions to an extreme degree, and may be unable to control their actions. Remember to be patient!

I'm Happy And I Know It!

If a child is having a difficult time controlling his emotions, try this adaptation of a familiar song. Singing may be just the tension reliever that is needed!

(sung to the tune of "If You're Happy And You Know It")

If you're happy and you know it,
   show a smile.
If you're happy and you know it,
   show a smile.
If you're happy and you know it,
   you can use your face to show it.
If you're happy and you know it,
   show a smile.

If you're sad and you know it,
   make a frown....

If you're mad and you know it,
   make a scowl....

Playacting Puppets

Since toddlers love to pretend, try this activity to help them explore their emotions. Prepare simple puppets by drawing either a happy face, a sad face, a scared face, or an angry face on each of four separate paper plates. Tape a craft stick to the back of each plate to make it a puppet. Seat two to three youngsters on the floor. In turn, ask each child to choose a puppet to lift up to her face. Talk about the facial expression; then practice making that expression on your own faces. Discuss situations that would cause that emotion. Continue until the emotion on each puppet has been explored, or until interest wanes. For added fun, combine the song in the previous idea with these puppets.

Squish And Pound

If you see emotions running high in the classroom, make some slime! To make a batch, pour an amount (such as a cup or more) of cornstarch into a bowl. Slowly add warm water to the cornstarch until the mixture has a liquid consistency but is not runny. (To test for the right consistency, pinch an amount between your fingers. It will feel hard at first; then it will become runny again.) Give toddlers the slime to squish as an outlet for natural physical impulses that come with many of their emotions. It's therapeutic for your toddlers, and for you.

Spinning Into Control

It's likely that you've seen a toddler's emotions change within a few moments. One minute he's happy; the next minute he's mad. Try this idea to help a young child practice getting control of his emotions. Ask a child to stand in an open space; then tell him to show you an angry face. Next explain that with a few spins, he can transform into a child with a happy face. Demonstrate this by spinning around and stopping with a smile right in front of the child. Have him practice spinning and changing his scowl into a smile. Then have him spin and change back again. One more spin and it's back to being happy. Yippee!

Where, Oh Where?

Many of a toddler's emotions deal with her need for security. Try playing Peek-A-Boo and Hide-And-Go-Seek to help children develop a sense of security while in your care. Or play the games using items connected to their emotions, such as favorite toys and photos of parents. For example, have a child hide a picture of her mommy, then find it again. Or play Peek-A-Boo using the photo. Where did Mommy go? Here she is!

Weave A Web Of Silent Play

Handling your emotions can be pretty exhausting. Give youngsters some quiet playtime and personal attention with this management idea. Using masking tape, make a hexagon shape on your floor with a center and six sections that are each large enough for a child to play in with several toys. Put several toys in each section; then invite a child to choose a section to sit in for a set amount of time. Sit in the middle of the web so that you can spin around to interact with each child.

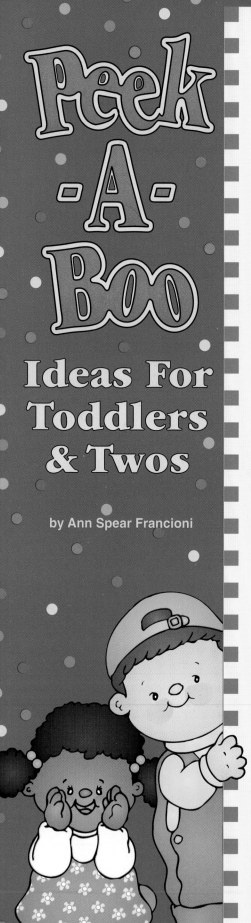

Peek -A- Boo

Ideas For Toddlers & Twos

by Ann Spear Francioni

Cognitive Development

● What makes toddlers tick? Two-year-olds have an innate desire to succeed! They use this willingness to try and try again, along with environmental clues and memories of past experiences, to help them reason through problems.

● Toddlers need to get physical! Touching and manipulating items in their environment helps them learn and feel in control.

● Cognitive skills include sorting and classifying, following directions, problem solving, and understanding relationships between objects and/or people.

One, Two—Toddlers Can Do!

Help your toddlers develop their emerging number sense with this activity that emphasizes the number *two.* Collect pairs of items from around your classroom, such as two red trucks, two green crayons, and two paper cups. Show each pair to the children and say the chant below, substituting the appropriate description for the underlined words. Then place one item from each pair somewhere in the room. Give a remaining item to a child and ask him to find its partner. As the child joins the pair, repeat the chant and encourage the children to join in. Continue with other items until every child has had a chance to find a pair.

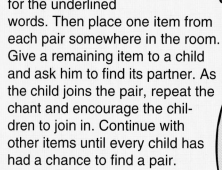

I have two red trucks!

Two [red trucks].
Two I see!
Two [red trucks]
In front of me!

Directed Dancing

"Put away your toy, sit at the table, and then take a cup from the stack." Wow! That's a lot to remember when you're two! Help toddlers practice following multiple-step directions in a fun, musical way. As you play a recording of dance music, demonstrate a short series of movements and give the verbal directions to match, such as "kick, clap, bend...kick, clap, bend...." Once your youngsters are able to keep up, make the directions more complex. Let the dancing (and the following of directions) begin!

What's Missing From The Basket?

Twos will enjoy this Easter hunt that builds memory skills. Put two or three different items in an Easter basket. Show each item to the children and say its name several times or even sing it so that your toddlers can remember the name and repeat it. Then ask the children to close their eyes. Remove one item from the basket; then ask the children to open their eyes. Ask them, "What's missing from the basket?" and see if they can name the missing item. Once your toddlers are memory masters with two or three items, try increasing the number.

Take A Peep

Here's an "egg-cellent" way to develop toddlers' memories! Place a different small manipulative into each of several different-colored plastic eggs. Invite a child to open each egg and name the object she sees before closing the egg. Then have her try to remember where a particular object is before opening an egg again to check. That's right—the cotton ball *is* in the blue egg!

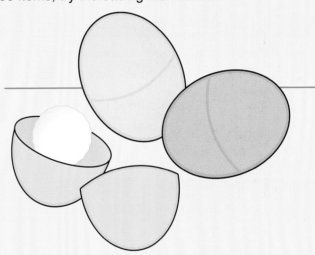

Sort-A-Snack

Your little ones will put this cereal-sorting activity in the "tasty" category! Provide a child with a clean muffin tin and a serving of fruit-flavored, O-shaped cereal. Show her how to sort one color of cereal pieces into a cup. Then encourage her to sort the rest of her cereal. Once she's sorted, it's time to eat this colorful treat!

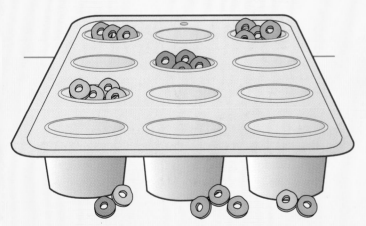

Cleanup Categories

Once toddlers get the hang of sorting, they can really help you out at cleanup time! Demonstrate what you want the children to do by making a pile of toys from various bins or areas of your classroom. (Start with just two or three types of toys.) Then help youngsters take each toy and find its appropriate bin or shelf. Let's see...dolls in the cradle, blocks on the shelf, books in the basket. Got it!

Peek -A- Boo

Ideas For Toddlers & Twos

by Ann Spear Francioni

Tidbits

Social Development

● Focusing on a toddler's social development helps him realize, "I'm a member of a group!" and "My behaviors affect those around me."

● A child may know what he wants or needs, but may get frustrated if he doesn't know how to get it. Developing a child's social skills helps him interact with others in order to meet his physical and emotional needs.

Oh, I'm waiting for my turn....

Oh, I'm Waiting, Darlin'

Teach your little ones this song; then encourage them to sing along when waiting is important.

(sung to the tune of "Clementine")

Oh, I'm waiting. Yes, I'm waiting.
Oh, I'm waiting for my turn.
I'll just smile and sit (stand) a while,
'Cause I'm waiting for my turn.

Yours, Mine, Ours

Is it yours, mine, or ours? Help a child distinguish what belongs to whom by gathering three sets of items: some belonging to you (book, scarf), some belonging to the child (shoes, school bag), and some belonging to the class (crayons, toys). Have the child sit with you; then enthusiastically offer him one item at a time to put away either in his cubby, in your lap, or on a class shelf. As he decides where to put each item, emphasize the words *yours, mine,* or *ours.* Also try playing this game with a small group of children to not only improve social skills, but name recognition as well.

Now boys and girls, today we'll have a story.

I'm The Teacher

Fulfill a child's fantasy by letting him pretend to be an adult in charge. Invite an older toddler to wear your apron, scarf, or shoes and pretend to be you. This activity enables the child to practice imitating roles and is sure to give you insight as to what he sees as your most memorable qualities!

I ♥ teaching toddlers!

Pretend Passengers

Imitating others is an important part of social and emotional development. Use this storytime suggestion to encourage children to engage in pretend play. Ask a child to sit in your lap and join you in reading *In The Driver's Seat* by Max Haynes (Bantam Books). The toddler with you is sure to enjoy being the driver in this wild ride over mountains and under water. When you have shared the story with a number of children, sit on the floor with a circular pillow (steering wheel) and pretend to drive a car. Invite children to join you in the car and tell you how to drive. Should you turn left? Turn right? It's amazing how far this game can go!

Patience, Patience

Here's a typical toddler thought: I want what I want when I want it! Waiting is easier for toddlers (and adults!) when it is known when the delay will end. Try using a song or fingerplay to help a child who's waiting. For example, you might say, "After we sing 'The Eeensy Weensy Spider' once, it will be your turn." These cues make waiting times easier and more fun.

Hugging Pillow

Showing affection appropriately is a wonderful attribute for toddlers to learn. Help them learn when and how with the hugging pillow. Use fabric paint to add a smiley face to a round pillow. If you notice a child hugging a friend who does not care to return the affection, offer her the hugging pillow. Explain that even though the child's playmate does not want a hug, the hugging pillow would love to receive one. While she hugs, have the child chant with you "1, 2, 3. Give a little huggie." Don't forget to ask for a hug yourself!

Bulletin Boards
And Displays

BULLETIN BOARDS

Your little farmhands are sure to crow over this barnyard display. Staple bandanas to a bulletin board. Prepare a large tagboard barn cutout; then cut a number of windows out of the barn. Take full-length pictures of your students; then cut the developed pictures around each child's body shape. Tape some of the pictures behind the windows. Mount the barn on the background; then arrange the remaining photos on the display.

Diann Kroos—Infants To Three-Year-Olds
Donald O. Clifton Child Development Center
Lincoln, NE

This progressive display reflects a year's worth of learning activities and themes. Use various colors of bulletin-board-paper lengths to divide a wall into as many sections as there are months in your school year. Label the sections with the names of the months. Fill each section with photos and student work from that month's theme or learning activities. As you add to the display, children will see the progression of time, and parents will see the progression of learning!

Darlene V. Martino—Pre-K, Palmyra Head Start, Palmyra, NY

This helper train will keep you on track when assigning classroom jobs. Cut simple shapes from tagboard to create a train. (Make sure the engine and cars together equal the number of classroom jobs you will have.) Label the engine and cars with different jobs. Mount the train on a scenic background. Assign classroom jobs by taping children's laminated photos to the engine and boxcars.

Amanda M. Brown—Three-Year-Olds, A Child's View, Newton, NC

This door display is the pick of the crop for welcoming preschoolers! Cover the door with paper; then add a border of apple cutouts. On a large apple cutout labeled "Welcome," glue large pom-poms and a pair of wiggle eyes to resemble a worm. Add the apple to the door along with students' personalized, sponge-painted apple cutouts. What an appealing door display!

adapted from an idea by Alicia Mia
   Dillingham—Pre-K
Denbigh Early Childhood Center
Newport News, VA

Pre-K Is Harvesting Fall Fun!

Gather your youngsters to help you make this display. Mount a bulletin-board-paper tree; then adorn it with students' sponge-painted leaf shapes. Have students glue orange and black tissue-paper pieces to paper plates to make a patch of jack-o'-lanterns; then pile the smiling pumpkins beneath the tree. You're really harvesting now!

Laura Fitz—Pre-K, Baltimore County Public School, Baltimore, MD

This display lets everyone know that you really give a hoot who's present each day! Mount a paper tree so that the branches are within students' reach. Enlarge and color an owl character; then mount it on the tree along with a caption. Mount a laminated basket shape below the tree. Each season, use Sticky-Tac to attach personalized, laminated shapes—such as apples, leaves, snowflakes, or birds—to the basket. Ask children to attach their shapes to the branches as they arrive each day.

Karen Eiben—Three-Year-Olds
The Kids' Place
LaSalle, IL

Amber

Anita

Milly

Tomas

Owen

Dustin

Keri

Michael

Demi

"Whooo's" Here Today?

Jon Kim Austin

AND DISPLAYS

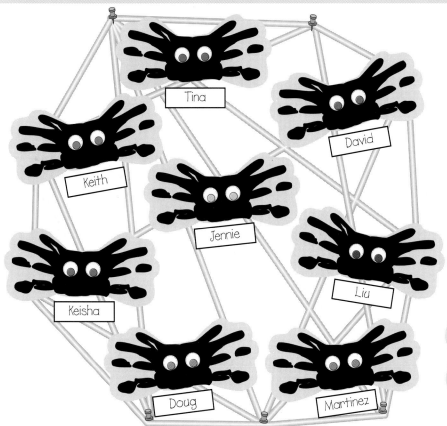

Tina

David

Keith

Jennie

Keisha

Liu

Doug

Martinez

Feeling creepy? Use pushpins and glittery yarn to create a web on a wall. Then fill the web with a handful of spiders. To make a spider, direct a child to dip both hands into black paint, then press them onto paper. When the paint is dry, cut around the shape, removing the thumbprints. Glue on wiggle eyes before adding the "creepy-crawly" and the child's name to the display.

Jennifer Liptak—Pre-K
Sonshine Preschool
Bensalem, PA

Watch
Out For
"Fall-ing"
Leaves

Watch out for compliments with this "color-fall" bulletin board. Post a sign on a background; then enlarge and color a character to add to the board. Surround the critter with student-painted watercolor leaves. If desired, add real leaves to the falling foliage.

Cathy Overton—Toddlers & Three-Year-Olds, St. Andrew's Preschool, Nags Head, NC

Splitter, splatter,
You'd better scatter—
This ghost is looking for YOU! BOO!

No one will scatter when invited to paint the background for this "spook-tacular" display. Give youngsters dishwashing-liquid bottles filled with orange, yellow or white paint. Then invite them to squirt the paint onto black bulletin-board paper. When the paint is dry, mount the paper along with a ghost-related poem or song. Tape a tagboard pedestal to the back of a ghost character (as shown); then attach the ghost to the board. Complete the display with students' ghostly projects.

adapted from an idea by Lisa Boyd—Pre-K, Nolanville Elementary, Nolanville, TX

Round up parents' enthusiasm for reading to their children by featuring youngsters' favorite books in this eye-catching display. Enlarge and color a western character; then mount it on a background along with a caption. Attach a book cover inside a ropelike lasso created from twisted strips of bulletin-board paper. Read 'em, cowpoke!

Amy Barsanti—Four-Year-Olds
St. Andrew's Preschool
Nags Head, NC

The Horse Ride

Howdy, "Book-a-roo"!

How about a friendly scarecrow to encourage youngsters' counting skills? Stuff a set of children's clothes with newspaper to create a scarecrow; then mount the fellow onto a bulletin board along with a title. Invite each child to glue his choice of construction-paper kernels on a paper cob shape. For each child's ear of corn, personalize a tag and label it with the number of kernels. Add the corn and labels to the display. It might be corny, but it's learning that counts!

adapted from an idea by Eileen A. Saad—Pre-K, Meadowbrook Nursery School, Troy, MI

Ask students to lend a hand in creating this display by inviting them to fingerpaint a length of paper brown. When the paint is dry, cut the paper to resemble a tree. Paint each child's hands with several fall colors; then have the child press his hands onto white paper. Cut around the handprints to resemble leaves. Mount the tree and collection of leaves with a caption.

Sheri McGarvey—Pre-K
Garrett's Way
Newtown Square, PA

"Tree-mendous" Accomplishments

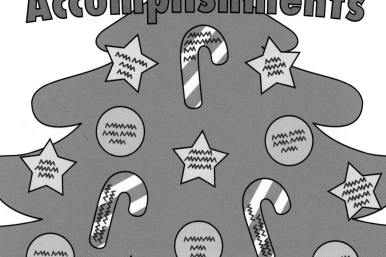

Students adorn this Christmas tree with decorations as they achieve group goals, such as cleaning cooperatively or eating politely at snacktime. Each time you would like to praise your group, note their accomplishment on a paper shape. Then ask a volunteer to mount the shape on the tree. Your star students are sure to shine with pride!

We cleaned our centers quietly.

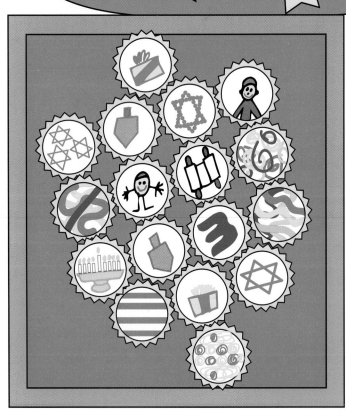

Use your little ones' artwork to create either of these holiday displays. Invite each child to paint or color on a white construction-paper circle. Glue each circle onto a larger yellow circle for a Hanukkah display or green circle for a Christmas display. Trim the larger circles with pinking shears. Mount these projects in the desired shape. Happy holidays!

Happy "Holly-days"!

Deck your door with this personalized wreath. Have students help you glue a number of construction-paper holly leaves to a tagboard doughnut shape. Attach a picture of each child to a separate red construction-paper circle. Display these photos as berries on the wreath. Add a real bow; then hang the wreath. Happy "Holly-days"!

This bulletin board changes with the seasons and holidays, but displays student work all the while! For each child, display an enlarged character. Each month, change the characters' hats and place different items in the characters' hands, such as awards or student-made projects. For example, in December, add Santa hats and student-painted presents. In January, add student-decorated party hats and students' illustrations or awards.

Count on your little sweeties having fun with this interactive display. Label ten paper cups with numerals from 1 to 10; then staple them around the outside of a large heart shape. On the background paper next to each cup, draw a corresponding number of hearts. Cut 55 construction-paper hearts; then glue each one to a separate craft stick. Store the sticks in an extra cup. Invite children to place the corresponding number of heart sticks in each cup.

Amy Nicholson—Pre-K
St. Thomas School
Thomaston, CT

This preschool puzzle shows parents how your class fits together! Using the pieces of a large floor puzzle as patterns, cut interlocking puzzle pieces from colorful construction paper. To each paper puzzle piece, attach a child's photo and a real, personalized puzzle piece. Have students embellish the pieces with glitter, if desired. Arrange the pieces together on a bulletin board, along with a border of real puzzle pieces. Finish off this display with the title "We Fit Together."

Growing Up!

Celebrate your youngsters' growing skills with this floral display! To prepare, snap a photo of each child engaged in a different classroom activity. Mount each child's photo on a paper plate. Write his dictated sentence about his abilities (as shown in the picture) on the plate. Then invite him to create a construction-paper flower using the paper plate as its center. Add green crepe-paper stems to the flowers; then mount them on a bulletin board, along with the title "Growing Up!"

Cheryl Gibson—Pre-K, Sedgefield Elementary, Greensboro, NC

Tell the world what a lucky teacher you are with this St. Patrick's Day door display! Mount a black posterboard pot on the corner of your door. Invite each child to decorate a yellow construction-paper circle with his choice of glimmering gold items, such as glitter, pipe cleaners, sequins, beads, and foil wrapping paper. Title your door. Then mount the golden circles on the door as if they are pouring out of the pot. Finally, add each child's name on a bright piece of construction paper near his gold piece.

"CHICK" IT OUT!

Spring Picnic

This Week!

Help Needed:

Use this clever display to get parents to take a peek at your current classroom events. At one end of a hallway, mount two halves of a large, cracked poster-board egg; then fill the remaining hall space with chick projects. To make each chick, use brads to attach a student's cut-out hand shapes to a paper egg shape; then add paper feet, eyes, and a beak along with feathers, if desired. Add to the display current announcements or pictures of your spring activities.

Help each child use different colors of bingo markers to create a pattern on a paper egg shape. Next fringe one side of a length of green bulletin-board paper to resemble grass. Staple the length on a display to create a pocket. Add more grass pockets, if desired. Tuck the decorated eggs in the grass; then put a real basket near the display. To use, a child takes an egg out of the grass. He then identifies the pattern before putting the egg in the basket.

adapted from an idea by Betsy Ruggiano—Preschool
Featherbed Lane School
Clark, NJ

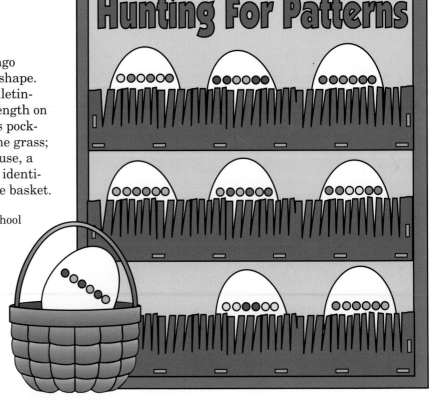

Hunting For Patterns

AND DISPLAYS

Celebrate the star qualities of every child with this display. Take a picture of each child standing in the position shown (arms straight out at shoulder height and legs apart). From each developed photo, cut out a star shape around the child's body. Mount the photo onto a piece of paper; then trim a larger star shape around the photo. Arrange the photos on a display along with star shapes that have been student decorated with glitter and other shiny materials. Brilliant!

adapted from an idea by Sheri Dressler—Pre-K
Woodland School
Carpentersville, IL

The Building Blocks Of Learning

Games & Manipulatives Area
- hand-eye coordination
- counting
- social skills

Sand & Water Table
- cause and effect
- measurement
- exploration

Reading Area
- reading readiness
- communication skills
- remembering details

Blocks Center
- size & shape discrimination
- spatial relationships
- physical coordination

Dramatic-Play Center
- communication skills
- problem solving
- social skills

Art Center
- fine-motor skills
- creativity
- visual perception

Here's a display that communicates the value of play to your students' parents. For each of your classroom centers, cut out a large bulletin-board paper rectangle. Label each rectangle with a different center's name; then list the learning outcomes from playing in that center. Mount the rectangles as shown on a wall along with a caption. When work is play, kids learn all day!

Lelia Eagloski and Barbetta Arnoldi—Preschool and Daycare, West Bloomfield Early Childhood, West Bloomfield, MI

Highlight the students in your summer program with this starfish-studded display. Have each child glue sand on a separate yellow, orange, or pink starfish cutout. Later, hot-glue a photo of each child to the center of her starfish. For a watery effect, cover a background with crumpled blue bulletin-board paper. Mount the completed starfish, name labels, and a starfish character along with a title to complete this star-quality display.

Aloha! If you have a year-round program, showcase summer fun with this vacation-themed display. Create a tropical-island scene by mounting a bulletin-board-paper palm tree onto a length of yellow bulletin-board paper that has been coated with sand. Have each child make a colorful flower by pinching the center of a tissue-paper circle; then have him glue it to the display. Invite each child to bring a photo of himself involved in a summer activity or excursion, such as a picnic or vacation. Display each mounted photo along with the caption "Aloha from [child's name] at [location of the picture]."

AND DISPLAYS

Here's an eye-catching way to display your students' seaworthy art projects! Suspend lengths of blue crepe-paper streamers from the ceiling so that they are several inches from a wall. Twist each streamer several times before securely taping its end to the wall. Next cut a piece of bulletin-board paper to resemble an ocean floor. Tape the paper onto the wall to cover the ends of the streamers. Tape youngsters' artwork to the streamers for a wonderful watery display.

Coming To School Is Just Ducky!

Get your ducks in a row with this attendance display. Mount student-fingerpainted paper onto a background to resemble a pond; then add details, such as twisted brown-paper logs and fringed green-paper grass. To make her duck, a child sponge-paints half a paper plate tan. Next she cuts out a head and beak from construction paper, then glues the pieces onto the dried plate. Personalize each duck and then store it in a tub near the display. As each student arrives in the morning, she takes her duck from the tub; then her parent pins it to the pond. You'll be able to tell at a glance which ducklings are at school!

Getting Your Ducklings In A Row

Getting Your Ducklings

Nifty Nametags

Your little ones will be happy to lend you a hand when making these self-adhering nametags for your tables or cubbies. To make a nametag, cut a square of clear Con-Tact® covering that is slightly larger than a child's hand. Remove the backing from the square. Have a child press his hand into tempera paint, then onto the adhesive side of the Con-Tact® covering. When the paint is dry, press the square onto a tabletop or the child's cubby; then use a permanent marker to write the child's name below his handprint. What a nifty nametag!

Carolyn Macdonald—
  Four-Year-Olds
Kiddie Haven Day Care
Brockton, MA

Snappy Center Management

Youngsters will independently choose and change learning centers with this photographic management system. Take an individual photo of each child and each of your classroom centers. Mount each picture onto a same-sized piece of cardboard. Cover each mounted photo with clear Con-Tact® covering; then attach a piece of magnetic tape to the back of it. Use masking tape to visually divide a magnetic surface into a grid with enough spaces for each center's photo and the number of children you will allow in that center at one time. Arrange the pictures of the centers on the grid. When choosing a center, a child places her picture in a space next to her chosen

center's photo. When all the spaces are filled, the center is full.

Christine Zieleniewski—Pre-K, Saint Cecilia School, Kearny, NJ

Stick 'em Up!

Tired of rolling tape in order to adhere calendar markers to your calendar? Try this sticky tip! Laminate your calendar, daily markers, and an extra sheet of poster board. Squeeze a drop of Aleene's™ Tack-It over & over glue onto the back of each marker. Allow the glue to dry. Stick the markers on the extra sheet of poster board to store them. During your calendar time, stick the day's marker on your calendar. These pieces will stick to your calendar over and over again!

Judy Kuhn Skaggs—Three-Year-Olds, Highland Preschool, Raleigh, NC

In A Row
Tips For Getting Organized

Here's The Ticket

Looking for a way to organize your learning center time? If so, then this idea may be just the ticket you need! Request that a home-supplies store donate countertop samples that are no longer in use. To make a ticket for each child, trim his picture; then tape it onto a sample. Personalize the tickets. In each of your classroom centers, screw as many cup hooks into a wooden surface as you will allow children in that center at one time. Store the tickets near your group area. To choose a center, a child hangs his ticket on one of the center's hooks.

Nicky Daigle— Non-Categorical Preschool
Thibodaux Elementary
Thibodaux, LA

Beautiful Bulletin Boards

Your bulletin boards will look appealing all year long when you back them with neutral-colored wallpaper before adding your display pieces. Wallpaper is durable, and its color won't fade. With this method you'll save time, and your bulletin boards will look great display after display.

Susan Dzurovcik—Preschool
Valley Road School
Clark, NJ

Rebus Calendar

Use this rebus calendar to help your preschoolers remember on which days they attend special classes or activities. On separate cards or sentence-strip lengths, write each of the days your class attends school and each of your weekly classes and activities, such as art and music. Draw a picture of each of your weekly classes on separate cards or use photos to represent each activity. To prepare the calendar, display the labels of the days, the pictures of the activities, and the activity labels on a chart or pocket chart as shown. Use an arrow cutout or other symbol to point to the current day. Replace the pictures and labels as needed to include field trips, parties, or other special events.

Mary Jenks—Preschool, Special Education (Hearing Impaired)
Briarlake Elementary
Decatur, GA

295

Getting Your Ducklings

Roly-Poly Portraits

Prepare these picture cubes and you'll roll right into games and transitions! Obtain a plastic picture cube for every six children in your class. Personalize a photo of each child. Insert a different child's photo into each side of each cube. (As an alternative, glue photos to the sides of empty mug gift boxes.) Use the picture cubes to work on classmate recognition or name recognition. Or roll the cubes to assign jobs and centers. When playing games, roll the cube to determine whose turn it is. With these ideas, you're on a roll!

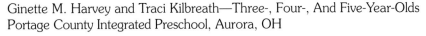

Ginette M. Harvey and Traci Kilbreath—Three-, Four-, And Five-Year-Olds
Portage County Integrated Preschool, Aurora, OH

Lovely Labels

When you use this easy tip for making picture labels for containers and shelves, children will know at a glance where everything belongs! Make a color or black-and-white photocopy of each item to be stored or shelved. Cut out the pictures; then use clear Con-Tact® covering to attach them to the appropriate shelves or containers. During cleanup times, students can refer to the pictures in order to replace materials easily.

Mandi King—Pre-K
Hubbard Pre-K
Forsyth, GA

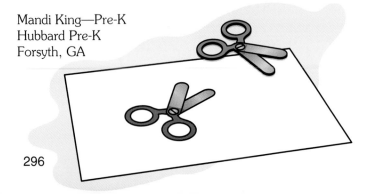

Zipper Chair

Do your little ones need an easy way to get help with their coat zippers? Try this adorable idea. Use fabric paint to paint a zipper on the front of a T-shirt. When the paint is dry, put the shirt over the back of a chair. (As an alternative, place a real coat with a zipper on the chair back.) Label the seat "Zipper Chair," and then cover the label with clear Con-Tact® covering. Next place the chair near your closet or the door. Encourage students to sit in the Zipper Chair when they encounter difficulty zipping up their jackets and coats to go outside. Or have a seat in the Zipper Chair and invite those children who need help to come to you. Zip 'em up and take 'em out!

Terry Steinke—Preschool
Emmaus Lutheran School, Indianapolis, IN

In A Row — Tips For Getting Organized

Puppet Posts

Organize your puppets with these easy-to-make puppet posts! First obtain a sturdy, medium-sized box with a lid and six to eight paper-towel or toilet-paper tubes. Trace one end of each tube onto the lid. Use a utility knife to cut out the resulting circles. Insert the tubes into the holes, securing them with hot glue. Pack the tubes with newspaper; then seal the ends with packing tape. Finally, spray-paint the box and the tubes. When the paint is dry, place your puppets on the posts. There you have it—perfectly pleasing puppet storage!

Leigh A. Allen—Two-, Three-, And Four-Year-Olds
Virginia Commonwealth University Child Care Center
Richmond, VA

Winter Dressing

Hung up on how to get all your little ones dressed to play in the frosty outdoors? Simply prepare a picture sequence of the necessary clothing; then display the pictures near your coat closet. Explain to the children to follow the order of the pictures when getting dressed for winter play. Youngsters will quickly learn that snow pants go on first, followed by boots, coats, hats, scarves, and mittens. All dressed? Let's go play!

Pam Waldrop—Preschool, Quality Care Child Care, Crown Point, IN

snowpants   boots   coat   hat   scarf   mittens

Easy-Care Decorating

Hey, toddler teachers! Do you find that the posters in your classroom are not as long-lived as you would like? Try this unique idea for decorating your room's walls. Use double-sided tape to mount children's educational picture placemats to your walls, making sure that the placemats are at toddlers' eye level. These vinyl mats are sturdy and can be easily wiped clean. Now you have long-lasting *and* educational decorating at *their* fingertips!

Judy Tanzone—Toddlers, Harmony School, Princeton, NJ

Getting Your Ducklings

Mega-Sized Mouse Pads

Give your preschoolers the advantage of an extra-large mouse pad while they're learning to use computers and honing their fine-motor skills. Replace your mouse pad with a sheet of craft foam, securing the foam to your table or cart with double-sided tape. Since children can move the mouse over a much wider area, they'll be able to focus more on the computer activity itself.

adapted from an idea by Patricia W. Mitchell, Eastbrook Elementary School, Winter Park, FL

Stylish Center Management

Manage your centers in style with this personalized T-shirt system. Cut a class supply of people shapes from tagboard; then write a different child's name on each one. For each center, also cut out the same number of people shapes as you will allow children in that center at one time. Next cut a class supply of T-shirt shapes from tagboard. Personalize each T-shirt; then have each child use crayons to color his T-shirt and his person shape. To make a starting chart, glue the decorated people shapes to a sheet of poster board. For each center sign, label a piece of poster board with a center's name; then glue the same number of people shapes to the sign as you will allow children in that center at one time. Laminate the starting chart, the center signs, and the T-shirts. Finally, attach the hook side of a piece of Velcro® to the back of each T-shirt, and the loop side of a piece of Velcro® to each person shape on the starting chart and the center signs. Attach the shirts to the chart; then display the chart in a group area. Display the center signs in the centers so they are within students' reach.

To use the system, a child takes his T-shirt off the starting chart, and then attaches it to a person shape on the sign in the center of his choice. When each person shape on a sign is wearing a shirt, that center is full.

Theresa Knapp—Preschool, Asbury Day Care Center, Rochester, NY

298

In A Row   Tips For Getting Organized

Window-Shade Wonder

With this clever idea, you'll have two display areas in the space of one, and a handy shelf, too! Construct a simple drapery cornice sized to fit over one of your existing bulletin boards. Paint the cornice as desired. When the paint is dry, bolt it to the wall over the bulletin board. Next use acrylic craft paints to create a display on a plain window shade. When the paint is dry, retract the shade; then mount it to the inside of the cornice (following package directions). To use the new display, pull the shade down; then retract it to use the bulletin board again.

Renee Farrand—Preschool
Union United Methodist Church Preschool/Kindergarten
Irmo, SC

Tissue-Box Storage Tip

Reuse empty tissue boxes as storage containers for learning-center pieces. You'll find their openings easily accommodate a child's small hands, yet prevent large spills. Gather a variety of empty tissue boxes. If desired, cover them with decorative Con-Tact® covering (being sure to keep the opening intact) or color-code them by centers. Drop game pieces, manipulatives, and other small center items into the boxes. At cleanup time, students simply return the items to the boxes, and the boxes to the centers.

Diane G. Williams
Seven Pines Elementary, Sandston, VA

Fish-Tank Viewing

Do you have an observation window so that adults can look into your classroom? If so, use this decorative idea to keep youngsters' attention focused inside the classroom rather than on the people outside the classroom. Tape blue cellophane to the outside of the window; then attach sea-life cutouts to the classroom side of the glass. Children who look at the window will tend to focus on the sea-life shapes, and observers' view of the room will remain clear.

Victoria Greco, Fairfield, OH

OUR READERS WRITE

Our Readers Write

ABC Art

Youngsters are sure to enjoy making these books throughout the year as they learn the alphabet and new art methods. To prepare, draw the outline of each letter on a separate sheet of paper. Duplicate a class supply of each letter. As you study each letter, give each child a copy of that letter to decorate using a related art method. For example, glue gold glitter on a *G*, or make rubbings with a red crayon on an *R*. Hole-punch each child's pages as they are completed, and keep them in a personalized three-brad folder. At the end of the year, youngsters will be proud of their art-and-alphabet collections.

Pat Coleman—Pre-K
Red Bridge Early Childhood Center
Kansas City, MO

Fabulous Frames

You'll be surprised at the variety of ways that youngsters can decorate magnetic frames. Use stickers, markers, colored glue, paint, glitter, fabric scraps, and more! What attractive frames—and creative, too!

Mary E. Maurer, Caddo, OK

Making Memories

If you're looking for a unique memento of the school year, then these memory books are sure to please. Throughout the school year, take pictures of each child participating in class activities, celebrations, and field trips. You could also use yarn to record each child's height at the beginning and end of the year. Store each child's photos and yarn in a personalized envelope. At the end of the year, make a booklet for each child by folding several sheets of construction paper in half. Attach photos, stickers, and die-cuts to the folded pages; then add captions. Insert the yarn lengths in paper pockets on one of the first and last pages. Tie ribbon around each completed booklet. On the last day of school, present the booklets to your students; then talk about how they have grown and changed throughout the year.

Sue Fleischmann—Preschool
Menomonee Falls Preschool Co-Op
Menomonee Falls, WI

No Oven Required!

A waffle iron to make cookies? You bet! Enlist the help of your youngsters in preparing the following recipe. In no time at all, you'll have a stack of "apple-licious," low-sugar treats just right for your apple unit!

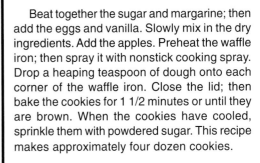

Apple Waffle Cookies
1/4 cup firmly packed brown sugar
1/2 cup softened margarine
2 eggs
1 teaspoon vanilla
1 1/2 cups all-purpose flour
1 teaspoon baking powder
1 teaspoon cinnamon
1/2 teaspoon salt
1/8 teaspoon nutmeg
a dash of cloves
1/2 cup peeled, shredded apples
nonstick cooking spray

Beat together the sugar and margarine; then add the eggs and vanilla. Slowly mix in the dry ingredients. Add the apples. Preheat the waffle iron; then spray it with nonstick cooking spray. Drop a heaping teaspoon of dough onto each corner of the waffle iron. Close the lid; then bake the cookies for 1 1/2 minutes or until they are brown. When the cookies have cooled, sprinkle them with powdered sugar. This recipe makes approximately four dozen cookies.

Jill Beattie—Four- And Five-Year-Olds
The Apple Place Nursery School
Chambersburg, PA

Handmade Tablecloth

This colorful tablecloth is sure to grab attention when placed on refreshment tables at Open Houses, parent meetings, and programs. To make the tablecloth, paint children's hands with various colors of fabric paint; then have them press their hands onto a tablecloth, an old flat sheet, or a large piece of cotton fabric. Use a pencil to write each child's name under his handprint; then have him use a fabric marker to trace his name. Once it's completed, you'll have a beautiful tablecloth that's one of a kind!

Michelle Link-Drey and Melinda Weeda—
    Preschool
Creative Beginnings Preschool, Creston, IA

Prizewinning Cake

Birthday children are sure to be delighted by the treats in this cake. To make a prizewinning birthday cake, cover the outside of an empty whipped-topping container with colorful paper. Fill the container with inexpensive birthday favors. Cut the number of slits in the container's lid that corresponds to the age your children will be turning this year. When a child celebrates a birthday, put the appropriate number of candles in the lid. Invite him to pretend to blow out the candles, then remove the lid and choose a treat from the cake.

Cindy Crosby—Preschool, Summerville Baptist Preschool, Summerville, SC

Remember When?

Make this class book at the end of the summer, and you'll have a way to chase away the wintertime blues later in the year. Record students' comments about summer—such as what they wore, the weather, and their favorite activities—on separate sheets of paper. Use photographs and youngsters' drawings to illustrate the pages; then compile the pages into a class book. Reread the book on a cold winter's day. Your little ones are sure to warm up as they remember their fun in the summer sun. As a variation, similarly compile a winter book to read during the summer months.

Gina Mahony—Four- And
Five-Year-Olds
Children's Preschool Workshop
Barrington, IL

Welcome!

Welcome students and parents with this warm and sunny display. Program each of seven construction-paper T-shirt shapes (or real children's shirts) with a different letter to spell "Welcome." Attach clothesline rope to opposite sides of a bulletin board; then use clothespins to hang the shirts on the line. Add personalized flower cutouts. Finally mount a smiling sun to keep the welcome warm and the flowers growing!

Carol Denny—Preschool, First Baptist Church, Conyers, GA

Overall Helpers

Use a pair of children's overalls to make this darling helpers chart. Sew as many different felt pockets as you have classroom jobs onto the pair of overalls. Use a marker to label each pocket with a different classroom job. Hang the overalls on a clothes hanger; then put the hanger on a hook. Or mount the overalls on a bulletin board. Personalize a name card for each child. To assign classroom helpers, simply tuck a name card into each pocket.

Janis Woods—Four-Year-Olds
Ridgeland Elementary, Ridgeland, SC

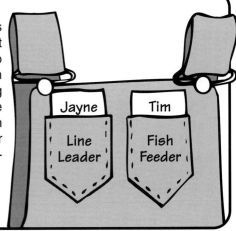

Science Story Extensions

Here's hoping these science extensions for the story *The Little Red Hen* really help you out!

- Show youngsters shafts of wheat (available at craft stores).
- Invite children to use a mortar and pestle to grind wheat berries (available at health-food stores) into flour.
- Plant wheat berries. In a few days, you'll have wheat grass!
- Fill your sensory table with flour; then add measuring cups, spoons, and sifters.
- Bake bread, of course!

Leslie Madalinski—Four- And Five-Year-Olds
Weekday Children's Center, Naperville, IL

Love Those Babies

Since bean-filled animals are a hit with preschoolers, invite youngsters to bring theirs to school for use in these learning activities. Focus on language skills by inviting each student to dictate and illustrate a story about his bean-filled friend. Or teach alphabet sounds using the toys' names. Classify the toys by different characteristics such as those with wings, legs, or tails. Finally find out which children share birthdates or birth months with the toys. Now that's learning that is worth a hill of beans!

Janet Comella Jansen—Preschool
Aardvark Enrichment Program, Ypsilanti, MI

Our Readers ▷ Write

Cap Counting

There's no cap on the amount of counting fun your little ones will have with these games. Program each strip in a supply of black construction-paper strips with an orange paper numeral; then add the corresponding number of orange paper circles to each strip. Laminate the strips. Use a permanent black marker to draw jack-o'-lantern faces on a supply of orange jug lids. To use these materials, a child counts as he puts the appropriate number of lids on each strip.

Similarly make Christmas-themed counting games by programming construction-paper tree cutouts with numerals and circles. Provide various colors of jug lids to represent ornaments.

Sharron Coletta—Three-Year-Olds
Chamblee-Methodist Kindergarten
Chamblee, GA

Marbleized Pumpkin

If you're looking for an age-appropriate art activity, pick this pumpkin idea. To make one pumpkin, trace a circular cake pan onto white or orange paper; then cut along the resulting outline. Next put the paper cutout in the pan. After dipping a marble in orange tempera paint, drop it into the pan and keep it rolling. Remove the paper from the pan. When the paint is dry, complete the project by gluing on construction-paper facial features and a stem.

Cheryl Songer—Preschool
Wee Know Nursery School
Wales, WI

The Family Tree

Invite your children's families to help you keep this year-round display decorated. Mount a large paper tree in a hallway or on a bulletin board near your school's entrance. Every month, provide each child's family with a seasonal construction-paper shape to creatively decorate. Arrange these projects on the tree's branches. Look what's on the family tree this month!

Suzi Dodson—Preschool
Growing Years Early Learning Center
Claysburg, PA

Painting Tip

Painting a lunch bag to make a pumpkin or puppet is easy when you insert an empty, rectangular tissue box into the bag. The box makes the bag easier to manipulate and easier to paint on all four sides. It also keeps the bag upright while it is drying.

Linda Gilligan—Pre-K
St. Hedwig School
Naugatuck, CT

Eight-Legged Pretzels

These savory spiders are easy to make and quick to bake. If desired, have your students help you mix up a batch of bread dough, or save time by using refrigerated dough. To make a pretzel, crisscross four dough lengths atop one another on a piece of aluminum foil. Press a dough ball on top of the lengths; then sprinkle the spider with kosher salt. Bake, cool, and then munch!

Lori Kracoff—Preschool
The Curious George Cottage Learning Center
Waterville Valley, NH

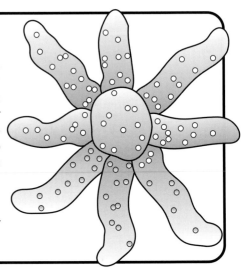

Platter Picture Frame

Parents never tire of cute ways to display youngsters' photos. To make a frame, cut a circle from the center of a small paper plate or seasonal party plate. If using a plain plate, have the child use art supplies—such as markers, glue, and glitter—to embellish it. Tape the child's photo to the back of the plate. Complete the frame by taping a second plate behind the first one. Then tape the frame at an angle to a poster-board shape similar to the one shown so that it can stand on a surface to be displayed.

Martha A. Briggs—Two- And Three-Year-Olds
Rosemont Tuesday/Thursday School, Ft. Worth, TX

Kachina Dolls

During your study of Native Americans, introduce your children to Pueblo Indian lore and *kachinas*—small wooden dolls carved to represent spirits. Then become a part of this tradition by making your own kachinas. To make the doll's head, use markers, feathers, or even magazine pictures of animals to decorate half of a cardboard tube. For the doll's body, glue a piece of brown fabric around an empty dishwashing-liquid bottle. Further embellish the bottle by gluing on scraps of material, fur, feathers, cotton balls (stretched to look like white fur), colored beads, and yarn. Use hot glue to secure the tube head in place on the top of the bottle.

Candida Connolly and Amy Ross
   —Junior Kindergarten
Lausanne Collegiate School
Memphis, TN

Leaf Banner

Crisp autumn air is the signal that it's time to make this colorful leaf banner or quilt. Direct each child to paint one side of a leaf with red, yellow, orange, or brown paint. Then have him press the leaf onto a six-inch square of cotton fabric to make a print. Let the print dry. Use a fabric marker to personalize the child's square. Sew the squares together to make a banner, bind the banner with batting, and then quilt it, if desired.

Janel Kieslich—Preschool, Emilie Christian Day School, Levittown, PA

Turkey Tracks

Follow these tracks to a creative background for any Thanksgiving display. Invite youngsters to dip forks into paint, and then to press them onto a length of bulletin-board paper to make turkey prints. When the paint is dry, mount the background paper. Which way did that turkey go?

Juli Betts—Three-Year-Olds
Tutor Time, Apex, NC

Totem Poles

Locate and share with youngsters some pictures of totem poles carved by Native American tribes of the Pacific Northwest. Then encourage each child to glue his choice of precut construction-paper shapes onto a large, brown construction-paper rectangle to create his own totem pole. Honor youngsters' hard work with a totem pole–raising ceremony in which you show each child's project, then mount it on a display.

Gina Mahony—Preschool
Children's Preschool Workshop
Barrington, IL

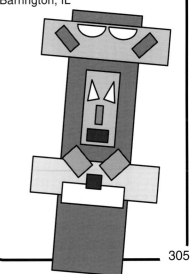

Show-And-Share

Turn your show-and-tell time into a real sharing time with this charitable idea. During your next nutrition unit or Thanksgiving unit, ask each child to bring in a box or can of a favorite food that he thinks another child would enjoy. During a sharing time, have him describe the taste, colors, or preparation of the food. Collect the food items; then donate them to a food bank or shelter. What a wonderful opportunity to learn about helping others!

Linda Bille—Preschool, Riviera United Methodist Preschool, Redondo Beach, CA

Our Readers Write

"Mousekin" Ornament

Looking for a cuddly holiday gift to make for your preschoolers? Try these adorable ornaments that double as finger puppets! To make one mouse finger puppet, cut two circles (ears) and two rectangles (body) from gray felt. Lay the two body pieces atop each other; then round the corners of one end. Next insert the ears between the body pieces. Leaving the bottom open, glue around the outer edges of the body pieces to form the puppet. Glue on wiggle eyes, a small felt nose, and three pieces of stiff thread on each side of the nose for whiskers. Cut two large mitten shapes from felt; then glue around the outer edges of the cutouts, leaving the bottom open. Next sew on a gold thread hanger. Tuck the mouse puppet and a copy of the poem shown inside the mitten. There you have it—an adorable mouse just right for preschool play and decoration!

Cheryl Cicioni and Jean Joyce—Preschool Director, Teacher
Kindernook Preschool
Lancaster, PA

Here is my little mouse.
He loves to play with me.
He lives inside this mitten
That hangs on my Christmas tree!

Magic Glitter Box

Do you like the sparkly effect glitter has on your students' art, but don't like the cleanup? Use this idea to neatly brighten up their projects! Decorate a clean, empty diaper-wipes container; then sprinkle a generous amount of glitter inside it. After a youngster applies glue to his project, have him place it inside the container, close the lid, and shake, shake, shake! When he opens the box, his project is magically sparkly without the extra cleanup. Best of all, he did it all by himself!

Patti Hawkins—Two-Year-Olds
Carousel Cottage
Clarksville, TN

Pasta Ornaments

Here's a pasta project that's perfect for even the youngest preschoolers! In advance dye a large amount of pasta wheels red and green. To make an ornament, pour a puddle of white glue in the center of a piece of waxed paper. Form a loop with a six-inch length of yarn and place the loose ends into the glue. Next put pasta into the glue, making certain that the wheel edges touch each other. Let the ornament dry overnight; then peel off the waxed paper. The "pasta-bilities" for these cute ornaments are endless!

Elizabeth Qualls—Two-Year-Olds
First Baptist Church
Greensboro, NC

"Three Little Kittens"

Remember the traditional nursery rhyme about the three kittens who lost their mittens? We've found some mitten activities just right for extending the rhyme.
- Invite each child to bring a pair of mittens to school.
- Discuss the differences between mittens and gloves.
- Hide the mittens and have children search for them (lost mittens).
- Use forks to sample different types of pie while wearing the mittens (soiled mittens).
- Wash the mittens and hang them up to dry (clean mittens).

What good little kittens your preschoolers will be!

Caro Brinkman—Preschool, Busy Bees Day Care
St. Cloud, MN

Countdown Calendar

The December holidays are a time of sharing and goodwill toward others. Foster youngsters' awareness of kindness with this activity-based countdown calendar. Prepare a December calendar programmed with tree-shaped day spaces. Program each tree shape with a simple activity for children to complete that day such as "Say a special thank-you to the person who drives you to school" or "Give everyone in your family a hug." Once a child completes the day's activity with his family, he colors that tree. These special calendars provide a kind-hearted way to count down the days of the month!

Patsy Dewey—Four- And Five-Year-Olds, The Lord's Lively Learners Nursery School, Lebanon, NJ

Seasonal Dice

These seasonal dice are great for little hands and minds! Measure up 2 1/4 inches from the bottom of each of two empty, clean eight-ounce milk cartons. Cut off the tops and discard. Fit the carton bottoms together to make one cube. Cover the cube with Con-Tact® covering; then program the sides with seasonal stickers. Use the dice with favorite classroom games or along with seasonal erasers for a simple counting activity. Get ready to roll!

Amy Aloi—Four-Year-Olds
Prince Georges County Head Start
    Berkshire Elementary
Forestville, MD

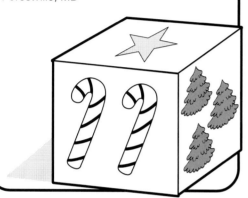

Money-Saving Border

Here's a pleasing patchwork bulletin-board border that will save you money! Cut wallpaper samples into three-inch-wide strips. Then staple the strips around your bulletin board for an inexpensive finishing touch.

Cindy S. Berry—Two-Year-Olds
Christian Kindergarten and Nursery School
Little Rock, AR

Button-Up Snowman

This frosty friend is ready to help your students sort. Collect three round, plastic lids that are graduated sizes (such as a yogurt-cup lid, a butter-tub lid, and a whipped-topping lid). Hot-glue the lids onto tagboard to resemble a snowman; then use permanent markers to add features. Supply a container of buttons. Encourage children to sort small buttons on the snowman's head, medium buttons on his middle, and large buttons on his base. Button up—it's cold outside!

Rhonda Monk—Preschool
Forest Hill Elementary School
Forest Hill, LA

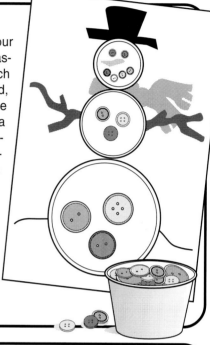

Holiday Manipulatives

Brighten up counting activities with some holiday sequins and your overhead projector. Invite your older preschoolers to work with these unique manipulatives in the following ways:

- Program each transparency in a set with a different numeral and corresponding dot set. Have a child place a transparency on the projector and cover each dot with a sequin. Ask her partner to count aloud the number of sequins projected onto the screen.
- Have a student place a plastic or die-cut numeral on the projector. Then have his partner place the correct number of sequins on the projector and count them with his buddy.
- Have a child make a pattern using the sequins on the projector. Have her partner read the pattern from the screen and continue the pattern.

Lorrie Hartnett, Canyon Lake, TX

Quik® Q Idea

Here is a quality center idea for teaching the letter *Q*. To prepare the center, locate a clean, empty box of Nestlé® Quik® chocolate milk mix. Next cut out a supply of drinking glass shapes from white tagboard. Color the bottom half of each glass brown to resemble chocolate milk. Program some of the glasses with the uppercase and lowercase letter *Q,* and the rest with other letters. To play the game, children look at the glasses and place only those with the letter *Q* into the Quik® box. Anybody thirsty for the letter *Q?*

Jill Beattie—Four- And Five-Year-Olds
Apple Place Nursery
Chambersburg, PA

Popcorn And Cranberry Ornaments

Shiny red cranberries team up with fluffy white popcorn to make these pretty ornaments. To make an ornament, thread popcorn and cranberries on midweight floral wire to create a simple pattern. When the wire is filled, bring the ends together, and then twist them to form a wreath. Hang these ornaments on a Christmas tree or outside your window so children can watch the birds feeding on them. The holidays truly are for everyone!

Jill Beattie—Four- And Five-Year-Olds

Our Readers Write

Valentine Mailboxes

Looking for an alternative to valentine bags? Collect a class supply of empty, square tissue boxes. For each child, cut a piece of bulletin-board paper sized to fit around a box. Invite each student to decorate his paper as desired with paint, glitter, and stickers. Personalize each child's paper; then tape it around his box. When it's time to deliver valentines, have students drop their cards into the correct boxes. These durable, attractive mailboxes will hold lots of valentines for your preschoolers!

Faith Heaviside—Four-Year-Olds
Fairmount Nursery School
Syracuse, NY

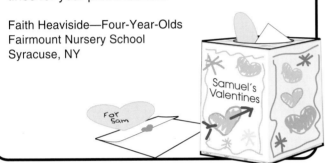

Stained-Glass Hearts

Once the valentine candy is gone, use those heart-shaped candy boxes for this art project that resembles stained-glass windows. Invite each child to trace various heart-shaped candy boxes onto a large piece of construction paper so that some shapes overlap. Trace over the heart outlines with black marker. Next have her use different colors of crayons to color the parts of the design. Now that's heartfelt art!

Jennifer Reisman
    —Four-Year-Olds
Christ Church Nursery School
Short Hills, NJ

Scoop A Little Love

Recycle laundry-detergent scoops for this sweet treat. Clean a scoop for each child; then fill it with valentine candy or other small treats. Write "Here's a scoop of love for you from [your name]!" on heart-shaped paper for each child; then punch a hole near the top. Wrap each scoop with pink plastic wrap; then tie the note onto the scoop with a ribbon bow. What a loving gift!

Carol Denny—Four-Year-Olds
First Baptist Preschool
Conyers, GA

Forever Foam Letters

Are your paper bulletin-board letters showing wear and tear? Try this tip for colorful, long-lasting letters. Purchase brightly colored craft foam at a craft store. Trace and cut out letters (or use a die-cut machine) for your bulletin boards. If desired, decorate the letters with Slick® paint, glitter, confetti, or permanent markers to match your themes. Attach these letters to your bulletin boards with pushpins for an unusual effect.

Pam Szeliga—Pre-K
Riverview Elementary
Baltimore, MD

Classroom Community

Turn your classroom into a mini-neighborhood when you study communities! Hang a sign on your door welcoming visitors to the neighborhood. Then add simple props and costumes to your centers to transform them into different neighborhood locations. For example, turn your housekeeping area into a restaurant with menus for the guests, and notepads and pencils for the waiters. Turn your block area into a fire station with fire hats, hoses (made of wrapping-paper tubes with silver tinsel water), and red and orange tissue-paper fire to attach to block buildings. Make the writing area a post office with a mailbox (made from a blue painted box with a slit cut in the top for letters), stamps, envelopes, paper, and mailbags. Convert your art area into a bakery with play dough, cookie cutters, rolling pins, birthday candles, trays, chefs' hats, and aprons. Welcome, neighbor!

Amy Aloi—Four-Year-Olds, Berkshire Elementary, Forestville, MD

Blooming Bouquets

These beautiful bouquets are a delightful gift for Valentine's Day. To make each flower, use an eyedropper to drop colored water onto a coffee filter. When the filter is dry, pinch and twist the center of it to form a bloom. Fold a green chenille stem in half. Twist the ends around the bloom for a stem; then secure it with green masking tape. Cut the tip off a paper snow-cone holder; then insert the flowers in the wide end to make a bouquet. Encourage each child to give her bouquet to someone special. Who wouldn't love getting these flowers?

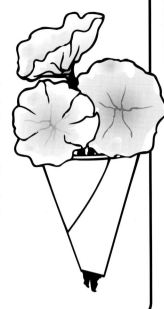

Linda Bille—Preschool
Riviera United Methodist Preschool
Redondo Beach, CA

A Printed Posy Valentine

Here's a pretty posy card made by printing with a bunch of celery! To make a card, fold a piece of construction paper; then glue a copy of the poem shown inside the card. Next cut off all the stalks from the base of a bunch of celery. Dip the base in Slick® paint; then carefully print the celery onto the front of the card as many times as desired. Add stems and leaves with Slick® paint. Happy Valentine's Day!

Jennette Shinkle—Child Development Specialist
Bush Early Education Center
Wilmington, DE

Roses are red.
Violets are blue.
Here are some flowers
That I made just for you!
Happy Valentine's Day!

Allison

Face Stamps

Use these face stamps to spread valentine cheer among your little smiling faces! To make one, hot-glue a small wooden heart to a wooden minicandle cup as shown. To use the stamp, use a sponge brush to apply a smooth layer of acrylic paint on the heart. (Acrylic paint does not stain the skin and peels off easily.) Carefully print the heart on a child's face, reminding him not to touch the paint until it has dried. You're sure to see some "heart-y" grins among your students with this idea!

Dayle Timmons—Preschool
Alimacani Elementary
Jacksonville, FL

What's Cookin'?

If you want safe make-believe food cans for your housekeeping area, then try this easy tip. Remove the labels from clean, empty plastic frosting containers. Next carefully peel the labels off fruit, vegetable, and soup cans. Use clear Con-Tact® covering to attach the new labels onto the frosting containers. Now you have safe, realistic-looking food cans for your little chefs!

Brenda Miller—Preschool
Kidecation of Camp Fire
Olean, NY

Handling Valentines

Do you have a supply of paper fruit bags or handled craft bags in your classroom? Use them for valentine mailbags that preschoolers can easily carry. Give each child a personalized bag; then invite him to decorate his bag with stickers, colored glue and glitter, or stamps. Valentine delivery is in the bag!

Susan Pagel—Preschool and Pre-K
St. Paul's Lutheran School
Moline, IL

Toothsome Necklaces

Since February is National Children's Dental Health Month, celebrate with these sparkly tooth necklaces! Mix 1 cup flour, 1/4 cup salt, 1/4 cup clear glitter, and 1/3 cup water; then knead the dough to get out any lumps. Have each child flatten a ball of dough, then shape it into a tooth by making a small dent at the top of the dough with a finger and a bigger dent at the bottom. Make a small hole at the top of each tooth with a drinking straw. Bake the teeth at 250° on a cookie sheet for an hour, or until they are hard. When each tooth has cooled, insert a length of yarn through the hole, and knot the ends to complete the necklace. Your students will be all smiles!

Alike And Different

Reinforce your preschoolers' understanding of *alike* and *different* with this stamping idea! To prepare, draw a circle in the corner of a piece of duplicating paper. Write "Different" below the circle and "Alike" at the top of the paper. Copy the page a number of times. Invite a child to stamp on one of the pages using one design inside the circle and a different design outside the circle. Then discuss how the designs are alike and different.

W. L. Harris—Preschool
Elite Christian Learning Center
Columbia, MD

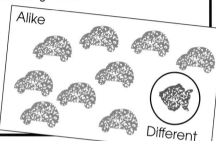

Clown Hats

Whether you're planning a circus unit or just feeling silly, these clown hats are easy to make and fun to wear! To make one hat, decorate a plain paper plate with markers or crayons. Next cut a slit to the center of the plate. Staple the plate into a cone shape. Glue colorful one-inch yarn pieces around the bottom of the hat for hair. Next glue a pom-pom at the top. Finally, punch a hole on each side of the hat, and then tie on a length of yarn to hold the hat in place during wear. Send in the clowns!

Barbara Cypert—Four-Year-Olds
First Baptist Church Learning Center
Tulsa, OK

It's A Jungle In There!

If you live in an area with palm trees, use the fronds to turn your room into a jungle. Cut real fronds from an areca palm tree. Simply staple or tuck the branches into nooks and crannies in your room until your room looks and smells like a wild place to hang out!

Gayle Callis—Pre-K
New Horizon Learning Center
Ft. Lauderdale, FL

Button, Button, Where Is The Button?

Here's an inexpensive game to send home with your older preschoolers to reinforce positional words and develop auditory memory skills. To make a game for each child, invite the child to choose five buttons from a collection to put into a resealable plastic sandwich bag. Include a copy of directions similar to those shown. Buttons high, buttons low—buttons, buttons, home you go.

Stephanie Larson—Preschool Speech/Language
Iola Preschool
Iola, KS

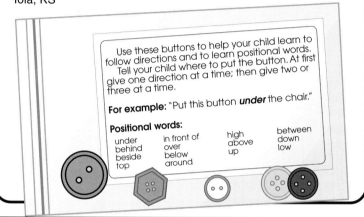

Good-Manners Tea Party

Remember your mother telling you to "put on your party manners"? Invite your youngsters to do the same at a good-manners tea party. Decorate your tables with tablecloths, pretty napkins, plates, cups, and a place card for each child. Invite each child to wear fancy dress-up clothes. After each child has found his place card at the table, serve decorated cupcakes and lemonade. Encourage children to eat and speak politely during the tea party, using "please" and "thank you" often. Miss Manners would approve!

Charlene Vonnahme—Four-Year-Olds
Carroll Area Child Care Center
Carroll, IA

Shaping Up!

Youngsters will review shapes and colors as they make these windsocks for decorating your room! To make one windsock, glue a collage of construction-paper geometric shapes onto a sheet of 12" x 18" construction paper. Turn the paper over, and tape colorful streamers along one long side. Staple together the short sides to form a loose cylinder. Staple a construction-paper strip across the top of the cylinder for a hanger. Suspend the windsock from the ceiling, and admire the shapes and colors!

Dayle Timmons—Preschool
Alimacani Elementary
Jacksonville, FL

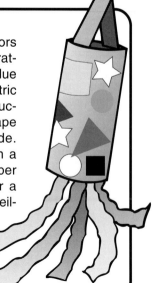

A Tissue, A Tasket, A Basket!

A-tisket, a-tasket, let's make a special basket! Collect an empty, square tissue box for each basket. To make one basket, cut the top off a box. Provide glue and an assortment of artificial flowers, ribbon, lace, rickrack, and buttons for decorating the basket. When the glue has dried, fill the basket with Easter grass and candy, or line it with foil to hold flowers or plants. These baskets are perfect for Easter, May Day, or Mother's Day gifts!

Patricia Duncan—Pre-K And Gr. K
American School For The Deaf
West Hartford, CT

Overheard

Pssst! Chances are that you've heard your little ones say some pretty funny and interesting things! Publish those quotes in a section of your class newsletter titled "Overheard." This section is guaranteed to become parents' favorite part of the newsletter!

Sharon K. Swenson—Preschool And Gr. K
Hazel Lake Montessori
Staples, MN

Jelly Bean Flip Book

Youngsters will flip when they are able to read this sweet book on their own! Draw a rabbit on the top half of a sheet of paper. Write the provided sentence on the paper, spacing it as shown. Duplicate a class supply of the page onto white construction paper. For each child, draw a jelly bean outline on each of a number of 1" x 8 1/2" strips. Staple the same number of strips into place between the lines of text on each page. To complete his book, have each child color the bunny and then color each of the jelly beans a different color. Label the strips. As a variation, make this a counting book by modifying the sentence and programming the strips with sets of jelly beans and matching numerals.

Bunny Rabbit found a *green* hiding in the grass.

Helen B. Kinser—Preschool And Gr. 1
Crosswell Drive Elementary School, Sumter, SC

Fluffy Fabric Bunnies

Help your preschoolers make these adorable bunnies this spring! To make one, place an eight-inch square of thin fabric, wrong side up, on a flat surface. Place a coin in the center; then put two or three small cotton balls on top of the coin. Next fold one corner into the center of the fabric; then repeat with the opposite corner. Roll the fabric from folded corner to folded corner so that you have a long, narrow roll. Thread both ends through a large wooden bead; then fluff the resulting rabbit ears. Finally, use a permanent marker to draw a bunny face on the bead.

Diane White—Preschool, Rotary Youth Centre
Burlington, Ontario, Canada

Organization On The Spot

Here's a tip to instantly organize valuable notes and ideas during teacher workshops. When you hear an idea you want to use, jot it on an index card and write the category (centers, circle time, and so forth) in a top corner. File the cards behind the appropriate heading in a file box. When you return to school, your new ideas will be organized and ready to use!

Julie Plowman—Preschool
Adair Care For Children
Adair, IA

Bunny Buckets

Feeling creative? Surprise your students or colleagues by crafting an adorable bunny bucket for each of them. To make one, collect a large, clean, empty can (from the cafeteria); then remove the label. Near the top of the can, drill two holes on opposite sides. Carefully inspect the can for sharp edges. Spray-paint the can white. When the paint is dry, hot-glue a pom-pom nose, pipe-cleaner whiskers, and wiggle eyes to create a bunny's face. Use Slick® paint to complete the features. Next bend two pastel-colored pipe cleaners into ear shapes; then hot-glue them to the inside of the can. Hot-glue a pom-pom tail onto the back of the can. Thread heavy string or ribbon through the holes to form a handle. Finish the project by writing the recipient's name and the year on the back of her bucket. There you have it—bunny buckets just in time for Easter giving!

Beth Gaskins—Four-Year-Olds, Bonner Elementary School, Moncks Corner, SC

Funny Feet

What walks like a duck or hops like a frog? Your preschoolers—wearing these fun feet, of course! To make one pair, obtain two empty macaroni-and-cheese boxes; then trim a small semicircle from the top of one side for a better fit. From poster board, cut two duck or frog feet sized to cover the boxes. Hot-glue each cutout to the top of a box. Punch a hole on each side of each box; then tie a piece of narrow elastic onto each box to hold the child's stocking foot in place. Get set to waddle and hop!

Liz Novak—Two-Year-Olds To Five-Year-Olds
Pumpkin Patch Preschool And Playcare
Davenport, IA

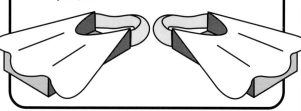

Chalk It Up!

This decorative paper is pretty enough to be displayed as artwork, but it makes terrific stationery as well! Gather a supply of colorful chalk, a cheese grater, white paper, and a tub of water. Invite a child to choose several different colors of chalk, then quickly grate some of each into the water. Within seconds, lay a sheet of paper over the chalk that is floating on the water. (Do not dip the paper; let it float.) Then carefully pick up the paper and set it aside to dry.

Dawn Marie Maucieri—Four-Year-Olds
Home Sweet Home, Fresh Meadows, NY

Rainbow Bowling

Bowl your youngsters right over with this colorful idea! Half-fill each of ten clean, plastic soda bottles with water. Invite little ones to predict what will happen when different combinations of food colors are added to the water. Next assist them in testing their predictions by dropping various color combinations into the water. When finished, hot-glue the lids onto the bottles. Mark a piece of poster board so that there is a bowling position for each bottle; then set up the bottles to bowl. Encourage children to take turns rolling a large rubber ball to knock down the bottles. Challenge them to get a rainbow strike!

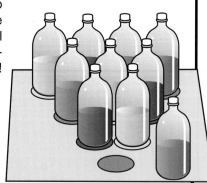

Terry Erickson—Pre-K
St. Martha Catholic School
Kingwood, TX

Seasonal Hot Potato Game

Need a quick circle-time game? Play the traditional Hot Potato game with a seasonal twist. Provide an object for students to pass, such as a plastic egg for Easter or a flower for May. Look out—this idea is hot!

Ashley Wyks—Two-Year-Olds
Kings Daughters Day Home, Madison, TN

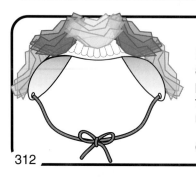

Flowery Bonnets

Have youngsters wear these colorful bonnets in a parade to celebrate spring! To make a hat, have a child scrunch the centers of large tissue-paper squares. Staple the scrunched part of each piece onto the back of a paper plate. When the plate is covered with flowers, punch two holes on opposite sides of the plate near the rim. Tie approximately 16 inches of ribbon on each side for securing the bonnet under the child's chin.

Gail Moody—Preschool, Atascadero Parent Education Preschool, Atascadero, CA

Balloon Blossoms

Use balloons to give these flowers pizzazz! To make one, inflate a small balloon; then tie it to a straw or balloon stick. Glue glitter onto a large, construction-paper flower cutout. When the glue is dry, cut a small slit in the center of the flower; then slip the straw through the slit. Tape two construction-paper leaves near the ends of a pipe cleaner; then twist the pipe cleaner around the straw. These large, sparkly flowers are just the thing to welcome spring!

Carol Rosell, Vineland, NJ

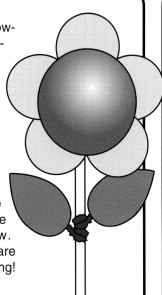

Footprint Butterflies

In years to come, these fluttering footsteps will provide parents with a happy reminder of days when their children were small. Draw a butterfly body in the center of a piece of copy paper; then write the phrases shown. Duplicate a copy for each child. To complete a butterfly, have a child remove his shoes. Place the paper over the soles; then have him rub over the soles with the side of a crayon to create the wings. Encourage each child to give his footprint butterfly to a loved one.

Beth Lemke—Pre-K
Heights Head Start
Coon Rapids, MN

Please keep these footprints
To remind you when I'm tall,
That once I was quite little,
And my feet were also small.

Handy-Dandy Caterpillar

Youngsters will enthusiastically lend a hand to create this adorable caterpillar display! Provide each child with paints and sponges, brushes, cotton swabs, and other creative tools with which to paint a paper circle. Next trace each child's hands onto construction paper; then cut them out. Help each child glue her hand cutouts to the bottom of her circle; then write her first name on the first hand cutout and her last name on the second hand cutout. Mount the circles together with a construction-paper head to create a colorful, cooperative caterpillar.

Keitha-Lynn Stewart—Four-Year-Olds, Little Kids Day Care, Sissonville, WV

"Bee-utiful" Board

Create a bulletin board youngsters will buzz over! Mount a large bee character onto a bulletin board; then surround the bee with close-up shots of your students. Title the board "[Teacher's name]'s 'Bee-utiful' Class." When you change the board, give each child his photo as a keepsake.

Ellen Marston
St. Mary Elementary School
Mobile, AL

Alphabet Mobiles

Use ceiling space to teach the alphabet! Make a large poster-board cutout of each alphabet letter. As each letter is introduced, have youngsters cut out magazine pictures of objects beginning with that letter. Invite each child to share her pictures during circle time; then glue the pictures to the letter cutout. When the letter collage is dry, suspend it from the ceiling. For a five-minute filler, give directions such as, "Everyone hop under the *H*" or "Point to the *P.*"

Tracey Dawson—Four-Year-Olds
Loving And Learning
Charleston, SC

Pop-Bottle Art

Put empty, plastic soda bottles to use with this flower-printing activity! Set out several different-sized bottles, corks, and shallow pans of tempera paint. Invite each child to dip the bottom of a bottle into paint, then press it onto a large sheet of paper to print flower shapes. Use small corks to print flower centers. Paint stems and leaves as desired. Now that's pop art!

Vicki Rhonemus—Preschool
Bentonville Preschool
Bentonville, OH

Our Readers Write

"Hand" Towels

These nifty beach towels will have your young ones drying off "with class"! In advance, have each child bring in a large, white bath towel. Enlist volunteers to help each student use fabric paint to make a handprint on every towel. Then use dimensional paint to label each print with the child's name. After adding your own handprint and name to each towel, write the year and your school's name on each one. Allow the paint to dry completely; then send your youngsters home with these wonderful class reminders!

Tina Springs, Main Street Methodist Preschool
Kernersville, NC

Fingerprinted Flowerpots

Thank your room mothers, volunteers, or student teachers with this fabulous fingerprint pot! Have each student use acrylic craft paint to fingerprint a critter on a clay flowerpot. Then use paint pens to label each child's print. When the fingerprints are dry, have students use the pens to add details to their critters. After spraying the pot with clear sealer, plant some flowers in it for the lucky recipient.

Barbara Meyers
Fort Worth Country Day
Fort Worth, TX

If You Give Your Class A Cookie...

Here's a sweet literacy activity that will also help foster friendship and cooperation. Have students bring in boxes and wrappers from cookie packages they have at home. Examine the packaging material with your students, pointing out brand names or other words such as *cookies* or *chips.* Have students create a cookie collage by cutting apart the packages and gluing the pictures and words onto a piece of bulletin-board paper cut to resemble a cookie. As your little ones work to create the collage, encourage them to discuss with each other their favorite cookies. Hang the completed collage in your room; then serve several types of the cookies depicted in the collage as a special treat!

Barbara Kennedy, Epworth Preschool, Indianapolis, IN

Shavuot Bouquets

Decorate a Shavuot table with this tasty cookie bouquet. Use a cookie cutter to cut flower shapes from sugar-cookie dough. Arrange the shapes on a baking pan, allowing enough room to insert a wooden skewer into the side of each flower. Make egg paint by mixing eggs and food coloring—using one egg for each desired color. Lightly brush each cookie with the paint; then bake the cookies. When the cookies are cool, insert the skewers into a block of Styrofoam® that has been inserted into a flowerpot. Place this scrumptious arrangement on a table and let the festivities begin!

Mimi Blumenkrantz—Four-Year-Olds
Yeshiva Shaarei Tzion
Highland Park, NJ

Preschool Days Poem

If you have an end-of-the-year ceremony, have your class recite this poem to the audience. If desired, mount a copy of the poem and a class photo onto paper for each child to take home as a preschool keepsake.

Now I know my ABCs,
Colors, shapes, and days.
I sang some songs,
Learned some poems, rhymes, and fingerplays.
I played outside on sunny days
And inside when it rained.
My little hands and little feet were busy every day.
My teacher was [teacher's name].
I kept her on her toes.
She tied my shoes, combed my hair, and even wiped my nose.
But now it's time to say "Good-bye"
To all my preschool friends.
School is over, summer's here,
But learning never ends!

Mary Hedman—Four-Year-Olds
Clayton, NC

Sunflower Wear

Your little ones will start their summer in style with these adorable sunflower T-shirts! Have each child use fabric paint to sponge-print a brown circle in the middle of a white T-shirt. Next help him make yellow handprints around the circle. Finally, have him sponge-print green leaves and paint a stem. Use dimensional paint to label the shirt with the child's name. When the paint is dry, allow your youngsters to wear the shirts home. Parents are sure to exclaim, "My, how you've bloomed!"

Cindy Rockney—Preschool
Katherine Thomas Elementary
Windham, OH

Three, Two, One...Contact!

This sense-stimulating idea is guaranteed to tickle your youngsters! Use duct tape to attach one or more strips of Con-Tact® covering to the floor—sticky sides up. Invite students to remove their shoes and socks, then walk barefoot on a strip of the sticky paper. What a way to keep them on their toes!

Leah Behrens—Preschool, Omaha, NE

Photograph Bookmarks

Have your little ones honor their fathers or other significant adults with these unique bookmarks. Take a photograph of each child in your class. To make one bookmark, cut the figure of a child from his photo; then glue the cutout onto a piece of tagboard. Trim the tagboard to match the shape of the figure. Write a Father's Day message on the back; then help the child sign his name. Laminate the shape. Finally, punch a hole in the top of the bookmark; then tie a yarn tassel through the hole. What a wonderful present for Papa!

Karen Eiben—Preschool
The Kids' Place
LaSalle, IL

Marshmallow Masterpieces

Jumbo marshmallows are marvelous when toasted over a fire. But did you know they also make wonderful painting tools? Stock your art center with a supply of jumbo marshmallows, paper, and several shallow pans of paint. Invite your little ones to create pictures by dipping the marshmallows in the paint, then pressing them onto sheets of paper. (Be sure to remind them that these tempting tools are for painting and not for tasting.) Keep a supply of fresh marshmallows handy to reward your little artists for their creativity!

Jill Rozman—Preschool, Special Education
Marathon Childhood Center
Middle Village, NY

I'm Nuts About You!

Dads and father figures will go nuts over this Father's Day card and treat! To make a card, cut out a peanut shape from brown paper. Label it as shown; then glue on a peanut shell. Next fill a brown paper lunch bag with unshelled peanuts. Fold down the top of the bag; then punch two holes through the layers. Tie raffia through the holes; then staple the card to the bag. Now there's a gift everyone will want to crack into!

Gayle J. Vergara
Willowbend Preschool, Murrieta, CA

Into The Deep Blue Sea

Your little ones will be swimming with excitement when you transform your classroom into an underwater arena. Begin by covering your windows with blue plastic wrap or cellophane. Next create waves by attaching strips of blue bulletin-board paper or cloth to your ceiling. Use fishing line to hang construction-paper fishhooks, fish, and other sea creatures from the ceiling. Finally, complete the transformation by displaying seashells, stuffed sea animals, and books on ocean life throughout your room.

Patty Wilson, Fairdale Elementary, Louisville, KY

Index

319